A Priv

A Private Affair

DONNA
HILL

ARABESQUE®

Recycling programs
for this product may
not exist in your area.

A PRIVATE AFFAIR

An Arabesque novel published by Kimani Press/July 2009

First published by Kensington Publishing Corp. in 1998

ISBN-13: 978-0-373-83162-3

© 1998 by Donna Hill

www.kimanipress.com

Printed in U.S.A.

Acknowledgments

My sincere thanks and appreciation to all of my readers who have supported me throughout the years. I feel blessed that *A Private Affair* is getting a second life and that my beloved character Quinten Parker will reach into your hearts once again. Be sure to collect the entire trilogy— *A Private Affair, Pieces of Dreams* and *Through the Fire*—love stories that will stand the test of time. Thank you all so much! Enjoy.

BOOK ONE

PART ONE
Quinn

Chapter 1

Quinn poked his head around the partially open bathroom door, shouting over the steam and rush of water. "I'll check ya later, 'round midnight."

Lacy parted the opaque shower curtain, shouting over the surge of water. "Not again, Quinten. You just got in. I thought you were staying for dinner. Maxine's coming over. When are you going to eat?"

Quinn chuckled deep in his throat. "Chill, sis. I'll grab a little somethin'."

She snatched the curtain shut. "Yeah, but what?" she grumbled, her question full of cynicism. She worried about her twin brother, more than she'd ever let on. The reality was, all they had was each other. And living in the heart of Harlem, New York, with its available drugs, rampant gang wars and random shootings, reiterated their oneness all the more. She also knew that no amount of haranguing would keep her brother off the street. The lure, the mystery, the danger and excitement, were his mistresses. He couldn't seem to get enough and kept going back for more. She knew Quinn had so much more to offer than just protection for local "businessmen." If they could just get out of the neighborhood, he stood a chance of surviving. They stood a chance.

"Later! Tell Maxie I'll catch her another time," he called, shutting the door behind him.

Lacy threw up a silent prayer for her brother's safe return, a proven ritual of her deep spirituality. They had to get out of this neighborhood, she vowed again. Quinn had no desire to move, and she'd promised herself she'd never leave him behind. But maybe when he saw the duplex apartment she'd found on the border of Greenwich Village he'd change his mind. The landlady was willing to hold the apartment for two more weeks. That's all the time she needed to get the rest of the money. "Two more weeks." She sighed, shutting off the water. "Just two more weeks."

Quinn sauntered down the semi-darkened avenue, assuming the rhythmic gait of the hood, his shoulder-length dreadlocks swinging to the hip-hop beat of his stride. He'd opted to walk this balmy spring night in lieu of driving his black BMW 750i. He needed to see and feel the pulse of the street, from the boom boxes that blared the outrage of inner-city life to the sweet-funky smell of greasy fried chicken, shrimp lo mein and chopped barbecue that wafted from the every-other-corner fast-food joints, Caribbean roti shops and Hispanic bodegas.

By rote he gave the barest rise of his chin in a show of cool acknowledgment to the rows of regulars who sat, posed, slumped, leaned, stood and harmonized along the stretch of Malcolm X Boulevard. He checked his watch. Twenty minutes.

As he continued toward his destination he wondered if his mother was holed up in one of the numerous tenements with yet another dude. His teeth clenched reflexively at the vision. He hadn't laid eyes on his mother in more than ten years. She'd walked out on him and Lacy when they were only sixteen. "Ya'll grown now," she'd said. "And can take care of yo'selves. It's my time now." She'd turned, walked out of the door and they hadn't seen or heard from her since.

Even now, after all those years, Quinn still felt that bottom-less emptiness in the pit of his stomach that burned like old garbage in the cans that kept the homeless warm. He felt some irrational guilt, that his mother's abandonment was somehow his fault. He'd tried to fill the void with everything from hurt to anger. He tried to fill his need with the warmth and brotherhood of the street. But the emptiness persisted. Lacy, on the other hand, had turned to the familial nurturing of the church, and the healing force of the Lord.

Stopping in front of B.J.'s, the local bar, grill and everything in between, Quinn pushed open the scratched, blacked-out Plexi-glas door and stepped into the smoke-filled room.

"Whatsup, brotherman?" greeted Turk, the bartender. "Whatcha tastin'?"

"My usual. Jack on the rocks." Quinn slid onto the well-worn wooden stool and perused his surroundings. The place was packed as usual for a Friday night. Women in all their finery lounged in various vogue positions to catch the eyes of available men on the prowl, their perfumed bodies cutting through the stench of stale cigars, cigarettes and body heat.

"Here ya go."

"Thanks, brotherman." Quinn absently raised his glass to his lips and took a quick swallow of the smooth amber liquid, its fire warming him. "Boys in the back?"

"Whatcha think?"

Quinn nodded, slapped a five dollar bill on the bar and headed toward the gray steel door.

"Luck to ya, brother," Turk called, wiping up the ring that Quinn's glass had left behind.

The small back room was even stuffier than the front. Smoke billowed like cumulus clouds, hanging over the tight, dark room like a canopy. One lone seventy-five watt bulb hung above the round, green, felt-covered table, casting grotesque shadows against the cracked and peeling lemon yellow walls. Sweat, perfume, Old Spice, cheap liquor and moldy carpet odor all blended together into one unique aroma. It was all an acquired taste, the boys in the back always joked.

Smalls, the bouncer, who was about the size of a Sumo wrestler and obviously nicknamed as a joke, expertly patted Quinn down, then gave his customary caveman grunt and hooked thumb over his shoulder, indicating that it was all right for Quinn to enter.

Several pairs of eyes momentarily locked on his approach, then quickly returned to the aces, queens and kings that beckoned them, daring them to make a move. Quinn spotted Sylvie, the hostess of sorts, and signaled her with a crook of his finger.

Sheathed in a tight-fitting red rayon dress, Sylvie strutted across the hardwood floor, leaving little to the imagination in her wake. Her heels clicked in perfect syncopation.

"Quinn," she cooed, looking up at his smooth, chiseled face, her full, red-painted mouth pouting seductively, as if waiting to be kissed. "What can I get ya, sugah?"

Quinn's dark eyes were shadowed by long lashes as his lids slid partially downward. The right corner of his artist-drawn mouth curled. "Remy set for the pick up? Time is money," he added, giving her the benefit of his dimpled smile.

"Follow me, lover. They're…just…about…ready."

Quinn slung his hands into the pocket of his Versace jogging pants, his Nike-sneakered feet moving soundlessly behind Sylvie's undulating form. She knocked twice on the brown wooden door, turned the knob and entered.

Remy, Charles and a face he didn't recognize were seated around a long table, counting and stacking Washingtons, Hamiltons and Franklins into neat rows of dead presidents.

"Be witchu in a sec," Remy acknowledged, briefly looking up from his task. He tilted his head in the direction of the young boy. "Dis here is T.C. He gonna run wit you tonight. I want you to school 'em on da route and da ropes."

Quinn's eyes narrowed to slits. "I ain't no damned nurse-maid," he grumbled, his ire directed at T.C., who seemed to shrink under the scornful gaze. "Send him with one of the other runners. I ain't got time for no baby-sittin'."

Remy's ink black face hardened as if suddenly tossed into quick-drying cement. "He goes wit you. You knows da street and the connections better than anyone. And, more important, 'they' knows you. Brothers see T.C. rolling wit you, they'll give him his props. Understood?"

"Yeah, yeah," Quinn reluctantly conceded. "But he better

pay attention." He threw T.C. a withering glance, then leaned his muscled frame nonchalantly against the doorjamb. His gaze slanted back in T.C.'s direction. The kid looked to be no more than seventeen. Quinn sighed inwardly—just about the same age he was when he started to build a rep for himself with Remy as his tutor.

Over the years Quinn had been elevated from errand boy to principal courier, responsible for the money transport between five of Remy's clubs. His cut was substantial for the safeguarding of the nightly takes. That took trust and nerves of steel. Trust—that he wouldn't run off with the goods—and nerves of steel when situations got dicey, as they did on many occasions.

As much as observers believed that Quinn had ice water for blood, he was anything but cold. Unfortunately, in his world there was no room for the soft of heart. So he played the role: hard, untouchable, unattainable, dangerous. The one person with whom he could truly be himself was his sister, Lacy.

Lacy didn't laugh when she read one of his rhymes, or when he played tunes off the top of his head on the antique second-hand piano. She'd just sit there all dreamy-eyed and listen with a pretty smile on her face. Lacy believed in him, believed that he could go places. *"Do something worthwhile with your God-given talents,"* she always preached. Sometimes she made him almost believe in himself, too.

His mouth twitched as he fought back a smile. Lacy, the dreamer, the idealist. What could he possibly do with a twelfth-grade education? He frowned, marring his smooth mahogany brow. Through the years the two personas who made up Quinn Parker had merged, one nearly indistinguishable from the other. Sometimes even he didn't know where one began and the other ended.

A thud near his feet pulled him back. He looked down to see two black duffel bags, packed to near bursting.

"Take my ride. It's out back," Remy said. He tossed Quinn the set of spare keys, then came from behind the table. He walked up to Quinn, clapping him roughly on the shoulder. He leaned close to his ear. "And take it easy on da kid. That was you once, remember?" Remy moved back, his gold front tooth sparkling against his skin of midnight.

"You never stop remindin' me."

Remy laughed loud and hard. "Dat's to keep you humble."

"Yeah, right. Come on, man," he called to T.C. over Remy's short salt-and-pepper head.

Quinn eyed T.C. up and down as they made their way to Remy's Lexus 400. His Tommy Hilfiger jeans were barely held up on poke-you-in-the-eyes hip bones, proudly displaying the red, white and blue waistband of his Fruit of the Looms. His Air Jordans flopped on his feet, for lack of tied shoestrings. Quinn slowly shook his head.

"Yo, man, when you gonna get you some clothes that fit?"

T.C. checked out his outfit. "What? All the brothers dress like this. These pants cost—"

"Yo, check this. All the brothers don't dress like that. Only the ones who don't know no better. Where'd that style come from?" he challenged.

T.C. shrugged and tried to look defiant, cutting his eyes up and down the length of Quinn's hard-packed body. He chewed his gum a little faster.

"From those fools who go busted and tossed in the joint. That's where. They can't wear no belts, so their pants are always saggin'. Can't wear laces in their kicks, so they're always gapped open. That's who you wanna represent? Not with me, my brother. Do what you want on your own time. When we rollin', pull up your pants and tie your shoes. The joint is one place I don't wanna go. And I don't wanna be reminded of the possibilities every time I look at you."

"Yo, man, don't nobody tell me what to do."

"Yeah. Well, guess what? I just did. Now get in the car, or find yourself somethin' else to do tonight. Didn't ask for no company, anyway." Quinn opened the door, slammed it behind him and started the engine.

T.C. stood there debating what to do and Quinn slowly eased the car away while he was thinking. T.C. ran alongside the car, struggling to hold up his pants while knocking on the window.

"Yo, man, hold up! Whatchu doin'?"

Quinn pulled the car to a stop and lowered the window. "Make up your mind yet?"

T.C. looked around, shuffled his feet for a minute, and then pulled up his pants.

Quinn unlocked the passenger door.

By the time Quinn returned to his apartment on 135th Street, it was nearly 3:00 a.m. He hoped that Lacy was asleep, because if she wasn't he was sure she'd stick her head out of her apartment door as soon as she heard his key turn in his lock. Lacy thought it was ridiculous that they should live in two different apartments, but as much as Quinn adored his sister, he needed his privacy. At least with this arrangement he had the best of both worlds: his privacy when he needed it, and the comfort and nurturing of his sister just a few steps away.

The door creaked on its hinges as he slowly pushed it open. The sound unconsciously caused his heart to beat a bit faster, and he had to stifle a chuckle. Like a kid sneaking in after curfew, he imagined that at any second the lights would come blazing on and irate parents would descend upon him: "Where you been, boy? Can't you tell time? Get to your room and don't come out."

No lights came on. There were no parents waiting. There never had been. He flipped on the light switch and closed the door. Tonight, though, he would have welcomed having someone there. He would have even settled for one of Lacy's lectures about the vagrancy of his life. He needed to feel cared about, especially tonight, and he couldn't seem to shake the feelings of melancholia. Working the spots and talking with T.C., he'd seen himself as he was years ago, eager, hungry and willing to please, to be accepted, to be one of the boys. Sure, he'd paid his dues over the ensuing years. He'd earned a reputation, a degree of respect from his peers. He had a decent crib, fancy ride, designer clothes and enough women's phone numbers to last him two lifetimes. And it all added up to zip. Outside Harlem, outside the security of the hood, he was nothing and nobody. This was his world. What else could he ever hope to be: the writer and musician that Lacy always talked about? Not in this world. Not in this reality.

Pulling off his jacket, he tossed it on the kitchen chair, then noticed the sheet of pink paper on the table with the familiar scrawl.

Hey, bro,

I know you didn't eat anything worth the time it took to fix it. Dinner is in your oven. Don't let me find it there in the morning. Max was here. She asked about you, though Lord only knows why. Get some rest.

Jesus loves ya and so do I.

Lacy

Quinn smiled and folded the piece of paper. The light was on.

It was about noon Saturday when Quinn bounded down the stairs of the apartment building and smacked into Maxine Sherman, who was coming through the door.

He felt her lush softness crush against the length of him, then bounce away with the force of their collision. His arm snaked out and grabbed her around the waist, halting her descent back down the stairs. "Sorry, babe. You all right?"

Maxine felt as if the wind had been sucked from her lungs, and it had nothing to do with their near calamity.

She smiled up at him. Her dark eyes sparkled. "I'm fine. I just need to watch where *you're* going," she teased. She begged her heart to be still. "Where are you off to in such a hurry?" She could feel his warm breath graze her face.

Quinn took a short step back and released his hold. "Have some folks to meet. What about you? Lacy's not here. She's pulling the early shift at the hospital."

She tapped her forehead with her palm. "Oh, I completely forgot." She shifted her purse from her right hand to her left. She took a quick look at her feet, summoned her courage and looked up into Quinn's penetrating gaze. "Mind if I walk with you?"

"Naw, not really. Actually, I was takin' my ride." He smiled, and her world seemed momentarily brighter. "Sure, come on. We ain't hung out in a while."

"So, how you been, Max?" Quinn asked, pulling the Beamer into the early morning traffic. The scent of rich leather mixing with the sounds of the rap group RBL Posse blaring from the speakers enveloped them. "Still at the bank?"

"I've been okay, I guess."

"You guess?" He turned toward her and smiled.

Maxine ducked her head and grinned. "What I mean is, things are just so-so. Nothing spectacular. And yes, I'm still at the bank. But I don't intend to stay there forever. I'm studying Travel and Tour at the community college. I'll have my own travel business one day."

"Hmmm. That's all good. I know it'll work out for you," he said, though he couldn't see how. But then again, things were different for women—better. Black women definitely stood a better chance of getting out and making a real life. As a black man he didn't even stand a good chance of catching a New York City yellow cab in Harlem. He had yet to meet a black man who owned his own business through legal means.

"Where's your man? I know there's got to be somebody takin' care of all that," he teased, moving away from the topic that haunted him.

She hesitated, weighing her response. "There's no one special."

"Fine thing like you. Brothers must be crazy not to snatch you up."

"Humph. That's what I keep saying," she rejoined.

"The right dude'll come along and sweep you off your feet just like in those romance books that you and Lacy love to devour." He chuckled at the thought.

Maxine poked him in the arm. "Very funny. Those books are good. There's a lot more to them than folks *like you* give them credit for."

"Yeah, right. You tellin' me those blond-haired, blue-eyed devils could tell you 'bout lovin' a man? What do they have in common with us? Arr-nold, pretty boy Tom Cruise, De Niro?"

"First of all, love is a universal thing, Q. Color has nothing to do with it. We all feel it and we all want to experience it with the right person. Besides, the new wave of romance novels that we read have black characters, showing black men who are about something, *and* the women. At least in those books it's a place where we can read about black people in a positive light. Not like how we're always played in the news and on TV. I know you think they're corny, but they have a lot of reality in them. They're about people just like you and me. About them struggling to get their relationships together while dealing with life. Just because they're about love don't mean that there's nothing to them."

Quinn turned his head and looked at her profile for a long, silent moment, maybe seeing Maxine for the first time. She was no longer a skinny little girl with braces and knock-knees. She was all grown up, smart, hardworking and a real beauty. And seemed as if she had a head on her shoulders. She was Lacy's best friend, and like a second sister to him. When they were kids he'd chased her up and down 135th Street, trying to pull her long hair. He would hide in Lacy's closet, then jump out and scare them witless when Maxine spent many a night. He'd seen her with her unpressed hair standing on top of her head when she woke up in the morning and teased her about the lumps of sleep in the corners of her eyes. That all seemed like another lifetime, when things were simple. Looking at her now, fine as she wanted to be, he wondered when she'd changed from the skinny little pain in the neck to the woman she'd become. Yeah, some man would be real lucky to have Maxine Sherman as his woman.

Chapter 2

I Don't Wanna Cry

Quinn was sprawled out on his sofa, just about to take a quick nap before his evening run, his belly full from yet another one of Lacy's lip-smacking meals, when the downstairs doorbell rang. Squeezing his eyes shut, he groaned. He was in no mood for company. He'd turned his phone down and his beeper off earlier just to have a little peace. He'd been working on a short story that he wanted to share with Lacy when she got back from wherever she'd gone, and hadn't wanted to be disturbed. Maybe if he didn't answer they'd just go away. Then he realized that his lights were on, that with his apartment facing the street anyone could just look up and see that he was home.

The bell pealed again. He practically threw himself off the couch. Maybe Lacy forgot her keys again—he hoped. He crossed the room in long, smooth strides, pulling his locks away from his face as he leaned toward the intercom.

"Yeah."

"It's me, man, T.C. Buzz me."

Quinn pressed his head against the cool wall and expelled a silent string of damns. It was rare that he ever allowed any of his "associates" into his crib. This was his refuge, a place to cleanse himself of where he'd been. He didn't want to dilute it by bringing the outside in. He could count on one hand the number of men and women who'd ever crossed his threshold. He guarded his privacy, and everyone who dealt with him knew it. Obviously nobody had schooled T.C.

He pushed the talk button, said, "Come on up," then pushed the button marked DOOR. The telltale buzz hummed through the control panel.

Turning, he retraced his steps and snatched up his discarded sneakers from the floor and the red T-shirt he'd worn earlier from the back of the couch, then took them both into his bedroom and shut the door. Returning, he took a quick look around, picked up Walter Mosley's *Gone Fishin'* and *Ecstasy,* a black romance novel by Gwynne Forster—which he'd sneaked from his sister just to see what they were like (it was actually pretty good)— and returned them to the bookcase. One lesson he'd adopted from his sister was cleanliness. He kept his place so immaculate that women who'd paid him visits always thought he had a woman living with him. He took one last look around and spotted his notebook, which contained all of his rhymes and short stories. He grabbed it and slid it under the couch just as T.C. knocked on the door. No point in giving anybody the opportunity to be nosy. Besides, if word ever hit the street that he wrote poetry, there wouldn't be a hole deep enough for him to hide in.

With great reluctance he opened the door. "Whatsup?"

T.C. sauntered into the room, taking in the decor. Black leather furniture, situated on clean-enough-to-eat-off floors, dominated the living area, which was separated from the cool, cream-colored kitchen by hanging ferns and standing banana plants at either end of the archway. A six-foot bookcase was filled with hardcover and softcover books. The state-of-the-art stereo system, encased in smoked-glass and chrome, pumped out the soulful sounds of Marvin Gaye's "Distant Lover." The scent of jasmine came from a stick of incense.

T.C. turned toward Quinn. "Nice crib."

Quinn gave him a short look and stepped down into the living room. "You sound surprised." He changed the radio station from R&B to all rap. The intangible words and driving beat vibrated in the background.

"Naw. I ain't mean it like that, man," T.C. stammered. He shrugged his thin shoulders. "I just meant, you know...living 'round here, you just don't figure—"

"To see people livin' halfway decent. Ain't that what you meant?"

He shrugged again.

"You sittin' down, or what?" He indicated the six-foot couch with a toss of his head. "Want a brew?"

"Sounds good."

Quinn's mouth curved into a wry smile. He opened the fridge and pulled out one beer and a can of Pepsi, which he kept around to mix with rum. He handed the Pepsi to T.C., who started to open his mouth in protest until he looked up and caught Quinn's stern expression and arched eyebrows. "I don't give alcohol to minors," he said simply. "Whatever you do in your spare time is your bizness." He popped the top of the beer and took a long, ice-cold swallow. Beads of moisture hung on the can. "Even in this game you need to have some ethics." He looked pointedly at T.C. "Don't ever forget that, kid, 'cause when you do you stop being human."

T.C. popped the top, gave Quinn a curious look, then nodded his head. He took a long swig of his Pepsi, tapping his foot to the beat.

Quinn plopped down in the matching recliner, flipped the switch and leaned back. The clock on the facing wall showed nine-fifteen. He wondered where Lacy was. Maybe it was one of her church nights. The last time he'd set foot in a church he'd prayed for his mother's return. She never did, and he never went back. Pushing the thoughts aside, he turned his attention to T.C. "What's with the visit? You ain't running with me tonight."

"Yeah, I know. I just wanted to...you know...say thanks...for the other night. I mean, I know you didn't want me hangin' around with you...so...thanks." He took a quick swallow of soda to hide his discomfort.

Quinn held back his smile. He remembered all too well how he'd felt on his first run: the rush of adrenaline, the eagerness to please. "Where are your folks, kid?"

"Around. I have six brothers and sisters. My mom waits tables. Don't know where my pops is. I'm the oldest," he added, and Quinn could hear the note of pride in his declaration.

He already knew the rest: oldest male in the house became the man of the house, and the man of the house had to take care of himself and his family by any means necessary. It was the tale of the inner city.

"You still in school?"

He nodded. "I graduate in June."

"Just make sure that you do," Quinn warned, suddenly seeing himself in T.C.—if he'd had the chance to start over.

They talked about this and that, their favorite athletes, which team was going to win the NBA championship, and the characters in the neighborhood.

"Did you hear about the shoot-out on Riverside?" T.C. asked.

"Naw. I been holed up in here all night. What went down?"

"The usual." T.C. shrugged, already jaded by the circumstances of life. "Cops got into it with some brothers. It got ugly and shots got fired. Coupla dudes got popped. Some girl, too, with a stray."

It was a story so typical you almost didn't pay it any attention, Quinn mused, shrugging off the sudden chill that surprised his body. "Where'd you say this was?"

"Down on Riverside, couple of blocks from that big church. They still had the area all taped off when I left a couple of hours ago."

Quinn nodded absently, took another swallow of his beer and a quick look at the clock. Ten forty-five.

"Hey, gotta roll. My moms is working late and I promised I'd make sure the kids were in."

Quinn grinned. "Then you better get steppin'." They both stood. "Hold on a minute, I'll walk out with you." He went into his bedroom and changed clothes. He didn't have to be at B.J.'s until eleven-thirty. He had time.

* * *

The three block stretch of Riverside was completely blocked off from traffic. Police cars and ambulances crowded the street. Swirling blue and red lights dotted the night sky. He spotted the meat wagon and immediately knew what that meant. From the look of all the uniforms that blanketed the street, the unfortunate victim was a cop. Guiltily, he released a sigh of relief.

Quinn was directed by a beat cop to move on. He made a wide U-turn and headed back down the way he'd come, passing a Channel 7 *Eyewitness News* van headed for the scene.

Quinn stepped on the accelerator. He'd catch it on the news.

Quinn arrived at B.J.'s a little early and was surprised not to see Turk behind the bar. He kept walking and stopped in front of the gray door, to be met by Smalls.

All eyes turned to him when he entered, but this time instead of refocusing on the poker game the stares remained fixed on his face.

He strolled past the gambling table, ignoring the odd looks. Halfway across the room, he spotted Sylvie heading in his direction. Her usual sunny smile was missing, her butterscotch face a portrait of sadness. When their gazes connected her eyes widened in surprise. An unnamed fear coupled with a rush of adrenaline snaked its way through his veins.

"Oh, Quinn. I'm so sorry." Sylvie pressed her head against his chest and wrapped her arms around his stiff body.

He wouldn't panic. Something had obviously happened to Remy. He would handle it. Gently he clasped her shoulders, peeling her away from him. He looked down into red-rimmed eyes. "What are you talkin' about? Sorry for what?"

Sylvie blinked several times before realization struck. Her hand flew to her mouth. "Oh, my God."

Just then Remy stepped from the back room and Quinn's pulse escalated its beat. "Hey, man, you know you don't have to be here. I wouldn't expect you to—" He caught Sylvie's warning look.

Quinn looked from one to the other. "Listen, I don't know what the fuck's going on, but somebody better damn well tell me somethin'—and quick."

Remy put his hand on Sylvie's bare arm. "Lemme have a minute with Quinn," he said softly. Sylvie nodded and stepped aside as Remy put his arm protectively around Quinn's wide shoulders. "Come on in da back, son, where we can talk private like."

Quinn threw off Remy's hold. "Talk about what?" he demanded. His heart started beating like crazy.

"Just come on, man. Come on." Remy ushered him into the back room.

All eyes trailed the pair as they walked into Remy's office and shut the door. Moments later, the door flew open with such force that everyone in the room flinched and held their breath. Quinn stormed out, his eyes glazed, with Remy hot on his heels.

"Quinn, wait. I'll go wit you," he called.

Quinn threw up his hand to halt Remy's pursuit. "No!" There was no room for argument. Suddenly the decor, the drab, stark nakedness, the shadows, the familiar scent of the back room, overwhelmed him.

Quinn raced from the building. His mind whirled in horrified disbelief. Of course it was some macabre mistake. They were wrong. Everyone was wrong. It happened all the time.

The Beamer assumed a life of its own as it hurtled down the darkened streets of Harlem, darting in front of cars and terrifying unsuspecting pedestrians. His entire life rolled before his eyes as if projected on some sort of larger-than-life screen.

He pulled to a screeching stop in front of the precinct house. For several moments he just sat there, staring at his hands that gripped the wheel to keep from trembling. Calling on something deep inside, he forced himself to get out of the car and put one foot in front of the other.

The rest of the night was a series of nightmarish snapshots taken from a house of horrors photo album—from the drive to the medical examiner's office to his return home, where he found himself staring at the snow dancing across his television screen.

He had watched himself mindlessly follow the short, pudgy doctor with tufts of hair protruding from his ears down the long, dull gray corridors, the effort of walking zapping his strength like the grip of quicksand. The only sound was his own heavy heart-beat, thudding like tribal drums in his ears. A thick metal door ahead swung inward to reveal a frigid, stark and sterile room with bright white walls bouncing off highly polished stainless-steel instruments and blinding him to where he really was, projecting the illusion of virgin purity. He cringed as teeth-gritting sounds of metal hitting metal played a chilly tune to the backdrop of the whir and hum of unseen machines and the snap and pop of rubber gloves, while technicians went about their business of un-covering the mysteries of death.

The motion of the doctor removing the stiff white sheet from her face flashed repeatedly like that of a high-speed camera shutter every time he blinked. Wrapped in a sheet like dirty laundry, with a tag for pick-up dangling over her exposed, pink-polished toenail. Something deep inside of him gave way, and he seemed to choke on his own air. Icy fingers of disbelief ran down his spine and he shuddered. Instinctively he reached for her, seeking the warmth and assurance he'd always known, come to expect. Her hand, it was so cold. All the life and the warmth that was Lacy was gone. Her face was just as peaceful and pretty as it had always been, except for that deep, dark, black hole in the middle of her forehead that could have easily resembled the blessing marks from Ash Wednesday.

But he kept staring at her, rubbing her hand, begging her in the silence of his heart to just get up so they could get out of there. Out of this place that was too quiet, too cold, too lifeless, with its stainless-steel tables and rubber blankets, the stench of embalming fluid more pungent to him than the odor of the back alleys. Lacy didn't belong in a place like this. She was too full of life, too full of energy. So why was she so still? Why wouldn't she just get up, so they could leave? Dread swept through him. He wanted to run, to scream at her to get up. But the words wouldn't come.

So he tried to blink the vision away. But it remained, un-changed. She could have been asleep, just as he remembered from tiptoeing into her room as a kid to tug her ponytails. She'd looked as though she'd open her mouth at any moment and make one of her smart-ass remarks, like when they were growing up and everyone always said how much alike they looked. "I'm just prettier," Quinn would say, and Lacy would remark, "But my boobs are bigger." And they would look at each other and crack up laughing. That's all he wanted to hear. Just hear her laugh, tell him to eat and not stay out too late. He wanted to watch her face glow with pride when she read his work or listened to him play.

He wanted to tell her how important she was to him. How she'd made life bearable after their mother deserted them. How much it meant to him to hear her words of praise, and how much he loved her.

All he wanted was for her to be asleep so he could walk across the hall and smell corn bread baking in her oven. Then everything would be all right and this sick, unspeakable torment that had infected every inch of his body would go away. His fingers dug into his palm. When had he told her he loved her?

From his eyes they fell, silently, trickling onto his clenched hands. He looked down at the unbidden wetness, blinking, momentarily confused. *"Big boys don't cry,"* he could hear his mother taunt. And Lacy would whisper in his ear, *"It's all right Q. It's okay."*

It would never be okay again.

"Comin' home from church," he moaned, the force of his sobs shaking his powerful body. "Church! Praying to her God. Where were you tonight? Huh? Why weren't you watchin' over my sister, like she said you always did? 'Cause there ain't no God. You ain't real. I knew that when you nevah brought my mama back. But Lacy kept believin', 'cause that's just the way she was. So why her? Huh? Why? She ain't never done nothing but good. And you took her. So whatta we got now, huh—*God?*"

Suddenly he lurched to his feet, staggering, his legs stiff and heavy from hours of immobility. He stumbled toward the window as the hazy orange sun began its ascent above the rooftop rows of tenements and high-rise projects.

Then, as if conjured from the depths of a personal hell, the agonized wail of a mortally wounded soul screaming to end its inhumane torture ripped from the bowels of his being, as his foot crashed through the curtain-covered windows.

"N-ooo!"

The service was a blur, packed with people he'd never even known were friends. His only moment of clarity was when Maxine stepped up to the podium and sang, "You Are My Friend," in a tribute to Lacy that rivaled Pattie LaBelle.

He could still hear the haunting power of her voice, the painful truth of the words humming through his veins as he and Maxine made their way toward home.

Maxine took periodic, countless glances at Quinn's drawn profile. He hadn't uttered a full sentence in days. She was afraid for him, and at the same time she needed him. She needed him to tell her that everything would be all right, to hold her and tell her they'd get through it. She was hurting, too, more than she would have believed was physically possible. But Quinn had left them behind, as sure as Lacy had. He was visible in body, but the spirit of the man was gone.

He turned to her when they reached her apartment building. His hair had come loose from the band that held it, and it blew gently across his black-clad shoulders, touched by the stirring breeze.

"You'd better go on up," he said in a barely audible voice. He wouldn't meet her eyes, because he knew that if he did, she'd see the hurt and the fear. He couldn't expose that part of himself to anyone—not ever again. *Big boys don't cry. It's okay, Q.* "Listen, I gotta go," he said abruptly. His gaze flickered briefly on her face. Leaning down, he kissed her cheek. "Later."

Maxine watched his long, bowlegged swagger until he was out of sight.

Several weeks later as Quinn was stepping out of the shower he was surprised to hear the faint ringing of the telephone. He had so isolated himself since Lacy's death that those who knew him had backed away after repeated attempts at offers of support. That being true, Quinn couldn't imagine who would have the heart to call just to get their feelings stepped on.

"Hello?"

"Mr. Parker?" came a voice, thin as a rail.

"Yeah. Who's this?"

"Oh, thank heavens," she rushed on. "I've been trying to reach your sister for days but she never seems to be home." Quinn's insides did a nosedive, leaving him momentarily speechless. "Such a hardworking girl, that one. It's the main reason why I decided to hold the apartment for the two of you. She left your number on the application in case of an emergency."

He finally found his voice. "W…hat?"

"The apartment. The one on Eighteenth Street. I've been holding it for weeks. She promised she'd come by with the rest of the money. When I didn't hear from her I got worried…"

Quinn's pulse pounded so loudly in his ears he could barely make out what she was saying. He felt as if he'd been tossed into someone else's nightmare.

"So I need to know if you two still want the apartment. I know how desperately she wanted to move. Said you'd be a hard sell, though." She chuckled. "It's such a lovely place. I told her she should let you see it first, but she insisted that she wanted to take care of everything and surprise you, so you couldn't say no." She chuckled again.

Quinn took slow gulps of air. He had every intention of just hanging up, ending the nightmare now. But something kept him on the line and pushed words through his mouth that he didn't know were forming.

"Why don't you gimme your address, and I'll come by. I think it's about time I saw this place."

The movers would arrive shortly. He looked around. The apartment was full of memories. All of which he wanted to put behind him.

He'd finally given in to Maxine's insistence that they go through Lacy's things. He'd let Max take what she wanted. He took the old second-hand piano, the one Lacy'd given him on his twenty-first birthday. He smiled, recalling the moment and the look of pure joy on her face when she saw his astonished reaction. His fingers lovingly caressed the keys. He moved away and took an accepting breath.

Boxes were packed and taped, his clothes bagged and ready. He checked the cabinets and closets for any overlooked items. He checked under the bed and behind the wall unit. He took a broom and swept it beneath the love seat and then the recliner. Satisfied, he ran the broom under the couch and was surprised to find it meeting resistance. He tried again and his notebook came sailing across the floor.

For several moments, he just stared at it. Bending, he picked it up. Remembering. He ran his hand across the pebbly black-and-white cover. One day perhaps he'd open it again....

The bell rang.

His eyes swept the room.

Time to go.

PART TWO
Nikita

Chapter 3

The professor's nasal voice continued its monotonous droning. The words blurred as if water had dripped on a penned page. The room was thick with the scent of sterility, body heat and morning breath.

Amidst it all, Nikita struggled to concentrate. She couldn't. The drone dissolved into a dull buzz. She wanted to giggle as she pictured the rotund Professor Cronin as a huge bee—buzzing, buzzing, flitting from one student to pollinate another, dripping words of "constructive criticism" all along the way. The room grew smaller. The buzz grew louder, closer. She had to get away. *Bzzz, bzzz.*

She heard him demanding in his astonished nasal voice that she return to her seat, calling repeatedly to her retreating back. It was the first time she'd heard any animation in the buzz since the start of the spring session.

No one ever walked out of Professor Cronin's anatomy class, under threat of expulsion. So at any moment she expected a firing squad to let off a round. She hurried. She wanted to run. But of course running through the sanctified hallways of Cornell University Medical School was against the Eleventh Commandment: *"Thou shall not digress from proper decorum."* Or was that her parents' commandment?

She pushed through the glass doors, greedily gulping the clean, fresh air, inhaling the pungent aroma of freshly cut grass and blossoming buds. Faster. She headed for her dorm, not quite sure what she'd do when she arrived, only knowing that she had to get there. She'd figure it out. *Rebellion felt exhilarating.* She smiled.

The buzz grew fainter.

Six and a half hours later, soothed by the sound of Kenny G on CD, Nikita pulled into the endless driveway of her parents' imposing Long Island estate. For the first time since she'd signed off the Cornell campus she questioned the veracity of her hasty actions.

Several moments passed—Kenny'd G'd, Al'd Jarreau'd and Grover'd worked his magic—before she took the key out of the ignition. She released a sigh. "It's now or never." *Never,* a little voice whispered back.

Nikita slid from behind the wheel of her silver-and-black Mercedes convertible—a gift from her father on her twenty-first birthday four years earlier—easing the door shut. Her honey brown eyes settled on the house.

Set on sixty acres of land, in Lattington—which was situated in the "Gold Coast" of above upper-crust suburbia—the Harrell home was the envy of many. It was an architect's delight, of Southern, turn-of-the-century charm coupled with modern accoutrements such as tennis court, swimming pool and gazebo. Their home had been the focus of many *Home and Garden, House Beautiful* and *Architectural Digest* issues. What seemed to impress everyone most, was that the Harrells were both black *and* affluent. Dr. Lawrence Harrell was one of the most renowned vascular surgeons in the United States, and Professor Cynthia Lewis-Harrell was the first black woman to head the mathematics department at Princeton University. Then there was Nikita.

Absently she ran her professionally manicured hands along the length of her ten-months-in-development dreads. They'd finally reached below her ears, and she couldn't wait until they were long enough for her to vary their style. Her parents, on the other hand...

She looked up. Second-floor lights twinkled against the impending nightfall, a sure sign that she'd missed dinner and that her folks were settling down for the evening. *Tradition.*

Determinedly she proceeded down the cobblestone walk, careful because of her heels. The smooth stones could tell many a tale of her skinned knees and bruised elbows.

She pressed the bell and listened for the familiar beeps of the alarm being disengaged. The door swung inward.

"Niki! What on earth? Your parents didn't say anything about you coming home," Amy rushed on, hugging Niki to her slender frame. She had been with her family for as long as she could remember. Amy was the real power behind the well-oiled Harrell machine.

Amy released Niki and set her away. Her sharp brown eyes narrowed. "What's going on? I've never known you to just come home without letting anybody know." She peered around Nikita, looking for something that would explain the unannounced arrival. "Come in here and let me look at you." She hustled Nikita into the house. "Are you sick?"

"No."

"In trouble?"

"No, no. Nothing like that, Amy," Nikita assured. "It was a spur-of-the-moment decision, that's all." She forced a smile.

"Humph. That doesn't sound like you. Not like you at all. Your folks are upstairs and you already missed dinner," she scolded, walking with Nikita down the Italian tile foyer.

"Amy! Who was at the door?"

Nikita's heart knocked at the sound of her mother's strident voice.

"It's Nikita. She wanted to surprise us." Amy threw Nikita a sharp look of disbelief.

Her mother, caressed by a pale peach satin lounging outfit and a cloud of Donna Karan's Chaos cologne, floated to the top of the oak staircase. "Nikita! Larry, Larry. Nikita's home."

"I've dropped out of medical school."

The silver teaspoon that her mother held clattered against a tiny demitasse cup. Cynthia's gray-green eyes rounded in disbelief.

Nikita's gaze darted across the table toward her father, who appeared to have not heard a word. The only indication that he had was the telltale flare of his nostrils.

Cynthia turned toward her husband. "Larry, for God sake, did you hear what she just said?"

"Of course I heard her. I'm not deaf. She's obviously joking," he continued without inflection. "Because no one for whom I've paid more than seventy-five thousand to finance their education would walk in here, sit at my table and tell me they're throwing all that in my face." His voice suddenly exploded. "She's obviously joking!" His fist slammed down on the table, causing everyone and everything within range to jump.

Nikita swallowed hard, and for a split second she contemplated telling them yes, it was a joke. But if she did do that, the joke would ultimately be on her.

Her tone was soft, but decisive. "It's not a joke. I've left medical school. I'm not going back." There, she'd said it, and the earth hadn't quaked and lightning hadn't struck.

"Oh yes, you are going back," her father spat out, rising to his feet. "And you're going to finish at the top of your class, as you always have." His hazel eyes blazed with barely contained fury. "After all we've done for you—"

Those words rolled around in her head like a beach ball out of control, and something as sharp as the sound of dry wood inside of her snapped.

Nikita sprang from her seat, leaning forward, pressing her palms against the linen-covered, hand-carved table. "What about all I've done for *you!*" She pinned her father with a defiant stare, then turned on her mother. "For as long as I can remember, I've done everything you've directed me to do. Joined all the *right* clubs, had the *right* friends—and the *right* color, of course. Excelled in every subject, attended the schools you wanted me to attend. Majored in a subject I hate. I was valedictorian for you. Summa Cum Laude for you, Mother, Father. What about me?" Tears of frustration burned her eyes and spilled. Her body trembled. "I can't do it anymore. I won't. Not…any…more." She sat down hard in her seat and wiped away the tears with the back of her hand.

"I should have seen this coming," her father said. He pointed a finger of accusation. "Ever since you started growing those weeds in your head—"

"They're not weeds, dammit. They're dreadlocks, a symbol of our heritage."

"Nikita! I will not have you use that language in this house," said her mother.

"The only thing you just heard me say was *damn?* Maybe I should say it more often, so someone around here would pay me some attention."

Her mother opened her mouth, then shut it when her husband continued his tirade.

"Weeds," he spat, caught up in his own rhetoric, ignoring the sparring between mother and daughter. "The first step toward your demise. No upstanding young woman would be seen in public like that. I don't know what heritage you're speaking of," he continued in his pompous tone. "It certainly isn't mine, or anyone's I know. All you need is a Jemima rag on your head to complete the look. We've come too far for this. We've worked too hard—"

"Why won't you listen? For once. I'm twenty-five years old, and I don't have a clue as to who I am, where I'm going, or even what I'll do for myself when the two of you are... I need to have my own life. Make some decisions for myself. And that means not being a doctor."

"So what do you intend to do?" her mother asked, perplexed.

Nikita took a long breath. "I want to be a writer."

"A writer!" Condescending laughter filled the room. "Have you completely lost your mind?" he sputtered. "Writing isn't a profession, it's a hobby. How do you intend to support yourself? Or are you going to be another starving artist, for art's sake?"

Nikita stood. "I knew I shouldn't come here. But I thought it was the right thing to do." With a pained expression she turned to her father. "I'll find a way to repay you." She snatched up her purse, turned and stalked away.

"Nikita." Cynthia hurried after her. "Where are you going?"

She kept her back to her mother. Her voice shook. "I don't know. Maybe I'll stay with Parris and Nick in the city."

"Of course you won't." Her tone softened as she turned her daughter to face her. "This is your home. You stay here as long as you want. It's obvious that you're terribly distraught. I won't have you driving around town half hysterical. Maybe some time off from school is just what you need. Now come along. Take a long soak. I'm sure you'll feel better in the morning."

Nikita looked at her picture-perfect mother with sad eyes. Cynthia Harrell didn't have a clue.

That was nearly three months ago, Nikita reflected. Her twenty-sixth birthday was dogging her heels, and she still had no job. Her savings were almost depleted and she refused to ask her parents for a dime. It was bad enough having to see her father's "I told you so" look every time they passed each other. The reality was, she had no experience or educational background to break into journalism. All she had was determination and a dream—one that she'd pushed to the back of her mind in pursuit of her parents' dream. God, she didn't want her parents to be right.

Maybe this interview would pan out. The woman said she was willing to train her as long as she didn't mind playing Girl Friday in the process.

She ascended the stairs from beneath the subterranean world of New York City, finally free from the press of damp flesh. She felt like taking a shower. Looking around to get her bearings, she fished in her pocketbook for the address: 803 Eighth Avenue, corner of Twenty-first Street. At least a ten-block walk.

She looked down at her low-heeled shoes, thankful. *"All God's Children Need Traveling Shoes,"* she muttered.

Turning off Fourteenth Street she walked along Sixth Avenue, peeking in the antique shop windows, outdoor cafés, absorbing the laid-back atmosphere. She inhaled deeply and smiled. She was growing accustomed to exhaust fumes and the intangible aroma of leftover garbage. She turned down Eighteenth Street, intrigued by the tree-lined block and stately brownstones. Sparkling plate-glass windows gave sneak previews of crystal chandeliers or high-tech track lighting, oversize living rooms, mahogany fixtures and hardwood floors. Couples in all shades and combinations sat on stoops, or strolled down the avenues. *This is a neighborhood,* she thought. Not the sterile, pristine, patrolled area in which she existed. She could like it here.

A moving truck was up ahead and she wondered if they were coming or going. She walked a bit faster, her thoughts outrunning her pace. If they were moving out, she'd ask about the vacancy. If she got the job, she'd be able to pay her rent. In the meantime, she could sell her Benz.... She slowed, nearing the truck.

The double-glass and wood door at the top of the stoop was propped wide open, like a woman awaiting her lover. She looked around and didn't see anyone. Taking a breath, she turned into the yard and was about to go up the steps.

"Lookin' for somebody?"

She looked up into dark, haunting eyes. Her heart pounded a bit too hard. "Uh, not really. I mean, I was just wondering if there's an apartment available." *He's gorgeous.* She cleared her throat and backed up as the lean, thoroughly masculine figure gave her a long, slow look that made her feel like he'd just undressed her, then bounded down the stairs.

"Not that I know of." *Damn, she's fine.* He towered over her— catching a whiff of sea breeze and baby powder—on his way to the van. A pulse pounded low in his groin, unsettling him with its suddenness. He turned back in her direction, his long black locks swinging across his bronze shoulders. Dark eyes held her in place for a brief moment before dancing away. "Sorry."

She shrugged, wanting to appear as cool and unaffected as he did. "No problem."

He leaned against the truck, his arms folded across his chest as he watched her walk away. "Good luck." He wanted to say more, talk to her and make her stay a minute. He didn't.

Nikita stopped and turned. Her insides seesawed when she saw him grin. It made his eyes kind of crinkle. She smiled, and his stomach clenched. "Thanks." She continued on, with just the slightest tremor in her legs, wondering what she could have said to a man like that to lengthen the moment. *Nothing.*

"Nice." Quinn hummed in appreciation as he watched her departure until she reached the corner and turned. For a moment he saw the light again.

Nikita looked up from the menu just as Parris stepped through the doors of B. Smith's. Every head turned and murmured whispers of recognition and speculation. Parris McKay had made her debut in the music world three years earlier, taking listeners and producers by storm. She and Nikita had met even earlier, while Nikita was an exchange student in France and Parris was in search of her mother.

To those who did not know her, Parris was an elusive beauty with the voice of Ella, Mahalia, Sarah and Whitney all rolled into one. But to Nikita, Parris was just her *girlfriend,* the one who told her like it was, borrowed her clothes, was light enough to be accepted by her parents and brazen enough not to care. Fame hadn't changed her one bit.

Nikita stood and they hugged, long and hard. "It's good to see you, girl," Nikita said into Parris's tumble of midnight hair.

"You, too. It's been too long, sis."

They both stepped back assessing each other with knowing up-and-down looks.

"That's my dress. I've been missing it since the last time you rolled into town," Nikita spouted, one hand on her hip and the other pointing at the red sleeveless linen dress.

"Just wore it so you wouldn't forget what it looks like," Parris taunted in a quick comeback. "You've finally grown into those dreads. Lookin' good, too."

"Yeah, they'd probably look real good with that dress."

"We'll never know, now will we?"

"We'd better!"

They bug-eyed each other and broke into sidesplitting laughter, collapsing into their seats.

"Whew. You still have that fast mouth, Parris."

"You just bring out the best in me. What can I tell you? Did you order?" She picked up the menu.

"No. I was waiting for you. As usual."

"Don't want to go changing on you. You'd be disappointed."

"I doubt it."

"It was that bad, huh?" Parris asked later over a mouthful of blackened salmon.

Nikita nodded her head slowly. "Worse. It wasn't so much the scene. It was the things that were said. I've never seen my father that furious."

"You've never had the nerve to go against him before. He was probably as stunned as you were."

"Yeah, well the shock should be over. That was almost four months ago. Even though I started working he still barely speaks. I can't wait to get out of there. I feel like I'm sitting on a time bomb."

"You're always welcome to stay with me and Nick. We're hardly ever there, anyway."

"Thanks, but no. I need my own space."

"I can understand that. Just remember the offer is always open." She shoved more food in her mouth. "Tell me about the job. I always knew you had a flair for the written word. I never could see you in the doctor getup. And your bedside manner is lousy."

Nikita laughed. "Yeah, how about that? But the job is great. My boss, Ms. Ingram, is a real character. A throwback to the sixties, and she must be about seventy-five. But she's determined to get her magazine out to the masses. I'm learning the business from the bottom up. Distribution, printing, layout, sales. She's even letting me edit some stories that have come in."

"Sounds great. How much does it pay?"

"Not enough, unfortunately. I get subsidized with hands-on training."

Parris eyed her speculatively. She leaned across the table. "Tell me. Is this really what you want, or are you just doing this to be a pain in the ass to your folks? I was only kidding about the bedside-manner thing. You'd be great at whatever you did. But you know how you have your moments—breaking up with Grant, then not going away to school, having *musicians* as friends…"

"The truth?"

Parris nodded.

"For as long as I can remember I've wanted to write. You know that. When I was little I saw myself standing in front of this massive desk with a huge floor-to-ceiling window behind me. And I knew I was a publisher, and that was my office. But you also know I was never encouraged in that direction. I was always pushed to fill my father's unfillable shoes." She paused, then looked at Parris. "I'm taking some writing courses at New York University, and I'm learning the business. I can feel it Parris, this is for me."

"Then go for it, hon. Give it everything you've given to all the other challenges in your life. This time put *your* heart in it."

Nikita keyed in the last page of a women's health article on the need for mammograms just as Ms. Ingram bustled through the door.

"Niki, you're still here? I thought you'd be long gone by now," she said, hanging her sweater on the brass hook behind the door. The scent of lavender wafted around her, cooling the room.

"I'm almost finished. I have a class tonight, anyway. Six forty-five, remember?"

"Oh, yes. How is it going, by the way?" She crossed the small room, her footsteps muffled by the Aubusson area rug. She went to her cluttered desk, which was scarred by years of use, and sifted through the stack of mail.

"So far, so good. I love my instructor."

"Glad to hear it." She wagged a brown finger at Nikita. "We'll make a journalist out of you yet."

Nikita pushed back from the desk and stretched her arms above her head. "Ms. Lillian?"

"Hmmm."

"I was thinking—what about adding an entertainment section to the magazine? I mean, I know the magazine is issue-and-health oriented, but I can't imagine that your subscribers wouldn't like to read about places in the city to go, interviews with entertainers who are in town."

Lillian stopped her perusing of the mail and settled her hazy brown gaze on Nikita's face. "Sounds like a wonderful idea, but who's going to write and edit that section?"

"Well…I'd like to, if you'd be willing to give me a try. As a matter of fact, Parris McKay is my closest friend. I could easily get an interview with her, *and* pictures."

"Parris McKay is a friend of yours?"

Nikita beamed. "She sure is. And she wears my clothes every chance she gets."

Lillian laughed her weatherbeaten laugh. "Niki, if you can get an interview with Parris McKay, I'll let you run the entertainment section anyway you want."

Nikita popped up from her seat, darted around the desk, and closed Lillian's lean frame in a bear hug. "Thank you. Thank you. It's going to be great. You'll see."

The weather had been unusually warm for late June. The temperature had spiraled into the nineties and remained there for more than a week. For the first time since she'd returned home she was grateful for the extravagance that her parents poured into the house. The entire structure was equipped with central heating and air. All of the major rooms had their individual thermostats. She had hers on frosty.

"You must have Parris out before she goes on tour again," Cynthia said, stepping into Nikita's dressing room.

Nikita sat in front of the oval mirror circled by professional makeup lights and looked at her mother's reflection. The entire top of the white-and-gold-lacquered tabletop was covered with a huge assortment of nail polishes, lipsticks, beautifying creams and ointments. She sprayed her locks with oil sheen and held back a chuckle when she saw her mother demurely turn up her nose.

"I'll ask her. But you know how busy she is." In actuality she didn't want to be subjected to her parents' monologues about how wonderful Parris's life was, what a wonderful husband she had, all compared to Niki's apparent non-accomplishments. Although in private they abhorred the "loose, debasing" life of singers and musicians, Parris was *different.* Sure.

"Do try. It would be so good to see her again. And tell her I said good luck with her performance tonight." Cynthia turned and floated away. Nikita just shook her head and finished with her makeup.

Parris had said dress would be extremely casual at the club. Nick had been having problems off and on with the air-conditioning unit. Some nights it was the Antarctic, some nights the Sahara. Nikita opted for a spaghetti strap, cotton knit T-shirt and a pair of khaki shorts. She grabbed the matching jacket and folded it over her arm, just in case.

She checked her purse: lipstick, notepad, tape recorder, two pens and a pencil. Grinning, she felt like a real journalist. Parris had promised to give Nikita the interview for the magazine after her set. Although Nikita couldn't imagine what Parris could tell her that she didn't already know, she wanted to do this the right way. "And anyway, I don't want you sneaking in any lies about me borrowing your clothes," Parris had warned.

Taking one last look in the mirror, she flipped off the lights, grabbed her bag and was on her way.

Nick stepped out of his office, drawn by the way-down soul that cried out from the black and whites. Clear, sharp, precise and so packed with emotion it gave him pause. He stood in the shadows of the archway, mesmerized.

When the music came to its stirring conclusion, Nick applauded. Not the kind of frenzied, hurried applause of concert-goers, but the slow, rhythmic beat of hands that comes from those who have been transported.

Quinn snapped his head in the direction of the clapping and quickly pushed away from the piano. Nick approached.

"Sorry, man. I didn't see anybody around, so I just kicked it for a minute." He held up his palms. "I'm out." He started to back away.

"Hold on. Hold on. I liked what you just did," Nick said to Quinn. "Where'd you study?"

"I didn't." Quinn raised a brow, uncomfortable being asked about his background.

"Meaning?"

"Meaning, just what I said. I taught myself. Listened to what I dug and copied it, that's all."

"Self-made man." Nick grinned, cautious, seeing the feral look of one caged and ready to pounce. "I like that." He stuck out his hand. "I'm Nick Hunter. I own the place. Me and you have a lot in common."

Quinn eased his guard down, relaxing his stance as he shook Nick's hand. He cocked his head to the side. "How's that?"

"Come on in my office. Let's talk."

"Naw, man. I got things to do." He turned to leave.

"If you can play like that I might have a spot for you here some nights." He waited a beat. "Interested?"

Quinn looked at him from over his shoulders, letting his eyes and his senses take in the man in front of him. Nick Hunter had the look of a man who had it all together. Money, clothes, his own business. What could he possibly have in common with him? It was only happenstance that he'd even wandered in. The heat on the street was unbelievable, and he'd ducked in to get a quick drink. Then it was as if something pulled him in the direction of the baby grand. He'd never played on a first-class piano before, and when he heard what it could do he couldn't seem to stop himself from drowning in the music.

It's okay, Q.

Quinn shrugged his broad shoulders and followed Nick into his office.

An hour later Quinn walked out of Nick's office with a job, one night a week, playing piano with Nick's band.

"Why don't you hang out a while and get a feel for the place?" Nick offered. "It usually gets pretty packed in here by ten. Besides, my lady is singing tonight. I'll introduce you."

Quinn nodded. "Sounds good."

"All right then, so I'll see you later."

"Bet."

Sitting at the bar, sipping a glass of his usual, Quinn tried to make sense out of the past few hours. Out of nowhere he was now employed as a musician, no less. The idea scared him. He had a mind to just tell Nick to forget it. He didn't have the time. But the reality was, he wasn't sure if he could cut it. He'd never played for a soul in his life, other than Lacy. Suppose he froze up like a punk when he was up there on the stage? What if his homeys ever found out he was some nightclub piano player? What would that do to his rep uptown?

But something greater than the fear of discovery pushed against him. The need for change, the need to be recognized for something other than a hustler. Maybe there was something to what Lacy had been saying all those years. Maybe he did have talent. Nick seemed to think so.

He looked around. This was no B.J.'s. The mirrored walls reflected shiny black tables, a dance-all-night floor, bathrooms that smelled as if they were cleaned on the hour. Even the smoke from the cigarettes didn't seem to hang on him and clog his lungs. The people who began to filter in wore suits, classy designer clothes, casual jeans with starched shirts, and jewelry that didn't blind him from a mile away. The women looked as if they'd just stepped off the cover of *Essence,* not *Player.* The bartender's shirt was pristine white, not a grimy Fruit of the Loom T-shirt splotched with grease and the underarm stains from failed deodorant. The music that filtered from car windows was classic R&B, not the booming sounds of hip-hop and underground rap.

He looked at his Nike sneakers, the large gold pinkie ring, and his customary oversize jogging suit. He didn't belong here. And he was a fool for thinking that he did. Even for a minute. To have a semblance of this kind of life and living behind the privacy of his own doors was one thing. To try to live it in the open was another.

He tossed the last of his drink down his throat, paid his tab and turned on the bar stool, ready to leave—then in she walked.

Chapter 4

Quinn and Nikita

She was whipped by the time she arrived, accompanied by a first-class attitude. She'd had to walk nearly four blocks in the suffocating heat from where she'd finally found a parking space, while listening to the cacophony of "Ooh baby's," "Can I get wit you's" and countless other comments she'd prefer to forget. If another fast-talking man had another one-liner for her, she wasn't going to be responsible for her actions.

Her clothes felt as if they'd been fastened to her body with Instant Krazy Glue, and if she hadn't known better she'd have sworn her "Secret" had been let out of the bag.

When she stepped through the door of the club she let out a silent *hallelujah* when a cold blast of air hit her smack in the face, lowering her body temperature to near normal. She adjusted her eyes to the semi-darkened interior, taking in the trendy patrons and classy decor.

Slinging her Coach bag onto her shoulder she threaded her way around the circular tables and walked with an easy grace toward the bar. Years of ballet classes and etiquette training were the only things that saved her from stumbling over her own feet when she looked down the length of the bar and saw him sitting there, as cool and collected as he wanted to be. And he was looking straight at her.

Lordhammercy. Now she knew what Parris meant about the unreliable air-conditioning. It was obviously busted again. What other explanation could there be for the rush of heat that closed around her like a cocoon? She felt like stripping. Her heart was hammering so fast she thought she was having some kind of fatal attack.

With as much calm as she could summon she averted her gaze, located an empty table as far away from him as possible, took a seat and prayed for an earthquake, tidal wave, something. Luckily, a waitress rescued her and brought her a quick drink of Pepsi with lemon. Heaven knows she hadn't forgotten him—that face, those eyes, *that body.* Every now and then, on her lunch hour, she'd walked along his block in the hope of seeing him again. Those times she'd been prepared with some cool and engaging conversation. Right now she couldn't even remember her own name. She slurped a sip of her drink.

When she walked through the door, he was sure he was seeing things. He blinked, and yes, it was her—that irrepressible sister he'd thought about almost constantly for the past few weeks. He took another swallow of his drink. Man, she looked damned good, just as if she belonged in a classy place like this. He didn't want to stare, so he just kind of played it off, as if looking for somebody. He wondered if she was meeting her man here or something. Didn't look like it. He blew it the last time he saw her, getting all tongue-tied and whatever. He wouldn't let another opportunity to get to know her slip by.

Damn, here he comes. What was she going to do now? *Mmmm. How does he walk like that, like he's floating on some cloud?*

"What if I joined you?" he asked as if he'd known her forever. "Would that be a problem?"

She looked up into those blue-black eyes and tried to focus on what he'd just asked her and not on the body that needed to be on the centerfold in *Playgirl.* She shrugged and gave him a half smile. "Suit yourself." What happened to the irresponsible actions she was going to launch into the next time a guy handed her a line? But this one sounded kind of good.

She tried to ignore him by signaling the waitress.

"Pepsi with lemon," he said when the waitress appeared.

Nikita looked at him, her eyebrow arched.

"What…I pay attention to those kinda things." He grinned. "Jack on the rocks," he said without taking his eyes away from Nikita. She was even finer than he remembered. The slope of her eyes, the arch of her cheeks and that clingy little T-shirt…

Dimples. She hadn't noticed the dimples before. But he sure had them and they were sure pretty. "You've been watching me?" she asked, both thrilled and apprehensive.

"Yeah, for a while." He paused and scanned the room. "You're not meetin' anybody."

"How do you know that?"

He watched her slender body adjust itself, ready to show she was indignant, and felt as if he were being pulled inside of her. "Because we've been waitin' to meet each other for a long time. Our last run-in was just an appetizer. You don't think I'd forget a woman like you, do you?" He took a sip of his drink and watched her over the rim of his glass. "And I know you didn't forget me. Tell me I'm wrong, and I'm outta here."

If this was a come-on line, she didn't care. There was just something about him. Something earthy and real, from the rich timbre of his voice, his don't-give-a-damn attitude, to his inaccessibility. Not like the sophisticated, suit-and-tie, Ivy League men that she was accustomed to. She felt out of *her* league in his presence, but she couldn't seem to stop herself from wanting more and had no intention of trying. She was about to take the leap of her life.

"You're right. I didn't forget."

He took her hand as if he had all the right in the world. "Quinn."

When she looked down at the large, smooth hand that swallowed hers, then upward into his dark eyes, she was a ship at sea. Somewhere, deep inside, she knew he was her anchor. "Nikita."

"Nice. It fits you."

His smile was slow and easy, like a hot, lazy summer afternoon, with Mama serving cool lemonade on the porch, by the swings. You just wanted to take your time with it and make it last.

"You from around here?"

"No. I live on Long Island." She hated how that sounded—all smug and above it all. But what else could she say?

He leaned back in his seat, cocked his head to the side, and kind of rolled his eyes up and down her body. "No doubt. Never met nobody from Long Island. So, you one of them w-a-y uptown girls."

"What's that supposed to mean?" She pulled her hand away and wrapped it around the cold glass to cool it.

"Whatever you want it to mean. You want it to mean something that's gonna piss you off, then it will. And from the look on you face, it does. Why's that?"

"It doesn't *piss* me off, as you put it." Defensive was not the sound she was striving for, but it came out, anyway. She took a sip of her Pepsi and tried again. "What I mean is, I like where I live. I didn't intend to sound otherwise."

He looked at her for a long moment. "Hey, that's cool. You're a big girl. Feel any way you wanna." He wanted to push her, to test her, test her sensibilities. Would she be put off by him? If he let her into his world, what would she do about what she saw?

"How's the apartment?"

The question pulled him back from the turn of his thoughts. "Comin' along. I'm settlin' in." He grinned. "Maybe you'll get a chance to see it for yourself."

Her stomach fluttered and she had to wiggle her toes to shake off a tingling sensation. "Who said I wanted to?"

He leaned closer across the table. "I know you do. Maybe not tonight, but you will."

"You sound awfully sure of yourself for someone who doesn't know me from Adam."

And then he said the most startling thing, in clear, plain English, and she wondered for a second if he were a ventriloquist. "No, I've known you all my life, Nikita. We've just waited until now to make it official."

He was one smooth talker, there was no doubt about that. "Is that right?"

"Yeah."

He grinned, and all those pretty white teeth sparkled against that good-enough-to-eat skin. Nikita was in creamy-black-chocolate heaven.

"So, you got a last name to go with that first one?"

Nikita laughed. "Yes. It's Harrell."

"Hmmm." Quinn nodded. "Nikita Harrell. Sounds important. You important?" His dark gaze probed her.

"I hope so."

Echoes of countless conversations with Lacy danced through his head. How many times had she told him that your worth, your own importance, could never be measured by the make and model of your ride, or the size of the roll in your pocket, or how many people moved out of your way when you walked down the street? He hadn't listened.

"You hope so. That's kinda lame, comin' from a girl like you. Either you are, or you ain't. Simple. Don't think about it. If you don't know, then who will?" She had that look again, like somebody'd just pinched her behind and she was rarin' to slap 'em. But he didn't even care.

"You have a very interesting way of making my words turn into what you want to hear."

"I call 'em like I see 'em. Ain't that what women look for in a man—honesty?"

"A little diplomacy wouldn't hurt your repertoire."

Quinn laughed, a deep hearty laugh, and Nikita struggled to keep the smile from her lips.

"You know you wanna laugh." He chuckled. "So why don't you just let go and give in to how you feel? You ever done that before, Nikita Harrell, just gave in to how you was feelin' without worryin' about tomorrow?"

Then, suddenly, his tone changed—softened—caressed. His eyes moved in on her and the world disappeared. It was just the two of them. His finger stroked her hand, setting off the electric currents.

It's getting hot in here. She opened her mouth to speak, but he just put that same finger to her lips. His mouth curved up on one side.

"Don't answer. Not now. I want that first to-hell-with-the-world experience to be with me."

She should have gotten up. She should have run as fast and as far away from this man as possible. But his presence held her there, as surely as if he'd tied her down.

"There you are." Parris bent down and pecked Nikita on the cheek, successfully snapping her out of her trance. "I was wondering if you were still coming." She looked from one to the other.

Nikita blinked and smiled up at Parris. "Of course I was coming. I've been here a while."

Parris raised her eyebrow.

"Oh, Parris McKay, this is…Quinn. Quinn, Parris. She's Nick's wife. He owns the club."

So this was the boss's wife. Damn, Nikita Harrell traveled in high circles. He'd seen Parris's videos and her face more times than he could count. He stood. "Nice to meet you. I was talkin' with your husband earlier. He said he'd introduce us, but Nikita here saved him the trouble."

"Oh, you're that Quinn! Nick hasn't stopped talking about you. When do you start?"

Nikita frowned. What in the world were they talking about?

Quinn shrugged. "Probably next week."

"Great. I'm dying to hear you play. Girl, you didn't tell me you knew such a fabulous piano player."

"Had I only known."

Parris squinted as if she couldn't see her. "Anyway, I have to run. My first set starts in an hour. Come to the office afterward, Niki. We can talk then." She stuck out her hand to Quinn, which he took. "Pleasure to meet you. Welcome aboard."

"Same here. Thanks."

Parris waved, then hurried across the floor and into the back room.

Nikita set her gaze on Quinn's don't-have-a-care-in-the-world face. "*You* play piano—here at the club?"

He chuckled. "I ain't even gotta look up the word *disbelief.* It's all over your face. What's so hard to believe?" His smile was gone. "Hard to believe a guy like me could do anything besides—what—find a short way into your pants? Everything ain't always how it seems on the outside. Take you, for instance." He leaned back. "Under the icy, uptown, Ms. Clean exterior, I know there's a hot-blooded, double or nothin', wanna-take-a-chance-with-you-Quinn woman dyin' to get out. All she needs is somebody to unlock the garage door."

She pressed her lips together to keep from smiling. "Oh, really?"

"Oh, yeah," he crooned and took her hand, pulling her to her feet and in line with his body, forcing her to look up at him. "I'm gonna show you, right now."

He led her out onto the dance floor and they flowed as one perfect unit to the moods of Whitney's "I Believe in You and Me." One song segued into the next, as they glided together across the smooth hardwood floor.

Although short women never held much appeal for him, this one was different, he thought. She felt perfect. She fit. Like some missing piece—of what he wasn't sure. Nikita Harrell was no Sylvie, that was for damned sure, or anyone else like her. She was more like those women on the cover of *Essence* and *Black Elegance.* You could see 'em, but not touch 'em. Getting with a woman like Nikita Harrell was that elusive dream. Would she be his dream come true?

Nikita closed her eyes. Allowed her senses to soar. She felt him everywhere, warm, hard, large and strong. Strangely enough she felt secure, as if this man could easily keep the bogeyman away. Keep her safe—from herself. He wasn't threatened by the foreign world she only imagined being a part of, because he lived it. Still, she felt that there was more to him than the hard, thug-like, don't-give-a-damn, too cool aura that he gave off like an expensive cologne. Against every bit of good judgment that had ever been ground into her, she wanted to find out what was beneath the surface.

"What do you do when you ain't hangin' in nightclubs and pickin' up strange men?" he said deeply into her ear.

A flood of heat roared through her body, jerking her away from her daydreaming. She arched her neck back to be able to look up at him. His eyes were crinkling at the corners. She swallowed. "I work for *Today's Woman* magazine. It's pretty local at the moment. But we're growing."

"Cool. What do you work at?"

She smiled. "I do everything—read manuscripts, answer phones, lick stamps. But I've finally gotten my big break. The publisher, Ms. Ingram, liked my idea for an entertainment section, and she's letting me write my first article. It's going to be an interview with Parris."

"You got my attention. Tell me more." He wanted to tell her about his own writings and his sister's dreams for him. He didn't.

The music moved from body-locking to hand-clapping, so Quinn guided Nikita back to their table.

"I'm listenin'." He held her chair while she sat down.

Niki looked up at him for a moment, the small, uncalculated gesture reaching her. So she talked. And he did listen. In small doses, she explained about her abrupt exodus from Cornell and the tension-filled four months at home.

"So, you gotta save enough loot to get your own crib?"

"Loot?"

He grinned. "You know, *Dinero,* cash, money—loot."

"Oh." She smiled in embarrassment. "Yes, I do. And soon."

Quinn nodded. "How long you been takin' classes at NYU?"

"I just started this semester."

He lounged back in his seat, splay-legged. "So now what— you're gonna be a writer—what happens to all your doctorin' skills?"

Nikita's soft brown eyes slowly traversed the room as though searching for the answer, or for the words that would bring her emotions to the forefront. She looked for understanding. "It just wasn't me," she finally said. "I tried to make it work—"

"Because your people wanted you to," he said, finishing her thought, "so you hung in there until you couldn't hang no more."

She nodded.

"Sometimes you just gotta do your own thing, ya know?

Everybody ain't gonna always understand or accept that. But you just gotta keep it real and go for yours."

Nikita looked at him. Even through the crudeness of his words she knew he understood. When had any man she'd ever been with ever grasped what she thought and felt, or even cared enough to voice an opinion that reached beneath the surface? Her male associates had always been too concerned with their own success to show any interest in her needs or feelings. Quinn was in total contrast to what she'd imagined he would be. With a little polish he could really shine.

"What about you? What makes it real for you?"

"Maybe I'll rap with you about it sometime." He stood. "But I gotta be pushin' on."

Nikita hid her disappointment behind the glass she lifted to her lips.

His eyes crinkled as he touched her cheek with the tip of his finger. "Take it easy, Nikita Harrell."

"You, too."

He turned, smooth as a velvet-toned Nat King Cole album spinning on a crystal turntable platter, and, like vaporous wisps of cigarette smoke, was gone.

She didn't know whether to be angry or insulted. He hadn't asked to see her again, or asked for her phone number. Even though he wasn't her type, anyway, he could have at least asked for her number, whether he called or not. Wasn't she interesting enough? Pretty enough? What kind of woman attracted a man like Quinn—Quinn? She didn't even know his last name.

"So, Miss Thing, what in the world was going on with you and Mr. Dark and Lethal?" Parris asked, breaking into Nikita's meandering thoughts. She took a seat.

"Nothing." She shrugged her right shoulder and frowned. "We were just talking. That's all."

"Really? Then what's with the look?"

"What look?"

"Like you just got your little ego stepped on."

"Not hardly."

Parris put on her best lecturing-her-girlfriend voice, targeted and launched. "He's not your type, Niki. Anybody can see that from a mile away. He has bad boy written all over him." She waited a beat, then broke into a grin. "And that's the turn on. Isn't it?" With Freudian accuracy she continued, "The other side of life that you only get to fantasize about. The whole *good-girls-don't* syndrome is tickling your imagination, like a bird feather flicking against your nose. Only thing is, sneezing is not what you have on…your…mind…to…do."

Nikita bit back a grin. Parris knew her as well as she knew the riffs and downbeats of her songs. Knew how to manipulate her as easily as she worked those notes up and down the scale. Parris McKay was a royal pain, and she loved her. "As usual, you're reading way too much into this. We were just talking."

"When you believe it, so will I." She pushed her chair away from the table and stood. "Don't look so lost, sister girl. Come back next week and you'll see him right behind that piano," she teased.

"Very funny."

Parris moved toward the stage, a raised platform in the center of the room, when the MC announced her name.

"See you in a bit."

"Parris," Nikita hissed between her teeth.

She turned, raised her brows in question.

"What's his last time?" Nikita asked, trying and failing to sound unconcerned.

Parris smiled. "Parker, hon. Quinten Parker."

Chapter 5

Wishin'

Chilling on his nightly run with T.C., who'd become his regular partner, Quinn let his thoughts surf to Nikita. She was all that. A fine sistah. No doubt. Had a lot going on, *and* she was a writer. The first female, the first anybody, he'd ever met who actually wrote for a living. And she gave up being a doctor to try her hand at what she really wanted to do. That took heart. He dug that. Dug it a lot. Smothering a grin, he thought that maybe she wasn't all high-toned and uppity, after all, even though he didn't go for her type.

He'd been a sentence away from telling her about his own writing and of Lacy's dreams for him. Somehow, he knew that she would understand, like Lacy had. But truth be told, he hadn't picked up a pen to write a single word since her death. He couldn't seem to bring himself to do it. Everything related to his other life was tied to his twin sister. To write again would only reinfect the wound of her loss, as would his playing at the club. And that's why he wasn't going to do it.

"Whatsup wit you, man?" T.C. probed, peeping Quinn's silence. Generally Quinn pumped him for information about how he was doing in school, listened to stories about his sisters and brothers, and offered the kind of older male advice that he couldn't find at home. T.C. had come to look forward to the evenings that he spent in Quinn's company. Come to expect the feeling of brotherhood that they shared. Even though Quinn had to be at least ten to twelve years older, he never talked down to him, or tried to make him feel stupid when he shared his thoughts. More often than not, Quinn told him he needed to get out of this life and lifestyle while he still could, before the money got too good and it was too late. Yeah, money was part of the reason he continued to make the runs, but the real reason was that he'd come to look at Quinn as the older brother, a missing father, that he needed. He didn't want to lose that.

"It's all good. You playin' *Jeopardy,* kid?" Quinn slid from behind the wheel and out into the flypaper night. It was the kind of evening when everything stuck to you—the air, your clothes, bugs. Even the dank smells of the street rose, wafted and clung to your skin. He cut his eyes over the hood of the car and pinned T.C. with his gaze, waiting for a response.

"Naw, man," T.C. said, catching his breath after stepping out into the clawing night, from the cool comfort of Quinn's ride. "My name ain't Alex. You just seem quiet."

The corner of Quinn's mouth tilted in a half smile. "It's all good, like a said."

Quinn's dark eyes scanned the length of 115th Street. Cars double-parked. Everything from run-down, rust-coated Chevys to this morning's off-the-lot Lexuses. Music blasting from everything that could send out a tune. Pushed upward to their limit in the hope of catching a whiff of something, the gaping holes of wide-open windows, set against the run-down buildings, resembled the missing teeth of the pushcart pedestrians in constant search of a stray anything. People in every size, shape, color and design seemed to have been stirred up in a big mixing pot, then dumped out on the street, any which way. They were everywhere. Fish frying in week-old grease seeped out of Shug's Fish Shack and hung around the mouths of the regular Friday-nighters gobbling down what looked to be their last supper. Gold twinkled around necks, in ears, on wrists and in mouths, as sure as the diamonds hidden in the mines of Africa.

This was his world.

He checked his left side and pulled his lightweight jacket securely over the bulge tucked neatly beneath his left arm. It was a calculated move. But necessary. Though he'd never had reason to use it in the past, everyone must know that he would and could in a heartbeat.

Quinn wound his way around and through the pockets of would-bes, could-bes and has-beens, accepting high and low fives, brotherhood hugs, the flavor-of-the-day handshake and the proverbial "Hi, Quinn" from the red-mouthed, everything-squeezed-in-so-it-could-pop-out, weaved, curled and braided hoochies who vied for his attention.

T.C. took up his post on Quinn's left side, etching the "I dare you" glare on his sixteen-year-old face. Watching Quinn as he parted the sea of humanity, accepting his props, T.C. knew that he wanted to be what Quinn had become. He wanted the ride, the crib, the women and the clothes. He wanted the money and everything that it could buy him. In Quinn he saw all of these things and knew that if he paid attention, worked hard, he could take Quinn's place on the street one day, or even have a territory of his own. But his mother wanted him to stay in school. "Get your education, boy. It's the only way out of the ghetto." Quinn even told him to stay in school, make something of himself. But he wanted that something now. Not ten years from now. Anyway, he'd probably be dead before he hit thirty. That was life.

Nikita tried to stay focused. To make the words in her head, on her tape recorder and on her notepad come to life. She'd known Parris for years. They were closer than sisters. Why was she having so much trouble making her real?

Sighing in frustration, she pushed away from her computer screen and stood up, stretching her arms high over her head and rotating her neck to get the kinks out. She stepped out of her calfskin sandals, immediately losing the added two inches that the heels gave her, and wiggled her toes. She padded over to the window, the cool of the wood tingling up her bare legs. From her second-floor perch, she could clearly see the lunch-goers, shop-keepers and local residents meandering up and down the block to their predesignated destinations. She pursed her lips and folded her arms beneath her ample breasts. One lock, weighted down by a seashell, dangled along the side of her face as she leaned closer.

Maybe what she needed to do was take a walk, get a better perspective on what she wanted to write. She couldn't let Ms. Ingram down, not after she'd promised she'd deliver the article. It had already been a week and she hadn't strung together one sentence that made any sense.

Be for real, sister, that annoying voice in her head whispered. She knew good and darn well what the problem was. Quinten Parker. Plain and simple. Every time she thought about writing the article, she thought about Quinn—the way his gaze rolled over her like hot lava, the way his dark eyes sparkled and crinkled when he laughed, the deep resonance of his voice that dipped down into her soul and shook it, and most of all, the way he listened and really heard her.

She'd been back to the club twice but she hadn't seen him, and neither had Nick. She'd even walked along his block, on the other side, of course, in the hope of catching a glimpse of him. No luck.

Anyway, why was she stressing herself out over a man who obviously had no interest in her? He hadn't asked to see her again and he hadn't asked for her number. She didn't have to be hit over the head. End of story.

She tossed her pencil across the desk. *Humph. Bastard. He has some nerve. Who does he think he is, anyway?* She had doctors, lawyers and Indian chiefs running after her—hard. They wanted her time and her number. What—she wasn't good enough? One thing was certain, she was a flight up from those hussies she just knew he was used to.

She turned from the window and stomped back across the room, stepping into her shoes. "Well, you don't have to worry about me worryin' about you," she mumbled, snatching up her purse with a vengeance. Grabbing the keys from the hook by the door, she locked the office and stomped out.

The muggy air closed in on her like a predator cornering its prey. She took a breath, adjusting her body to the change, posed for a moment while looking out at the comings and goings on the avenue—and there he was.

He wasn't quite sure why he'd rolled up here. He stepped out of his vehicle and slid his dark glasses up the bridge of his narrow nose. She wasn't his type. She was too damned short and too green. She didn't know nothin' 'bout nothin' except what she'd heard or read. Damn, she didn't even know what *loot* meant. That should have been his exit cue right then. But there was just somethin' about her. Maybe it was that innocence. The way she acted—all nervous and shy with him, not like those females who'd be ready to pop him where he stood if he said something they didn't like. Quite frankly, he was tired of that. Tired of women who acted just as tough, just as hard, as he did. Shit, a real man wanted a woman, not another real man. And he was getting to the point where he'd like someone sweet, someone soft and feminine who could talk about something besides having babies and videos. So here he was. Now what? He wasn't even sure how to rap with a woman like Nikita. Hey, he'd been around. He'd think of something.

He leaned against his car and waited. He hoped she'd turn up soon. *Man, it was hot.*

Nikita didn't know whether she should run back upstairs before he saw her, stroll down the block as if she didn't see him or just act as if she hadn't noticed him and find out what he was going to do.

Maybe he wasn't even there to see her. He did look as if he was waiting for someone, leaning against that pretty BMW, fine as he wanted to be with that red T-shirt against that chocolate skin that she could almost taste. Her mouth started to water. *Could he see her, with those dark glasses on?*

There she was, all decked out in a b-a-a-d lime green number that stopped just above her knees and those dynamite legs. *Yeah, I see you, baby, tryin' to act like you don't see me. Let me make it easy for you.*

He inhaled deeply, slowly removing his shades, and their gazes connected.

With practiced ease, Quinn uncrossed his long, CK-clad legs, the precision-creased sandstone linen pants flowing around them in lazy-river fashion.

She watched him glide toward her like a director calling for slow motion. *Why was she holding her breath?*

Quinn stopped at the bottom of the steps, placed one foot on the first step, and looked up at her. His eyes crinkled. "Whatsup, Nikita Harrell?"

She kind of smiled. "I was on my way—to get something to eat. Whatsup with you?" Did she just say *whatsup?*

He grinned. She sounded funny, but cute. "That's what I'm here tryin' to find out. But in the meantime, why don't I take you where you're goin'? My ride's across the street. Come on."

"Was that a question or a command?" She arched her brow.

His dimples flashed and she felt even hotter. Quinn gave a mock bow. "It was a question, your high-ness." He looked up at her from beneath those long lashes—grinning.

She pursed her lips as if trying to decide, knowing good and well that she was going. Finally she shrugged. "I guess."

Purposefully, she took her time coming down the stairs. There was no way she could miss the salivating look he gave her legs, and she figured she might as well give him a bit of entertainment, show him what he wasn't getting.

Nikita remained mute during the short ride, afraid of saying something nerdy. Quinn, on the other hand, seemed perfectly content to listen to endless unintelligible lyrics by rap artists with names that sounded lethal. She'd definitely have to do something about his music-listening habits if he planned on spending any time with her.

Then, as if he'd been reading her mind, he pressed the SCAN button and the cool sounds of pre-programmed CD 101.9, the city's premier jazz station, filtered in all around them with a haunting ballad by Phyllis Hyman.

Nikita's eyes slightly widened. He was just full of surprises, wasn't he? And he even had the station programmed.

Quinn, from the corner of his eye, could see her tight little body relax, as if someone had mercifully snatched her out of a too tight girdle. He almost laughed. Instead, he just hummed along with Phyllis. Now, Phyllis could blow. Why she'd decided to snuff herself was a mystery to him. *Ain't nothin' that bad.* And he should know.

"This the spot?" he asked, slowing down in front of Zuri's, a little outdoor café on Fourteenth and Sixth.

"Yes. This is it. There's a parking space across the street," she offered, pointing to a vacant spot.

"What kinda time you got—regulation one hour, or what?"

She turned her head to look at him and her heart knocked hard. Quinn had angled his body so that he faced her. His long, cottony-soft locks hung loose around his wide shoulders. Dark eyes, partially hidden by half-closed lids and sinfully long lashes, gazed back at her. The beginnings of a smile played around those luscious, can-I-get-a-taste lips.

She blinked. What had he asked her? Something about time? Oh, yeah. "I have some work to take care of at the office." She checked her gold Cartier watch. "I suppose a couple of hours wouldn't hurt. Why?"

Quinn chuckled, pressed his foot on the accelerator and took off. "I'ma take you uptown, for some real food. That cool with you?" She nodded, too surprised to do much else. "I wanna check you out with corn bread crumbs around that pretty little mouth of yours."

"Very funny. You don't think I eat corn bread?"

He slanted his gaze at her. "Do you?"

"Sometimes," she lied. The truth was, her parents were so removed from their roots and black culture in general, that her diet growing up had been strictly European. As she grew older, she'd just never acquired a taste for "soul food." Her dates generally took her to French, Italian and anything other than black ethnic restaurants. It was a status symbol to be able to read French menus and make reservations a week in advance to get a table. That was her world. But the possibility of entering his thrilled her little "I thought I had arrived" suburban soul.

* * *

Without further ado, Quinn jumped on the FDR Drive and headed uptown. He'd intended to give her a real culture shock, an awakening. But then he thought better of it. *What if she freaked?* He didn't want to scare her off. There would be plenty of time to show her the other slice of life. Then again, maybe not.

He snatched a quick look at her, taking her all in with a blink of an eye. Small, smooth-looking hands were folded neatly in her lap, ready for a class picture or something. That compact body of hers was pressed so close to her side of the car that if she moved any farther she'd be outside. She was staring straight ahead, like she wanted to make sure she knew what was coming at her. And she was tapping that right foot like she had that shaking disease.

Naw. He couldn't do that to her. Nikita was a lady. No doubt. Those females up on the avenue would eat her alive. Nikita was the type of woman you wanted to protect, not use to protect you. She was used to the smell of cut grass, not the stench of piss in an alley; nightclubs that didn't have secret back rooms; meals that were served on real dishes, not on foam with the little pockets and had to be stapled closed. Damn. What was on her mind? He didn't have any business being with her.

He checked her out again—lookin' all scared, but trying to be cool. And then he knew why. He needed someone like Nikita Harrell in his life. Someone to remind him that there was a whole world that existed outside the one he found himself confined in. He needed to be reminded that there was still some goodness in the world. She could do that, and that made her special.

Yeah, that's why he was with her. And the thought scared the hell out of him, as sure as if he'd stepped into a pitch-black room with no telling what was inside.

"You ever been to the Soul Cafe?" Quinn asked, exiting at 42nd Street.

Nikita released a silent breath when he made his exit. At least they weren't going too far *uptown.* "No. I never heard of it."

"I think you'll like it. It's owned by that brother on *New York Undercover,* Malik Yoba."

Her eyebrows raised. "Oh, really! I love that show. I watch it whenever I can. I hadn't heard that he had a restaurant."

"It's a pretty new spot."

"This is great. Maybe we'll see him," she added, sounding like a schoolgirl.

Quinn slanted his eyes in her direction and smiled, seeing the look of anticipation on her face. So that's the kind of stuff she digs. This was nothing. He couldn't count the number of famous faces he'd either met, eaten with or seen. Everyone at one time or another came uptown to get a taste of can't-be-beat cooking, no matter how much loot they were making.

"Yeah, may-be."

She breathed a silent sigh of relief. This wasn't too bad. He'd had her a little nervous at first when he just took off from Zuri's like that. Although she really did want to see where he was talking about, she just wasn't sure if she wanted to see it today. She'd heard such awful things—the people, the violence, the filth. All she could imagine was what she'd seen on the evening news. Then again, anyone with a grain of sense knew that the news only showed what they wanted to show. They always interviewed the most snaggletoothed, illiterate black person they could find to represent whatever the issue was for the day. She promised herself she'd keep an open mind.

"So, what nights are you playing at the club?"

"I'm not."

"Why? I mean, I thought you were. It was set."

"Changed my mind."

"Oh."

"Problem?"

She shifted for a minute under his gaze. "No. Why should it be? It's like you told me. I'm a big girl. You're a big boy. Right? Do what you want."

"Yeah. Exactly." That was easy. No pressure. He should feel relieved. Then why did he feel like somebody had just let the air out of his steel-belted radials? He kind of wanted her to ask some more questions. He wanted to explain that he'd never played for anybody besides his sister, Lacy. That Lacy was dead. That things hadn't been the same for him since. That the time in the club was the first time he'd played since her death. He wanted to tell her that the pain was still too strong, so bad sometimes that he just wanted to disappear so he could stop being afraid. He didn't have anybody to keep him from being afraid anymore. He wanted to tell her.

He didn't.

Nikita wrinkled her nose. She sure hoped he wasn't one of those trifling Negroes. Supposed to do things, make commitments and then back out. If this was any indication of how he handled his business, well—well, she just didn't know.

Quinn took the liberty of ordering for both of them. Lunch was a combination of hot and spicy jerk chicken, peas and rice, callaloo, fried chicken fingers, a side of homemade coleslaw, not that supermarket stuff, and melt in your mouth corn bread—cooked to a perfect golden brown and served up in healthy chunks.

"How's the food?" he asked.

"Delicious," Nikita mumbled over a mouthful of corn bread.

Quinn reached across the table and brushed the tip of his finger against the corner of her mouth.

A bolt of electric energy shot straight through her. She went perfectly still.

Quinn smiled. "That's what I wanted to see," he said in a tone so low it seemed to reach down to her soul, "what that pretty mouth would look like with golden crumbs around it."

She swallowed. "What does it look like?" she whispered in a tone to match his.

"Very tasty." He grinned.

She bit back a smile and shifted her gaze to her plate. "Is that right?"

"Yeah."

He ran his finger across her lips again and the thrill was twice as strong. She fought down a shiver.

"So what are we gonna do about that?"

She put her fork down, folded her arms on the tabletop and

leaned closer. Her cinnamon-colored eyes held his. "We're going to have to work that out, Mr. Parker. One day at a time."

"I like the sound of that. Night and day meeting at dawn."

"You sound like a poet."

"Naw. Ain't nothin' like that at all. Classy lady like you brings out the melody in a man. Sometimes," he added. "So don't get no wild ideas in your head." His eyes crinkled, and she smiled in return.

"I'll keep that in mind."

And Quinn thought about the fact that he'd never told her his last name. *So she's been askin' about me. Nice.*

He pulled up in front of the building where she worked exactly two hours later. He turned off the engine. They sat in silence for several moments.

Now what? Should she just thank him and get out? What if he tried to kiss her? She knew she probably tasted like some kind of spice and peppers. But then again, so did he. If he tried, she was going to let him.

He unfastened his seat belt and angled toward her, draping his arm along the back of her seat. His fingers played across her exposed neck.

Uh-oh.

"So why don't you give me your number and I can call you sometime?"

"Is that another question or a command?"

The corner of his mouth curved up in a grin. "A question, your high-ness."

"In that case, I guess I can give you my number so you can call me sometime." She dug in her purse, found a pen, and tore off a piece of paper from her pocket notebook and wrote down her number. "That's the number at my office."

He took the paper and checked out the number, then stuck it between the sun visor and the roof of the car.

"Got a man at home that's gonna get ticked if I call you?" he teased, fishing.

"No."

"What if I feel like hearin' your voice after hours?"

"One day at a time. Remember?" She smiled, closed her purse and pressed the button to release the lock on her door. "Thanks for lunch." She got out of the car, shut the door behind her and trotted up the steps, giving him one last look at her legs.

"Thank *you*, Nikita Harrell," he whispered, watching her disappear beyond the door. "Thank you."

Chapter 6

From Here to There

Once again Parris was out of town, and Nikita desperately needed someone to talk with. She sat up in bed and dialed Jewel's number. They'd met several years earlier when Jewel's lifetime partner, Taj, started working at Nick's club. Although Jewel was at least eight years older, they'd become fast friends. Jewel'd had her own battles to wage when she met and fell in love with her much younger mate. She'd bucked the odds and the comments, and come out on top. Next to Parris and Nick, there wasn't a couple more perfect than Taj and Jewel. All she could hope for was to find the same kind of happiness one day.

The phone rang three times before Jewel's eighteen-year-old daughter, Danielle, picked up.

"Hey, Dani. It's Nikita."

"Hi, Aunt Niki. How are ya?"

"Just fine." Nikita laughed. She was tickled every time Danielle called her "Aunt." Jewel had a strict rule in her house: adults were addressed as Ms. or Mr. so-and-so, or they were inducted into the family as honorary aunts or uncles, an African practice. Nikita had opted for family status.

"How's everything with school?"

"My second year at Howard was phat! I had a ball, and the most gorgeous men—chocolate-chip heaven with a little macadamia for variety."

Nikita laughed along with Danielle. "Sounds good, but what about your classes?"

"Oh, those. I aced them. No prob."

Danielle had been an above "A" student since grammar school, skipped grade levels twice and received a full four-year scholarship to Howard.

"Keep it up. I know your mother is proud."

"She oughta be. Maintaining my social calendar and a 4.0 ain't easy." She chuckled.

"I can imagine. Where is the lady of the house?"

"She just got out of the shower. Hang on, I'll get her. Take it easy, Aunt Nik. Come out and see me before I go back."

"I'll try."

A few moments later Jewel's softly Southern voice came on the line.

"Hey, girl. It's been too long. How are you?"

"Pretty good. Just needed some girl talk."

"In that case, let me assume the girl talk position." Jewel fluffed two oversize down pillows behind her, crossed her legs and sat back. "All right, who is he?"

"Why does it have to be a he? Maybe I'm just calling to get your opinion on a new outfit."

"Girl, pleeze. I know good and well you didn't make this toll call from Long Island to Connecticut to ask me about some clothes. Unless we're trying to devise a way to keep that thieving Parris out of our closets!"

They both erupted in a fit of laughter, thinking of all the missing items that mysteriously turned up on Parris's long, lean body.

"Yeah, Parris thinks she's *in* Paris when she shops at my house," Nikita said, chuckling.

"I just don't understand it," Jewel continued. "Girl makes enough money to buy her own department store."

"Don't I know it. But she says it keeps her close to us because she's away all the time. She keeps a little piece of us with her."

"I know," Jewel replied, sobering. "Whatever helps. I know I couldn't lead that kind of life for all the money in the world. I need roots."

"That's the truth. At least she has a man who understands and accepts her lifestyle."

"Which brings me back to my original question—who is he? And take as long as you want to tell me all about him. It's your quarter."

Nikita took a breath. "Well, his name is Quinten Parker…"

"So, you have nothing in common. He acts and talks like the characters in that *Sugar Hill* movie with Wesley Snipes. You're not sure what he does for a living and don't want to think about it, and you can't wait to see him again. That about right?" Jewel brushed another coat of clear polish on her toes.

"Gosh, Jewel, you don't have to make it sound like that." The scenario did sound rather awful.

"If it's not like that, then tell me what it is like. I mean, be real and tell me."

Nikita took a long, thoughtful breath. "I know he represents everything I've been told to stay away from. And on the outside he seems like a real character. But beneath it all is a humanity, a sensitivity, a goodness. I can just feel it. I know this all sounds crazy, but—"

"Listen Niki, nothing is crazy when it comes to a person and their feelings. They can't be explained most of the time. There are no real rules or regulations. Sometimes you just have to go with how you feel and hope for the best. Don't worry about how everyone else is going to feel about your decision. You're the only one who has to live with your choices. If I'd worried about how everyone was going to feel about me and Taj, I would have never married him, and I'd have missed out on the greatest experience of my life.

"Sister, I can't sit here polishing my toes and tell you he's the wrong one for you. I can't tell you he's *the one,* either. Only the two of you and time can tell."

"Yes. You're right. I was feeling the same way. I guess I just needed to hear my thoughts out loud. The truth is, I don't know how it is," she blew out in frustration. "He scares me—in an I-want-to-get-back-on-that-ride-again kind of scary. He's not like the men I've dated. He's crude, but sensual, and as much as he puts on the tough guy act, there's something else there. Something gentle and needy."

"The only advice I can offer is to go slow. And be sure of your reasons for getting involved."

"Yo, Max!" Quinn called out of his car window, simultaneously blowing his horn.

Maxine slowed her long-legged strut and turned in the direction of the familiar voice. When her gaze rested on Quinn's smiling face, the heavy baggage of her day, of dealing with corporate backstabbing and annoying customers, seemed to slide from her shoulders. She hadn't seen Quinn since he moved out of the neighborhood. She'd asked around and heard through the vine that he was still looking good and doing well. He'd taken some time off from working for Remy, but word had it that he was back.

Quinn pulled alongside Max and put the car in park. "Hey, baby. Long time. Lookin' good."

Maxine jutted her hip and accessorized it with her hand. "You don't look so bad yourself—stranger. Just forgot all about your friends." She adjusted her shoulder bag. "How you been?"

He shrugged and half smiled. "Awright. Hangin' in . Where you headed?"

"Home. Where else?" she joked.

"Get in. I'll take you."

"That's what you better have said," she teased.

Quinn broke out laughing and realized that he actually missed seeing her.

Maxine slid in next to Quinn and all the months without seeing him slipped away. His scent, those delicious dimples and that cool arrogance. Damn, she'd missed him.

"So what's been happenin', Max? I been kinda out of touch, ya know."

"Yeah, I know."

Their gazes touched in silent understanding.

"I finished that course I told you about," she said, moving away from the painful memories. "Got my certificate and everything."

"Congrats, baby. Knew you could do it. No doubt. We gonna have to celebrate," he grinned. "What you wanna do? Name it, you got it."

"No shit?"

Quinn looked at her and burst out laughing. "Yeah, no shit." He'd forgotten how regular Max could get when she wanted to. "So, what's it gonna be? Your call."

"You know what I'd really like to do, Quinn?"

"What?"

"I'd like to see your new place. See what you've done with it."

Quinn nodded. "Cool. Here we go."

Chapter 7

Letting It Go

"This is n-i-c-e, Q," Maxine said, walking through the spacious duplex. "You always did keep a fly place." She ran her hands along the polished wood of the old piano and her chest constricted with memories. She'd gone with Lacy the day she'd picked it out for Quinn's birthday. "I know he'll love this," Lacy had said. "And he'll never do it for himself, so it's up to me. Crazy man needs a gentle push every now and then," she'd added, giving Maxine a *you-need-to-take-this-advice-and-run-with-it* look. But she hadn't. She just couldn't. She needed Quinn to see for himself without any pushing from her. "You still play?"

"Naw. Not really."

"Because of Lacy?" she asked gently.

He shrugged and crossed to the other side of the living room and turned on the stereo. "Somethin' like that," he mumbled. He sat down on the couch and stared down at his folded hands. Maxine took a spot next to him, placing her hands atop his.

He looked at her, then turned away.

"Lacy wouldn't want you to stop being all you could just because she's not here to nag at you, Q."

They looked at each other and kind of smiled reminiscent smiles.

"I keep tryin' to tell myself that, Max. It don't work. Everytime I even think about playin', writin'—I just lose it."

"It's hard. I know it is. She was my best friend for as long as I can remember. Sometimes I get ready to pick up the phone to call her because I know she can lift my spirit, and then I remember." She swallowed back the swell that rose to her throat. "But you gotta hang tough. You gotta." She reached out and squeezed his hand.

They sat in silence for a long while, just easy in each other's company. Relaxing in the memories they each had of Lacy.

"Funny thing, ya know," Quinn said after a while. "One day last week, I stepped into this club. It was empty 'cept for the bartender, and I checked this phat baby grand, ya know," he said, his voice building in enthusiasm. "So I just sat down and played this joint I had been savin' to play for Lacy…" His voice trailed away.

"Yeah, Q, I'm listening. So, tell me, what happened. You just plopped yourself down there like you owned the place." She grinned. "And what else?" She wanted to keep him talking, to let him get it out. Over the years she'd seen how quickly he could close himself off, shut down and Fort Knox people out. As if there was so much inside that he didn't know how to share. Lacy had been the only one that could ever get to him. And Max had watched and listened on those rare occasions when she got to witness Lacy working her magic on Quinn.

"Well, this brother, Nick, he owns the joint. He heard me play, ya know—"

"And…" She grinned, hunching him in the ribs. "You're killin' me with the suspense."

"He offered me a gig."

"What!" she squealed. "Get out. Just like that." She snapped her fingers. "You know you bad, Q. Just admit it and go head on."

He couldn't help but laugh. Max was funny. "I ain't all that."

"You a liar. We been trying to tell you for years. But seriously. You got the job. So when can I come down and hear you rock?"

He blew out a breath and stood. "You can't, 'cause I ain't gonna play."

Maxine watched him, that tall, proud, handsome black man, trying to hide his pain, anger and confusion from her. She was the only person other than Lacy who knew how truly gifted Quinn was. Many a night she'd stood outside his apartment door and listened to his grab-you-by-the-heart music wafting to her ears. Without Quinn's knowledge, Lacy had shared some of his poems and short stories. They were great—at least she thought so. But she also knew how fiercely Quinn guarded that part of his life.

"Listen, Q, I'm not the one to tell you your business, or how to feel. I just think you're making a mistake. Not giving yourself a real chance. But that's on you. Whatever you decide is cool with me. You know that."

"I hear you."

"Nuff said. Now, how much congratulations do I still have left?" she asked, grinning, that toothpick-wide gap in her teeth winking at him.

"Say what?"

"You heard me. I'm not a one-stop shopper. What else do I get to ask for?"

"Whatever your pretty little self desires."

"I'm hungry. That club you were talking about, do they serve food?"

"Yeah."

"Then let's get ta steppin'."

"Woman, you're pressin' your luck." He chuckled. "Better be glad I kinda like you. Get your stuff before I change my mind."

The band was in full swing when they arrived. Couples were on the floor, at tables, talking nose to nose and just hanging out.

"This is sweet, Q," Maxine said, taking a look around before he helped her into her seat.

"Yeah, it's cool," he responded absently, wondering what he was gonna tell Nick if he saw him, or Nikita's friend Parris. Man, what was on his brain rolling up in here? He was gonna look like a real punk. He should have taken Max someplace else. He didn't have any business in here. But the truth was he'd wanted to come back. Had been thinking about it for days. But he figured since he stood Nick up like that, there wouldn't be anything he could say. That's just how it was. Man can't be making excuses for reneging.

"Is that the piano you were talking about, Q?" Maxine asked, cutting into his thoughts.

He slanted his eyes in the direction of the baby grand and that old tingling sensation started in his fingers.

"Yeah."

"You'd probably sound real good on *that.* It looks like they haven't found anybody yet," she hedged, peeking at him from the corner of her eye.

"Naw, it don't." He crossed his arms in front of him, leaned back and stretched out his long legs. Maybe he still could give it a shot. Nick seemed like an all right brother. He knew Max was right when she was talking about not giving up just because Lacy wasn't around to nag at him. He needed to do this because deep inside it was what he loved doing. Well, it was all over but the shouting, anyway. He was supposed to have started a week ago and never showed, which shifted his thoughts to Nikita. What was Nikita thinking about it? Females like her must be used to dudes acting correct. Even though she acted as if she understood, she couldn't.

The waitress came to their table to take their order. Max and Quinn had both loved shrimp in a basket since they were kids, and ordered one large basket each with a side order of onion rings. Just like old times.

"You sure haven't changed." Quinn chuckled.

"You should talk. I can only aspire to consume as much shrimp and onion rings as you have in your lifetime, my brother."

"You don't have no problem holdin' your own, my sistah," he teased.

Maxine rolled her eyes and smiled.

Their drinks arrived.

Maxine lifted her glass of rum and coke to Quinn's Jack Daniels.

"To better days, Q," she saluted softly.

"No doubt." He took a long swallow. "So, what's gonna happen with this certificate thing?"

"Well, I'm going to look for something part-time at a travel agency so I can get some hands-on experience." She took a sip of her drink. "I've been saving my money and I'm with this investment plan at the bank. I'm hoping I can open my own place in about a year. At least, that's the plan."

Quinn slowly nodded his head, taking it all in. Knowing how determined Maxine always was, he figured she'd pull it off. "Maybe I'll be your first customer."

"Yeah. I'll send you someplace exotic, like to one of the islands or something."

He chuckled. "If you need any help, ya know, like with paying for your spot, or anything, you just tell me. I got some loot stashed. No problem."

Maxine smiled, feeling warm all over, and knew it had nothing to do with her drink. She looked down at the remains in her glass. "Just knowing that you have my back means a lot, Q. But you know," she said, looking into his eyes, "I have to do this on my own. Prove something to myself—that I can do it." She shrugged and half smiled, looking at him. "Know what I mean?"

"Yeah, I hear ya, Max. It's all good. Just don't forget what I said, anyway."

"I won't." She grinned, flashing that toothpick gap. She put her glass down and leaned closer toward him. "Q, I've been thinking a lot about Lacy's death and all the B.S. the cops gave us about what happened."

He felt that old knot tighten in his gut, but he forced himself to listen. He took another swallow of his drink and signaled the waitress for another one.

"Q." She placed her hand on his, knowing how hard it was for him, but she needed him to know what she was planning and she wanted his support.

He tugged on his bottom lip with his teeth. "I'm listenin'."

"Not talking about Lacy, putting aside everything that she was, what she meant to the both of us, is not going to make this fuckin' pain go away. We're never going to walk through our doors and see her again, or hear her singing in her kitchen. All she ever wanted for anybody was the best, Q. She gave everything that she was to everyone that mattered to her. So we need to do her some justice, too."

His nostrils flared as he sucked in air. He swallowed, but his voice still came out gravelly and hoarse. "What're you talkin' about, Max?"

"I've been talking with a friend of mine. You know Valerie?" He nodded. "She works at the bank and goes to law school at night. She thinks we may have a case. Wrongful death. We may be able to sue the police department."

"Sue!" He threw his hands up in the air. "What the hell for? All the gottdamn money in the world ain't gonna bring her back, Max."

"No. It won't. But it can bring to justice the bastards that killed her. Somethin' ain't right, Q. The cops have been playing games with us for months. They think because we're black we're automatically too stupid to care, or if we do care, too dumb to do anything about it. To them it's just one more black body out of the way."

He was listening now, really listening, fueled by Maxine's energy. "So what're you sayin', get a lawyer and file a suit?"

"Exactly."

He rolled the idea around in his head. For the past few months, he'd done everything in his power to seal up the hurt, the anger. The only way he found he could do that was to distance himself from all the things that reminded him of his twin sister. New neighborhood, everything. Maybe that wasn't the route. He sure as hell knew it didn't work. It was like putting a Band-Aid on a wound from an Uzi; everything still kept seeping out.

"Let's do this, Max," he said finally. He leaned toward her and ran his finger down her cheek. "For Lacy."

She smiled, her insides twirling from the sensation of his touch. Instinctively, she clasped his finger in its wayward stroke of her cheek and held it pressed to her face.

"It's gon be all right, Q. It just takes time."

That's how Nikita saw them when she stepped into the club.

Chapter 8

Checkin' Things Out

She'd needed to get out of the house, away from the illusion of peace and tranquility, from the scornful, disappointed glare of her father and the trivial conversation of her mother.

Her first thought had been to call Quinn, be daring and take a ride with him somewhere. But she didn't have his number and she hadn't seen or heard from him since that day at her job. She was totalling the days. Eight days and counting.

After her talk with Jewel, she'd made up her mind that she wanted to see where things could go with them.

All of her life she'd played by the rules, followed the white line, lived up to expectations, never deviating, no surprises. Her life was as pale and lifeless as limp, blond hair. What she wanted was some color, some spark, a little fire. Quinn Parker was all that, and then some. And there was this energy between them that snapped, crackled and popped. The men she'd been with barely got the match lit.

So with that in mind, she'd decided to give Rhythms one more try. She'd been itching to talk to Parris and find out if Quinn ever turned up, but she wouldn't be back in town for another two weeks. And Nick was on business on the West Coast.

Maybe, just maybe, Quinn had changed his mind and decided to play at the club. Maybe that's why she hadn't heard from him.

She took a chance, and he was there all right, fine as he wanted to be—in the face of some other woman.

With an expert's eye, she sized her up.

Probably about five foot seven, from the length of her legs crossed beneath the table. She was sporting one of those short, precision cuts, and it fit her rather delicate face like a cap. There was no doubt about it—even from where she stood, half a room away, she could tell that Ms. X had a knockout body. And her even-toned, black-beauty skin was *working* up against a pale peach tailored suit. The girl could definitely dress. As a matter of fact she had a suit almost just like it. Cost a pretty penny, too. She wondered what she did for a living.

Just then the waitress momentarily broke her line of vision when she brought their food. *Looks like they both ordered the same thing—and they're laughing about it.*

Quinn was turning to say something to the waitress. Nikita ducked between two people seated at the bar. She ordered a Pepsi with lemon. *Now what?*

When the waitress moved away, Quinn's gaze landed on the line of bodies at the bar. He'd know those legs anywhere.

Since the last time he'd seen her he'd tried to push her to the back of his mind. It hadn't worked, but he hadn't called, either. He wasn't sure what he wanted to do about Nikita. Part of him wanted to pursue her, get something going. Another part of him told him to steer clear. They were from two different worlds. But if he was going to start making some changes in his life, maybe Nikita Harrell was the missing ingredient.

"'Scuse me for a minute, Max. I see somebody I know."

Watching him thread his way around the press of bodies, she couldn't imagine who Quinn would know in a place like Rhythms. No one that he hung with would think about crossing 110th Street.

"Still drinkin' lemon Pepsi?"

Nikita felt the hairs on the back of her neck begin to tickle. She put her glass down to keep the contents from spilling and slowly angled her head around.

"Well. We meet again," she said as casually as she could. "How have you been?"

"I'm feelin' better already. How 'bout you?"

"I'm fine, thanks."

"You by yourself?"

"Why?"

He leaned against the bar so that he faced her. "'Cause if you're by yourself, I'd invite you to join me and my friend for dinner." He shrugged. "But if you got plans, no problem."

"I wouldn't want to interrupt."

He grinned. "If you was interrupting I wouldn't have asked you."

"If you're sure it's okay." Obviously whoever he was with was just a friend. Why else would he invite her to join them?

"Yeah, I'm sure. It's okay. Come on."

With her heart pounding a mile a minute, she followed him to his table.

He grabbed an empty chair from a nearby table and held it out for her.

"Maxine, this is Nikita. Me and Max go way back."

"Hi," Nikita said, taken by Maxine's stunning looks up close. "Nice to meet you."

Maxine forced a smile. "Same here." *Where did he meet her? Definitely not from the neighborhood. Must be somebody from around here. And from the hungry way he keeps checking her out, he really digs her.* Her spirits sank.

"You wanna order somethin', Niki? Me and Max are celebratin'."

"Uh, no thanks." She looked from one to the other and caught the brief look of something akin to jealousy in Maxine's eyes. "What are you two celebrating?" she said, shaking off the bad vibes that she was getting.

"Max just got her certificate as a travel agent."

"Really? Congratulations. Are you working at an agency?

I'm sure I could send you plenty of business. My friends love to travel."

Maxine gave her a saccharine smile. "I'm sure they do. But I'm not with an agency at the moment. I'm planning on opening my own place." She stabbed her fork into a shrimp and popped it into her mouth.

"That's great. Good luck."

Maxine popped another shrimp into her mouth. "What do you do?"

"Right now, I'm trying to be a journalist." She smiled. "I'm working for Lillian Ingram, the publisher of *Today's Woman* magazine."

"Never heard of it."

"It's pretty local. Distribution is mostly in just the Village and lower Manhattan." Maxine was making her nervous, for some reason. She felt a string of perspiration trickle down her spine.

Maxine took a sip of water. Just great. So they had something in common. She was a writer, too. Pretty, intelligent and, by the looks of her clothes, she had money. And she actually seemed nice, much as she wanted to dislike her. She was starting to feel worse by the minute.

Quinn ate his food, letting the ladies talk.

They were getting along. That was cool. It seemed kind of tense at first, but he figured that was because Nikita was nervous about meeting Max. Probably figured Max was his woman or something. It seemed important to him all of a sudden that Max like Nikita. Not that he would back off if she didn't. But he would like to know that she thought Nikita was okay. He realized she wasn't the kind of woman Max was used to seeing him with, but hey—to better days.

"So where did you two meet?" Maxine asked, pushing the rest of her food aside.

Quinn suspiciously eyed the half-full basket.

Nikita turned toward Quinn and smiled. He slid his arm along the back of her chair, then turned toward Maxine. "We kinda ran into each other a coupla times. Still gettin' to know each other."

"How long have *you* two known each other?"

"Since we were all in kindergarten together," Maxine stated—
real clear.

"Long time. I wish I could say I had friends that went back
that far." The truth was that until her senior year in high school
she'd never had time to cultivate friendships. She'd always
attended all-white schools and they tolerated her, even pretended
to like her, but they were never really her friends. Her parents
pushed her so hard to excel at everything, and those few who
weren't pretend friends were just out-and-out envious of her
achievements. Until she met Parris, she hadn't known what it was
like to really have a close female friend. Men, on the other hand,
were never really a problem. It was just the type of men she attracted—or to be honest, those she allowed herself to be attracted to—who wouldn't turn her parents inside out.

"I need to be gettin' home, Quinn," Maxine said suddenly.
"I'm beat, and I have an appointment in the morning." Both
things were lies, except for the part about her getting home. She
rose and so did Quinn.

"You sure you're okay, Max? You didn't even finish eatin'."
He looked at her, but she turned away.

"I'm fine, just tired." She took a breath. "Nice to meet you,
Nikita. Maybe I'll see you again."

"Yes. And good luck with your business."

"Thanks."

She moved from behind the table and started to walk away.

"Hold up, Max. 'Scuse me, Nikita." He walked away from the
table and ushered Maxine farther away with a hand in the small of
her back. "Whatsup with you? I brought you. I'm takin' you home."

"I can get a cab, Quinn. It's no big deal."

"It's not goin' down like that, Max. Now you just wait here
a minute. I'm takin' you home. End of story."

She tried to act annoyed. "Okay. I'll wait," she said, secretly
pleased that he'd have to leave Ms. Nikita sitting all by her
lonesome.

Quinn returned to the table and leaned over Nikita from
behind, enveloping her with his hands braced on either side of
her. Her heart began to race.

"Listen, I gotta run Maxine home. You wanna wait and I'll come back for you, or what?"

Her heart sank. "No. You go ahead. I have my car."

"It's still early. You gotta get back to Long Island, or what?"

She swallowed. "Eventually. Why?"

"I wanna spend some time with you." His smile ran over her like warm sunshine. He was taking a chance letting her cross the line. He reached into his pants pocket and pulled out a spare set of keys and placed them on the table. "These are the keys to my crib. You remember where it is? Eighteenth and Sixth. Three oh one. The apartment at the top of the steps. First door on your right."

"What am I supposed to do with your keys, Quinn?"

"Open my door, go in, make yourself comfortable and wait for me. I should be back in a coupla hours. You with that, or what?"

She pressed her lips together. *Decide, girl.* "So long as you're sure you'll only be a couple of hours."

He grinned. "No doubt." He leaned a bit closer and pressed his lips to her cheek. Her heart slammed in her chest. "See you in a few."

As she watched him walk away, her head began to pound and her hands started to shake. What was she doing? She had keys to the apartment of a man she hardly knew. Her stomach started to do a dance. And she was planning to go.

She caught a fleeting glimpse of him walking through the door with his arm possessively around Maxine's waist. Just how good was their friendship?

"You wanna tell me what's buggin' you?" Quinn grumbled, pulling his car out into traffic.

"Nothing. I told you I was just tired."

"You wasn't tired a minute ago. I thought we were celebratin'."

"So did I," she mumbled under her breath.

"What?"

"Nothing."

"Women."

Maxine folded her arms and stared out the passenger window. Quinn cut a look in her direction.

She sure was acting strange. He'd never known Maxine to flip the script like that. She was always cool, easy to be around. Hey, maybe it was that time or something. If he didn't know better he'd swear she was jealous.

He slanted another look. Naw. They were family. It wasn't like that between them. Not that he hadn't thought about it from time to time, but hell, she'd probably really freak if he came on to her—like he was her brother or something.

"So when you gonna let me know about this lawyer?" he asked, trying to draw her out of her mood.

"I'll talk to Val on Monday," she said without turning around. Then she did. "Listen, Q, I'm sorry about tonight. I guess I was more tired than I thought." She paused. "Maybe we can pick it up another time."

"Sure. Whatever. So long as you're okay." He grinned, feeling better. "Had me worried there for a minute, girl—leavin' all that food."

She smiled. "First time for everything." She took a breath. "So where'd you meet Ms. Uptown?"

He laughed. "Ran into her the day I was movin' into the new crib. What do you think?"

She shrugged her left shoulder. "Not that my opinion counts for anything." She gave him a look and half smiled. "She seems okay. A little stiff, but friendly. Can't see her hangin' in B.J.'s, that's for damn sure."

They both laughed at that one.

"I hear ya. She's different. No doubt."

They drove in silence for the balance of the trip, each caught in private thoughts about Nikita.

He eased to a stop in front of Maxine's apartment building.

"Thanks, Q." Maxine fidgeted with the lock for a minute, got it open, then turned to him. "See ya. You have my number. Give me a call one day next week. I'll let you know what's happening."

Quinn nodded and looked at her hard. "You straight, Max?"

"Yeah. I'm fine. Nothing that a good night's sleep won't cure." She opened the door. "Later." She wanted to ask him about Nikita. She wanted to know if he was going to see her later—again—ever. She didn't.

"Yeah, later," he mumbled. He waited until she was safely inside the building, then pulled out.

He shook his head, pushing thoughts of Maxine Sherman temporarily aside. He had his run to make and then home— where Nikita was waiting. He smiled. That sounded real good.

She wasn't stupid. Every grown woman with a grain of sense knew what to expect when she got invited to a man's apartment. Her hands shook as she tried to fit the key in the lock. The keys clanged to the concrete steps.

Oh, Lord, what in heaven's name was she doing? Was this what she really wanted? She stared at the keys. She looked around, up and down the quiet, tree-lined block. Maybe she could leave the keys where he could find them and just go home. That would certainly put a quick end to their short relationship.

When are you going to get some heart, girl? she thought. *This is supposed to be all about change.* She bent down and picked up the keys. This time she got the key in the front door lock.

After her fumbling with the keys again and trying each one, the last one, of course, finally fit in the lock to the apartment door. Cautiously, she stepped inside. Feeling along the wall, she found the light switch. The large, airy front room was bathed in soft light from the track system up above.

Quietly closing the door behind her, she stepped into the room. Her eyes widened. The gleaming, high-gloss wood floors supported black leather furniture with smoked glass and wood coffee and end tables, a complicated-looking stereo system situated near the floor-to-ceiling windows, and a bookcase loaded with books. Books! He even had plants. Dead in the center of the room was a fireplace, with a piano holding a place of honor to the left. The smooth, cream-colored walls were beautifully adorned with examples of black art—she was familiar with some, and with others she wanted to be. On either side of the fireplace hung magnificent reproductions of John Biggers' *Harvest From the Sea* and *Crossing the Bridge,* a poignant depiction of rural black life. *Wow.* She approached the piano to get a closer look at the portrait of a jazz band that hung above it. A Doris Price original.

She looked around and noticed a pair of heavy sliding doors at the back of the room. She tiptoed across the floor and opened them. A full dining room with a rectangular smoked-glass dining table atop what appeared to be a polished tree trunk, surrounded by six chairs covered in African fabric, took up the center space. Beyond was a sunny yellow-and-white kitchen with every kind of gadget imaginable. Did he cook, too?

Uhmph, uhmph, uhmph—well, wonders never ceased. Quinn Parker lived well, seemed to have excellent taste in furnishings, art, literature. Yet, on the outside he presented himself as a crude, unworldly thug. Beyond closed doors he was an entirely different person. Why? It was almost as if he were two different people.

She shook her head in confusion. What in the world did he do for a living? She wondered if he shared this classy abode with a woman. It was just so neat for a man. But he couldn't be so arrogant as to give her a set of keys if his girlfriend could just walk in. Could he? She discarded that idea.

She jumped when the ringing phone pierced the silence. On the third ring the answering machine came on and seconds later she heard the voice of a sexy-sounding female who didn't seem to feel the need to identify herself. *"Hey, baby. Long time no hear from. Give me a call so we can get together. Soon."* Click.

Well, whoever she was, at least she hadn't seen him in a while and she obviously didn't live there.

She retraced her steps and went back out into the front room. The bedroom must be upstairs. She thought about going up, just to see, but that would probably be the moment Quinn would arrive and find her in his bedroom. No thanks. No point in asking for trouble.

Crossing the room, she approached the stereo and pressed open the Plexiglas panels. Not wanting to take a chance on messing with anything, she opted for listening to the radio and was pleasantly surprised to find it programmed to 98.7, better known as KISS FM, which only played classic R&B. The throaty sounds of Anita Baker's "Been So Long" filled the room. *How appropriate,* she thought.

Letting the music soothe her, she took a seat on the couch and leaned her head back, closing her eyes, thinking how comfortable she felt. Just as he'd said, she mused, a smile touching her lips. She hummed along with Luther's "A House is Not a Home," true understanding of the lyrics finally taking hold.

Quinn understood it, too, standing in the doorway, watching her without her knowledge. Feeling what it felt like to come home to someone. Someone who mattered.

He took a short inhale. Nikita could really matter to him. If he let her. It was gonna take time. She wasn't one of the "around the way girls" that he could play on. He would have to be for real, up-front and correct with Nikita. But the life he led didn't allow for diversions. And she could sure become one. Having someone close always caused problems. They became your weak spot, a way for your enemies to get to you. That's why he'd stayed free of any heavy relationships. They weighed you down, slowed your step. But she looked real good sitting there, just like that's where she belonged. Maybe she did.

She sensed his presence. Instead of being startled at being caught unawares, she felt comforted, secure. Slowly she opened her eyes and turned her head toward the door. He was almost beautiful, like a black Messiah, framed in the doorway, haloed by the light from the hall.

"Hi," she said softly, as if she'd always sat in that very spot waiting for him to come home.

That lazy smile slowly spread. "Hi, yourself. Lookin' mighty relaxed on my couch," he teased, stepping in and closing the door.

"Per your instructions." She sat up straighter as he languidly approached.

He leaned down, placed a hand on each side of her head. "Let's try this," he said, leaning a bit closer, "and get it out of the way. Then we can spend the rest of the time gettin' to know each other."

Ever so slowly he drew nearer until she just wanted to snatch him by his shirt and pull him to her, to stop the unbearable anticipation. When his lips touched down on hers, tiny sparks started popping in her head like a million flashbulbs. He pressed a little harder, letting the tip of his tongue brush across her lips, asking for access. She heard her own sharp intake of breath when he penetrated her mouth and felt the rush of heat that followed, flooding her body.

Did he moan or did she? She couldn't be sure with so many new sensations and emotions tumbling around at once.

His hands caressed her face, his fingers tracing her jawline until they reached her chin and he gently withdrew.

Quinn pressed his head against hers, closing his eyes, letting the impact of that kiss subside. He hadn't expected to be taken like that, not over some kiss. Something happened. He couldn't explain it. Nikita was trouble. He didn't need trouble. But some part of him needed her.

"How much time you got?" he asked, looking hard into her eyes, because he knew this was going to take a while.

Chapter 9

Taking Chances

"Where's Nikita tonight?" Lawrence asked, stepping into the bedroom.

Cynthia, sitting in front of her vanity mirror, continued applying a heavy coat of cold cream to her smooth, red-tinted complexion in practiced strokes—up and out, just the way her masseuse and the beauty magazines advised.

"She said she was going out for a while. She didn't say where." Gray-green eyes with just a hint of crow's feet at the corners stared back at her. At fifty, Cynthia Harrell was just as striking as she had been at twenty-five—her daughter's age. Her daughter, by some genetic twist of fate, had acquired a prior generation's dose of melanin, resulting in her warm, caramel tones. Cynthia pursed her thin lips at the thought.

"If she's going to continue living here indefinitely, she will not be traipsing in here at all hours." He loosened his tie and removed his jacket, hanging it in perfect alignment with his others in the walk-in closet.

Cynthia watched his movements in her mirror. "Don't marry a man darker than you," her mother had warned. "You'll wind up with black babies with nappy hair." Well, she hadn't. Lawrence Harrell was about as close to white as you could get without crossing the line. Lawrence was what was referred to in some circles as "high yella," with jet-black wavy hair and gray eyes. And still, nature had fooled her.

"We have to have rules in this house," he added without conviction.

She took a tissue from a lacquered box and began removing the cream. Nikita would never have to worry about sunburn and premature aging of her skin. Cynthia wiped some more. She'd have other things to worry about. Like being an obviously black woman in a white world. Having to work twice as hard to get half as much—to never truly be recognized for her accomplishments by whites and her own people, if not more so.

"How was your day, dear?" she asked, not in the mood to debate with her husband.

"The usual. Two major surgeries today. Both successful." He sat on the edge of the bed and removed his shoes, covertly looking at his wife. When did the woman he'd married turn into the woman in front of him—distant and cold—he wondered. Somewhere during their thirty-year marriage they'd become so absorbed in their own careers and their accomplishments that they'd forgotten about each other.

He released a sigh. The only times he'd been truly happy were when Nikita was born, when she soared to new heights, accomplished new goals. Which was why he was so devastated when she dropped out of medical school. He wanted to talk with Cynthia, tell her how he truly felt. But they had stopped really talking a long time ago.

Cynthia studied her reflection. Nikita, Nikita, that's all he ever seemed to care about from the moment she was born. Cynthia wiped some more. She resented Nikita, so she pushed her, and punished Lawrence for sharing the love that she craved for herself alone. She envied the very harsh reality that at least Nikita, for all that she might or might not be, was accepted in a world that had turned its back on her mother. *"A credit to her race."*

Cynthia, on the other hand, had been rejected by her own.

Her fair skin might have won her easy entrée into the white world, but black doors were always shut in her face. "You think you white," was the favorite taunt. "You think you too cute," others would say. Then there were those who believed she'd steal their men, with her white-girl looks and long, sandy blond hair.

She brushed her hair, remembering how many times it had been pulled, twisted, even doused with food coloring—by ninth-grade girls. And how she'd cut it up to her ears in tenth grade, in the hope that maybe they'd like her then. They never did.

So Cynthia withdrew into a world of books, concentrating on her studies, excelling, besting all of those who had thought so little of her. She made friends with the white girls in college, and then at work. They became her contemporaries, her confidantes, her role models. And just when she thought she had pushed that dark, painful world behind her, there was Nikita, her little brown baby, there to remind her of all the women who'd always hated her. She'd never get away from the humiliation of who she was. Nikita would always be there to remind her.

So she demanded more than Nikita could ever give. More than she could hope to deliver. Whenever Nikita could not meet or exceed expectations, Cynthia felt vindicated. She proved that she was better than those "cullud" girls who had tormented her. Nikita's return home was her supreme triumph, and still Lawrence dwelled on Nikita, even in her failure.

Slowly, Lawrence pushed himself up from the bed, rising to his full six-foot height. "I'm going to take my shower," he announced.

"I think I'll read for a while. I have a meeting with the department heads in the morning," Cynthia replied, brushing her hair.

Lawrence walked toward the master bathroom, then stopped. He turned to his wife. "Why did you marry me, Cynthia?"

She swiveled around in her chair. "Larry, what a ridiculous question." She turned back around and continued brushing her hair until it gleamed. "This isn't one of those mid-life crisis things, is it?" She chuckled.

"Yes, it is ridiculous, isn't it?" He stepped into the bathroom and shut the door.

Moments later Cynthia heard the rush of water.

Mechanically she returned the brush to the tabletop. "Why did you marry me, Larry?" she whispered to her reflection.

Quinn eased back, then took a seat in the space next to Nikita. He studied her, saw the eagerness and doubt drift and change places on her face. He lifted the lock that dangled with the tiny shell, and tucked it behind her ear. He felt her shiver.

"You didn't answer my question," he said, stroking her ear.

Nikita swallowed. Did he really expect her to spend the night with him? "About how much time I have?"

"Yeah." He grinned.

She didn't want him to think she was totally uncool and had to run home to Mommy and Daddy. But then again, she didn't want him to think she was easy, either. "Uh, I guess I have some time. Why?"

He shrugged that easy-does-it shrug. "I figured we could listen to some music. You could tell me 'bout yourself, and then take it from there."

Nikita nodded, then smiled. "That sounds okay. But what about you telling me about yourself?"

Quinn stood up and chuckled. "You hungry?"

"A little." He hadn't answered her question, but that was answer enough. If he thought she was going to be giving the 411 and he was just going to listen, he had another think coming. She smiled to herself. Maybe she could finally put her reporter skills into practice.

"How's your story comin' on your friend?" he asked, reading her mind again.

"I finally finished," she said, standing and following him into the kitchen. She leaned against the counter while he rifled through the fridge.

"Burger and fries cool?"

"Sure. Can I help you with something?"

"Hey, I'm down for equal opportunity." He grinned, and his dimples winked at her. "What's your pleasure, seasonin' the meat, or arrangin' the fries?"

Why's my heart doing a tap dance because of a simple question? It wasn't so much what he said, just how he said it. *Season the meat, huh?* "I'll handle the fries."

Quinn placed an unopened bag of frozen french fries on the counter. "Work your magic, babe. The oil is in the cabinet over your head."

They worked together in a comfortable silence, the music from the stereo mixing with the cling and clang of pots, utensils and popping grease. Soon the kitchen was filled with the aromas of sizzling ground beef that Quinn had molded into two perfect patties, sauteed onions and steak sauce.

Nikita's stomach gave an embarrassing shout out, which she tried unsuccessfully to camouflage by shutting a cabinet.

Quinn smiled but figured he'd give her a play and not tease her.

"You have anything to make a salad?" Nikita asked, turning just in time to catch the tail end of his smile.

"Check the fridge," he said, flipping a burger.

Nikita was pleased to find a fresh bag of spinach, mushrooms, cucumbers and cherry tomatoes. He kept surprising her.

"We can eat up front," Quinn said, taking the plates into the living room. He placed them on the coffee table, then went to the bar. "Fix you a drink?" he asked, pouring a shot of Jack Daniels over two cubes.

"I saw some Pepsi in the fridge. That's fine with me."

"Help yourself. There's a lemon in the vegetable bin."

She angled her head over her shoulder as she walked to the kitchen. Their smiles met.

"How long you gonna be livin' with your people?" Quinn asked over a bite of the burger. Juice dripped out and he caught it with his tongue.

"Every day is too long," she moaned. "But I'm trying to save. It's just taking a long time."

"Make the most of it."

Nikita frowned. "The most of what?"

"The time you have with your folks. Can't get it back, ya know?"

She watched his profile for a moment, trying to see beyond his words. She took a sip of soda. "Where's your family?"

She saw the slight flare of his nostrils as if he were struggling for air. His eyes drifted away. He seemed to be looking beyond the window that faced them. "Just me," he said finally.

His voice sounded as vacant to her as an abandoned building.

Quinn got up from the couch, took their empty plates and put them in the dishwasher.

She watched him walk away, distracted, as if he were traveling to some other place. So family was off-limits. It was obviously something he didn't want to discuss. Maybe some other time.

Quinn returned and went straight to the stereo. Nikita silently prayed that he wouldn't turn on that rap music, but that's just what he did. She cringed when the first pulsing wave jumped through the air with a life all its own. Initially, she couldn't make out a word of what was being said, and didn't want to. If he was planning on their talking and getting to know each other, how in the world could they do that over all the noise?

Quinn seemed oblivious to her discomfort, his long, muscled body rocking to the beat as he sorted through his cache of CDs. The pounding of the drums vibrated through her, pulling her unwillingly along. She knew all they were talking about was how women were just "hos" and "bitches," how they were going to kill cops and get high. Wasn't that what everyone said? She wanted to tell him to turn it off, that she didn't want to listen to the noise, but the lyrics began to make sense, pushing past the barriers she'd erected. The singer was talking about his mother and how hard she'd struggled to raise them in the projects. How much he respected and loved her, no matter what she did to bring the money in. It was sad, powerful and filled with a painful kind of love.

"Who's singing?"

Quinn turned. "Tupac."

"Oh." The name sounded vaguely familiar. "Is he the one who was killed in Las Vegas?"

"Yeah. Didn't think you kept up," he teased.

"I don't, at least not with the music, but I do listen to the news."

"Hmmm. The news…" His voice drifted away. "Believe

what's on the news and you'll keep a twisted picture of what's real." Her body tensed at the sudden underlying anger that tinged his voice. "They tell you what they want you ta hear, how they want you ta hear it. Especially when it comes to black folks."

"That's probably true, sometimes. But not always."

He just looked at her, a half smile curving his lips. "Yeah," he said without an ounce of belief.

"Why do you feel that way?" she asked, wanting to know, even if the question made her sound silly and naive.

He took a breath and changed to "Jook Joint" by Quincy Jones. His smooth, unlined features seemed to distort into a mask of hatred. "I been there," he spat. "Seen it all the way live and then watched it get twisted in the papers and on the news."

"I'm sure there are plenty of reporters who look for the truth and tell it."

Quinn crossed the room in slow, easy strides. "Yeah, baby. You probably right. No doubt." Sarcasm dripped from his lips, like the juice from the burger. "The reality is, the ones who report the news ain't large enough to be in charge. Everything is run by somebody with their own agenda." He gave her a long look. "Same thing with you. Your boss got her own opinion about what she wants said in her magazine, what stories she wants told. Right or wrong?"

Nikita was thoughtful for a moment, taking in the enormity of what he said in his own unorthodox style. Regretfully, she had to admit that Quinn was right. It was a scary concept, that the entire world was manipulated by the thoughts and opinions of a handful of people. How long had she lived in this vacuum? And what happened in his life to make him so cynical and bitter? "I guess you're right."

Quinn joined her on the couch. "I ain't tryin' to be right. That ain't what it's about," he said, the easy, crooning resonance of his voice returning. "I'm just tellin' it like it is."

He looked at her for a moment before turning away. She was green. No doubt. But at least she had thoughts in her head—even if they were bent out of shape—and she was willing to listen, wanted to hear somebody talk besides herself. The only females he knew like that were Lacy and

Max. Now, those two could definitely hold their own in a conversation, but they always wanted to hear the other side, whether they agreed or not. He dug that. And he really dug Nikita, too.

"Let me show you the rest of the place," he said, shifting gears. He stood and took her hand.

Her heart began to pound. "Sure."

He opened the door and went up the stairs, with Nikita close on his heels.

"Do you have the whole house?"

"Naw. The landlady lives on the ground floor. Nice lady, but she wears me out runnin' errands for her." He chuckled. "Every time she sees me she finds somethin' for me to do. But it's cool."

That's sweet, she thought. It was hard to picture big, tough, macho Quinn Parker running errands for old ladies. But hey, her horizons were opening up by leaps and bounds.

He opened the door at the top of the stairs and flipped on the light.

A thick, mint green carpet covered the floor of the huge bedroom. Black lacquer furniture consisting of a six-drawer dresser, armoire, two nightstands and a bed straight out of *House Beautiful,* complete with a built-in stereo system in the headboard, filled the room.

"Come on in."

She timidly stepped across the threshold, feeling as if she'd just fallen into a lion's den. A mud-cloth bedspread and matching valances were the only decorations.

A television hung from brackets in the ceiling in the far corner of the room. Along one wall were two doors. He opened one.

"This is the bathroom." He stepped in. "Come on." He grinned.

Nikita stepped inside a totally masculine bathroom done in beiges and browns. He walked across the cream-colored tiles to a door in the opposite side. He opened that door and Nikita beamed when she saw another room.

Although sparsely furnished compared to the rest of the house, it was just as tastefully done in cool, creamy leather with brilliant art on the walls.

"I'm not sure what I want to do with the room yet. I guess it was supposed to be a bedroom."

"This place is fabulous, Quinn," she breathed.

"It's cool." He shrugged. "Got a little patio out back that I can use. Haven't gotten to it yet."

"You really lucked out when you found this place." She looked up at him and smiled, but was taken aback by the sudden closed look that shadowed his handsome features. It seemed as if the light had suddenly gone out of his eyes.

"Is something wrong?"

"Naw."

The sincerity of the word was missing. She saw him clench his jaw. "Quinn, what did I say?"

"Just forget it. It's nothin'. Serious." He forced a smile and draped his arm across her shoulders. "Let's go back down."

Nikita frowned, wondering what had just happened. What had she said that changed him from day to night in an instant?

Quinn started down the stairs. He wasn't ready to tell her about Lacy, that this was Lacy's dream and he'd only stepped in it. Naw. Not yet. If ever.

Back downstairs, Quinn removed the Quincy Jones CD and replaced it with Regina Belle's "If I Could." He turned toward Nikita, his eyes so dark they were almost black, haunting. He extended his hand and she sensed a deep sadness, something untouchable, and it reached her in a place that had never been chartered. She wanted to find the hurt that pained him, that turned him from an easygoing charmer to a brooding stranger. She wanted to make it right—like Regina said. *If I Could.* Quinn was the ultimate challenge, and hadn't she been groomed for challenge all of her life?

She moved into his embrace and felt the air leave her lungs when she became cocooned in his warmth. She pressed her head against his chest and listened to the steady heartbeat. She closed her eyes, letting the words wash over her.

"Stay with me tonight, Nikita," he whispered in her hair.

Her petite body flooded with heat. She arched her neck and looked up at him, her soft brown eyes searching his face.

"Call home and tell 'em you'll be back in the mornin'." How could he tell her he didn't want to be alone again tonight without soundin' like a punk? He just wanted her to say yes. To keep the light on for just a while longer.

"Quinn—"

"You can stay in my room." He grinned. "By yourself. The couch turns into a queen-size bed. Or the guestroom. Whatever."

A part of her was relieved. Another part of her was disappointed that he didn't want to sleep with her. Because she realized that, against all of her ingrained inhibitions, she wanted him.

"If you promise to stay put," she said, giving him the *"I ain't too sure about you"* eye.

"No doubt. 'Sides, it's too late for you to be drivin' all the way back to the Island. It's almost two o'clock."

She let out a breath. "Okay. But I'll have to be up and out early."

"Yeah," he said softly, pulling her closer. "No doubt."

PART THREE
Maxine

Chapter 10

Maxine alternated between sleep and waking for the better part of the night. Her thoughts were filled with images of Quinn and that woman Nikita. The very idea that thoughts of a man—even a man like Quinn—could keep her up at night had her out of sorts. She was still at a loss as to what he saw in Nikita. She was pretty, yeah, but definitely not his type. Anybody could see that from a mile away. But men were such babies when it came to relationships. The real thing could be smack in front of them and they'd walk right past it to the next pretty face.

She stepped into her shoes, grabbed her keys, purse and briefcase. No time to dwell on Quinn and his man-mentality self. She'd promised to meet her friend Valerie for an early breakfast before work, to talk about the lawsuit. Next to Lacy, Val was her dearest friend. Although the three hadn't hung together regularly because Lacy was not a club girl, they were all pretty tight. Val had been Maxine's shoulder, the one she leaned on when they lost Lacy. That was Val—the rescuer, always looking out for the other girl. She'd promised to be Val's first client when she opened her own law office.

The ride on the A train from uptown to lower Manhattan was as eventful as usual. The cacophony of dialects—Jamerican, Spanglish, Southern soul, urban slang and everything in between—melded with the metallic rumble of the train. Dancing-for-dollar kids, who entertained the travelers with acrobatic feats along the length of the car, competed with homeless representatives pleading their causes over the garbled static of the announcements of the conductor. The usual aromas of garlic, curry, stale beer breath and an assortment of designer perfumes clumped together into one indistinguishable scent.

Yeah, just another day on the A train, she thought.

Maxine swayed back and forth from the overhead strap, bumping and grinding with a hefty man behind her. Luckily, after five stops, she was able to squeeze into a seat. She adjusted her headphones and relaxed, rocking her foot to the beat of Notorious B.I.G., the latest victim of the rap world's East Coast-West Coast rivalry.

So much is senseless these days, she mused as the train rocked and rolled along the track, searching for the light at the end of the tunnel. Black folks were dropping like flies in all walks of life from drugs, poor health and random violence. *When are our dues gonna finally be paid?* she wondered, inhaling a powerful whiff of White Diamonds perfume. She held back a sneeze. If, in fact, black folks were the chosen ones, as Lacy had so often said, what were they chosen for? Destruction?

She rocked her foot a bit harder. Well, Maxine Yvonne Sherman had no intention of being a casualty in the war against black folks. She was gonna have her own. God bless the child, and all that. It was the only way. On that score, she, Lacy and Val had always agreed. She wiggled her hips a little to get the man next to her to close his legs.

Funny how so many of the females from the neighborhood were moving on, doing their thing, while the guys just kept hustling, thinking that their whole future was only what they could see right in front of them.

It was harder for black men. She knew it, saw evidence of it every day at the bank. There was not one black man in management, compared to three black women—she and Val being two. Oh, they had plenty of custodians and security men, but nothing that required a suit and tie and an above-high-school education.

Looking around her now, she could count on two hands the number of brothers who had "white collar" jobs.

The underground railroad screeched to her stop at Chambers Street, and she squeezed out with the rest of the indentured servants.

Maxine exited the subway and took a big gulp of exhaust fumes mixed with hot, muggy air. Even at the early hour of seven forty-five, the streets bracing City Hall, the World Trade Center towers and Pace University were bustling with life. Delivery trucks carrying everything from the *Daily News* to Nathan's hot dogs jockeyed for position with the madmen of Manhattan, who drove the yellow cabs like Indy 500 professionals.

Her pearl gray Donna Karan suit hugged her body in all the right places, and she knew it from the admiring glances she received along the way to meet Val. She prided herself on her physical fitness, making it a point to go to the gym at least three days per week, and keeping her bi-annual appointment with her doctor. Couldn't be too careful these days. Though she practiced safe sex, there were days in her past that she'd just as soon not think about.

She hurried along Chambers Street. Her sneakered feet, de rigueur, helped speed her journey. She reached the door of Hogarth's at eight on the dot. But Val, never one to be outdone, had arrived moments earlier, securing their table.

Val waved when she saw Maxine enter. "Hey, girl," Val greeted as Maxine slid into the red leather booth and planted a kiss on her cheek.

"Hey, yourself. One of these damned days I'm gonna arrive *somewhere* before you. Girl, I swear," she said, a bit breathy from her five-block walk, "I don't know how you do it."

Valerie laughed her "all is right with the world" laugh. "Chile, don't even try it. You might hurt yourself."

"You got that right." Maxine tucked her purse and briefcase between her feet. "Did you order?"

"Yep. I'm starvin'. Been up since four-thirty."

"You are crazy."

Val laughed. "So I've been told. But—" she wagged a finger

at Maxine "—I get so much done at that time of the morning. That's when I do my studying."

"I guess so. What other fools are up to bug you?" Maxine chuckled. "I hear you. Gotta get it while you can."

The waitress arrived and took Maxine's order.

"So I guess you've had a chance to talk with Quinten about the possibility of a lawsuit?" Val asked, taking a sip of freshly squeezed orange juice.

"He wasn't going for it at first," Maxine said, keeping her eyes focused on her glass of water. "But he finally came around. He told me to get the ball rollin' and let him know what needs to be done."

Valerie eyed her speculatively. "You sounded more enthusiastic *before* you got him to agree. What's up?"

Maxine pursed her lips and planted her elbows on the table. Finally she looked up. "Why can't I get beyond Quinten Parker, Val? Why can't I get it through my thick skull that all we'll ever be to each other is 'good friends'?"

"'Cause for one thing, he's about the finest thing I've seen since whenever. And second, you don't really want to accept that friend thing because you want it to be more. The question is— what are you going to do about it?"

Maxine tilted her head to the side and half smiled. "Nothing."

"Exactly." She paused for a moment, her light brown eyes resting on her friend. "Listen, we've been friends for a while. And as long as I've known you, you've had a thing for Quinn Parker. But I also know you're not the type of woman to let one monkey stop her show. You have it going on, girl, and you know it. If Quinn can't see it, it's his loss, my sister, not yours. You have a new man in your life that digs you, good job, new career on the horizon, and you kinda look okay," she teased. "So just push on."

"I know. And I'm not moping about it. Don't have the time. But you know, every now and then those feelings just sneak up on me."

"Like Friday night," Val stated, knowing.

The waitress placed a plate of pancakes, scrambled eggs and sausage in front of Valerie and an identical one in front of Maxine, minus the sausage. She'd opted for Canadian bacon.

Maxine cut up her pancakes and doused them in thick maple syrup until it created a little pool around the edge of the off-white plate. "Yeah, like Friday night. Everything was all that until this chick walks in the club." Maxine proceeded to tell Val what happened.

"Well, sis, one thing I've learned about men is that you can lead them by the nose to your heart, but no telling if they'll take it. They have to find their own way, on their own, in their own time."

"Don't I know that, too. But hey, this diva's gonna keep, keep keepin' on."

They gave each other a high five.

"Now that's what I want to hear."

"And I didn't get my behind up at the crack of dawn to talk about Quinn, anyway. Tell me what we need to do to get some justice for our girl."

Three o'clock. Amen.
Maxine had opened and closed her last account for the day. Sitting in front of her computer, she wiggled her toes inside her gray pumps, which she'd donned at the start of her work day. Keying in her activity log, she was pleasantly surprised when a single rose was waved beneath her nose.

She turned. "Dre. Hi, baby," she greeted, raising her lips for a quick, discreet kiss. "How'd you get in?"

"You know me. Besides, Clarence the security guard is cool. Told him that I had a very important appointment with a very special lady. The rest was a breeze." He grinned, displaying his boyish smile with the tiny chip in his front tooth. Max thought it was cute.

"Dre, you are a piece of work." She shook her head. "What are you doing off so early, or are you taking a really late lunch?"

André pulled a vacant chair up to her desk and straddled it. "A little of both. I thought if I could leave a little early today, maybe we could go to a movie or something. I hear the new Denzel movie is good, and I missed seeing you over the weekend." His brown eyes, set in a sienna-complexioned face, sparkled at her. He was a dead ringer for Michael Jordan, minus about five inches.

Maxine swallowed back her momentary bout of guilt and beamed. "You sure know how to rescue a girl."

Maxine had met André Martin almost a year earlier when he'd come into the bank to open an account. He'd just started his job as Assistant Supervisor of Security for Tower Two at the World Trade Center. He'd moved from Philadelphia to New York and was eager to get his finances in order. She'd liked that.

He was easy to talk with and had a raw sense of humor. He'd always made it a point to pop into the customer service station and say hello whenever he did his banking. Then one afternoon, he dropped in just before closing and asked if he could take her out for a drink after work. That was three months ago. They'd been a "couple" ever since.

"So you think you'll be ready to break out of here by five?"

"Absolutely. Maybe earlier. If I can, I'll beep you."

He checked his watch and stood. "I have a couple of runs to make, but I'll be out front at five."

Maxine smiled up at him. "See you then."

Dre turned and sauntered out, nodding and waving to familiar faces, his navy slacks and white shirt fitting his long, slim body like an *EM* model.

Maxine went back to her work with just a bit more enthusiasm. Val was right. She did have a good life, and if her request for a small business loan was approved it would get even better. Then she could look forward to a future as a small business owner.

During her talk with Val, they'd decided to secure the services of a small black law firm that specialized in civil cases. If she didn't hear from Quinn by the next day, she'd give him a call and let him know the plan.

Maxine turned off her computer and any further thoughts of Quinn, directing her attentions to her upcoming date with Dre. He was good for her, filling many evenings, making her laugh. He was one of the few men she'd dated over the years who was trying to be about something. That in itself was rare. Maybe this relationship could be "the one." She hadn't given *it* up yet. And Dre wasn't dogging her to get in her pants. He'd been real patient, since this time she wanted to be sure. She was tired of drifting in and out of relationships. She wanted some permanence in her life, and Dre kept hinting that he was in the market for the long haul.

She'd just have to see.

Five o'clock arrived at a snail's pace and Maxine was out of the door like a shot. As promised, Dre was parked out front in his slate blue Honda Accord. There was definitely some wear and tear on the "ole girl," but she rode like a cloud. Dre boasted that in the ten years he'd owned the car, the only work he'd had to do was regular tune-ups.

"Hey, babe," he greeted as she slid into the passenger seat.

"Hey, yourself." She offered him a quick kiss.

"Get all your work done?"

"Oh, yeah. You know I hate having leftover work greet me in the morning. I'd rather stay late before I let that happen. But today was pretty slow. Not too many problems. How 'bout you?"

He switched on the car stereo to the sexy bantering of Ashford and Simpson on KISS FM. He kept his eyes on the road. "No complaints."

Maxine gave him a sidelong glance. Dre was always eager to talk about his job and the oddballs that came in and out. Since the bombing a few years earlier, the World Trade Center was more secure than the Pentagon. The slightest little thing and the security force was on you like milk on cereal.

"Everything okay?" she asked, her curiosity itching like a mosquito bite.

"Yeah, yeah." He turned his head toward her and smiled. "No problem. What's happening with your business loan? Hear anything?" he asked, quickly changing the subject.

"No. Not yet. I probably won't hear anything for a couple of weeks."

"I know that waiting can be a killer." He patted her thigh. "You'll get it. Don't even worry about it."

She smiled. "It's just hard to believe that I'm even at this point in my life." *Damn, a businesswoman. Who would have thought it?*

"Why. You don't think you deserve it?"

"No. Nothing like that." She took a breath. "I mean, I just barely made it out of high school with my life. I was runnin' with a gang, fightin', cuttin' classes." She shook her head. "I thought I was all that. Tough girl, didn't take no mess. We were the fly girls that all the guys wanted. It was my girl, I mean my friend, Lacy—the one I told you about—who really pulled my coat. There was a plan to break into the school and steal some of the computers. When Lacy heard about it, she convinced me not to go. She really got me to see that there was more to life than what was right in front of me, but I had to want it."

Her throat tightened as an image of Lacy's nut brown face and smiling eyes filled her vision. She blinked away the burn in her eyes and swallowed. "She said, 'Girl, we been friends since kindergarten. You're like a sister to me. You go out and get yourself all messed up, then where's that gonna leave me? What am I gonna do for a sister? Who's Quinn gonna bug? Want more than just today, Max. The good Lord's been watchin' over your fool behind all these years. Don't make him think he's been wastin' his time.'"

Her mouth trembled at the edges as tears spilled down her cheeks. "She was like that, ya know." She sniffled. "She always knew what to say, as if she really had some special vision, some insight into things." She wiped her eyes.

"Shit," she sputtered. "I just miss her so damned much. God was so busy watchin' over my sorry behind, he took his eyes off her."

Dre checked traffic and pulled the car to a stop at the curb. He unfastened his seat belt and then hers. "Come here," he said gently.

Max leaned her head on his chest, inhaling his Farenheit cologne. He stroked her hair, letting her get out the last of her tears.

"I'm sorry." She sniffled, moving away, her head lowered. "Sometimes it just gets to me, ya know."

"No sweat. She sounds like she was really a great person."

"She was all that, and then some." A smile wavered around her mouth. "Funny thing, I'm not sure if it was the words, or because she talked for so damned long," she said with a shaky laugh. "By the time she'd finished, I knew those girls were long gone. So I just stayed with Lacy. And the next day it was in the papers that the girls had been caught breaking into the school and were arrested." She shook her head. "Turned me around." She chuckled softly. "After that I even let her drag me to that church of hers every now and then. Lacy was always a firm believer in the power of prayer, the power of change. But she was never preachy, like some folks you run into, always talking about 'Praise the Lord' and 'Amen this' and 'the good Lord that,' and five minutes later they're sleepin' with your man."

Dre laughed. "Yeah, I've run into my share of holier-than-thou rollers."

"That's why it's so important to me to make sure that right is done by her. My girl Val is gonna help. She recommended a black law firm that's down to take civil cases."

"Didn't you mention that she had a brother? What about him?"

Quinn. "I talked with him about it. We're gonna push it through." She didn't want to dwell on Quinn. She took a breath, then brightened. "Hey, are we gonna sit here all night or what?" She dabbed under her eyes.

"Sure you're okay?"

"Absolutely."

He checked his mirrors. *Rush hour.* Slowly he pulled the car into the snarled, narrow streets of lower Manhattan. The towering skyscrapers were casting long-fingered shadows along the pebbly gray concrete. Pedestrian traffic was just as heavy as the mélange of buses, trucks, cars and squawking yellow cabs.

He settled back and concentrated on maneuvering toward the FDR Drive. He'd wanted to tell her what happened at work today, hoping that maybe she could give him some leads. But the last thing she needed to hear tonight was a sad story about him losing his job. He'd have to be real careful with his finances until he found something. He could probably live off of his savings for about two months before his stuff started getting raggedy. What happened to him at the job was foul. He knew he was set up, but he couldn't prove it.

He gave Maxine a quick look. With all she had going for her, where would their relationship be if he remained unemployed?

Damn, Maxine was the best thing to happen to him since before he left Philly. He didn't want to blow it.

They stood in front of Maxine's apartment. Dre took the key and opened the door. They faced each other.

"I had a great time, Dre. Thanks for the movie and dinner. Just what I needed."

"You deserve the best, Maxie. I wanna be that for you. If you give me a chance."

"Let's just take it a day at a time," she said as gently as she could. "I got a lot going on in my life, Dre. I don't know if I'm ready to handle more than that right now."

Slowly he nodded his head. "Do I have competition?" He grinned.

Maxine heard the underlying tone of disappointment lacing his lighthearted words. "No. Nothing like that." She reached for his hand. "Everything's cool. Call you tomorrow?"

"Yeah, sure. Uh, just beep me." He didn't want her to call his former place of employment before he had a chance to tell her himself.

"I will." She leaned forward and placed a long, slow kiss on his lips. "Night, Dre."

"Night, Max." He turned and left.

Dre was really a nice guy. She put her keys in her bag. He was good-looking for sure, paid her plenty of attention and was ready for a committed relationship. So what was the problem?

The old wooden door creaked on its hinges as she pushed it closed. She flipped on the light, bathing the narrow hall in soft yellow. She dropped her purse on the hall table, kicked off her shoes and walked the length of the railroad-style apartment to her bedroom on the right.

As she switched on the bedside lamp, the first thing that caught her attention was the flashing light of her answering machine.

She unbuttoned her suit jacket and slipped out of her skirt, hanging both in the small closet. Off came the cream-colored blouse and half slip.

Dre deserved a chance and so did she. She knew she'd been half stepping with him. And starting tomorrow, things were going to change. She was putting her life in full gear. No more looking over her shoulder. *Press on, my sistah.*

She unhooked her black push-up bra, took off her sheer black hose and black panties. Fully disrobed, she sat on the edge of her bed and pressed the play button to listen to her messages. She took her silk paisley robe from the foot of the platform bed and slipped it on while she listened to Val reminding her that tomorrow was gym night. There was a message from Mr. Hines, her landlord, lying about the paint job he'd promised and telling her not to forget her rent. *Like he forgot the paint job? Ha.* Then Quinn's deep, pulsing voice filled the room.

"Yeah, Max. It's me, just checkin' on what you found out from Val." Maxine closed her eyes. "I'll be in and out, so just beep me and I'll get with you. Yeah…I start that gig next week."

She popped up from her bed, beaming. *You go, Q. I knew you would do right.*

There was a pause. "Thanks, Maxie. Later."

Her heart beat just a little faster. She spun around ready to beep him and tell him about her talk with Val and share her congratulations. She punched in the numbers. Then, halfway through punching in hers for the return call, she stopped.

She returned the black cordless phone to the base. *Whatsup with you, girl. It's damn near midnight and you're salivating to call that man.*

She took a deep breath and relaxed. Q could wait till the a.m. She smiled and decided to take a nice hot shower. She touched her fingers to her lips. The sensation of Dre's kiss still lingered. *Yeah.*

Chapter 11

"What do you mean, you spent the night at his house and nothing happened?" Parris squealed into the phone.

Nikita grinned. "Just what I said. Nothing happened."

"Is he gay?"

"W—hat?" she sputtered, then burst out laughing. "No!"

"You sure about that, girl?"

"Yes, I'm sure. Trust me. He's all male and then some, with enough to go around."

"Humph. I thought chivalry was cremated."

"Parris, you are too crazy." Nikita laughed, pushing her chair away from her desk.

She and Quinn had been seeing or talking to each other practically every day for the past week. She couldn't seem to get enough of him. She thought of him constantly, wanted to be in his company every chance she got.

When she was with Quinn, she didn't feel that she always had to meet some expectation, as she had with the other men she'd dated. She knew she was nothing like the other women in his life, and for that very reason she felt special. She'd never felt special before. For once, she didn't feel that she was in competition with the man in her life.

"So what do Mom and Pop think about Mr. Parker?"

"They haven't stopped lecturing me yet about staying out all night without calling. I think it'll be a while before I bring him home to dinner."

"I hear you." Knowing Cynthia and Lawrence Harrell, Parris couldn't imagine that they'd ever accept Quinn, even at lunch. He was straight out of their worst nightmare, and she wondered if that was Nikita's real reason for her interest in Quinn, the fact that she knew her parents would hate him on sight. Well, she'd always prided herself on her "wait and see" approach, her ability to withhold judgment until all the facts were presented. So, for the time being, she'd keep her mouth shut. "Where did you tell them you were?"

"At your apartment. I said I was too tired to drive home."

"Your folks sure didn't pay all that money educating a fool." She chuckled. "How's the job going?"

"Wonderfully. Lillian loved the article. It's going to run in the next issue."

"Great. You didn't tell any lies about me, did you?"

"Of course I did. That's what makes the story interesting," she joked.

"Girl, pleeze, don't make me jump on the next plane to New York."

Nikita giggled. "Believe me, your honor and all your little secrets are intact."

"I'll be back early next week. Then we can really talk. Nick told me that Quinn called him and he's going to start playing this Friday night."

"Yes. I'm so excited. He's trying to act cool, but I know he's nervous. He's been rehearsing with the band all week."

"Nikita, what does Quinn do—exactly?"

"He works with a guy in the evenings, helping him to run his clubs."

"Hmmm. So he's a manager or something?"

"Yes. He's a manager," she said, thankful for an answer and

wanting to change the subject. As much as she and Quinn were getting to know each other, there were areas of his life that he didn't discuss. What he did for Remy was one of them.

"Who are you going to profile for the next issue?"

"I'm not sure yet, but I have to figure something out, and quick. I don't want this career to be a flash in the pan."

"Give Nick a call. I'm sure he can hook you up with someone."

"That's an idea. I'll probably see him Friday at the club, anyway. I'll try to talk with him then."

"At least he can point you in the right direction."

"Speaking of which, I'd better get the rest of this work done before I leave today. I've been falling behind lately."

"That doesn't sound like you, Niki."

She sighed. "I've just been trying to take some of the pressure off. Ease back a little."

Parris frowned. "I've never known you not to try to reach for the moon with everything you did. Deadlines were never a problem before."

"They're not a problem now."

"Uh, unh. Hey, do your thing, Niki."

"Whatever that thing may be," they said in unison.

"Okay, I'm off, sister-friend. See you next week."

"Can't wait. Have a great show and a safe flight."

"Thanks. Talk to ya."

Nikita hung up the phone and leaned back in her seat. There was so much she wanted to tell Parris, questions that ran around in her head, feelings that she was trying to sort out, happiness that she wanted to share. But something held her back. There were still so many shadows and unanswered questions surrounding Quinn. There seemed to be a part of him that was sealed shut.

She sighed. It was still early in the relationship. She hoped that over time he'd open up. In the meantime, she had work to do.

She'd just finished reviewing and keying in two articles: one on childbirth after forty and the other about a new wave of sexually transmitted diseases among women twenty-five to thirty-five. That article gave her food for thought. She hoped that when the time came, and she felt sure it would, that Quinn wasn't the kind of man who balked at using a condom. There was no debating that point, and he'd better be very clear about it.

She hit the save key with a definitive pop.

There, finally done. She checked the rectangular wall clock. Four-thirty. Switching off the computer and activating the answering machine, she turned off the lights and locked up.

Going home wasn't at the top of her list of things to do, but she had no other plans for the evening and no journalism classes. She hadn't heard from Quinn all day, and she'd promised herself she wasn't going to become one of those women who were always beeping "their man" and sitting by the phone waiting for return calls. And neither was she going to leave "where are you?" messages on his machine.

Nikita stepped out into the humid early-evening air and across the street to her car. Her bare arms were quickly covered in dampness, and she thanked good sense that she'd given up on perms. She turned up the air conditioner and popped an Anita Baker cassette into the deck. Anita's throaty alto told her man that she was giving the best she had to give.

She could do the same for Quinn, if he'd let her. Over the years the only times she'd extended herself were in school. Her personal and social life were almost peripheral—not her focus. She endured the chitchat from the women she'd known—except for Parris and Jewel—the damp, passionless kisses and less than earth-shattering sex from the few men she'd known. But she craved more, needed more. She felt sure that she was the main ingredient missing from Quinn's life. She could be the stabilizing force that he needed. Everyone needed some stability and structure, a plan for the future. She could help him with all that. And he could be that missing puzzle piece of her life, finally fitting into that undefined space.

Amy was the only one there when she finally arrived home. The mouthwatering aroma of roasting chicken greeted her as soon as she walked in the door. She'd always felt guilty that Amy was more a mother to her than her own. She never could understand her mother's detachment from her, her inability to really listen or show an interest in the things that bothered her. "Your mother's just busy with that job of hers," Amy would always say. "Of course she loves you, Niki. And so does your daddy."

Lawrence Harrell was an entirely different enigma. The only times he ever seemed to show any emotion toward her were at report card times, when she won awards, or when evaluations came in and she remained at the top of her classes. At those times her mother seemed to withdraw even further, barely commenting, or only saying, "That's what we expect."

"You're home early today, Niki. No classes?" Amy asked as she hustled around the kitchen with the final preparations for dinner.

"No. No classes tonight. So I thought I'd just come straight home." She sat on a bar stool at the kitchen counter.

Amy peeked over her shoulder from basting the chicken, catching the forlorn look on Nikita's face. She closed the oven door. "What's wrong, chile? Look like you lost something." She began kneading the dough for the apple pie crust.

Nikita forced a half smile. "Oh… I don't know, Amy. I just think coming back home was a bad idea." She picked a green seedless grape from the bunch that rested in a ceramic fruit bowl on the island counter and popped it into her mouth. She chewed thoughtfully.

"You saying you think you should have stayed in school?"

"No. Definitely not." She picked up another grape. "I just should have planned better so that I wouldn't have to stay here. They don't want me here."

Amy stopped kneading. "Now you listen here. Of course they want you. They's just disappointed that you dropped out of school like that, no warnin', no nothin'. That's all."

"That's not all, Amy, and you know it." Nikita looked deep into the soft brown eyes of her mother-friend. "They've never wanted me around. They were always shipping me off somewhere—to camp, this lesson, that lesson, boarding school, the student exchange program. I thought Mom would have a heart attack when I decided to stay in the country and attend Cornell. The only time they pay me any attention is when I screw up."

Amy sat down on a stool on the opposite side of the peach Formica counter. "Chile, your parents have only wanted the best for you, give you opportunities they never had. I know they may seem difficult and stiff in the ways of thinkin' and doin' things, but they always had your best interests at heart. Even now. Might not seem so, but they do."

"But sometimes, Amy, giving a person *things* is not what they need. I can't remember a time when they ever asked me what *I* wanted. It's always been what they wanted for me. All I ever wanted was their love."

"Everyone has a different way of showing love, Niki. It's easier for some than for others. Some folks show their love the only way they can—by doing things for ya, giving ya things, like that. Other people express their love in words and open affection. Doesn't make it that one loves ya more than another."

Nikita let the words settle over her for a moment.

"Maybe," was all she could say.

Quinn unlocked the door to his apartment just as the phone rang. Maybe it was Nikita. He'd been running all day and hadn't gotten around to calling her.

He picked up the phone expecting to hear her voice, but was equally pleased with the one he heard.

"Yeah?"

"Hey, Q. It's Max."

"Hey, babe. How's it goin'?"

"It's all good. How 'bout you?"

"Cool. Whatsup?" He walked with the cordless phone into the kitchen and took a beer from the fridge.

"Just wanted you to know that I spoke with Val."

He clenched his jaw. "What she say?"

Max ran it down for him and gave him the number of the law firm.

"I'll go with you when you're ready, Q."

"I can handle it."

"That ain't the point. I want to go."

He pushed out a breath through his nose and took a big gulp

of the ice-cold beer. "Yeah, awright. I'll call 'em tomorrow and see what they got to say."

"Just let me know."

"Yeah, I will. How's the job hunt goin'?"

"I'm going to check out a travel agency tomorrow. See what happens."

"Good luck and all that."

"Thanks. Oh, yeah, congrats on the gig. You're playin' Friday night, huh?"

He grinned. "Yeah. Don't get all hyped, now."

"Listen to you. I know you just cheesin' it up on the other end of this line, my brother."

He had to laugh. "You comin', or what?"

"Would I miss your debut? Hell, yeah, I'll be there." She took a quick breath. "Your friend whatshername comin'?"

"Who? Nikita?"

"Yeah."

"I guess. Why?"

"Nothin'. Just askin'. What time is this shindig?"

"'Round midnight."

"I'll be there."

"I'll get the owner to reserve a table for you up front."

"Ooh, chile, talkin' like a star already." She chuckled.

Quinn just laughed and shook his head. "Just don't be hootin' and hollerin'."

"Hey, listen, this around the way girl knows how to act in public."

"Yeah, it's behind closed doors that a brother has to watch out."

"Now you'll never know, will ya? Later, Q. See ya Friday."

"Later, Max." He hung up the phone with a big grin plastered on his face. *That Maxine was somethin' else.*

Maxine slowly returned the receiver to the cradle. "Yeah, you'll never know, will ya?" she whispered.

Quinn pulled up a seat and pressed the play button on his answering machine. There were calls from three of his women friends, each wanting to see him and wanting to know why he hadn't called.

"'Cause ya'll ain't got nothin' to talk about. That's why," he said out loud.

There was a call from his landlady, Mrs. Finch, wanting him to take her food shopping in the morning, even though she knew he slept late.

Well if ya know I sleep late, why ya want me to take ya shoppin' in the mornin'? Women. Young, old, didn't make any difference. Difficult.

No call from Nikita.

She still hadn't given up the number to her crib, and he wondered why. Maybe she was really living with some dude. He frowned, the thought taking all kinds of twists and turns. He didn't like the feelings that were building. It wasn't like him to care one way or the other.

He tried to shake the sensation off by turning on the stereo. The sultry voice of Phyllis Hyman's "You Know How To Love Me" pumped through the speakers. He trotted up the stairs to his bedroom and the music followed him through the sound system built into the walls.

He changed out of his jeans and denim shirt into his standard night attire. Checked his piece and was ready to roll. He frowned. If Mrs. Finch ever found out— She just *wouldn't* find out. He didn't bring his business home. That was a strict rule. He shook off the twinge of guilt.

He bounded down the stairs, double-checked the locks and windows—old habit from the hood—and went out.

Cruising up the West Side Highway to the sounds of Heavy D, Quinn thought about his nightly commute. Not that driving bothered him or anything, though the trip would eventually put some wear and tear on his ride. But he had to admit he was growing to really dig where he lived. He liked to be able to come home to a quiet block, without the wail of the ambulance and the scream of police sirens which always followed the *pop-pop* of gunfire.

He could see a woman like Nikita fitting right into this new world that he was building for himself. Just as she had the other night. He'd begun to feel safe and warm again, knowing that she was right in the next room. More than once he'd been tempted to break his promise and creep into her room. But he'd never do that. A man had to be held by his word and he was a man of his word.

The way he knew he could allow himself to feel about Nikita scared him. The women who'd ever meant anything to him had left—one through choice, the other through death. He wasn't going to ever live through that kind of bottomless pain again— the unending emptiness that ate through your soul, leaving you barren as a desert. He'd have to go really easy with his feelings, keep his heart locked down and out of reach.

He pulled up in front of B.J.'s, double-parked his ride and pushed through the blacked-out door.

"Turk, my man," he greeted, giving the old bartender a five. "What it look like?"

"It's all good. Jack?"

"Yeah. I got a few minutes." He slid into a vacant seat at the bar and took a look around while Turk fixed his drink, his eyes quickly adjusting to the dim smokiness of the room.

Music pumped from the decade-old jukebox and couples bumped and grinded on the miniature dance floor, while the rest of the regulars huddled in corners, leaned against walls and sat at old wooden tables that wobbled from side to side, depending on who was leaning which way the hardest.

All so familiar. It felt good.

"Here ya go." Turk put the glass in front of Quinn.

"Thanks, man."

"I hear they lookin' for some other suspects in that shootin' that took out your sister, man."

The glass stopped just before it reached his lips. His stomach rolled. "Say what?"

"Yeah. That's the word on the street, brother. I thought you knew."

Quinn tossed the drink down his throat, the burning liquid boring through the sudden chill that iced his belly. His gaze narrowed. "Who's lookin'?"

"Cops. Been sniffin' 'round the neighborhood all day. Quizzin' people 'n shit."

Quinn pulled a five from the knot of bills in his pocket and slapped it on the table. Standing, he finished the rest of his drink. "Later."

"Yeah. Take it easy, money." Turk wiped down the bar, watching Quinn as he moved toward the back room.

Once inside he didn't see or smell a thing. His focus was on getting with Remy. If anybody knew what was going down, it was Remy. He brushed by Sylvie, barely acknowledging her when she smiled her smile. He pushed into the back room, and Remy's eyes momentarily rolled up from the cash in front of him.

"Whatsup?"

"Need to kick it with you for a minute." His dark eyes cut across the faces of the two men counting and stacking. "Private."

"Gimme five, ya'll."

The two men hauled themselves out of their seats and ambled out of the room.

"Rest ya self," Remy said, indicating a chair with a toss of his head.

Quinn shoved his hands in his pants pockets, his fists balled. He remained standing.

"What's the deal with the cops askin' questions 'bout the... shootin'?"

"SOS. Askin' questions 'bout who was where. Said they had the 411 'bout it being someone from 'round here that fired on the cops."

"Yeah, but what about the dudes they locked up?"

Remy shrugged. "Way I hear it, dem boys swearin' they ain't do it. Said only ones shootin' was the cops."

A rock settled in Quinn's stomach. He swallowed, trying to douse the burning that scorched his insides. "You sayin' it was a cop's bullet?"

Remy looked at the man who had been like a son, knowing what he was about to tell him could change his whole life. "Yeah. Dat's what I'm sayin'."

Remy's eyes, which always looked as if they carried the burdens of the world, held his in a silent moment of reckoning.

Slowly Quinn sat down, taking in the implication of what he'd been told.

He clenched his jaw. It was as Max had said, and what a dark corner of his heart had held at bay. They were trying to cover up what they'd done. Trying to use their "black-on-black" crime slogan as their reason for the lie. He stood. "I got a run to make. Be back in about an hour."

"Q." Remy stood up. "Don't do nothin' stupid." His voice held a warning edge from too many years of knowing what moves made on raw emotion could do.

Quinn just cut him a look from dark, angry eyes. "Later."

Maxine was curled up on her couch, cuddled in the curve of Dre's arm. Tonight was the night. She was kicking her doubts to the curb and taking her relationship with Dre to another level. She was ready.

Her eyelids fluttered closed as Dre's soft lips brushed against her neck. Tiny tingles scuttled through her body. It had been a long time since she'd had some good loving, and her deprived body was shifting into overdrive with anticipation. She wiggled a bit closer when Dre's hand drifted from her shoulder to cover her right breast.

He felt her shudder and squeezed just a little. "You feel good, baby," he whispered in her ear, catching the soft whiff of Eternity. He felt sure that once he'd made it with Maxine, she'd be his—finally—and wouldn't so easily walk away from him when she found out he was unemployed. Maybe she'd even let him stay with her for a while if things got too tight financially. He intended to tell her. He just wanted to be sure the time and timing were right.

Dre angled his body so that his face was inches from hers.

The doorbell rang like a shock wave shooting through her body. She jerked back.

"Leave 'em out there," Dre groaned, trying to hold on to the intimate moment and the one that was slipping from his fingers and getting up from the couch.

"It could be important," Maxine said, disconnecting herself from Dre.

He hung his head in disbelief as he watched her walk down the narrow hallway to the door, straightening her blouse and buttoning the top button of her pants.

The lock clicked and he heard the distinct rumbling timbre of a male voice. He sat up straighter, straining to hear. He sure as hell hoped this wasn't gonna turn into an ugly throw down.

"Q?" Her heart rocked in her chest. *Damn, fine time for you to be showin' up, lookin' and smellin' good, too.* "Whatsup?"

"Need to rap with you for a minute."

She blinked, sensing the rumbling vibes pulsing from Quinn's body, thought about Dre for a hot second. "Sure. Come on in."

Quinn stepped inside while Maxine relocked the three locks. He followed her sinewy form down the hall, noting how good she looked in her cream silk shirt and the way her pants hugged her hips and full behind. He came up short when he spotted a brother lounging on the couch like he owned the joint. His muscles tightened.

"Quinn, this is André Martin. Dre, Quinn Parker, Lacy's brother."

Dre stood, extending his hand, and they exchanged the handshake of the day.

How men could ever figure out which of those intricate handshakes to use was always a mystery to Max. Must be a secret brotherhood thing.

"Heard a lot about you," Dre said.

"Yeah?" *Never heard about you, my brother.* He slanted a look at Max and wondered what she saw in this cut-off version of Michael Jordan with a chipped front tooth.

"Me and Quinn need to talk for a minute, Dre."

"No problem." He resumed his spot on the couch.

"Come on in the kitchen, Q. 'Scuse us, Dre."

"Have a seat," Maxine offered, pulling out a chair from beneath the butcher-block table. She couldn't recall a time when Quinn had sat in her kitchen. It was kind of nice. "So…what's with the visit?"

Quinn sat, long legs stretched out in front of him. He crossed his arms, leaned forward. "Word's out that it was a cop who did Lacy," he said, a shaky edge to his voice.

"I knew it!" She slapped her palm on the table, her eyes blazing.

"That's why they been slippin' and slidin' about gettin' to the bottom of things." Her brown eyes settled on his stern expression.

"Yeah, but 'cording to Remy they're lookin' for some other dudes. Been through the hood askin' questions."

Maxine's smooth, dark brown features bunched up in a frown. "You think it's true?"

He pushed out a breath. "I ain't sure what to believe, but we definitely gotta press on with these lawyers, see what they can find out. Ya know?"

"Absolutely. This week. When's the best time for you?"

"Whenever. I'll make time."

Maxine nodded. "I'm calling them tomorrow."

"Cool." Quinn rose from his seat. "Listen, I gotta roll. Just wanted to, ya know, drop that on you."

Maxine got up. Her heart beat a little faster. She pressed her lips together and clasped her hands in front of her. Her gaze rose and rested on his face. "I'll, uh, walk you to the door."

Quinn turned his head down the hallway and saw Dre sitting in the same spot. "Later, man," he called.

"Later," Dre called back, relief in his voice.

Quinn stopped at the door and looked down at Maxine, his loose locks swung across his shoulders. "He treatin' you cool?" he asked with a lift of his chin in Dre's direction.

"Yes." She gave a half smile.

Quinn nodded. "Better be. I don't wanna have to hurt nobody." He grinned.

"What do you think?"

"About him?"

"Yes, about him." She planted her hand on her hip and arched her neck.

Quinn shrugged. "If it's what ya like, baby." He flicked her chin with the tip of his index finger. "Go for it." He gave her a wink. "Talk to ya." He turned and left.

Maxine slowly closed and locked the door behind him. She turned and saw Dre watching her. Smiling, she walked toward him.

He got up and met her halfway. "Meeting turn out okay?"

"Yeah. No problem." She ran her hands down her hips, wiping

away the dampness, and looked at him. "Uh, can I get you somethin'? Thirsty?"

"Naw. Thanks. Listen, it's gettin' late. I'm going to get moving."

Maxine took a breath and nodded. "It *is* getting kinda late."

He picked up his jacket from the couch. "I'll call you." He walked down the hallway to the door, then turned to Maxine. "I think you oughta think about what you really want, Max."

"What do you mean?"

A half smile curved his lips. "I think you know. We'll talk." He stepped out of the door and closed it behind him.

"Damn," she whispered, staring at the closed door.

"Hi, Nick. It's me, Nikita."

"Hey, how are you?"

"Not bad." She ran her fingers through her locks. "Well, actually, I have a favor to ask."

"Shoot."

Nikita explained that she needed a lead on an entertainer for an article in the magazine.

"Hmm. Would a phone interview work?"

"Sure." Her hopes spiraled.

"I'll make a few calls and get back with you. Are you comin' down tomorrow night?"

"I was planning to."

"I should have something for you by then."

"Great. Thanks, Nick."

"No problem."

"Nick? Um, have you heard from Quinn?"

"He just left. Mmm, maybe about twenty minutes ago."

"Oh, thanks." She absently hung up the phone. She hadn't heard from Quinn in several days and didn't know why. Quinn was like night and day. At times he seemed caring, thoughtful, almost romantic in his own cool way. At others he was remote, distant, as if a deep sadness weighed down his spirit. Almost as if he turned inward, shutting the world out.

She looked at the stack of mail and unread manuscripts. She pulled one from the pile and began to read just as the phone rang.

"*Today's Woman*. Good afternoon."

"Hey, baby."

The air stopped midway in her chest. "Quinn."

"Yeah, Quinn. How are ya?"

"Kind of busy at the moment," she answered, her tone tight and curt.

"That's too bad. I'm outside. I was thinkin' of stealin' you for a coupla hours. But since you're busy—"

"I haven't heard from you in days, Quinn, and you call out of the blue and want me to stop what I'm doing and hang out with you?" Ooh, she really wanted to run to the window, but couldn't, silently cussing Ms. Ingram for not investing in a cordless phone.

"Yeah, somethin' like that." He grinned, peeking up at the window hoping to get a glimpse of her, knowing that she had that pretty little honey-dipped face of hers all puffed up. "But hey, I hear ya. You got things to do. So why don't I pick you up after work? Maybe we can do a little somethin' somethin'," he crooned in that sexy tone that made her blood run hot and hotter. "What time you gettin' off?"

She fought back a smile and tried on her indifferent voice. "Four-thirty."

"I'll be out front. Think about that somethin' somethin' you wanna do."

"I certainly will, because you have some making up to do."

"That's the best part." He chuckled. "Later."

Nikita held the phone to her breasts, a big Kool-Aid satisfied grin on her face. Then she dashed to the window just in time to catch a look at his black BMW zooming down the street.

She looked at her wall clock. One-thirty. The end of her work day couldn't come fast enough. She had things to do to get ready for her date with Quinn.

Quinn exhaled deeply and hung up his cell phone. Adjusting his shades, he shifted the Beamer into drive and pulled into the flow of traffic heading uptown.

Yeah, he'd been lax, he knew it. But sometimes the real side of his life took a front seat. He'd just make it up to her, that's all. He wasn't used to answering to anybody, anyway. Didn't have any intention of starting now. But there was something about Nikita that made him wanna do the right thing—do things differently. Still, there was a big piece of him that was tied to the life he'd made—it was all he knew. Change was hard. He wasn't sure how much of it he wanted.

He turned onto Sixty-first Street and was surrounded by the towering buildings that made up Lincoln Center. He pulled up to a meter and dropped in a quarter, looking at one of the imposing buildings. ASCAP.

So this was the spot where Nick handled his *real* business. He'd asked him to drop off a package and deliver it to his manager. Yeah, right. He knew he had to have something going on. Things were too straight at the club. It was the same deal with Remy, except that Remy handled his business in the back room. Nick bumped up a step and handled his with a bit of class. He looked around and spotted the bubbling fountain across the street, the rows of outdoor cafés, all the folks dressed in designer suits, carrying briefcases. Yeah. He nodded, heading toward the building. Perfect front.

Quinn took the elevator to the eighth floor and stepped into music history. For a moment, he was thrown off. He was expecting…he didn't know what…but it wasn't this.

All along the pristine white walls were photographs of music greats for decades—Lena, Sarah, Quincy, Celine, The Count, Prince, The Temptations, Whitney, Toni, Sinatra and countless other faces he couldn't even name. Music, not the dental office kind, but the real deal, floated seamlessly through the air.

Groups of seating areas were filled with young kids and their parents, older teens, and other groups of kids who were passing jokes between them and sheets of paper that looked like musical notes. He could tell that the cases sitting at their feet held instruments. What was this place, *really?*

He walked a little farther down the hall. Gold and platinum records encased in glass held places of honor on the walls. *Whatever this place was, it was phat.*

"Hi. I'm Simone. Can I help you?"

He blinked away images of himself framed and covered with glass hanging on the wall. "Yeah. I have a package from Nick Hunter."

The young woman's face brightened. Her contact-lensed hazel eyes widened. "You're a friend of Nick's?"

"Somethin' like that." And then for some reason he wanted her to know. "I play with his band."

"Really?"

"Just started. Play piano."

She flipped her shoulder-length weave over her shoulder and tilted her head to the side. "Good luck. His band is fabulous. I have all of his CDs."

Quinn smiled. He handed her the package. "This is for Paul Conner."

"Let me buzz him for you. I think he's still in with the accountants. Why don't you have a seat?"

Moments later, a tall, rather slender man with just a hint of a pot belly came out of one of the rooms. He wore no jacket, with the sleeves of his bright, white shirt rolled halfway up his light brown arms.

He stuck out his hand. Quinn spotted his Rolex. "You must be Mr. Parker. I'm Paul, Nick's business manager."

Quinn shook his hand. "Nick wanted me to drop somethin' off for him."

"Signed contracts," he said offhandedly, his thick mustache quivering as he spoke. "He's told me a lot about you. He said you're a gifted piano player. Ever play with a band before?"

"Naw. I mean, no." He shrugged. "Just for myself, mostly."

"Well, if you hang in there with Nick, a lot more than just yourself will be hearing your music. Nick has been responsible for launching quite a few careers. I always told him if he ever wanted to get out of playing there was definitely a spot for him as a talent scout." He chuckled. "If you have a few minutes, I'll show you around."

"Sounds good."

"We do a variety of things around here, Mr. Parker."

"Quinn."

"Quinn. We give music classes, seminars on the business of the music industry. A lot of the managers and accountants meet here to discuss their clients, knock out contract deals, make sure everything is on the up-and-up."

He showed him some classes that were in session, the music rooms and studios. If Quinn didn't know better he'd swear he'd just seen Nick Ashford and his wife, Valerie Simpson, walk across the corridor ahead of them.

"Was that—?"

"Yes, it was. They're here quite a bit. They do a lot of the lectures. Sometimes they even write their music here."

Returning to the reception area, he chuckled. "Well, that was the fifteen-cent tour."

"Thanks a lot."

"Maybe your picture will be up on these walls one day."

"Naw." He smiled.

He slapped him on the back. "Think positively. Anything can happen if you put your mind to it. Fifteen years ago, Nick never thought he'd be where he is today. He was just another street hood with no dreams of a future. Found an old saxophone in an alley one day," he said, shrugging, "and the rest is history."

"No sh—no doubt." Maybe there was a lot more to Nick than he thought. No wonder they connected.

Paul looked at him and grinned. *Nick Hunter all over again,* he thought. All he needed was some guidance and some polish, and if he was half as good as Nick claimed, he could have a real future ahead of him. He hoped seeing this side of things would give him some inspiration.

"Well, Quinn, it was a pleasure meeting you." He stuck out his hand. "Hope to see you again."

"Yeah. Thanks for the tour."

"Any time. Maybe you might want to think about taking one of the classes. Simone can give you a schedule, if you're interested."

Quinn nodded.

"Got to run. Good luck tomorrow night." He turned and

hurried down the hall, disappearing behind the same door he'd come out of earlier.

A bit overwhelmed, Quinn headed toward the elevator.

"Do you want a copy of the schedules?" Simone asked, holding up a thin pamphlet.

Quinn turned around and walked back toward her desk. "Thanks." He stuck the information in his back pocket.

Waiting for the elevator he stood behind two men. One looked vaguely familiar.

"That's Nick Hunter's band," one said, pointing to a picture Quinn had missed earlier.

Sure enough, there was Nick, decked out in black and white and surrounded by his band members.

"The man is awesome. I have to try to get my agent to get the two of us together, maybe cut an album," the second man said.

"With you on keyboards, Herbie, and Nick on sax, it would go platinum in no time."

Herbie? Hancock?

The ding of the elevator snapped him out of his daze. The doors opened and he stepped in. He turned and faced the front.

The trademark glasses were a dead giveaway.

Herbie smiled. "We're going up," he said.

Quinn nodded and pressed the button for the ground floor. *Yeah. Going up.*

For a few fantasy-filled moments, as he watched the little yellow light bounce from one number to the next, he saw himself again, his own gold and platinum albums hanging on the walls. The melodic voice of Sade wrapped around him.

"Anything is possible, Q, if you just put your mind to it," he could hear Lacy say, almost the exact words that Paul had uttered moments earlier.

"Yeah. You believed, Lacy. It got you a bullet," he whispered. He hung his head and the image vanished.

Stepping back out into the light of day, everything around him bursting with life, the possibilities seemed endless. He adjusted his shades, slid behind the wheel and pulled out.

Chapter 12

I Apologize

"I'll give Quinn a call and see if five is good," Maxine said into the phone to Sean Michaels, the attorney who would be working on the case.

Maxine hung up and beeped Quinn. Minutes later, her office phone rang.

"Maxine Sherman."

"You beep me, Max? It's Quinn."

"Hi, Q. Listen, I spoke with the attorney. He can meet with us today at five. I'm off at four-thirty. Can you pick me up at the bank?"

He paused and thought about his promise to Nikita, then said, "Yeah, I'll be there."

"See you then."

As fast as she hung up, the phone rang again.

"Maxine Sherman."

"Hi, Maxine. It's Dre."

Her stomach did a little dance. "Hi, Dre."

"Listen, about last night...ya know...I'm sorry."

"You don't have to apologize, Dre. Really."

"I was hoping we could pick up where we left off. I could come by for you after work—"

"Well, Dre, I wish I could, but I'm supposed to meet Quinn after work. We're—"

"No problem. Hey, tell him I said hello, and uh, I'll call you…maybe tomorrow."

"Dre, maybe we could still get together later. It shouldn't take too long."

"We'll see, okay? Listen, I gotta run."

Click.

"Damn." She slammed down the phone. There was no reason for him to get bent out of shape. She and Quinn were just friends. Just friends.

Quinn called Nikita's office. After three rings the answering machine came on. He started to leave a message, then changed his mind. He'd said four-thirty. He'd just shoot by her job a little early and let her know what was going down. They'd have to make it later.

He replaced his cell phone and headed home to change clothes.

Nikita rushed out of the boutique with two shopping bags. It was already after three. She had enough time to get back to the office and change before Quinn came to pick her up. She wanted tonight to be special, to make up for lost time. She wanted him to see what he'd been missing.

Pulling up to the last parking space on the block she hurried into the office building. She was surprised to see a folded piece of paper stuck in the doorframe. She pulled it out and dug in her bag for her keys, juggling the bags.

Kicking the door shut behind her, she dropped the bags by her desk and opened the note.

Can't make it at 4:30. Something came up. Meet me at my place at 7:00.

Q

"What!" She crumpled the piece of paper into a ball and threw it across the room. "Can't make it! What came up, Quinn? And what in the world makes you think I don't have anything else to do but wait on you for two and a half hours?"

She flopped down in her chair and kicked the bags away from her feet, spilling the contents on the floor. She looked at the aqua knit dress, new stockings, satin and lace Victoria's Secret underwear, and the 8 oz. Bottle of Oscar de LaRenta's Volupte.

She sat tapping her foot for a good five minutes. Fuming. Hadn't seen him in days. Calls finally, then puts her on hold until later.

The phone rang.

She snatched the receiver off the hook.

"Today's Woman." She knew she sounded like she hated her job, but she couldn't help it.

"Nikita? Is something wrong?"

"Oh, Ms. Ingram. Uh, no. I just…banged my knee against the desk."

"Do be careful. Are you all right?"

"Yes. I'm fine." She tapped her foot a bit faster.

"I just wanted you to know I won't be back in the office until Monday. And I also wanted to find out how the next issue was coming."

"I laid the last story out this afternoon. Just the entertainment section needs to be done, and it'll be ready for the printer."

"Have you found someone?"

"I have a good lead. I should know something by tomorrow night," she said, hoping that Nick would come through.

"Wonderful. Well, dear, you have a good weekend. And don't stay too late. I know how you can overwork sometimes. Get out and enjoy yourself."

"I will." She smiled, the tightness in her chest beginning to ease.

"See you first thing Monday."

"Bye, Ms. Ingram."

She pushed out a long breath. The heck with Quinn. She was going home, much as she didn't want to.

The phone rang again.

She rolled her eyes. *"Today's Woman."*

"Niki, sweetheart."

Her spirits sank even further. "Hi, Mom."

"I just wanted you to know that we've invited the Colemans over for dinner tonight. Grant is home on leave from the air force, and I thought it would be wonderful if the two of you saw each other before he left again, maybe make some plans to get together."

Grant. Would her misery today never end? She and Grant Coleman had a thing before he joined the air force. He'd wanted marriage. She'd wanted—what, she didn't know, but it wasn't marriage. Grant took it badly, hounding her for months. He called every day, until it got to the point where she didn't want to answer the phone. When he finally went off to the Philippines, the calls stopped. Then the letters started. She'd stayed in a state of guilt for nearly six months after their breakup, and her mother didn't miss an opportunity to tell her what a big mistake she'd made.

The letters finally stopped about a year ago. And she hadn't heard from or seen him since. Now he was home.

A part of her wanted to see him, see how he was. Then there was another part that was afraid it would lead to other things. Things she didn't want to indulge in—not now.

"I have plans tonight, Mom. I was going to stay in the city."

Cynthia frowned. "I thought Parris was on tour."

"She is. But I have a spare key to her apartment."

"Where's her husband?"

"He's here."

"And you're going to be staying in their apartment—alone—with her husband?"

"Yes."

Cynthia drew in a quick breath and expelled it in a rush of words. "That is entirely inappropriate, Nikita. I insist that you come to your own home. No decent young woman would spend the night alone with someone else's husband."

Her temples began to throb. "Who is it that you don't trust, Mother, me or Nick?" she snapped.

"Nikita!"

"I'll be fine. I'll see you tomorrow evening. Late. Give my apologies to the Colemans and say hello to Grant for me." She hung up before her mother could reply.

She squeezed her eyes shut and wished the pounding away.

"Looks like you'll get the booby prize after all, Quinn."

Snatching up her bags, she marched off to the bathroom, briefly wondering how Grant looked these days.

Maxine's long legs, encased in sheer black, paced the pebbly gray concrete in front of the First Trust Bank building. Harried workers walked around her and into her on their way to their end-of-the-day destinations.

Her lime green DKNY two-button suit hugged her curves like a long-lost friend. She peered over her shades to check out oncoming traffic.

No sign of Quinn.

The Tower clock showed 4:45.

Didn't men know that the longer they made you wait, the more time you had to think of the things they'd done that ticked you off?

She dug in her purse for a stick of gum. Since giving up smoking several months ago, she'd resorted to gum chewing and candy sucking. The last thing she needed was to gain weight by eating to replace the smoking urge, so now she just chewed every time she was edgy—on the verge of reaching for a cigarette. Like now. Her dental plan was in full force and a new set of teeth would suit her any day over the "Big C."

Traffic stopped for the red light, and a car horn started blowing, catching her attention. Quinn was in the center lane.

Maxine checked the flow and dashed around a tan Lexus and a steel blue Volvo to reach his car. He leaned over and opened her door.

She hopped in, flipping her gum to the street just before closing the door.

"Hey, Q." Damn he looked good. And why did he have to smell like that? All the time.

"Hey, yourself." He spun the wheel and made a quick left. "Lookin' all good in your suit."

Maxine tugged on her bottom lip with her teeth to keep from grinning like a fool. "Don't even try it, Q. You know you're late."

"No doubt. But we'll get there. Can't have a meetin' without us," he joked, fighting back the nervous beats that fluttered in his stomach. Talking about Lacy—it was going to be hard. Had been. The only conversation he'd had with anyone since her death had been with Max, and that ate at him like battery acid, leaving him more empty than before. He knew this was something that had to be done. Way down, he knew it. But dealing with it was another story.

"Where's this place?"

"Thirty-fifth and Madison." She settled back in her seat and snatched a look. She wasn't sure when he looked better—in his casual, too-clean-for-you clothes, or when he was slamming like he was now in his hunter-green baggy jacket, money-green T-shirt and wide-legged pants. His Hershey's chocolate skin was so smooth it looked good enough to lick, and his black locks glistened with health.

"Can I open a window?"

"Open the window?" He looked at her, his thick brows bunching up. "The air is on, girl. Want me to turn it up?"

"Yeah. Thanks." She dug in her bag for a stick of gum and proceeded to chew.

They rode in silence until he hit the FDR Drive. "So what's supposed to go down with this dude?" Quinn asked, his stomach getting tighter as they approached.

"They're gonna want all the info we have—ask questions—and take it from there." She turned to look.

His large hands gripped the wheel with such force that she could see the veins pulsing. The hard line of his jaw protruded, from the flexing of his teeth. Even behind his shades she noticed the tightly drawn impressions between his eyes.

"You cool, Q?"

"Yeah, yeah. Why?"

She shrugged. "I don't know. Tense vibes that you're giving off. That's all.

"It's all good, Max." He took a breath. There was no one he could talk to about how he felt about Lacy—losing Lacy—but Maxine. She'd understand. But it was still hard, and he couldn't stand for her to see him weak and breaking down. That wasn't his role. So he kept everything sealed up inside, but sometimes he just felt like he was gonna explode if the words, the hurt, the confusion and the rage didn't find a way to come out.

The sounds of Hot 97, pulsing through the radio, with DJ Wendy Williams's intermittent chatter, kept up the conversation that they couldn't hold.

Maxine finally broke the silence. "Q, you wanna talk for a minute before we go in? I mean, I know this isn't easy…for either of us."

He sat there for a few minutes, staring straight ahead, his hands in a death grip on the wheel. Slowly he let out a breath.

"Maybe some other time, Max." He turned glistening eyes in her direction. "Thanks."

She covered his hand with her own. "You know I'm always here for ya, Q."

"Yeah." He nodded and put the car in park. "Come on. Let's get this done."

The law offices of Michaels and Phillips, a husband-and-wife team, were by no means like those on *L.A. Law,* but they had class.

He looked around while the receptionist buzzed Sean Michaels. The beige leather furniture was cool—nothing he would put in his crib, but it served its purpose. Guess there was no point in getting nothing too top-of-the-line, with all kinds of people sitting on it all the time.

The steady flow of nervous energy propelled him back and forth across the beige carpeted floor.

Nice lights. He would have chosen track, but the recessed ones were cool, too.

On one wall were photographs of Johnnie Cochran and a smiling couple. On another was the same couple, looking as if they were talking with Al Sharpton.

He had turned to look at the plaques when a tall, well-built,

Armani-bedecked man just about Quinn's height stepped out into the reception area and greeted them.

Same dude as in the pictures. High-powered, connected, Quinn decided. Maybe he *could* make something happen. He'd have to see.

"Sorry to keep you two waiting. I'm Sean Michaels."

"Thanks for seeing us on such short notice," Maxine said. "Valerie recommended you highly." She shook his out-stretched hand.

Sean smiled. "I taught a litigation class last semester. She was one of my best students. I'm expecting great things from Val." He turned his attention to Quinn. "Mr. Parker." He extended his hand to Quinn, who seemed to take it reluctantly and merely nodded his head in response.

"Why don't we talk in my office?" He ushered them into his office and shut the door.

Sean asked all the basic questions about where they'd lived, for how long, names of friends. He told them about his legal background, that he'd started off in New York and then relocated to Atlanta, where he'd met his wife and business partner, Khendra.

As he talked he gauged Quinn's reaction: the subtle relaxing of his body and facial expression. He'd run into brothers like Quinn all his life. Men who'd come to experience violence and poverty and day-to-day survival as the norm. The mistrust, that belief that everyone was out for himself, the quick buck, the fast hustle, was part of their makeup. They believed that there was nothing but more of the same on the other side of the elusive rainbow. In Quinn Parker, Sean saw something of himself as he'd been, growing up on those very same streets, watching friends and family fall victim to drugs, violence and early death. Sean had found a way out, and so could Quinn. He needed Quinn to know that he understood.

"I know this will be hard, but I need to hear about Lacy." He looked at Quinn and then at Maxine. "As your sister, and as your friend."

Quinn had known this time was going to come. Thought he was ready. But the knot in his belly grew, taking up all the space, squeezing out the air in his chest. How could he tell this man, who had it all, what it was like to only have one thing, one person, in your life who mattered, who made you feel that *you* mattered, and have it taken away? How could he ever explain that she was the wind beneath *his* wings, the wind that kept him afloat, away from being completely consumed by the life he lived? There were no words.

So instead he listened to Maxine, and he ached. That twisting sensation got tighter, and he couldn't breathe. He kept seeing her face as she'd looked that night, laid out on that cold metal table, and he wanted to cry—again.

But he couldn't.

Wouldn't.

Quinn finally snapped, unable to stand listening to the recollections. "What's all that she was about got to do with what *you* got to do?"

Sean sat back a little, glad that he'd finally gotten Quinn to react. He folded his hands on the desktop. "I know this is hard. I can only imagine what it must be like for both of you. But I need to know as much about Lacy Parker as possible. When I present our case, I want it to be so powerful that a jury will have no recourse than to find in our favor."

Quinn swallowed. "Do you think we have a shot?"

"I don't take cases I can't win."

Quinn pressed his lips together, assessing the man in front of him. "Then you'd better check the rest." He told him of the word that had been circulating in the hood. How the cops were looking to pin it on somebody else, not the dudes they had locked up. But the real deal was that the cops were scurrying around trying to cover their own asses, because it was one of them that took out Lacy.

"That's right, Mr. Michaels," Maxine said. "That's the word on the street." She looked to Quinn and squeezed his hand, her reassuring smile loosening the knot.

Sean nodded. The ramifications were more complex than

he'd anticipated, and that pushed his buttons in all the right places. Since his own false arrest years earlier for the murder of his ex-wife, and vilification in the press, he'd been a staunch advocate for the rights of those wrongly accused, especially the families of victims. Though he didn't press a civil suit, the real perpetrators would never see the sun shining through their backyard windows again.

"Then we take them on," Sean said. "But I have to warn you, this could be a long, ugly fight. It could last for months, or years. I'm up for the challenge." His eyes zeroed in on Quinn. "Are you?"

Quinn took a breath, and for the first time since he'd sat down the shadow of a smile haloed his lips. He stuck out his hand, which Sean shook. "Yeah, I'm down."

Sean smiled, hoping to reach Quinn in that dark place that he stored his emotions. "It's gonna be all right, my brother. We're gonna do this together."

The knot in his stomach was still there, but it seemed to be loosening its grip.

"No doubt."

"He seems pretty cool," Maxine said as they drove back uptown.

"Yeah. Seems like he knows what he's rappin' about. I don't have no problems with him—so far. We'll just have to see if he's all about what he says."

"You want to grab something to eat?" Maxine asked as Quinn entered the FDR Drive.

His eyes jumped to the digital clock on the dash. Seven-thirty. "Damn."

"What?"

"I told Nikita I'd meet her at my crib at seven."

"Oh," bubbled out of her mouth. She adjusted her bag on her lap, then opened it and took out a piece of gum. "You can drop me off at the train station. I can find my way home—since you're in a hurry."

"You want me to dump you out at a train station in the middle of where—the FDR?" He gave her a what-is-on-your-mind look, shook his head and kept driving. "You trippin' again, Max. I'm takin' you home. End of story."

She blew out a breath through her nose, chewed a little harder, and fixed her gaze out of her window. *Damn.*

The twenty-minute ride seemed endless. She wanted to just smack some sense into him. Men! Were they born stupid, or was it an acquired thing from hanging around other stupid men—ya know, something they caught like a cold? What other explanation could there be?

She sighed silently. *Don't even stress yourself, girl. Whatever will be, just will. What's that sayin', the grass ain't greener?* she reminded herself.

Quinn cruised to a stop in front of Maxine's apartment building. He turned and caught her profile. Humph, Maxine was all that. Had it going on. *Wonder how she and her man are doing. Didn't look like her type.* In his mind, he shrugged. *Whatever.* "Here ya go, babe. Safe and sound."

She turned toward him.

Did she just roll her eyes? Must be imagining things.

"Thanks, Q." She opened her door.

"You still comin' tomorrow, right?"

"Sure."

"You bringin' that dude with you from the other night?"

"Yeah. Why?"

"Just askin'. No prob. Later."

"See ya. Tell, um, Nikita, I said hello."

"Yeah."

She got out and strutted, with purpose, to the building entrance. Quinn could hear the "Hey, beautiful's" and "Yo, baby's" even through the closed windows.

"Ya'll wish," he mumbled, and sped off.

Nikita checked her watch. Seven forty-five. Just how long did he expect her to wait? She was beginning to feel really silly. She shouldn't have come in the first place. Now he'd had her sitting in her car for forty-five minutes. She didn't want to go to Nick and Parris's apartment in Midtown, and she definitely didn't want to go home. Now she saw more than ever how much she needed her own place—and quick.

She absently twirled the lock of hair with the shell on the end around and around her finger. The disk playing Anita Baker's greatest hits came to an end. She leaned over and popped open the glove compartment and searched through her assortment of tapes. Finding an older Patti LaBelle, she slipped the tape into the slot. She rolled down her window and leaned back.

He had ten more minutes, then she was leaving. Going where, she wasn't sure. But suppose something had happened to him? How would she know?

She began to worry, getting more nervous by the minute.

Quinn turned the corner onto his block and spotted Nikita's Benz parked in front of his building. Mrs. Finch was in the front yard sweeping again. That woman did more sweeping, for an old lady. Guess it made her happy. He sure hoped she didn't have a list of errands for him to run.

He parked on the opposite side of the street, anticipation of seeing Nikita building like a campfire.

He glided out of his ride and started across the street. The faint strains of "You Are My Friend" drifted through the air and right to him, sucking the air from his lungs. He hadn't heard that song since Maxine sang it at Lacy's funeral.

That old, tight sensation got a grip on his stomach.

It's just a song, man. Get it together. But the memories were so stark, so very real.

He breathed deeply, placing one foot in front of the other until he was across the street.

Nikita saw him approach, walking that slow, easy stroll that made him look as if he were gliding on air. She felt her heart beat just a little faster, realizing at that moment how much she really wanted to see him.

Quinn approached her car and leaned on the hood, peering down.

"Waitin' long?"

"Yes. I was. I thought you said seven."

"Somethin' came up. I had some business to take care of."

Was that his explanation? She just looked at him.

He'd seen that "aren't you gonna tell me what it is?" look too many times. He wasn't biting today.

"You gettin' out, or what?"

She didn't answer. She turned off the music, raised the windows and grabbed her purse. She had a good mind to just drive off and leave him standing there, but there was something in his tone, his manner, his stance, that made her feel unsettled. Whatever had kept him away had chipped away at his cool exterior, leaving him exposed—as much as he tried to hide it. She couldn't begin to imagine what could have done that to a man like Quinn Parker. Maybe he would tell her if she were patient.

She opened the door and stepped out. He placed his hand at the small of her back, guiding her toward the house. Warmth flowed through her body as if she'd stepped into a warm house after a snowstorm.

Hmm, good.

"Hey, Mrs. Finch."

"Hello, Quinten."

Quinten. How many people got away with that, Nikita wondered.

He grinned like a little kid. "This is Nikita Harrell, Mrs. Finch."

Mrs. Finch leaned her broom against the steps and dusted her hands on her pink flower-print housecoat, which hung from her thin brown frame like a Superman cape.

"Nice to meet you. Fine young man, this one," she said, poking Quinn in the chest. "Just sleeps too late. Lets the day get away from him."

Nikita chuckled and looked at Quinn, who had visibly relaxed. The harsh lines that had tensed his eyes had smoothed. The smile was softer, real, and his body seemed to have unwound.

He leaned down and pecked Mrs. Finch on her smooth, baby-powder-scented cheek.

"I'll get to the backyard this weekend, I swear." He grinned, his eyes crinkling.

She swatted his arm. "Told you 'bout swearing," she scolded, peering up at him over the top of her Ben Franklin-style glasses. "Hardheaded, that's all," she said to Nikita, winking.

Quinn took Nikita's hand and chuckled. "Come on, Niki. See you tomorrow, Mrs. Finch."

Esther Finch watched the two young people trot up the stairs. "I have a roasted chicken in the oven…if you're…too busy to cook, and you get hungry."

Quinn turned at the top of the steps. "B-y-e, Mrs. Finch."

"Just a suggestion," she mumbled, retrieving her broom. She slowly looked left, then right, to see who was coming and going. She resumed her sweeping.

"She's a real character," Nikita said, chuckling, when Quinn had closed the door.

"She's all that. But she's cool. Keeps me hoppin'." He inserted the key into the lock of the apartment door, then stepped aside to let Nikita in. Fact was, Ms. Finch filled a small corner of the empty space. She treated him like the child he'd never had the chance to be, but still respected him as a man. He appreciated that—needed it.

Nikita walked in and immediately felt right at home. Everything was just as neat and orderly as on her previous visit, so she guessed it wasn't just a fluke.

"Didn't get to do any shoppin'. So we'll have to order somethin' if you're hungry, or we could go up on Sixth."

Nikita smiled. "Or, we could take Mrs. Finch up on her offer."

"Naw. Don't think so. Don't want to get her started. Then she'll be bringin' me dinner every night." He laughed. "Turn on some music. I'ma go up and change."

She nodded and went over to the stereo, picking up and putting down CD cases. She finally settled on Mary J. Blige's "What's the 411?" wanting to hear what all the hoopla was about over a girl whose reputation seemed to be built more on her attitude than her aptitude.

While she listened, not really getting it, she strolled over to the bookcase, looking over the wide range of selections. He had everything from mystery to poetry to contemporary fiction, as well as an array of nonfiction titles.

Had he actually read all of this? Then why did he talk as if he'd never seen a written word?

Her slender fingers grazed over the spines of the hardcover and softcover titles until she ran across a romance novel, which stopped her cold.

Romance? Now that was a twist. Must belong to one of the women he knew.

She picked the book up from the shelf and opened the front cover.

"To Lacy,
      May all of your dreams come true.

                              Gwynne Forster."

"Who's Lacy?" she mumbled.

Footsteps on the staircase snapped her out of wondering. Quickly, she returned the book to its space.

"Mary J., huh?" His eyebrows rose.

"Why not?"

"Hey, whatever."

He pushed open the sliding doors that separated the living room from the dining area and strolled into the kitchen. She followed him.

When he turned from checking out the fridge, Nikita was posed against the counter.

"Nice outfit," he said, popping the top of his beer, admiring how the clingy aqua knit hugged her every which way. He took a breath.

"Thanks." Her lowered lids shielded her eyes. She looked up and he was still staring at her. "So what did you do today?"

He looked away and took a swallow of his beer. "Hmm, this and that. What about you?"

"Why won't you tell me anything about yourself, Quinn? Why is your life such a big secret?" she added, tired of the cat-and-mouse game.

"My life ain't no secret. It just ain't that interestin'. At least, nothin' you'd be interested in."

"How do you know that if you don't tell me?"

"'Cause I know." He crossed the room, seeing the hurt seconds before she averted her gaze, the defiant crossing of her arms. He stepped up to her. Close.

She kept her eyes focused on the yellow-and-white tile floor. He tilted her chin upward with the tip of his forefinger.

"It's really not that interestin'," he said in a soft voice, hoping to ease the harshness of his last response.

"Maybe it is to me, Quinn," she said, matching his tone. "Ever think of that?"

"Why?"

"Because I want to know you—really know you. You're such an anomaly. You present yourself to the world as this…this rock-hard, can't-be-touched, too-cool thug. But anyone with one eye could see that there's so much more to you than the front you put on."

"Umph." He stuffed his hands into the pockets of his sweat-pants. "Maybe *this* is the front. Maybe what everyone sees *is* the real me. Has been for twenty-odd years. Think of that?"

"So which is it, Quinn, this or that? Tell me so I'll know who I'm dealing with."

"Strange as it seems, both. It's all me, Nikita. I choose how I wanna be, who with and when." He shrugged. "I just don't mix 'em together. Simple."

"Is it?"

"Yeah, it is."

She let out a breath, then looked him in the eye.

"Listen, I've been led around by the hand all of my life. Told what to think, what to believe, what to do. I want to move past that phase of my life. So I don't need to backtrack by dealing with yet another man who thinks that I'm some airheaded, fragile princess who doesn't have an original thought in her head. I know we're different. I think that's part of the attraction. But in so many ways we're the same. You're making changes in your life, major changes. I can see it, feel it. The resistance is still there, but change is coming. Just like it is for me. I don't know about you, but I don't want to do it by myself."

He looked at her for a long moment before speaking.

"You think you wanna make those changes with me?"

"Yes. I do. But only if you're willing."

His eyes roamed over her face, searching for any hint of a game being run. He'd never met a woman in his life—except Lacy—who didn't have some plan going on when they met a dude. But Nikita seemed different—for real. She actually seemed honest. And on the serious tip, he didn't think she had it in her to be otherwise.

He took his hand from his pocket, reached out and stroked her cheek. "We'll try it your way." The corner of his mouth turned upward. "Just be careful what you wish for."

Chapter 13

'Round Midnight

They'd had a light dinner at a little Chinese restaurant on Sixth Avenue. Then Quinn announced that he had to go uptown. This time, he broke all of his own rules. He took her with him.

Quinn turned onto St. Nicholas Avenue. "I gotta stop and pick up my man, T.C."

Nikita looked around at the towering tenements, the gutted and boarded buildings, and pockets of people who congregated on every available corner. Children, countless children, everywhere, racing up and down the garbage-strewn streets as if they were let loose in an amusement park. *Who did they all belong to? Where were their mothers, fathers?*

Quinn pulled to a stop in front of Shug's Fish Shack, where a line ran from the counter out into the street.

Was the fish free, or was it that good? she wondered.

The smell of fish grease, fried onion rings and something else she couldn't decipher seeped into the cool, filtered interior of the BMW.

"Be right back."

She wanted to scream: *Don't leave me here!*

Quinn eased out of the car and rounded the front. The alarm engaged with a soft beep in time with the door locks clicking into place. She suddenly had an eerie picture of a prisoner being led down a cell block with the clang of the metal door shutting behind him. A shudder skittered through her.

Nikita stole a glance at Quinn as he moved easily among the knots of boys-to-men, passing a word here, a high five there. Everyone knew him, and they went out of their way to catch his eye, gain his favor—a blessing, with a wave or a nod of acknowledgment from him—like the pope.

A tiny, electric shock of realization hit her. He knew all of these people.

This is where he grew up, lived and breathed, where he'd learned most of everything he knew, an earthy, street-savvy intelligence that he shed like snakeskin when he stepped across the threshold of his home.

Seeing him through new eyes made her wonder how, if ever, she could find a place in his life. Where did she fit? Here, or back in the Village?

A tingling sensation akin to fear floated around in her stomach. Yes, she was afraid. Afraid to get out of the car and walk through this neighborhood. Afraid of the men who stayed in a perpetual state of anger, rage and hopelessness. Afraid of the women in their body-hugging clothes, hip-grabbing skirts and five-pound-weight earrings, who cut her dirty looks as they strolled by the car, snickering as if they had a secret she'd never know.

She tried to appear cool, assuming the same stare-you-down look as the women who passed.

Her heart thudded.

Did that make her afraid of Quinn, too?

She jumped when the alarm popped again and the front and back doors opened and closed in unison.

"That's T.C.," Quinn said with a toss of his head to the back of the car. "This is Nikita. My lady," he added, his smile asking her if she had a problem with that. She returned it, her pulse fluttering. "So treat her nice and watch your mouth."

"Yeah, yeah. Hey, what's happenin', Nikita?"

She didn't know what to say, so she just said, "Hi."

Quinn turned his head toward her. "We got a few stops to make, then we'll head back. Cool?"

"Sure." She nodded. What other choice did she have? *Be careful what you wish for.*

He patted her clasped hands and pulled out.

Nikita sat alone in the car, the blunt beat of hip-hop her only company, while Quinn—with the long, rangy T.C. trailing behind him—went in and out of five "spots," doing who knows what. The duffle bags that they carried in always seemed much bulkier when they came out. Finally they made their last stop, but this time they came out empty-handed.

Where are we headed now? she wanted to ask, but didn't.

Before long, they were back where they'd started, in front of Shug's, and at one o'clock in the morning there was still a line. Made her want to try some—just to see.

"Hungry?" Quinn asked, as if reading her mind.

"Kind of." She smiled.

"Shug's has the best fried whiting in the city. You wanna check it out?"

"Sure."

"Cool."

"Later, Nikita," T.C. said from the back and hopped out.

"Later," she mumbled.

Quinn looked at her for a minute, then grinned. "Be right back."

She had to admit this fish was the best she'd ever tasted. Crispy, with just the right amount of batter, and seasoned to perfection.

"Good, huh?" Quinn grinned, his eyes crinkling at the corners, from across his dining room table.

Nikita raised her eyes and pulled her finger out of her mouth. She smiled sheepishly.

"How can you tell?"

"'Cause I can't figure what you wanted to suck on more, the fish or your fingers."

"Very funny." She wiped her hands and mouth on the little napkin that Shug's had provided.

"Here, let me get that for ya." Quinn reached across the table and took her hand. One by one he took each finger and dipped it in his mouth, flicking his tongue, momentarily, across the sensitive pads, his eyes glued to her face.

A pulse way down between her legs started to beat like those drums in the music she'd been listening to, the heat of it building, rising and spreading through her body. Her temples began to pound and she could have sworn she heard her own heartbeat above the sound of R. Kelly's "I Believe I Can Fly." A shudder rippled up her back, and she shivered.

His voice reached down and stroked that throb. "Cold?" He placed her hands between his.

All she could do was shake her head in denial.

"Hot?"

She swallowed.

"Let's see what we can do about that."

He came around the table and gently pulled her to her feet. He kissed her forehead, a kiss so featherlight that she wasn't sure it had happened.

Taking her hand, he led her upstairs.

He opened his bedroom door and she followed, her heart racing in first place, her thoughts a strong second.

How would it be? How would she be? Why was she here? Oh, God.

He opened the second door which led to the bathroom. He turned on the shower, while Nikita stood in the doorway, not sure what "wuzup."

The room filled with steam while Quinn removed fluffy oversize towels from the tall linen closet, which she hadn't noticed before.

He walked over to her, a gentle warning in his eyes. Slowly he leaned down until his lips touched, captured and explored hers.

Her arms had a will of their own as they glided up his back, her fingers threading through his hair.

Steam enveloped them. She felt the dampness suck her dress to her skin, dewdrops dotting her arms, her face.

Quinn's warm, wet hands moved down her sides, finding the bottom edge of her dress, easing it up and above her hips.

Nikita shivered in the heat, whispering a moan of pure pleasure to Quinn's ears.

He pulled her dress over her head to reveal the satin and lace.

Quinn's eyes roved over her petite body, marking his territory.

"You're beautiful, Nikita." He slipped one strap from her shoulder and then the other, then pushed her bra down, forcing her breasts to reach out to him, which he took—one by one—until Nikita began to whimper, her legs growing weak.

How or when she didn't know, but Quinn had removed his shirt, because she realized that she was feeling his bare chest against her.

"Come on," he urged. He took her hand and led her into the shower.

"But—"

"Just step in—just as you are."

She blinked away her confusion and stepped into the shower stall, where she watched Quinn remove his pants, leaving on his briefs, and join her, shutting the door behind him.

"We're gonna stay just like this, 'til we know it's right." His eyes glided over her face. "Awright?"

What else could she say? That she wanted to strip down right this second, wanted him to do to her what she'd been dreaming about, and the hell with waiting?

"All right," she whispered.

To her ultimate delight she'd never experienced a more erotic interlude. The fact that they still kept their underwear on, even as they touched, massaged and intimately explored each other's bodies, was more of a turn-on than being fully nude. It raised the whole experience to a level of anticipation that was indescribable.

They laughed, sighed, moaned and whispered until the water began to grow cool.

Quinn turned off the shower, stepped out and grabbed a towel, wrapping Nikita in the downy-soft cocoon. He followed suit.

Then, without a word of warning he picked her up, cradling her in his arms. She closed her eyes and snuggled closer, listening to the rapid beat of his heart.

He laid her down. She felt a cushiony quilt wrap around her. Her eyes fluttered open and rested on his face. And then it registered where she was.

Her eyes widened in surprise. This was the guest bedroom! Why—

"Get some rest," he whispered, leaning down for one last deep-down kiss. "See you in the mornin'." He turned and closed the door behind him.

She stared at the closed door. Stared at the ceiling. Her entire body was a mass of tightly strung nerves. She was on fire. Everything throbbed.

What had happened? She knew without question that he was just as aroused as she was. There was no debating that. Then why had he stopped?

She flipped onto her side and stared at the wall, questions but no answers tumbling through her head. Still, she found herself drifting to sleep. She unwrapped the towel and slipped out of her damp undies. At least she wouldn't have to worry about washing them out.

She slid down between the sheets, her nude, tingling body slowly beginning to calm. The heat, the hot water and the total body massage began to take their toll.

Quinn dimmed the lights next to his bed, then got in.

He could have had sex with Nikita. There was no question about that. It probably would have been great, too. Had it been anyone else that he'd been dealing with, he would have just taken what was offered and called it a day.

He didn't know what it was about Nikita. She was different— special—and he just wanted to make sure that he didn't make any mistakes with her. He wanted what they did in bed to really mean something. For once.

She wasn't like those other women. He knew her heart was going to be in it, and he had to be sure his was, too. Women he'd been with had only one thing in mind, having a good time and just "seein' what he was like." It wouldn't be that way with her. She'd want more. She already did. Could he handle it?

Sleep didn't come easily.

When Nikita opened her eyes again it was eight o'clock in the morning. She blinked and sat up, when reality struck.

The house was tomb quiet. Quinn was obviously still asleep.

She stretched. She couldn't remember the last time she'd slept so well. She actually felt invigorated.

She got up, wrapped herself in the discarded towel and tiptoed across the room to the bathroom, carrying her emergency toothbrush. Quietly she pressed her ear to Quinn's side of the door. Not a sound. She turned on the water in the sink.

Tiptoeing back to her room, she started to get dressed when she heard knocking on the bathroom door.

"All clear," she shouted, pulling her dress down over her head.

Quinn poked his head in. "Mornin'." His dimples winked at her.

"Hi."

"Sleep okay?"

"Fine, and you?"

"Coulda been better," he said, stepping fully into the room, beautiful and bare chested. "Maybe we can do somethin' about that at a later time."

She swallowed. "May-be."

"What time you gotta be to work?"

"Well, Ms. Ingram won't be back until Monday. So I need to open the office and get things going."

"Hmm." He took a breath and ran his fingers through his hair.

"You're up early. Have plans?" The last time she'd stayed over he'd slept right through her departure, and she hadn't had the heart to wake him.

"This and that." He grinned. "Found a note under my door from Ms. Finch. She wants me to take her everywhere but to heaven today." He chuckled. "Besides, I didn't want to miss seein' you before you left."

Heat infused her face. "Oh."

"You comin' tonight, right?"

"Of course. I can't wait. I know you're going to be fabulous."

"We'll see." He came closer. "You're stayin' with me tonight." It wasn't a question.

Her breathing picked up a notch when he ran his hand along the side of her face.

"In my room." His eyes bored into hers. "So bring some clothes and stuff. We'll make it a long weekend."

Leaning down, he brushed his mouth across her ear and along her jaw until he reached her mouth and clung there for the briefest moment.

"You better get rollin', or you're gonna bc late," he said, the depth of his voice reaching the center of her heat and stoking it.

"You're right." Even she heard the breathlessness of her voice. *This was going to be a heck of a long day.*

Chapter 14

And the Band Played On

After running Mrs. Finch all over town he finally made it to the club, and he was still early for rehearsal. *Maybe there was somethin' to this gettin' up early stuff.*

He'd already squared it with Remy about getting somebody to take over his run for the night. Personal business, he'd said. He trusted T.C., but he was still too young and too green to take on that responsibility by himself or even to play the lead, as much as T.C. had protested otherwise. Remy agreed with Quinn. End of story.

"Sounding real good, man," Nick said, patting Quinn on the back during the break.

They'd been rehearsing one of the compositions Nick had written for the band.

"It's a phat number, man. Easy to follow." Quinn stood and stretched, flexing the tight muscles in his back.

"You could probably put something together yourself," Nick hedged, watching for Quinn's reaction.

He shrugged. "Nothin' full scale."

"Maybe you might want to take one of those classes up at ASCAP. Teach you everything you need to know."

Quinn eyed him. "Yeah?"

"That's how I got it together. Like I told you, man, I was just like you. Had a natural ear. Now, man, they have computers to do all the work. You just lay down the sounds you want."

He tossed the idea around. Sounded interesting. Maybe it was something he could do. It's not as if he didn't have the time or the loot.

He stuck his hands in his pockets. "How long somethin' like that take to learn?"

"As short or as long as you want it. You work out a schedule that suits you and fits with what they have to offer."

Quinn slowly nodded his head, taking it in.

"I'll think about it."

"Good enough. Take your time. You don't want to jump into something before you're ready. If there's anything I can do, or any questions you have, just let me know." He turned back to the band. "Come on, fellas, one more run-through."

Quinn took his seat behind the piano.

School. Classes. Damn, he hadn't been inside a classroom in more than ten years. Study. How? But the idea of learning to write his own stuff… Maybe he really could.

He stole a glance at Nick, who was absorbed in blowing his sax notes.

Yeah. He could do it. Changes. They were coming. No doubt.

Maxine hung up the phone and jumped up from her seat. Cloud Nine was her next stop. Her small business loan had been approved. She was a sho nuff bizness woman! And there was no better time than right now to start celebrating, beginning with an early lunch. She picked up the phone and dialed Val's extension.

"Girl, I told you you were going to get that loan," Val enthused, taking a bite of her salad. "Now you don't even have to bother about getting hands-on training. Hire your own staff."

"Ain't that the truth! But you know what, Val, it's kind of scary. Ya know, being on my own."

"Listen, this is something you've been working toward for more than a year. You deserve this. Don't even stress yourself."

"Yeah, you're right. I'm ready."

"So what are you going to do first?"

"Start looking for a good computer system and set up shop at home, just like I'd planned, until I find a space I can afford. I've been lookin' but the rents are so high in the city. My plan is to set up my agency on the Internet. Everyone can book their travel arrangements right online, through me. When the business takes off, then I can quit this dump."

"It's going to take off, girl, you just wait and see." She sipped from her water glass. "Have you told Dre yet?"

"No. I wanted to surprise him. I'll tell him tonight at the club. Then we can really celebrate—later," she said with a lifting of her eyebrow.

"It's about time you finally checked that out," Val said.

"Who you tellin'? Been so long I may not know how to act."

"Oh, you'll know, my sister. Just like ridin'—a bike, that is. Once you learn it, you never forget it."

They gave high fives and bubbled with raucous laughter, drawing the attention of an elderly couple at the next table.

But as much as she enjoyed sharing her moment of triumph with Val, she wished she could run over to Harlem Hospital, grab Lacy from behind her desk and share her news. Knowing Lacy, she'd tell her how the Lord always makes a way, even for backsliders like her. She'd laugh and cry with her and tell her she needed to go to church on Sunday and give thanks, but seeing that she knew Max probably wouldn't make it, she'd say something on her behalf. Yeah, that was Lacy.

"Thinkin' about Lacy, huh?"

Maxine's gaze drifted back to look at Val. "Yeah." A soft smile touched her lips. "Wish she was here. Ya know. The three of us talked about this for forever. You wanted to be a lawyer, I wanted my own travel agency and Lacy wanted to get her R.N. license. We were there for each other."

"We're still there for each other. You think Lacy didn't have a hand in this, somehow? She's probably been up there twisting the arms of the saints and pleading your case." Val laughed softly, remembering.

Maxine laughed, wiping away the tears that had formed in her eyes. "And I'm not gonna disappoint her—or you, Val. I swear."

"We know. Or I just might have to sue your butt."

Dre was scanning the want ads. Had been for the past couple of weeks, with no luck. He'd sent his résumé to a number of security agencies and hadn't received one call.

He tossed the *Times* aside and took a sip of his lukewarm coffee. He didn't know how much longer he could keep up the front with Maxine. He dreaded "the look" that he knew he would get when he told her he was out of a job.

Maxine, his woman, was on her way up. The last thing she needed or wanted was a man that was two steps behind. All women were like that. His mother was like that. Walked out on his father like Rhett Butler did to Scarlet. Only his mother's line was, "I can do bad by myself." Took him and his brother and never went back.

A breath shuddered through him.

He had no intention of being another André Martin, Sr. He never wanted a woman to look at him the way his mother had looked at his father that last day.

But time was running out and his savings would only last so long. In the meantime, he had to try to hold his relationship with Maxine together, on top of everything else.

If he hadn't seen how she'd looked and acted around that Quinn dude—all soft and fluffy—he wouldn't be quite so edgy. Something about how they acted around each other just shook up his basic instincts. They were a little too damned close for his taste. And everybody knew men and women could never be "just friends." That lasted all about a New York minute.

"Damn."

He pushed away from his small, round kitchen table, the remnants of his coffee swishing and spilling onto the newspaper, leaving a big brown stain on the "Want Ads" page.

"Figures."

But at least he'd see her tonight, even though he wasn't all that happy about having to spend half of their time together listening to Quinn play piano. He shook his head as he used a napkin to blot up the coffee spill. Can't figure that one. Didn't seem like the type. Maybe he'd screw up, and Maxine would see that Quinn Parker put his pants on one leg at a time just like everybody else.

He had to have Max. That's all there was to it. He wasn't going to lose her, too. No matter what it took. All he needed was a plan.

"Are you planning on coming home tonight?" Cynthia asked, stepping into Nikita's bedroom without knocking.

Nikita turned from rifling through her closet to look at her mother. "I doubt it."

Cynthia pursed her lips. "Will you be staying with Nick again?" Her tone was clear.

Nikita inhaled. Tonight was not the night to get into a sparring match with her mother, but it looked like it was unavoidable.

"Is that what you think? Is that what you think of *me*—so very little—that I would sleep with my best friend's husband?"

"What else can I think?" She thrust her chin forward, her eyebrows arching.

Suddenly Nikita felt like a thoroughly shaken can of Pepsi whose top had just been popped. Words spewed in every direction, landing wherever. She just didn't care.

"How about something simple like, I wouldn't do something like that." She laughed softly, sadly. "But since you really want to know, I won't be staying with Nick. I'll be staying with someone else. His name is Quinn Parker. He's a musician. He has dreadlocks down to his shoulders. He drives a black BMW with tinted windows, and I don't know what he does for a living besides play the piano occasionally. He grew up in Harlem. Yes, Mother, Harlem—that place *you* only hear about on the news. And he took me there. And I liked it."

She felt the blood pushing against her temples, and her chest heaved as she drew in air. She just wanted to scream, realizing that she was actually enjoying the stricken look on her mother's face.

"I've only known him for about two months, and I've never felt more alive in my life. Now, is that what you wanted to know?"

"It was only a matter of time," Cynthia said, visibly trembling with fear or outrage, Nikita couldn't tell. "You're set on ruining your life and everything we've planned for you. Now you've taken up with some hoodlum from the ghetto and you seem thrilled. What next? You've had every opportunity in the world placed in your lap. You could have any one of countless eligible men who could offer you something."

"Offer me something. Something like what? More of a half life, like the one I've been living?"

"You deserve more than what some street musician can offer you, Nikita."

"Do you really think so, Mother? Isn't this where you really always wanted to see me—what you think I really deserve, so that you can somehow feel vindicated for disliking me so?"

She turned away to hide the tears that scorched her eyes. Her fingers trembled as they pulled clothes out of the closet. She heard her mother's muffled footsteps as she hurried down the hall, and the tears spilled down her cheeks.

And I could keep slipping between the sheets with white guys—or brothers with their noses so far up in the air they couldn't smell their own stink—just to satisfy you, just to prove to myself that I was worthy. Wasn't that what you wanted, Mother?

Nikita thought these thoughts, felt them deep within her. But she could never speak the words out loud. To do that would be to admit how truly shallow and meaningless her life had been. Until now.

Chapter 15

High Notes

The notes were running around in his head faster than Michael Johnson on the Olympic track. He needed to rein them in so he could think. What he really wanted was a drink, but he was afraid it might mess with his playing.

Quinn pushed away the glass of Pepsi and got up from the bar, wondering how Nikita could drink that stuff. Maybe that's why she always added lemon.

He'd already walked through the club twice. No sign of Nikita or Maxine. The table he'd reserved for them was still empty.

The knot in his stomach tightened. Suppose he screwed up. Suppose he just folded in front of the whole crowd. Suppose…

"Hey, man." Nick clapped him on the shoulder. "Loose?"

"Yeah. Yeah. No doubt."

"Good. I know everyone usually gets first-night jitters." He chuckled. "Hell, I remember my first time on a real stage was in some dive in North Carolina. Humph. Scared witless. Saw all those people out there just staring at me and I froze. But when that spotlight came on and I hit my first note, m-a-n, that fear was gone. It was all about me and doing my thing. I couldn't see the audience anymore. It was like I was alone in my room, playing for nobody but me."

Nick's eyes drifted to the present and rested on Quinn's face. "Understand what I'm saying?"

"Yeah." Quinn looked at Nick and slowly nodded. "Yeah."

Maxine untied the scarf that held down her hair, added a dab of gel and gave her hair a quick brushing until it shone.

Peering closer in the bathroom mirror, she stroked her lashes with waterproof mascara, just in case she started bawling when she saw Q onstage.

Damn, she just couldn't believe it. Lacy would be so proud. She pressed her lips together, added a hint more plum lipstick and dusted her nose with translucent powder. Returning her makeup to a small pastel pouch, she took it and rushed off to her bedroom to finish getting dressed.

Dre would be there any minute, and she hated to keep people waiting. Especially tonight.

She held up the black slip dress she'd just bought and wondered if Q...Dre would like it. She knew *she* did. It showed off just the right amount of "somethin' somethin'" without giving it all away.

Just as she stepped into her shoes, the doorbell rang. Nine. Right on time. She liked that.

When she opened the door and saw Dre standing there looking all handsome she just kissed him—one of those get-up-closer, wrap-your-arms-around, go-down-for-the-count kind of kisses.

"Whoa, what's gotten into you, baby?" Dre asked, grinning, and trying to be cool, but wanting more.

"Nothin'," she teased. "That's probably the problem." She gave him a wicked look.

"We can fix that right now." He stepped in.

"We can fix it," she said, pressing a finger to her lips, then to his. "But not now. Later."

He held her hand to his mouth. "I'm gonna hold you to that." He kissed her palm.

Maxine spun away and strutted down the hall, giving Dre a Kodak moment.

"Lookin' real good, girl. That dress is just where it's supposed to be. On you."

Maxine smiled, glad that he was pleased. She was feeling good and she wanted him to be feeling good, too, when she shared her news about the loan. There were plenty of reasons to celebrate, and that's just what she was going to do.

"I'm ready," she announced, picking up her small black sequined purse and the waist-length jacket that matched her dress—just in case she got chilly in the club. Worst thing in the world was to be sitting around thinkin' you looked cute with chill bumps running up and down your arms.

Leaving the apartment, she locked all three locks and they were on their way.

She hoped Q remembered to reserve a table. She still hadn't figured out how she was going to handle sitting with "his lady" all night.

She sighed as Dre sped down Seventh Avenue. Nikita did seem nice. And Quinn seemed to like her. There wasn't anything she could do about it, anyway. Besides, she had her own man. She moved a little closer to Dre and put her hand on his thigh. Dre had his act together, was a decent brother, treated her good, and she dug him—a lot. That's what counted.

Her father hadn't gotten home by the time she was ready to leave, and it was just as well. She'd had about enough parental supervision for one night.

She was still shaken from the confrontation with her mother, but determined to put it behind her, at least temporarily. Tonight was her and Quinn's night, and she wasn't going to let anything spoil it. She just wished she had someone to sit with while Quinn was playing. He'd told her he'd reserved a table for her. All she had to do was tell the hostess at the door.

During the hour-and-a-half drive back to the city, listening to CD 101.9 helped to get her back in balance. By the time she arrived at the club and found a parking space, she felt like her old self.

She should have told Jewel to come. At least she would've had some company.

She reached the glass door and pulled it open, a blast of cold air slapping her right across the face.

It was a good thing she'd decided to bring the jacket to the dress. She slipped it over her bare arms and stepped into the semi-darkened nightclub.

It was barely nine-thirty, and the club was already crowded—she observed—her eyes adjusting to the dim lights.

Everyone was dressed to impress tonight. There wasn't a sign of a T-shirt or a pair of jeans in the house. Jewelry, real and fake, twinkled around necks, wrists and on fingers. The mélange of perfumes, colognes and oils blended together into one unique, expensive assault on the senses. It was definitely Friday night in New York.

"Hello. I'm your hostess, Michelle. May I help you?"

Nikita blinked, realizing she hadn't moved since she crossed the threshold. "Oh, yes. I'm sorry," she apologized to the woman, who was at least a good head taller than her and model-thin. "There should be a table reserved for me."

The striking woman, who was a dead ringer for Tyra Banks, picked up her clipboard. "Name?"

"Nikita Harrell."

She scanned the list, then looked up with a toothpaste-commercial smile. "Right this way."

Nikita followed her pencil-thin form across the room to a table directly in front of the stage—already occupied.

Maxine and Dre looked up at the same time. All three pairs of eyes bounced from one face to the next.

"Here's your seat, Ms. Harrell. A waitress will be around to take your order."

"Thank you." She turned to the occupants at the table, addressing Maxine. "Hi. I'm Nikita. We met—before."

"How are you? This is André Martin. Dre, Nikita, Q's friend."

"Pleased to meet you," he said, standing and helping her into her seat.

When Nikita moved directly into the light, Maxine nearly

choked on her Kahlúa and milk. They had on the same damned dress! Nikita's was more filled out up top, where hers was making its statement around her hips.

Lord help us if she takes off that jacket.

"Have you two been here long?" Nikita asked, ignoring their similar attire with practiced diplomacy.

"Maybe about twenty minutes," Dre said, happier than a kid with ice cream that Quinn had someone to keep him occupied tonight. He assumed that's what Maxine meant by "friend." "So how do you know Quinn?"

Maxine cringed inside and took a swallow of her drink. She really didn't want to hear "the story" again.

Nikita smiled and Maxine noticed the tiny dimple that twinkled beneath her right eye.

"We met a couple of months ago when he was moving into his apartment. Then we ran into each other again here at the club. After that…" She lifted her shoulder and smiled.

After what? Maxine wanted to know. No, she really didn't need to go there.

Nikita turned her cover-model looks on Maxine. "How's everything going with finding something part-time with a travel agency?"

Was she going to ruin her *entire* night? She hadn't told Dre about the loan, and this certainly wasn't the time. "Slow but steady. How about you? What's happenin' at the magazine…um, what's the name again?"

"Today's Woman."

"Yeah. Right. How are things?"

"Hectic. But challenging. I'm still learning a lot."

The waitress approached the table and asked for Nikita's order. "Are you both having dinner?"

"We ordered already," Maxine said.

Nikita scanned the menu. "Shrimp in a basket, fries and a Pepsi with lemon." She handed back the menu.

"I can't wait to hear Quinn play," Nikita said, her dimple winking at Maxine. "It's so exciting."

"This is definitely his night to shine. Been a long time comin'." She sipped her drink.

Nikita pulled her chair closer, placed her arms on the table and leaned forward. "How long has he been playing? I know he hasn't done anything professionally, but how did he get started?"

Maxine took a breath, then a sip. "Q's been playin' piano since grade school. Used to sneak into the music room when all the kids were gone and fool around on the piano. The music teacher, Mr. Howard, walked in on him one day and heard him playin', tried to convince him to take music classes. Q told him just where to go." She laughed at the memory. "Said it would ruin his rep. So Mr. Howard said he'd give him private lessons twice a week after school. Q agreed as long as Mr. Howard kept it secret."

She shook her head. "But like with everything else, somebody found out and told the principal, nearly got Mr. Howard fired. So he had to stop the lessons. Q never set foot in that class again, but he still liked to play. His sister bought him a secondhand piano for his twenty-first birthday."

"Sister? I didn't know Quinn had a sister."

Maxine stared at her for a moment, wondering what Quinn *did* tell her—about anything. "He *had* a sister. Lacy. Let's just leave it at that. It's not something he, or I, like to really talk about."

Nikita blinked back her surprise, her mind full of questions which apparently were not going to get answered. So *that* was *Lacy*. The name in the book.

Dre sipped his rum and coke. Now maybe they'd talk about something else. He had Quinn's name coming out of his ears.

The waitress brought Nikita's drink and Maxine's and Dre's food. "Yours is coming right up," she said to Nikita.

Nikita looked around, hoping to catch a glimpse of Quinn, but he was nowhere to be seen. She knew if she went in search of Nick, he'd tell her where Quinn was. But she didn't want it to seem as though she was hunting him down.

She turned her attention back to her tablemates, realizing that she'd hardly said a word to Maxine's friend, which was terribly rude of her. Quinn seemed to have dominated the conversation and he wasn't even there.

"What do you do, Dre?" she asked, noticing that the question seemed to cause his fork to stop midway between his mouth and his plate.

He bit off a piece of chicken finger, then took a swallow of his drink. He turned his head in her direction for a brief moment. "I, uh, work security, for the, uh, the World Trade Center."

Maxine cut a look at him. Why was he acting like that?

"Really? Were you there during the bombing?"

"Naw. Before my time."

He halfway smiled, and she noticed the slightly chipped front tooth.

"Lucky you. That was awful."

"Yeah. It was."

Her gaze included them both. "So, how did you two meet?"

Before either had a chance to respond, Nikita's food arrived and the house lights lowered, moments before the band assembled on the small center stage area.

Nikita forced herself not to jump up out of her chair when she saw Quinn take his seat behind the piano. *Gosh, he looks good.* The stark white collarless shirt stood out against his dark brown skin. He'd kept his locks in place with a black band, tied at the nape of his neck.

Nick stepped into the spotlight and welcomed the crowd. Told them to sit back and enjoy, and let them do their thing.

The band ran through a montage of jazz and R&B classics, as well as two of Nick's original compositions, for more than an hour.

Quinn's fingers floated across the black and whites, zeroing in on every note with precision.

Nick was right. All that nervous energy was gone. All he could feel was the rhythm of the music. The spotlight blinded him to the audience. All he could see was what was in front of him and hear the sounds of clapping and shouts for more every time a number ended. And he wanted to play more. He wanted this feeling, this sense of power, to go on forever.

But the biggest blast came when Nick introduced the band, and him as the newest member of the Nick Hunter family. The crowd roared their approval.

"We're outta here," Nick announced. "So eat up and be merry."

The band filed off stage to another round of applause.

Quinn hopped down and walked over to the table. Both Nikita and Maxine stood up as he approached.

Maxine took his hand and reached up to kiss his cheek. "You did it, Q. I knew you could," she whispered.

"Thanks, Max."

"Hey, man, good to see you," he said to Dre, shaking his hand.

"Congratulations. Sounded real good."

Quinn focused all of his attention on Nikita and felt his insides shift when he saw the soft smile and sparkle in her eyes, remembering last night and envisioning later.

"Hey, baby." He moved closer to her, shutting out everything and everyone.

"Hey, yourself," she whispered. "You were fantastic, Quinn."

"Just doin' my thing." He grinned. "I'm finished for the night. You wanna hang out here for a while, or you ready to cut out?"

She felt the heat rush through her body, anticipating the rest of their night together.

"I'm ready when you are. I just need to see Nick for a minute."

"You do that and I'll meet you back here. I think he's in his office."

He watched her until she was swallowed up in the crowded dimness, then turned back to Maxine and Dre.

"Ya'll gonna hang for a while?"

"Naw," Dre said, giving Maxine a long, slow look. "We're gonna head in." He took her hand.

Quinn glanced from one to the other, pushing down a twinge of unease.

"Cool." He shoved his hands in his pockets. "Thanks for comin' down, ya know."

"No problem," Maxine said, suddenly wanting to get away before Nikita returned. "Come on, Dre, let's get going."

"Right with you, baby. Take it easy, Quinn."

"Yeah. Talk to ya, Max."

She just sort of smiled.

Quinn pulled up an empty chair at the table and straddled it.

He wanted to leave, too, and wished that whatever Nikita had to take care of would be quick. A waitress passed and he flagged her down, ordering a shot of Jack on the rocks. He had finished his drink by the time she returned.

Her face was beaming. "Guess what?"

"Clueless."

"Nick got me a phone interview with Anita! Can you believe it? I have to call her on Wednesday." She clutched the piece of paper to her chest.

"That's awright." His dimples flashed. "Nick really has some pull, huh?"

"Definitely. And he acts like it's no big deal."

"Humph. I know." Just thinking about his trip to ASCAP had him knowing Nick was all that.

"You ready?"

"I sure am." She looked up into his eyes. "Have been for a while."

Her words raced through him like a forest fire and he felt that old, low-down throb begin to pulse.

Chapter 16

About Last Night

Quinn turned on the stereo and adjusted the dial to the jazz station. She'd like that. He kind of liked it, too, from time to time.

He turned and she was sitting on the couch, looking all small and fragile. He wanted to take her right then and there, but he wanted everything to be right.

"You want anything?" He crossed the room and sat beside her, draping his arm across her shoulders. His fingers played in her hair.

"Yes. I do."

She could feel the little pulse beating in her throat. "You, Quinn. The you that you want to be with me."

He smiled that soft, little-boy smile, and her insides did a dance. His dimples hollowed his cheeks.

"All that, huh?"

"Yes. All that."

He looked at her for a moment and knew that he was going to lose himself to this woman. He'd never done that before, hadn't wanted to. Maybe still didn't. But just maybe...

He lowered his head until his mouth touched hers. And he

kissed her, gently at first until he felt her soften and yield to him, then with more pressure, his tongue deftly exploring her mouth.

He pulled her closer, needing her closer, wanting her to ease the weightless sensation that was spinning through him.

Nikita's sigh filled him like needed oxygen, and when she eased away he suddenly felt adrift.

Her fingers trailed across his face, savoring the *before* moments. Knowing that from this time forward, there was no turning back.

"Will you take me upstairs…to your room?"

The question was so simple, so direct, but he knew it meant much more.

Quinn closed the door behind them and crossed the room, where Nikita met him halfway. Her eyes lowered as her trembling fingers began to undo the buttons of his shirt.

One by one.

He threaded his fingers through her hair, looking down at her lowered head as she unfastened his belt and slid down the zipper of his pants.

Quinn's hands clasped hers, holding them in place. He tilted her head up so that he could see her eyes, maybe into her heart. What he saw was a genuine giving, an openness, a willingness to share a precious part of herself with him.

A warm surge of protectiveness, a need to make her happy, whatever it took, flowed through him.

He reached around and unzipped her dress, easing the smooth black fabric from her body. Taking her hand, he walked her to his bed, opened the nightstand and took out a condom.

"Let me." Her soft, slender fingers caressed and teased, feeling the strength of his sex pulse against her fingertips.

He sucked in air through his teeth as she slid the condom along his length, and she felt him tremble, and her own fluids released.

"Touch me. Everywhere, Quinn. I want you to know me."

And he did.

His touch felt like fire, searing her skin, and still she trembled, needing to be wrapped in the heat of his embrace. Wanting more. Wanting to be absolved of the constraints that her life had been. This loving was going to change her. She knew it. Her beliefs, her vision of herself. Within Quinn rested the soul secrets that she'd always desired to know, that had been denied to her.

No more.

She opened herself to him, letting him take all that she had to give, discovering a wantonness about herself that she hadn't known existed.

Enveloped in her heat, it didn't matter to him about the afterward. This was their moment, never to be duplicated, only to get better. It was a moment that he'd waited until now to know.

They were everywhere together, uncovering the mysteries of their union, whispered words, soul-deep sighs, body to body, wet and wild.

He felt the steady building rise, the tightening of her body as it began to drain him. She arched her hips as the intensity of her climax gripped her, tore through her, and set his off.

For those sacred, fleeting seconds, the two worlds from which they'd come united.

Quinn spooned Nikita against his body. "You okay?"

"Mmm. I'm fine." She turned over to face him. Her finger wiped away a trail of perspiration from his brow. "What about you, Quinten Parker—are you okay?"

He grinned and his eyes crinkled. "Yeah. No doubt. You could spoil a man, ya know. For a way uptown girl, you got a lot with you," he teased.

She raised up on her elbow.

He could swear her eyes were twinkling, like in that romance book he'd read.

"Is that right?"

He kissed her swollen lips. "Yeah, that's right, Little Bit. You intendin' to spoil me, or what?"

"That's the plan." She grinned.

"I think we should work on it a little more. What do you think?"

She pressed her body closer, feeling his rise. "The plan has to start somewhere," she whispered.

* * *

The sun was high in the sky, beaming in through the partially opened blinds.

Nikita let out a little moan, her body slightly aching and gloriously sore. She grinned and snuggled closer to the warm, hard body beside her, feeling the stickiness between her thighs.

She felt like an entirely different person, or at least a revamped version of herself. Something magical happened between them last night. She knew he felt it, too, by the searching look in his eyes, the way his voice shook when he'd whispered her name. The way he gave himself to her. There was no way that she'd ever believe he could be that way with anyone else. He'd made love with her— they didn't just have sex. She'd had that, and knew the difference.

She listened to his even breathing and knew that this was only the first of many morning-afters.

Quinn felt her move against him. She was probably awake, maybe wanted to talk. Yeah, it felt good waking up knowing that Nikita was there beside him. It was like getting the Oscar after a great performance. Could it be every day? Did he really want every day? Or even sometimes?

Part of him did. That part that needed to be really cared about—looked after. But there was that other part of him, the streetwise, wary part of him that stood on the outside and peeped into his life. That part of him that was too damaged from the past and his life to risk anymore.

Nikita's question about "who he really was" haunted him now. He'd tossed it off at the time, saying he was both whenever the mood hit him, and he just never mixed the two. If he let Nikita fully into his life, his two worlds would mix, become blurred, and maybe he'd have to make some sort of choice about who he really was—who he really wanted to be. Every instinct told him that at some point Nikita would demand a reckoning, a total accounting. She wouldn't take halfway for an answer.

She moved against him again, running her baby-soft fingers along his spine, and he felt his nature start to rise. He turned over, settling himself atop her, pinning her down with his weight, and gave her what she wanted, realizing in that instant that he always would.

Maxine moved around the kitchen putting together a quick breakfast of scrambled eggs with cheese, grits, pancakes and Canadian bacon.

She opened one of the overhead cabinets hoping to find some coffee, even though she knew she hadn't bought any.

The bacon sizzled in the pan.

Her eyes were bleary and her body could sure use a few more hours sleep. She and Dre had finally finished celebrating at about 5:00 a.m. He definitely had stamina. She had no complaints in that department. And although she was thoroughly satisfied, physically, there was still this empty feeling that she couldn't quite shake which had propelled her out of bed at the unholy hour of nine when she really wanted to sleep.

She should be dancing around her kitchen. She had been to sexual heaven and back more times than she could count, last night and into the morning. But she couldn't. Actually, she didn't want to.

"Hey, baby." Dre eased up behind her, wrapping his arms around her waist. He kissed the back of her neck.

"You're gonna make me mess up what I'm doing." She wiggled away, out of reach, and continued beating the eggs in a blue-and-white bowl with a little chip along the rim.

She needed some space.

"Couldn't nothing mess up what you do, baby."

"There's some clean towels and stuff in the hall closet by the bathroom, if you wanna take a shower before breakfast," she said, steering clear of his comment.

"Something wrong, Maxine? You're actin' real strange." He moved closer, cupped her chin and turned her to face him. "Especially after last night. What gives?"

She gave him a "say cheese" smile, with no teeth. "Just tired, I guess. I'm really not a morning person."

"You're sure?"

"Positive."

She pecked him on the lips and returned her attention to beating those eggs. "Go on and take your shower. Everything will be ready in about ten minutes."

Dre looked at her for a moment, not sure what to make of the vibes he was getting. "You still want me to take you computer shopping today?"

"Yeah. I figured we could be on our way around one."

He nodded, took a breath and walked out of the kitchen.

Maxine exhaled a shaky breath and sniffed back the tears that were burning her eyes.

By the time Sunday afternoon rolled around, Quinn and Nikita had moved into an easy routine. If he cooked, she cleaned up. When he showered, she promised not to use the dishwasher.

They'd gone food shopping, stocking his cabinets and refrigerator with every kind of everything. Nikita insisted on splitting the bill, even though Quinn had a problem with that.

They took turns listening to their favorite music, and Nikita silently admitted that there was a little somethin' somethin' to rap and the countless "urban contemporary" singers that Quinn had her listen to, even though her "thing" was jazz.

She didn't even flinch when his phone rang and he lowered his voice to a throb or took the call in another room. Whoever was on the other end was out there. She was here.

She'd sat on the stoop with Mrs. Finch while Quinn made a "quick run uptown," and was educated on the history of the block, the gentrification of the neighborhood and all the juicy gossip about the neighbors.

By the time Sunday evening came around and she began making preparations to leave, she realized just how much she didn't want to go. She never wanted to go back home, not just to her parents' home, but back to the way her life had been.

Quinn stood in the doorway of his bedroom watching Nikita pack away her clothes and suddenly felt that emptiness returning, like a hole had opened up inside of him. The light that had been there since her arrival seemed to dim.

It felt good having her there, to laugh with him, talk with him, just be with him. He'd never let a woman spend the weekend before. It had always been the other way around. But it felt good, too damned good, knowing that when he went out she would be there when he got back. He was scared of losing the feeling, and just as afraid to hold on to it.

"When am I gonna see you again?"

Nikita turned, startled. When she looked at him, her heart beat a little faster and she felt the flutter in her stomach. "When do you want to?"

He stepped into the room, pushing his hands into the slit pockets of his favorite gray sweatpants. Thoughts tumbled through his head. His feelings pushed them aside.

"Later tonight. Tomorrow mornin' when I get up. When I get in off the street at night." He looked down at the floor, then across at her. "Can you handle that?"

Nikita put down the blouse she was folding.

"What are you asking me, Quinn?"

He hesitated. "I ain't sure, Niki. I just know that I want to see you, ya know, be with you."

"It's up to you, Quinn. I want to be with you, too."

He nodded and pursed his lips. "Why don't you leave those things here?" The corner of his mouth inched up. "Since you're gonna be spendin' time."

"Are you sure?"

He wasn't too sure how things would be with her in his life, but he knew how things would be without her.

"Yeah, I'm sure." *Changes. Yeah, they were happenin'.*

Chapter 17

Makin' Moves

Nikita and Parris, worn out from hours of window and real shopping, walked down Fifth Avenue, sidestepping the steady flow of human traffic on the famous New York avenue, juggling their packages and keeping their balance.

They bypassed St. Patrick's Cathedral and headed for Rockefeller Center to the outdoor café, catching the last vestiges of the warm fall afternoon.

"You haven't said a word about your mother or your father," Nikita said, shifting her packages. "How are they?"

Parris adjusted her brown Italian-leather duffel bag on her left shoulder. "They're both fine." Parris exhaled. "I think Emma is happy. Michael has finally forgiven her for lying to him for twenty-odd years. I think they've made peace with each other."

"What about you, Parris? Have you made peace with them?"

"As much as I can, I suppose."

The waitress showed them to a table. They settled themselves in their seats.

"It takes a lot of getting over to discover that your near-white mother told your Italian father that you'd died at birth, because you couldn't pass for a white baby."

"Your mother was young and made some wrong choices, Parris. But she paid for those choices—dearly—and you know that."

"I know," she said. "And I know that sometimes circumstances force people into making decisions that they regret. And what about you? Have you made a decision that you'll regret?"

"What, by moving in with Quinn?"

"Yes." She looked at her hard. Nikita was the first to look away.

Nikita took a long breath, played with her water glass, then took a sip. She looked across at Parris's patient stare.

"I've thought about it. Long and hard. The more I'm with him, the more I want to be with him. He gives me something I need, and I think I do the same for him. I spend all of my time over there, anyway."

"That's not a reason to move in with him, Nikita. You've only known each other for a few months."

"I know that. It's just that… I've never felt like this before… about anyone."

Parris smiled. "And who knows that better than me? I've seen you run circles around men. And the only one who ever came close to locking you down was Grant. And we see now what happened to that relationship. It's just that I want you to be sure. Quinn is handsome, charming, talented, and has a quiet danger about him that's irresistible. Just be with him for the right reasons, Nik. Not because you think you can reform him."

"You of all people should know how I feel, Parris. Nick wasn't much different from Quinn, not that many years ago."

"Exactly. But I also went into my relationship with Nick knowing who he was, what he was about. I had no delusions about steering him onto any course but the one he'd chosen before we met. Nik, when two people change to please the other, no one winds up happy. I just want you to be happy."

"I am happy, Parris. Happier than I've ever been." How could she tell her that she felt this was the only way to keep Quinn? That she felt threatened by his other life, which he wouldn't talk with her about? That she felt she could never compete with the mystique of the street that was more potent than the scent of any woman? That if she was there, with him every day, she could find a way to help him see that there was so much more out there that he could be a part of? All Quinn needed was someone in his corner. That wasn't reform. That was love.

"Then I'm with you one hundred percent. When's the big move, and what do Mom and Pop Harrell have to say?"

"She's moving in?" Maxine chewed her gum a little faster. "You're kiddin', right?" Any minute he was gonna tell her he was joking. If they hadn't been sitting in Sean Michaels's waiting room, she would have simply screamed.

"Naw. This weekend."

She felt her stomach dip and rise like a ride on a roller coaster. "It's like that, huh? 'Bout time somebody locked you down." She forced herself to smile. She chewed a little faster.

Quinn chuckled. "Never thought it'd be me."

"Yeah. Who you tellin'?" She swallowed, but her throat was so dry she almost choked. How in the hell did that happen? Quinn Parker had never been with one woman more than a few weeks at a stretch. Never had the time or the inclination, he'd always said. And as long as she'd known him, no woman had ever spent more than a night with him, if that long. Now here comes Ms. Goody Two-shoes with her white-girl ways and upstate education, and the man done flipped the script. *What in the world did she whip on him?*

"Hey, if it makes you happy, go for it."

"No doubt."

"Need any help with anything?"

"Naw. Most of her stuff is already at my crib, since she's been stayin' there most of the time."

Her stomach took another nosedive. "Oh."

He wasn't sure why he'd told Max. Except that when he looked around at his life, the one true friend he had was Maxine. Yeah, he could kick it with Remy, even Nick, but he could never explain how he was feeling, especially about Nikita. Remy would just say something about how her stuff would be easier to get, and Nick, well…he was Nikita's best friend's husband. He didn't want all his business spread during pillow talk.

Truth was, he was scared as all hell. This wasn't just taking their relationship to the next step; it was a leap. He wanted to talk it over with Max, but she seemed to have closed up on him, as if she wasn't really interested. That wasn't like Maxine. She'd always been one of his noisiest cheerleaders whenever any major change happened in his life. It was in moments like this that Lacy would have just the right thing to say, whether he wanted to hear it or not.

He snatched a glance at her smooth, dark brown profile, and those jaws were working that gum. But she was just staring straight ahead, as if she were in the room all by herself.

"What's happenin' with Dre?"

"Huh? Oh, he's good. We've been spending a lot of time together. He's been helping me get my business set up. I just found a guy to do a Web page for me on the Internet to announce my services. I hope it'll be up and running in a couple of weeks. Then it's just wait and see."

"It'll work."

"That's what I've been telling myself." She finally turned and looked at him. "How about you—I mean, besides this moving-in thing with Nikita?"

"I…started writing again."

"You have?"

Her exclamation drew the attention of the receptionist, who quickly reverted her attention back to her files.

"Yeah. A little. Just foolin' around." He hadn't shown any of his work to Nikita. There was just something stopping him. Nikita was taking courses at NYU. She'd studied in Europe, gone to boarding school. All he had was a twelfth-grade education. She was pretty much running that magazine by herself. Naw. He couldn't tell her. At least not yet.

"That's great, Q. I know it was hard."

"At first. Then once I got started, it got easier."

"Quinn, Maxine," Sean said, stepping into the reception area. "As usual, sorry for the wait. Come on in."

"I know it's been a while since we've talked," he said, taking a seat and extending his hand to the two vacant ones for them to do the same. "And it's not because your case is on the back burner. Actually, I didn't want to contact you both until I had something concrete to talk about."

Quinn unfolded his arms and sat up a bit straighter in his seat. It had been nearly six weeks since that first meeting, and they hadn't heard one word from this dude. He was beginning to think the "best-dressed brother" was just B.S.-ing them.

Sean folded his hands in front of him just as there was a light knock on the door. Everyone's gaze swung in that direction.

Quinn took a quick inventory. She was the woman in all of the photographs with Sean. She looked a hell of a lot better in person. Reminded him of somebody…couldn't figure out who.

Maxine turned back around. Humph. That suit was slamming. *Wonder where she shops. Man, she looks just like…um, Sheryl Lee Ralph from the TV show* Moesha.

"Sorry, folks. I'm Khendra Phillips."

"My wife and business partner. Khendra's been behind the push for an investigation."

Khendra took a seat to the right of her husband, crossed her long legs and flipped open a zippered leather folder. She started talking in a "this is important" voice.

She looked directly at Quinn. "I've requested the autopsy report on your sister, Mr. Parker." She was slightly startled to realize just how much he and his sister looked alike. Losing a family member under any circumstances was always devastating, she thought, but to lose a twin… She'd read some of the studies scientists had done on twins, and death between twins was invariably life altering. It was truly like losing a part of oneself, they said. Some twins reported never feeling whole again—almost like those who have lost a limb, but still have the sensation. She took a breath. "It appears that they've lost the report."

Quinn was out of his seat as if hit with a stun gun. "What?"

"Quinn," Maxine whispered, grabbing his arm.

He snatched it away and leaned forward, bracing himself on

his palms against the desktop. "What're you sayin'? That the rumors are true, they are tryin' to cover their asses?"

"To put it mildly—yes," Sean responded. "I wanted you both here so that we could talk with you face-to-face." He turned to his wife. "Khendra…"

"I've made an appointment to meet with the district attorney early next week. We're going to demand a full investigation of everything associated with the shooting."

Quinn spun away and began cutting a trail in the carpet. "What do you think you're gonna find out? Do you really think they're gonna let you get to the bottom of it? Hell, no!"

"Mr. Parker, we have no illusion that there is going to be anything easy about this case. Nothing," Khendra said. "It's obvious that they'd prefer we just shut up and go away."

"It's not going to happen," Sean added. "I know that you want this resolved. So do we. You've got to believe that we're going to do everything in our power to make sure that justice is served."

Quinn took a long breath. Looked from one to the other. "Do whatever you have to do. No matter how long it takes, no matter how much it costs. Just do it." He turned to leave. "You need me, you know how to reach me."

He stalked out, leaving the door standing open.

Maxine stood. "Thank you…both. We appreciate everything you're doing. Quinn's just upset."

Sean stood, also. "No apologies are needed, Ms. Sherman. We'll keep you both posted."

"Thanks. Nice meeting you," she said to Khendra and hurried out of the office.

Quinn was sitting behind the wheel of his BMW, music blasting.

Maxine got in the car, took one look at his stiff profile and knew this was not the time to talk. Not that he could hear anything she had to say over the blare of the music, anyway.

In no time he pulled up in front of her building.

She turned to look at him. "You cool?"

"Yeah."

"Well, good luck with the move…and everything."

"Yeah."

She opened the door. "It's gonna work out, Q."

For the first time since they'd gotten in the car he looked at her, his eyes filled with a pain she knew she'd never understand. The anguish in his voice tore at her heart.

"When?"

If looks could kill, he would certainly be laid to rest. The daggers that Nikita's parents threw at him when he came to help her with her things felt real. It wasn't anything they said—because they didn't say a word—but the blatant disgust for him was obvious in their every move.

Quinn picked up a bag. *Hey, they'll get over it,* he decided. *Nikita is a big girl and can make her own decisions.* But briefly, while moving some of the boxes into the house, he wondered what it felt like to have parents who cared enough about you to get pissed off when you did something. Humph, he'd never know.

"That's it," Nikita puffed, dropping the last box on the living-room floor.

They looked at each other and the dozen or so boxes and bags that surrounded them, and fully realized what they were embarking on. There would be no more getting up and going home for her. Privacy, a thing that he relished, would be cut back. All the little annoying habits that they'd hidden from each other would be right there in their faces. Every day.

They got scared, and both started talking at once.

"You can, uh—"

"Where should I—"

"Go 'head," Quinn said.

Nikita took a breath. "First, I think we're going to be great together." Her gaze ran across his face. "I've never lived with anyone before, other than roommates at school." She smiled. "I don't want your life to change because I'm here. I know there are things in your life that don't include me. Maybe they will one day, maybe they won't. I…just want us…to be happy when we *are* together. And to just work toward making us work."

Us. Damn. He'd never been an "us." "Sounds cool. We'll just take it one day at a time."

He bent down to pick up a box. "I'ma take this upstairs. You can put all your clothes in the closet in the guestroom. I'll find some space for your…other stuff in my dresser."

He took the box and walked toward the door, stopped and turned. "I'm glad you're here."

Chapter 18

Revelations

Nikita floated through her days at work, eager to get home to Quinn. More often than not, he was there when she got in, and they talked a bit, shared a meal, but by ten o'clock he was gone, usually not returning until the early morning hours.

Her mother called her at work practically every day, telling her what a mistake she'd made, that there was no way it would last. Her father was bolder, calling her at the apartment but refusing to acknowledge Quinn if he answered the phone.

She saw the sting of her father's treatment reflected in Quinn's eyes, the tight set of his jaw, the momentary faltering of his proud stance. And she hurt for him, pushing her parents even further away. And the further she pushed, the closer she clung to Quinn.

"Can we do something this weekend?" Nikita asked, stacking the dishes in the dishwasher.

"Don't know, Nik. You know I got things to take care of." He walked across the kitchen, took the pot off the stove and emptied the wild rice into a plastic container.

When she moved in, she'd had only an inkling of how Quinn

spent his time. Three months later, she didn't know any more now than she had in the beginning. She just sort of accepted things the way they were—as the norm. It was only now and then, like now, that it bothered her.

She didn't want to ask too many questions, pressure him or demand too much of his time. She just didn't want to rock the boat. She wasn't going to prove her parents right. She didn't say anything when he stayed out half of the night. She didn't tell him how she felt about being left home alone. She didn't say how much she resented all the time that he spent with Maxine. She wanted to be the one to go with him to see the lawyers. And she already knew that talking about Lacy Parker was out of the question. He'd made that perfectly clear when she'd asked him what happened to Lacy, though he'd finally told her what had happened to his sister. He'd been distant and almost analytical about the tragic details, as if the only way he could relay the events was to remove himself.

Tonight, she was tired of being shut out.

"Why do you have to be in the street every night, Quinn? I know you could get a real job and just work during the day like everybody else."

Slowly he turned to face her and her heart went on a rapid-fire rampage. She'd never seen such fury emanate from him. She swallowed, determined to stand her ground. She watched him bite down on the inside of his lip and shake his head. She wasn't sure if it was in disbelief or dismissal.

"Later." He grabbed his jacket from the back of the chair, snatched his keys from the table and walked out.

Quinn sped down Seventh Avenue, racing the lights, swerving around cars, barely missing getting sideswiped by a yellow cab. He turned the music louder, hoping that it would block out the thoughts that ripped through his head.

It ain't gonna work.

He was a fool to think that it could. Nikita couldn't understand his life. The way it had been. The way it was now. Naw. Never. Even if he tried to explain, it wouldn't come out right, and she'd try to find a way to make it better.

His heart settled down a bit and he took in a long breath. That's just the way she was. Always striving, trying to do better, make things better. And it was all good. He dug that about her, except when it came to him. She had to know that.

He jumped onto the FDR and headed uptown.

He'd never been able to talk to anyone about himself, explain all the whys. They just understood, or didn't care enough to want to know. Most of the time it didn't matter, anyway.

He pulled up in front of B.J.'s, looked around, saw the usual sprawled out here and there, smelled the pungent smell of marijuana that left a permanent aroma in the air, the streetlights—every other one lit—that cast hazy shadows along the gray concrete and brownstone buildings.

Yeah. He saw it all. Saw where he fit into the puzzle. And he saw himself behind the black and whites in a club where you didn't have to go through a metal detector to get in.

He opened the car door. The alarms beeped into place. Where did he belong…really?

He moved easily among the brothers and sisters who society had written off, but had been like distant relatives to him all his life.

Middle ground. Where was it?

Nikita wandered aimlessly around the house, turning lights off and on, turning the stereo up, then down, but the sinking sensation just wouldn't go away.

Was she wrong for wanting more from him, knowing that he was capable of giving it? Why should he want less than the best for himself? She couldn't understand that.

Restless, she finally found herself in the bedroom that they shared, and she suddenly felt so alone. She needed to be close to him, hear him say that it was going to be all right between them.

She strolled over to his closet and opened it, inhaling his scent. She looked at the array of suits, shirts, sports outfits, rows of shoes and books on the shelf. She started to close the closet when she noticed several black-and-white notebooks tucked in the corner.

She'd never gone through his things before, and had made a silent oath to herself that she wouldn't. But her curiosity went into fifth gear.

She stretched. She tiptoed. She couldn't reach them without knocking everything down in the process. Now her curiosity was beginning to heat up like a fever. She hurried across the room and dragged the small nightstand from next to the bed and pulled it up to the closet.

Climbing up, she reached the trio of books and took them down.

Her heart was racing, expecting a security guard to tap her on the shoulder at any moment and hustle her off to a back room for interrogation.

Hopping down, she pushed the stand back in place and took the books to the bed. Fluffing the pillows around her, she sat cross-legged on the bed and opened the first book.

Never in her wildest dreams had she expected to discover what she'd found.

Starin' out my window, lookin' for the sun to shine
There ain't nothin' there but more of the same
More of yesterday
That same beat of the street, a mood all its own
The only place I know.
Only place I've been, can ever go.
There's nothin' beyond the sunshine
Just more of the same hurt, anger and pain.
Move with it
Not against it.
'Cause there's nothin' you can do
All those stories about gold at the end of the rainbow
They ain't talkin' about you.
Tomorrow is just more of today.

There were more. Dozens and dozens of poems, short stories, song lyrics. Some finished, most incomplete. Many brought tears to her eyes and others made her laugh, but all of them left her feeling the weight of his hopelessness.

Throughout all of the work ran the single thread of a buried hurt. Many were half-written stories about a little boy who had to become a man too soon, who did what he needed to do to survive.

She closed the last book, trying to absorb the enormity of what she'd read. Through his writing he was able to express his feelings, his outrage, even weakness, which he'd never dare to show anyone.

Retracing her pattern, she returned the books to his hiding place.

Quinn had talent. Raw, phenomenal talent. But he hid it, kept it to himself, unwilling to share.

She couldn't let that happen. She had to find a way to get him to see how important it was to sharpen his skills and share them. And from all that she'd learned about him, it wouldn't be easy.

Quinn returned around 2:00 a.m. She heard him try to be quiet as he moved around the room. She lay perfectly still until she felt the weight of his body push down on the bed.

Usually when he came in he'd wrap himself around her, kissing and caressing her body, warming her by degrees until she was hot with need. Tonight he made no move in her direction. He kept his back turned.

She opened her eyes. *So this is how it's going to be. Whenever he's upset he's going to pout. That's not how things are going to work.*

"Quinn."

He knew she'd say somethin'. Had to. That was Nikita. Couldn't let anything rest. But, bottom line was, it was his intention, anyway. He'd wanted her to make the first move.

"Hmm?"

"We need to talk, Quinn."

"About what?"

"Could you at least turn around?" She sat up in the bed.

He turned on his side and propped up on his elbow. "What? I'm listenin'."

She blew out a breath, then wrapped her arms around her bare knees.

"About earlier… I'm sorry if I said something to upset you. It's just that I want so much for you. I get afraid for you when you're gone all hours, who knows where. I look at the news and hold my breath, hoping and praying that I don't hear your name connected with something awful. I can't take a decent breath until I hear your key in the door."

"Nik, I been takin' care of me and my sister since I was sixteen years old. I did what I had to do. Being out there, turnin' a dollar into two, runnin' numbers…whatever. I did it. I got good at what I did. I got respect from everybody on the street, and then I got better. The world you talkin' about… Naw, it ain't no place for me. Corporate America is lookin' for people they can control. I control what *I* do."

"But what about tomorrow, Quinn, and the day after? What about when you have a bad week and the money doesn't come in? What if you get sick? Does Remy provide health insurance, a pension plan?"

Quinn looked at her dejected profile, the way her shoulders hunched over, and the way she kept biting on the inside of her lip like she was going to cry.

She'd better not cry. That was the one thing he couldn't handle—a woman's tears. Put a gun to his head, and he wouldn't feel as weak and helpless. He hadn't meant to hurt her.

Damn. There was that first tear, running right down her cheek. Sniffles, too? Damn. But how could he ever explain how alien he felt out of his environment? How scared he was of failure? Not to her. Not to his lady.

"Niki, baby…" He sat up and pulled her into his arms, and her sobs broke like a burst water main. He shut his eyes and stroked her hair. "Come on, baby. It's gon be all right. I just gotta do things my own way. Ya know. You need to understand that."

"Quinn… I get so scared. I…just want the best for you." She sniffled and wiped. "You have so much going for you. I…I don't want anything to happen to you." She buried her face in his chest. "I don't want to be without you, Quinn. I love you."

His heart slammed in his chest and he would have sworn his stomach was trapped in his throat.

Love? Who'd ever told him that they loved him? Only Lacy. Sure, women had said they loved him in the middle of hot sex, but he knew good and damned well it wasn't *him* they loved, but what he was doing.

Love?

He eased back and lifted her face. Her beautiful brown eyes glistened. So many things he wanted to say with her looking at him as if he was the most wonderful thing in the world. He ached to make things right for her. Sure, he could tell her he'd do whatever would make her happy. But he might be lying. And he never wanted to lie to her.

Instead, he kissed her. Really kissed her. Long, slow, searching, pouring into that kiss all that he couldn't say. Hoping she'd understand.

She clung to him, needing his nearness like a fix—desperate for a part of him. The longing made her feel weak and lightheaded. She knew that the unquenchable desire she had for Quinn was a dangerous thing. It blinded her to the realities all around her. But she couldn't help it and she didn't care.

When she felt his large hands stroke her heated flesh, his fingers separating the tiny folds, she shivered, whispering his name. She moved closer, not able to get close enough. She wanted him to know just how important he was to her, that being with him like this was not just a physical need, but an emotional fulfillment.

Feeling her wet heat surround and draw him in, he let loose his doubts, if only for the moment, succumbing to the comfort and security of her giving, hoping to convey with his body all the things he could not say.

If only for the moment, the gap that separated them was bridged once again.

Chapter 19

Tell It Like It Is

Maxine and Val stood by the watercooler in the employees lounge of the bank.

Val tossed her plastic cup in the gray trash can. "You have your things for the gym tonight?"

"Yeah. I definitely have to go tonight. I've been fallin' off big-time, but I've been working so hard trying to pull everything together for my business. It's been straight from this job to the one at home. I've been so tired, girl, my eyes are crossin'."

"That's just why you need to go to the gym to unwind." Val looked at her friend and missed the usual sparkle in her eyes. "When's the last time you saw Quinn?"

"Coupla weeks… I guess." She shrugged. "Why?"

"Nothing. Just asking." She waited a beat, then put her hand on Maxine's shoulder. "You wanna talk about it, Maxie?"

Her throat closed up. She shook her head. "Maybe some other time."

"You know I'll listen, hon. No judgment. No 'free' advice," she teased, getting a half smile from Maxine.

Maxine took a deep breath. "It's just… Shit, I don't know

what it is. I guess somewhere in my stupid head I just figured Quinn would suddenly realize that I exist. Me… Maxine Sherman. I am woman." She shook her head. "Then he winds up keepin' house with Nikita, the last person on earth anyone would ever imagine him being with. I just don't get it."

"I know the whole thing threw you for a loop. It would have done the same thing to me. But the reality is, Quinn has made a choice. For how long, we don't know. But you have *your* life to worry about, your growing business, and your own relationship with Dre. Don't waste any precious time sweatin' something you can't do anything about." She lowered her voice to a pseudo whisper. "Besides, man look that good, probably *ain't* that good. Know what I mean?"

Maxine laughed. "But, g-i-r-l, I just wanted to check it out for myself. One good time!"

It was just about quitting time. Maxine checked her appointment calendar for the next day, ticked off all the items she'd already accomplished and shut down her computer.

Hmm. 4:50. She should give Dre a call and see if he wanted to do something later.

She picked up the phone and punched in the first numbers of his pager, then hung up. There was no way she was sitting there a minute past five waiting for a return call. She dialed his office directly. Either he was there, or he wasn't.

The phone was answered on the third ring.

"Security. Tower Two."

"André Martin, please."

"Who?"

Are you deaf? "André Martin."

"Sorry, miss, he doesn't work here anymore."

"'Scuse me?"

"He doesn't work here anymore. Gone about two months."

She frowned. What was going on? "Uh, thanks."

Absently, she hung up the phone.

Why didn't he tell me? Better yet, what's he been doing for the past two months? No wonder he started tellin' me to just beep him, said management was cracking down on personal calls.

Yeah, right. Lyin'… Humph.

Now she was ticked. He could have told her. She felt like a fool calling his job like that.

She slammed her desk drawer shut and locked it, dropping the tiny gold key into her empty "You're the Greatest" coffee mug. *I'd really like to hear your story, my brother.*

She snatched up her purse and her gym bag, practically stomping down the main corridor to Val's office. She was locking up as Maxine stormed in.

"What in the world is wrong with you?"

Val picked up her gym bag and slung it over her shoulder, giving Maxine the once-over.

"Guess what?" Maxine planted her hand on her hip, daring Val to guess.

"I'm stumped." She closed her office door and they walked back down the hall.

"Dre doesn't have a job."

"What are you talking about? He *never* had a job, or he doesn't have one now?"

"He doesn't have one now, and hasn't for two damned months! Man's been lyin' to me through his teeth. And for what?"

Val was silent until they'd been checked by security and let out of the bank. "Why do you think he didn't tell you?" she asked, in her patient, soon-to-be-lawyer voice.

Maxine twisted her lips as they trekked down Chambers Street, bumping into and dodging the after-work mélange of human traffic.

"I…don't…know."

"Of course you do. But you're so intent on being the one put upon that you aren't looking beyond your feelings. I'm sure he didn't lose his job for the express purpose of tickin' you off."

Maxine switched her gym bag from her left shoulder to her right. "I guess he was embarrassed."

"Of course he is. Look at you… Beginning businesswoman, secure in your position at the bank—"

She released a long sigh. "Yeah, and there he is trying to make things work between us and bam, he loses his job. He just let his male ego get in between. I would have understood."

"He doesn't know that, Max. He's probably figuring you're gonna see him as just another brother out of work, looking to cash in on you."

Maxine looked at Val. "Yeah, and he's probably feelin' even worse because I'm doing so well. He's been so helpful and thoughtful. Never said a word about his own troubles. It musta been killin' him."

"Exactly."

"I'm calling him as soon as I get to the gym. We have to talk, work out a plan. If we're gonna have a relationship, we have to be honest with each other. Good times with the bad, and all that."

"Now you're talking."

Maxine grinned. All they needed was a plan.

Dre drove up to his neighborhood bank, found a parking space that was meter-free and got out. He needed gas, his light bill was due and rent was coming up in another two weeks.

He pulled out his thin brown leather wallet from the inside pocket of his jacket, took out his ATM card and slid it into the opening until the little red light flashed and the door clicked open.

Standing behind an obviously pregnant woman who wore one of those finger-wave hairdos that he hated, he concentrated on the flakes of dried gel in her hair instead of how much money he probably didn't have in his account.

It was his turn. He stepped up to the window, selected English as his chosen language and dipped his card in the slot. He pressed Withdraw, then $100.00.

The machine's humming and whining made his stomach churn until he saw the money slide through the little door. He threw up a silent "Thank you" and pressed No when the machine asked about further transactions.

He knew all he had left was about two hundred dollars, minus the monthly service fees. The World Trade Center had denied him unemployment, saying that he was fired for insubordination.

He was out of cash and out of options.

Returning to his car he headed back home. Maybe there was

a message on his answering machine in response to the dozens he'd left about job possibilities.

When he got home and checked, there were no messages about job offers, but there was one from Maxine, who'd called from the gym. She wanted to talk. Tonight.

His stomach seesawed.

Maxine took a good long shower, letting the steamy hot water massage her overworked muscles. Otherwise, she knew, she'd be one big knot in the morning.

Wrapping herself in a thick towel, she hurried to her room, dried off and rubbed some generic baby oil all over her skin. She did some quick maintenance on her toes, then slipped into her favorite pink panties and matching push-up bra. She dabbed some Eternity behind her ears, at her wrists and between her breasts, then put on her sea green silk sweater and matching pants. She untied her head scarf and brushed her short hair back into its precision cut.

Ready.

Now she just had to wait for Dre.

Bing. The timer on the oven sounded and her stuffed chicken breasts had come out mouthwatering perfect. The steamed veggies were ready and the yellow rice had about another five minutes to go. She'd bought a bottle of wine on her way home from the gym which she'd stuck in the fridge to chill.

As she took a quick survey of the small but neat apartment, everything seemed to be in order. She wanted Dre to feel comfortable, full and relaxed when she talked with him.

The bell rang. She took a breath, repeated her mantra—Be cool—and opened the door.

"Hi."

"Hey, babe." She kissed Dre lightly on the lips. "Come on in." She took his hand and looked over her shoulder as they walked down the hall. "I fixed up a phat dinner, got some wine and the night is still young."

"What's the special occasion?"

"Does there have to be an occasion?" She turned off the pot

of rice, then faced him. "Maybe I just wanted to do something nice for you. You've been so good to me, Dre, hangin' in there with me tryin' to get my business together. I figured it was my turn. Ya know."

He stuck his hands into the pockets of his gray slacks, lowered his head, then looked up. "Uh, listen, Max, there's something I need to talk with you about."

She leaned against the light green kitchen counter. "I'm listening, Dre."

He took a breath. "I lost my job, Max. I been outta work for two months."

She kept a serene expression on her face. "Why didn't you tell me?"

"I couldn't." He looked at the floor, the stove, the table, everywhere but her face, her eyes. He didn't want to see that look—the look that his mother gave to his father. He couldn't handle that. Not from Maxine. "I felt like you would lose respect for me—as a man. Ya know?"

"No. I don't know, Dre. Why would I think any less of you? Folks lose jobs every day. It's what you do about it that matters." She pulled out a chair from beneath the kitchen table and sat down. "Wanna tell me what happened?"

Dre blew out a breath of relief and began telling Maxine how he and his supervisor got into a confrontation over Dre's handling of checking passes of all employees and visitors to the Tower.

"It was the same dude I've been seeing for months. He was late for a meeting and forgot his pass. I let him up on the floor and my boss found out and went ballistic. He wasn't tryin' to hear nothin' I had to say. Told me it was a breach in security policy, whether I knew him or not. Even after I told him it would never happen again, he says, 'You bet it won't. You're fired.'" He shook his head in disgust. "Come to find out from one of the guys on my shift it was all a setup. Dude I let through has his nephew working in my old job."

"Damn," she whispered. "Dre, you should have told me, baby." She reached out and took his hand. "So what are you gonna do? You been lookin'?"

"Yeah, I've been looking. Filling out applications, answering ads. No luck."

"How are you fixed for money?"

"Oh, that. I'm good. Got everything taken care of."

She watched his eyes dart back and forth while he talked, and knew he was lying. But she wouldn't push the issue. "If you need anything, Dre, all you gotta do is ask. Okay?"

"Sure. Okay." He sort of grinned, showing his chipped front tooth. "Something sure smells good. What you got cookin' in that oven, girl?" He came up to her and pulled her to her feet, wrapping his arms around her waist, easing her closer. He closed his eyes, letting her nearness push aside his fears.

While she held him close, she silently prayed that Dre would find a job soon. She'd seen too many times what despair did to black men.

Chapter 20

Lookin' Fast Forward

Nikita and Parris were relaxing in Parris's apartment when Nikita dropped her news.

Parris put down her cup of tea on an end table. "He writes?"

"Yes. Poetry. Short stories. And they're good, Parris. Really good. I couldn't believe it myself."

"I suppose you haven't talked to him about it because he doesn't know you were looking through his things."

Nikita looked away. "Right. But they're too good to just sit up in his closet."

"Maybe that's what he wants, Niki. Some people write simply for the personal pleasure of it, or to get things off their minds."

"But that's ridiculous. He could make something of himself as a writer. I know he could. He's light-years ahead of some of the stuff I've seen come through the office."

"Are you asking my advice?"

"Sort of."

"Leave it alone. If he hasn't told you about it, it must be for a reason. Did it ever occur to you that Quinn is exactly who and where he wants to be?"

Nikita uncurled her legs and leaned back on the couch. "Everyone can improve himself, do more with what he has," she insisted. "Look at us…Nick…Jewel. Come on, Parris."

"*If* they want to." Parris took a sip of her apple cinnamon tea. "*He* has to want to."

Nikita pursed her lips, then ran her manicured hands down her denim-clad legs. "Maybe he just needs a little push, some encouragement. I'm sure I could convince Ms. Ingram to publish some of his work. He could get some exposure."

"Are you listening to yourself? You can't map out that man's life."

"I'm not trying to—just giving it some direction."

Parris looked at her friend and shook her head.

Quinn checked out the clothes that he needed to take to the cleaners, tossing the selected items on the bed. The house seemed strange without Niki humming around, like something was missing. He kind of wanted her around right about now. Wasn't sure why. He just did.

Yeah, he understood her worries. Lacy was the same way, always thinking he wouldn't come home. But he knew how to take care of himself, had been doing it most of his life.

He dug into his pants pockets and pulled out some change, tossed it on the dresser. But he had a woman now. A real somebody in his life.

He piled the shirts together. Maybe it *was* time to take a new look at where his life was going. Nick had been bugging him about playing more than just the one night, and he was talking about cutting a new album.

Quinn took in a deep breath. Yeah, maybe it was time for some changes.

He picked up the last pair of pants, checked the pockets and pulled out a folded piece of paper. It was the workshop schedule for ASCAP. He looked it over. There was an orientation session set up for that afternoon to explain the programs. The one that caught his attention was about writing music.

He checked his watch. Eleven-thirty. The session started at two. If he hurried and took care of his running around right quick, he'd make it on time.

Grabbing his bundle of clothes and his keys, he shut the bedroom door and ran down the stairs.

Dre punched in the numbers from the ad he'd seen in the paper. This morning, just before he'd left Maxine's apartment she'd asked him if he wanted to stay with her for a while, save some money until he found a job.

And for a hot minute, he'd almost said yes. But when he looked at her, success and moving on up written all over her face, he knew shacking up with Maxine would just be the beginning of their end. She'd grow to resent him, feel she was taking care of him, just as his mother had with his father. He didn't intend to be another statistic—another black man moving in with his woman. That wasn't for him.

"Allied Systems. May I help you?"

"I'm calling about the ad for representatives." He figured it was real estate. He could handle selling homes and showing apartments. But the last thing he expected was what he was told.

All he needed was his own video camera and a car, the woman had said. Allied would provide the client list and the one-week training. All he had to do was get clear videotapes of insurance scammers.

He hung up the phone and laughed loudly. The job was made for him, and his brother in Philly had a video camera. If he could just convince his brother to lend him his camera, he'd be in business.

Maybe things were finally beginning to look up.

Nikita hurried home, taking turns and whizzing around cars with the same aggressive savvy that she'd watched in Quinn. She reached their apartment in no time, parked and hopped out of her car. She didn't see Quinn's car on the block.

Good.

Running up the stairs, she went to their bedroom, pushed the nightstand over to the closet and took down his notebooks.

There was a stationery store with a copy machine around the corner. She'd copy the poems that were finished and put the books back before Quinn realized they were missing.

On Monday morning she wanted to show them to Ms. Ingram and see what she thought. If they were as good as she believed they were, she was certain she could convince Ms. Ingram to publish them in the magazine.

As she dropped in dime after dime, making the copies, she knew that Quinn would be angry at first, but he'd get over it. All he needed was a chance to show off his work. Maybe when he saw how proud she was of him and how talented he really was, he'd change his tune and take his writing more seriously. Maybe he'd even take a class with her at NYU.

Then why did she have this sinking sensation in the pit of her stomach?

Quinn pulled up in front of Rhythms, hoping to catch Nick. He wanted to tell him about the class he'd signed up for and get his advice.

He stopped at the bar.

"Nick around?" he asked Jimmy, the newest bartender.

"He was in his office. Didn't see him go out."

"Thanks." He walked to the back and knocked on the office door.

"It's open."

Quinn stepped in. "Hey, man. Sorry to bother you. I wanted to kick somethin' with you."

"Rest yourself and let's hear it." He pushed aside his papers.

Quinn took a seat on the opposite side of Nick's desk, leaned forward and rested his arms on his thighs.

"I went up to that place you sent me to a few weeks ago."

Nick nodded.

"And, uh, I signed up for a class."

"That's great. Which one?"

"Computers and Music, the one you told me about."

Nick smiled. "You'll really dig that class. I took it and it blew me away."

"Yeah, but ya know, like how much do you have to already know about reading music?"

Nick leaned forward. "That's just it. All you gotta have is drive, man, and a good ear. You already have both. You don't have to know anything about reading scales."

He knew that was what was bugging him, and he had a pretty good idea that Quinn hadn't gotten very far in school—not due to lack of intelligence, but because of circumstance.

"Listen, man, I'd be happy to help you in any way I can. Just say the word."

Quinn smiled. "Thanks."

"Parris would help, too. She's a whiz with that stuff."

Quinn suddenly got up from his seat. "Naw. I don't want you to say nothing to Parris. She'll wind up sayin' somethin' to Niki, and I ain't ready for her to know yet."

"I hear ya. No problem."

Quinn nodded. "Listen, uh, I was thinkin' about, ya know, workin' another night. If it's cool with you."

"Sure. I've been asking you for months. Which night?"

"I was thinkin' maybe Wednesdays."

"Sounds good. That's the after-work crowd. So we close early."

"Yeah. Works for me."

"Done deal. So when do you start classes?"

"Next week. Three days."

Nick grinned. "Before you know it, you'll be producing your own music."

"Yeah, may-be."

Chapter 21

Crossin' the Line

"Ms. Ingram, I want you to take a look at something and tell me what you think. Honestly." Nikita handed her the photocopies of Quinn's poetry.

Lillian pushed her glasses up the bridge of her narrow nose and sat down to read.

Nikita anxiously tapped her foot and crossed her fingers while she waited for the verdict. Her tummy turned every time Ms. Ingram made a sound or her usually stoic face changed expression.

Twenty minutes later, Lillian put the pages on her cluttered desk. She looked across at Nikita, who was twirling her lock of hair with the shell on the end.

"They're good. Actually, better than good. Crude but moving. Are they yours?"

Nikita popped up out of her seat. "No. They belong to a friend," she said, finally breathing easy. "You really think they're good?"

"I wouldn't have said so if I didn't." She handed the papers back to Nikita. "Your friend has a lot of potential. They could use a little polish, but the foundation and the passion are definitely there."

Nikita beamed with delight. She'd been right. It wasn't just her blind love that made her think Quinn's work was good.

"What would you say if I asked to have one of them published in the magazine?"

Lillian frowned, looking long and hard at her protégé. "You want to take on an awful lot, little miss. You know that once you open the door to something like this we'll be deluged with all sorts of would-be poets. Don't you think you already have your hands full?"

That meant yes! She just knew it. All she had to do was convince her that she could handle it.

"I can handle it, Ms. Ingram. You see how the entertainment section is taking off. I don't even have to hunt down leads anymore. The calls from publicists are coming in every day, wanting their clients to be featured."

"I'll have to think about it. And you know I'll have to have permission from the writer. Who is it, by the way? Have they been published before?"

"His name is Quinn Parker. And you would be his first publisher."

Lillian thought about it for a minute and was pushed into her answer by the eagerness on Nikita's face. She'd been just like her when she was Nikita's age, always striving for more, wanting to outdo her last effort. Nikita had come a long way in the months she'd worked for the magazine. Sales were up. Her own job was easier. And Nikita was turning into one darned good editor and businesswoman. She would go a long way in this business.

Lillian took off her glasses and placed them on the desk. "You get permission from the writer, as always, and we'll try it for six months and see how it works." She wagged her finger at Nikita. "This is your baby. You handle it, and all the fallout."

"Thank you, thank you, thank you!" She scooted around Lillian's desk and gave her a big kiss on the cheek. "You won't regret it. I promise."

Now all she had to do was convince Quinn.

* * *

Quinn knew he was taking a chance, just rolling up on Maxine without calling first, but hey, they were friends. It was cool. What if her man was up there? Too bad.

He found a parking space about two doors away from Maxine's apartment building. As usual, the front door was open, so he just trotted up to the third floor and rang the bell.

Standing there, he realized he was nervous. He felt jumpy, and didn't know why.

"Who?"

"It's me, Quinn."

Maxine's heart knocked one good time in her chest. She pulled the door open and it hit her again. There he was, in the flesh, looking cool and in control as usual.

"Quinn. Whatsup? Come on in." Did she sound as shaky as she suddenly felt?

Quinn dipped his head as he stepped in, wondering why all of a sudden he felt like fifteen instead of twenty-seven. He stopped halfway into the hall, while Maxine squeezed by him and headed for the living room. He caught a whiff of her soft scent, and had she brushed just a little closer…

Her stomach was doing a real number on her and she *re-ally* wanted a piece of gum.

"Rest yourself. Want something to drink? I was making some tea. It's getting kinda chilly."

She smiled and that toothpick gap peeked at him. That made him smile, too, and he slowly began to relax. *No sign of whatshisname.*

"Naw. Nothin' for me. I wanted to talk to you about something."

"Sure." She sat down in the beige-and-brown-striped armchair that matched the couch and tucked her bare feet beneath her. "Is it about the case?"

"Naw. It's about me."

Lord, please don't tell me this man is marrying that woman. She's nice and all, but…. "I'm all ears." She smiled.

"I'm takin' some music classes."

"Get out!" She sat up and her bare feet hit the floor. "Come on, come on. What's the 411?"

Quinn started to laugh. "Take it easy."

"No. You takin' it easy enough for the both of us. Let's go. I wanna hear every minute detail. And don't leave nothing out," she warned, pointing a finger at him.

Quinn told her about the classes at ASCAP and his extra night at the club, and all the while that he spoke his spirits lifted higher and higher, with her "You go, boy's," "Ain't you some-thing's" and squeals of delight.

"Q, I'm so happy for you. You're going places, baby. Nothin' can stop you now but you."

"I feel like it, Max, ya know. But it's strange, almost like it's happenin' to somebody else. I mean, in the year since Lacy died my whole life has changed. At least, some of it." He grinned, giving Max a "you know the deal" look. "There's still that big part of me tied to my life uptown, the runnin', the hustlin', the brothers. Then there's this other part, a small part, that's startin' to break out."

"I know exactly how you feel, Q. It's happening to me, too. I know I can be more than just an account supervisor. And I can't let where I live, the color of my skin, or the fact that I'm a woman stop me from anything. We've been set up to fail. All the odds are stacked against us from the jump. It's up to us what we do with what we've got. Life's too short to let it pass you by 'cause somebody says that's the way it is."

"No doubt." He looked around for a minute. "How's André doing? Ya'll still hangin' tough?"

"He's doing good." She didn't want to tell him that her man was out of work. "What about Nikita? How's the living together life?"

He shrugged just a little. "It's pretty cool. Takes some gettin' used to."

"Hmm." She didn't want to think about them spending nights together, waking up together, sharing things together. "Lemme go get my tea. Sure you don't want any?"

Quinn got up. "Naw. I'm gonna roll. Just, ya know, wanted to tell you what was happenin'."

She walked him to the door. He turned and looked down at her in her peach sweat suit and bare feet. *Yeah. Real regular.*

"Talk to ya."

She reached up and wrapped her arms around his neck, hugging him to her.

Shock waves ricocheted all over his body when he felt hers against his. A sudden, powerful erection startled him. For a minute his mind was scrambled eggs, and before he knew it he was hugging her back. Hard. Like he couldn't let her go.

"Good luck, Q," she whispered against his neck.

"Thanks, babe." He kissed her hair and slowly released her, looked down into her upturned smiling face, then walked away.

Maxine closed the door, shaking all over. *You shouldn't have done that, fool. Nearly lost it.*

She walked into her bedroom and threw herself across her bed. Several minutes later she dialed Dre's number.

That night Quinn made love with Nikita as if his life depended on it, as if with each descent and ascent of his body, he could push aside the visions, the feel of Maxine.

Finally he did.

Nikita had been debating with herself for an entire week about how to approach Quinn about publishing his work.

First on her agenda was trying to figure out how to tell him she knew. She got up from the couch and walked over to the thermostat. The temperature outside had dropped considerably. She adjusted the temperature to seventy degrees. With the large, airy rooms and high ceilings, it took a while to warm up when a chill got in. She tugged on her tube socks and sat back down.

Maybe she should just be honest and tell him the truth. She was going through his things and found his notebooks. What other choice did she have, except to lie? She couldn't put it off much longer.

She grabbed the remote control and aimed it at the large-screen TV. *Seinfeld* was just going off. *Eleven-thirty.* It would be at least two more hours before Quinn came back home.

Tonight. She'd talk to him tonight.

* * *

Quinn was beat. His night had run longer than he'd figured on, and T.C. had talked his ear off nonstop. *Boy act like I'm his father or big brother or somethin'. Always askin' questions, needin' advice.* Now he wanted to know how to deal with some girl from the neighborhood who wouldn't seem to give him a play.

"Ignore her," he'd said. "Works every time."

Quinn laughed as he pulled onto his block. As much as he might pretend to be annoyed, he really got a kick out of talking with T.C. It felt good to try to steer him in the right direction. But T.C. was a hardhead. Had to tell him things a million times. Humph. Him all over again.

He found a space across the street, and pure skill was the only thing that got his 750i into the small space.

Putting his key in the lock, he knew Nikita would be halfway awake, trying to wait up for him, even though she had to be up and out early. He liked that. It reminded him that someone cared.

Lacy used to do that.

He closed the door with just enough noise to let Mrs. Finch know that he was home. She'd said on too many occasions, "Can't understand why a good-looking boy like you has to be out in the street till all hours of the night. Keeps me up nights— worrying." She'd looked him straight in the eye. "Understand?"

"Yes, ma'am." He'd grinned, and she'd popped him on the back of the head for being fresh.

Ever since that day nearly six months ago, he'd made it a point to make some noise when he came in. *No sense in worrying the poor woman.*

He smiled as he trotted lightly up the stairs. *Mother downstairs, and my woman upstairs. Not half bad.*

The light by the bed was still on, and Nikita was propped up with pillows and all of her schoolbooks spread out around her.

She was knocked out.

Quinn collected her books and stacked them on the floor near the bed. Cradling her like a baby, he eased her under the down comforter and pulled it up to her chin.

He took a quick shower, crawled in beside her and switched

off the light. He put his arm across her waist and pillowed his head on those breasts that he loved.

She moaned softly in her sleep.

He snuggled closer. *Damn, this felt good.* His body began to uncoil. His thoughts smoothed out and began to recede to that hazy phase just before slipping off to dreamland.

The sound of his name being called tugged him back like a fish on a hook.

"Quinn." Her voice sounded soft and fluffy, cushioning him back to sleep.

"Quinn."

His eyes flew open. "What? Whatsthematter, baby?"

She thought she'd had it planned, but the words just tumbled out, like an overstuffed closet whose door had been pulled open. "I want to publish some of your poetry."

"Say what?" He was definitely awake now. He sat up in the bed and turned on the three-stage light full blast. "You wanna run that by me again?"

Nikita blinked at the look of fury that blazed in his dark eyes, the deep furrows that creased his brow and lowered the timbre in his voice to a growl.

"I...found some of your writing...and it's really good, Quinn. Really. I want to get some of it published in the magazine." She held her breath.

Quinn got up out of the bed, cut his eyes at her over his shoulder and walked out of the room.

He tried to clear his head as he went down the stairs, but his thoughts wouldn't stay focused.

One, she'd gone through his things. Two, she'd read his work. He'd never let anyone besides his sister read his work. Why did she do that? *How* could she do that? What next?

He flipped on the lights in the living room and went to the bar. He poured a glass of Jack Daniels, no ice, and tossed it down his throat.

Publish his work! *Yeah, right.*

"Quinn."

Nikita stood framed in the doorway, her oversize nightshirt—that did nothing to disguise her curves—hitting just above those beautiful knees. His eyes rolled down her legs for a minute, then back up, and rested on her heart-shaped face, the picture of innocence.

"I'm sorry. I shouldn't have done it." She took a deep breath and walked into the room. She looked up at him, her chin jutting out. "But I'm glad I did. And I'd probably do it again. You may think it's okay to have all the gifts you have and just keep them to yourself. I don't think so."

"Lemme get this straight. Because *you* don't think so, *I* shouldn't. Is that the deal?"

"All I want is the best for you, Quinn. That's all. I want the world to open up to you, to let your talents, your dreams, take you places."

"What about what I want? Huh? Did it ever occur to you that maybe I wrote because I had to, Nikita…to keep from losin' it…to keep from doin' somethin' to hurt somebody or myself? And that after all the words were done *I* was done with what was eatin' me alive…at least for the moment? What makes you think I want to share the things that make me feel less than a man with anyone…including you?"

He would have done less damage if he'd smacked her. He saw the sting of his words bounce her around harder than a prize-fighter's best shot.

She pressed her lips together and breathed…slowly.

"Fine." Her voice barely crossed the short distance between them. "Did you show them to Maxine?" She turned and stormed up the stairs.

Quinn paced. Relentlessly. Moving back and forth across the expanse of the gleaming, high-gloss floors, trying to find a way to break free of unseen bars.

He was exposed. His insides turned out. The one person who could cast a critical eye, whose esteem he wanted to remain highest, had seen his every weakness, his every pain, his every dissolved dream.

How could he face her and still be the man he wanted her to see, the one she had met and claimed to love? How? That was not the same man who poured himself onto those pages.

"I want you to be whoever you want to be with me." Her words echoed in his mind.

Did she really mean that?

Finally he sat down, heavy, on the couch, his thoughts outweighing his body.

"It's okay, Q," Lacy whispered.

His body shuddered as his hands came up and covered his face.

For the first time since the night he'd seen Lacy's lifeless body, he cried.

Chapter 22

Just Do It

Everything ached, and the aches finally woke him up. His legs were stretched one way, his body turned another, and his neck was propped against the arm of the couch.

Slowly he opened his eyes and blinked against the brilliant morning sunshine. He sat up, and a blanket slipped off his bare chest and dragged on the floor.

He half smiled. Nikita must have tossed it over him during the night.

Nikita!

He sat straight up and heard his neck crack in protest. He'd slept on the couch and left Nikita upstairs all night… Why? His thoughts struggled for organization. Then it all came back to him in a wink. She'd read his work and wanted to publish it.

He settled back for a minute, letting the events of the previous evening replay. He shouldn't have left things the way he had, or spoken to her the way he did. There was no way for her to know how he felt. What was worse, he had her believing that Maxine had a spot with him that she didn't.

Slowly he stood and stretched. It wasn't the first time she'd said something about him and Maxine. But it wasn't like that. They were just friends. Period. Always had been. Nikita was just going to have to understand that.

He looked at his watch. Nine-thirty.

Damn. She'd already left for work. He was sure of that. Must still be ticked, because she hadn't said goodbye.

Grabbing the blanket, he took it upstairs, folded it and put it in the hall closet. He went into his bedroom. It was empty. Just as he'd figured.

A tingling sensation suddenly ran through him. He opened the connecting door, stepped into the bath and across to the extra bedroom. He flung open the closet and released a breath of relief.

She hadn't left him. But that flash, that millisecond when he thought she had, rocked his world.

She knew she must look a fright. She hadn't slept a good ten minutes after Quinn came home. There were shadows beneath her swollen red eyes, and her body felt as if she'd run the Boston Marathon without a warm-up.

What was worse than all that was that her emotions were all tied up in a knot. It was all she could do to keep herself from totally falling apart.

Parris was right. She should have just left it alone. But she'd thought she was helping. She couldn't understand why he would be ashamed of who he was, of the deep feelings that he had about life.

Methodically, she began opening the stack of mail from the weekend, wondering how she could turn around what she'd begun.

"Mr. Martin?"

André looked up from the four-year-old *Sports Illustrated* magazine that he'd been reading and put it back on the imitation wood table. He stood up, adjusting his bronze-and-black-striped tie, standing at least a head over the very bald man.

"I'm Mr. Hargrove." He stuck out his pudgy pink hand, which was enveloped by Dre's. "Why don't we step inside so we can talk?"

An hour later Dre walked out of Mr. Hargrove's office with his first assignment—to get video coverage of an allegedly injured truck driver who was believed to be scamming the insurance company. All Dre had to do was get footage of the driver doing any activity that could prove that his back "injury" was a fake.

The insurance company would pay him for up to five hours of surveillance per day for two weeks, with a bonus if and when he caught the culprit in the act.

This was going to be a cinch.

He whistled all the way back to his car with the name, address and photograph tucked in his pocket. He would start this afternoon, along with a guy who was going to show him the ropes. The quicker he wrapped it up and got his bonus, the quicker he could get a new case. The faster he got the hang of this surveillance thing the better. 'Cause he had a plan.

Maxine looked up from her pile of applications for new accounts into Val's smiling face.

"How's it going?"

Maxine rubbed the bridge of her nose. "Too slow." She smiled a tired smile. "Whatsup?"

"Just passing through. Thought I'd stop and see if you wanted to go to lunch later."

"I'm just gonna go down to the lounge and catch a few winks. I'm beat, girl. This two-job thing ain't all it's cracked up to be."

"So business is starting to pick up, huh?"

"Definitely. In the past week alone, I've processed two cruises and three trips to the Bahamas and arranged for the hotels, and booked another half-dozen flights around the country."

"Sounds like you're going to need an assistant before long."

"I know. I'm just not too crazy about having somebody up in my house when I'm not home."

"I hear ya. But maybe you could find someone who'd be willing to work the same hours you do, and you take a break on those nights."

Her eyebrows raised as she tossed around the idea. "Hmm.

Not bad. It just might work." She looked up at Val and grinned. "So you *are* good for somethin'."

"Yeah. How 'bout that? At least every now and then. How's Dre doing? Find a job yet?"

"No, girl. That's a whole 'nother story."

"Well, you're going to have to catch me up when you have the time…and the energy."

"Are we still on for the gym tomorrow after work?"

"Can't miss my workout, since that's the only workout I've been gettin', if ya know what I mean." Val gave Maxine "the look," and they broke out laughing.

"Girl, you need to stop."

"Stoppin's not the problem. It's getting something started. Hey, listen, I've got to run. Talk at you later."

"Have a good one," Maxine called out.

Maxine took a moment to refocus on her work, but her thoughts kept bouncing back to Dre. She was really beginning to worry. He seemed to get more depressed each day, with no real prospect of a job in sight. When she'd told him that she'd be willing to help in any way that she could, she'd meant it. Yeah, he'd tried to blow it off as if he had everything under control, but how long could his finances hold out without an income?

She turned to her computer and pulled up the accounts file. Her heart started to race. She'd never done anything like this before, especially on the down low. Her eyes darted quickly around. She keyed in André's name and pulled up his account. Within seconds she saw his remaining balance. *$75.00.*

Damn. She exited from the file. How was he gonna make it?

Her heart ached for him, and he was too proud to say anything to her. Well, that was coming to an end.

Tonight.

Nikita picked up the phone and dialed the house. Somehow she'd have to find a way to make it up to him. She didn't want to lose him, couldn't lose him. Not over this.

The phone rang.

And rang.

The answering machine clicked on and Quinn's smooth voice came on the line. She listened to his request to the caller—"Tell me what you want me to know"—and then she hung up.

She needed to talk, to try to sort out her feelings, figure out what she was going to say to Quinn, to do about their relationship.

She picked up the phone again, intending to call Parris, then quickly hung up. Although Parris would listen and empathize, she wasn't up to hearing the censure in her voice, even though she would never actually say, "I told you so."

A knock on the office door pulled her away from her thoughts. She looked up at the wall clock. Eleven-thirty.

Must be Federal Express.

She went to the door and pulled it open.

"Quinn." Her heart beat in triple time, making her suddenly light-headed. He was coming to tell her to pack her things, that it wasn't working, that she'd—

"I…I'm sorry, baby." He put his hands on her shoulders and looked down into her eyes that looked as if they needed sleep. His stomach tightened. "I was rough on you… I shouldn'ta been. Ya know."

She had just grown roots, because she couldn't move from the spot in front of the door.

"Quinn, I'm the one who should be apologizing. It was wrong of me to go through your things. It's just that… I was feeling lonely…and—"

"Forget it, Nik. You don't have to explain." He blew out a breath. "Can I come in outta the cold?"

He smiled that baby-boy smile, his dimples twinkling, and her knees went weak.

She took his hand from her shoulders and led him into the office.

When he came in, he realized it was the first time he'd actually been right inside where she worked. They'd been together for months and he'd never seen the place, and up until recently she'd never known he wrote. *Humph. Strange.*

He looked around.

"This isn't what I expected."

Nikita tried to tidy up her desk. She smiled. "What did you expect?"

He shrugged. "I don't know. I guess somethin' like what you see on the box. A bunch of desks, people runnin' around, stuff everywhere. This is more like an apartment."

"It was, until it was converted. Lillian used to live here before she bought her house. She knocked out a few walls and had office furniture and computers put in. Come on, I'll show you around."

She took him on a five-minute tour, pointing out the two bedrooms that had been turned into work and storage rooms, the dining room that was the copy room, the kitchen, bathroom—equipped with a shower—then back to the large living room that was the main office.

"Not bad." He looked at her with a newfound pride. "So you really run all of this by yourself, huh?"

She grinned. "Most of the time. Lillian comes in less and less now that I've got the hang of everything. But I really could use some help. Between the mail, bills, reading manuscripts, writing copy and laying out the magazine, it's a lot of work."

The phone rang.

"Not to mention all the calls. Excuse me, just one minute." She picked up the phone. *"Today's Woman."*

Quinn wandered around, looking at the stacks of previous issues and what appeared to be the layout for the next one.

Funny, he'd just sort of assumed he knew what she did every day. Taken it for granted. Sure, she rattled on about her day, but it had never really sunk in, until now. Nikita really did have it going on. She was doing something she was good at and handling it, and when she'd wanted to make him a part of it he'd blown up, because he was scared.

He looked across at her as she took notes, checked something on her computer and answered the caller's questions.

She hung up and caught him staring at her. Her face got hot. "Sorry. It took longer than I thought."

He stuck his hands in the back pockets of his jeans. "So…ya know…you think my stuff is good?" He chewed on the inside of his bottom lip.

"Quinn." Her gaze moved over his face, seeing and sensing his doubts and insecurities, and she couldn't understand them. "Your work is so wonderful, moving. It touches you. It's the part of you that no one knows." She stood up and crossed the room to stand in front of him. She looked up into his eyes, taking his hands in hers. "But I'm glad that I do, now."

"You are?"

"Of course. Did you really think it would make me feel different…love you any less?"

"I don't know, man. It's like stuff punks do. None of my boys would be sittin' 'round writing rhythms unless they were for some rap music. And stories, sh—forget it."

"Maybe it's because *they* can't, Quinn. But you can. Why hide that?"

He let out a long breath. "So… What are you gonna do with them?"

She heard the cautious note in his voice, but also the beginnings of hope.

"You'll probably flip your lid again." She looked down at the floor, then up at him. "I showed them to Lillian and she's willing to publish one if I get your written permission," she said quickly.

Did she just say her boss would *publish* them? His heart started beating faster. He swallowed. "She did?"

"Yep! She loved what she read."

His dimples made a brief appearance. "Yeah?" He sort of shrugged as if it was no big deal, but his insides were going crazy.

"Yeah." She beamed.

He thought about it. Thought about having his innermost thoughts on display. Thought about seeing his work actually published in a magazine. He thought about how his sister had always encouraged him, and how Maxine had said the only thing stopping him was him. And he thought about this itty-bitty woman standing in front of him who believed in him from the bottom of her heart. And he thought… *What about me? What do I really want?*

"So tell me about this permission thing." He sat down on the edge of the desk and pulled her onto his lap, nuzzling her neck while she spoke.

Nikita's spirits shot straight to heaven. She couldn't wait to tell Parris how wrong she'd been about Quinn. And maybe this would shut her parents up, too, especially since she planned to bring Quinn home for Christmas. Everything was going to work out just fine.

But how could she concentrate and figure out what was best with his hands roaming all over her body, his mouth finding exposed skin?

She started to feel shaky again, just as she had that first night, and the night after that, and after that. It was always that blissfully helpless sensation that floated through her like gentle, lapping waves, building a steady rhythm, until her entire body pulsed and the sweet wetness between her legs felt like liquid fire.

Like now.

"I missed you last night, Niki." He ran his tongue along her ear. "I don't wanna feel like that again." His hand slipped up under her sweater.

"Neither...do...I." She shuddered against his chest, feeling the snap of her bra come undone.

So they made love on her desktop, on the imported area rug in front of Lillian's desk, on the couch and finally in the shower, as if each act would somehow bind them, erase the doubts, silence the fears, make everything all right.

Again.

"Woman, you could wear a brother out." Quinn chuckled, watching her replace her clothing, while he ran a towel through his damp locks.

She looked at him from beneath her mascaraed lashes. "You can hold your own, too, buddy."

He grinned. "So what else do you do around here besides seduce unarmed men?"

His offhand comment made her realize that they hadn't used any protection. For a minute, a nervous knot tightened in her stomach. That was the last thing she needed, or wanted, especially now. She had too much to accomplish, and Quinn didn't even have a real job. Well, she wouldn't worry about it. For now.

"A little bit of everything. Read a bunch of stuff to see if it's worth publishing, for one."

"What kinda stuff do you get?"

She looked at him for a minute, an idea forming. "See for yourself." She lifted her chin in the direction of the stack of papers on the shelf behind her desk.

Quinn strolled over, his eyes grazing across the neat rows. He reached up and pulled down a folder marked *Features*. "You looked at this stuff already?"

"Some of it. But it's getting so hectic, I'm falling behind. I can't read everything that comes in." She paused for a moment. "I've been thinking about asking Ms. Ingram for an assistant."

He looked up. "Oh, yeah? What kind of assistant?"

"Just somebody to go through the stuff that comes in and make recommendations. Things like that."

He took the folder and sat down, flipping it open.

While he read, Nikita replied to correspondence and sorted through the bills to be paid.

The phone rang. Nikita answered and Quinn checked the time. He had class in an hour.

Nikita hung up and he closed the folder.

"Not bad, I guess." He stood and plopped the folder on her desk. "See anything interesting?"

He shrugged. "There was one in there about a bunch of single mothers who opened their own business. Sounded kinda cool."

"Thanks. I'll take a look. Maybe we'll use it."

He shrugged again, feeling that he'd made a difference. "Listen, I gotta roll. We'll talk about this publishin' thing some more tonight. Cool?"

She smiled and nodded. "Where do you have to go?"

He leaned down and kissed her lightly on the lips. "Got things to take care of. See you later."

"How much later?" she called out to him.

His hand held the doorknob. "We'll see."

Maxine was anxious to see Dre. He'd called and wanted to pick her up after work. She needed to find a way to let him know she'd lend him some money, and that her offer to stay with her if he needed to was still good.

She pushed through the glass doors of the bank and spotted Dre's car parked across the street.

He saw her coming, clean as she wanted to be with her bronze Burberry trench, to-the-waist printed scarf which she'd draped around her neck, and those long legs with just the right amount of heel to make them fabulous.

His woman.

Maxine pulled off her shades as she got in the car. "Hey, babe." She gave him a quick kiss. "This is a treat."

"I thought I'd take my lady for a quick bite and share some news."

She strapped herself in and crossed her legs instead of her fingers. "What news?"

"Chinese sound good?" he teased, wanting to delay his announcement a while longer.

"Your news would sound better. Come on, you're making me nervous."

He chuckled lightly and pulled off into the rush-hour traffic. "First of all, I just wanna tell you how much it meant to me that you stuck with me, Maxine. You were in my corner all these months, even after I tried to keep things from you." He looked at her profile for a brief moment, then back at the road. "All that means a lot, baby. I never felt less than a man. You didn't do that to me. Not once. I mean, even your offer to let me crash at your place… I know it was from the heart.

"I know things have been tight. But all that's about to change. Got me a sweet gig. And I been thinkin' how I can turn what I do into my own business. But I'm gonna need your help."

Chapter 23

'Tis The Season

Quinn started stopping by Nikita's office on the mornings that he had classes at ASCAP. There was nothing official said, but he'd come in, look over the stories and story ideas, and make comments. More often than not, Nikita agreed with him.

On some days he watched Nikita lay out the magazine on the computer, and sometimes he'd add a few suggestions.

His own computer skills were getting sharper, and he surprised Nikita with his knowledge.

He still hadn't told her about his classes. He wanted to wait until Christmas. It was when his poem would be in the magazine and his first music track completed.

Nick had listened to pieces of it as he was putting it together, and was eager to hear the finished piece. He wanted to include it on his next album when they went into the studio in the new year. Quinn was psyched. Things were really coming together.

The only thing that kind of bothered him, maybe more than he'd ever admit, was that he missed Maxine.

They didn't see each other much anymore. Since that day in Nikita's office and that same night when he'd actually come in before 2:00 a.m., Nikita told him that she wanted to have more of a place in his life. She wanted to be with him when he went to see the attorneys. She wanted to hear him play on Wednesday nights, instead of staying home. And he noticed that Maxine came down to the club less and less.

He'd have to make it a point to stop by and check her out during the holidays.

It just seemed that Nikita was filling up more and more of his life.

"So how much longer you think you'll be at the bank?" Dre asked, stringing tinsel on Maxine's six-foot tree.

"Hopefully just until the spring. The business is making some solid money now, and it's building every day."

Dre put the box of tinsel on the table and turned to Maxine, who was spraying furniture polish on the coffee table.

"Max, you know things have been picking up for me, too—thanks to your help with my business plan. I'm figuring that by the new year, if things go right, I'll be able to open my own surveillance office. I already have some potential clients, and some of the brothers from my old job are interested in working for me part-time."

Her heart started beating a little faster and her stomach started feeling funny. Something was up, and it was making her nervous.

"Sounds good, Dre. I know it's gonna work out. You have a good plan."

"Yeah." He stepped closer, cutting off the distance between them. "So I've been thinking real hard about…you and me, Max, and where we're going." He swallowed and looked across into her eyes. He took her hand in his. "I was trying to wait until Christmas," he said, smiling nervously, "but I guess Christmas Eve is close enough."

He led her over to the couch and they sat down. He took a breath.

"I love you, Maxine. I think you know that. You've made me happier than I've ever been, given me the confidence to go for myself just by watching you. I can't see my future without you in it."

He reached into the pocket of his jacket and pulled out a little black velvet box.

Now her stomach was really spinning.

He popped the box open and a beautiful diamond, set in platinum, gleamed up at her. "Marry me, Maxine. Be my partner, my friend and lover...my wife."

Maxine's thoughts and feelings swirled, blending, merging. She looked at Dre and the love that he offered, then at the diamond. And in its brilliance she saw where her life was, where it had been, and where it was going, who had been in it, who was and who would no longer be. Her eyes filled with pain, memories and joy. The muscles in her throat tightened. And realization settled over her as gently as the falling snow. She could no longer sit back and wish on a maybe. "Press on," she heard Lacy whisper.

She inhaled a deep gulp of pine-scented air and squeezed Dre's hands. "Yes," she breathed, and the elusive dream popped like a pin-pricked bubble. She closed her eyes and wrapped her arms around Dre's neck. "Yes."

And silent tears trickled down her cheeks.

"Your people hate me, Nikita," Quinn grumbled as he eased her Benz, which she'd insisted they take, onto the snow-covered street. "Let's just make this as quick as possible. I wanna get back and check out Maxine."

Nikita's insides seesawed for a minute. "How is Maxine?" she asked, pushing back her pangs of jealousy.

"That's what I don't know. Haven't had time to see her much anymore."

"And that's my fault?"

"Is it?"

"Just forget it, Quinn. It's Christmas. Let's not fight, especially about your friends."

"Humph. Don't seem like I got too many of them, no more."

"What's that supposed to mean?"

"Like you said, forget it." He was in a foul mood. Had been

ever since she'd said she wanted them to spend Christmas day with her family. Humph. If he'd wanted to be miserable, all he had to do was look at the news.

They settled down to an uncomfortable silence, the jazz sounds on the car stereo filling the gap between them.

He wasn't quite sure when or how things had changed. He just knew that they had. He didn't seem to have much time for anything anymore except work, which had gone from two nights to four. If he wanted to spend some time with his boys, Nikita sulked. Somehow or other, he was practically employed at her job. What had started out as just "something to do" had turned into a regular gig. Ms. Ingram even sent him a check once a month for his "services."

It was as if Nikita was trying to keep tabs on him 24/7 or something. It was beginning to get to him.

Even seeing his poem in the magazine didn't have the kind of kick he'd thought it would. Humph, he guessed Nikita had enough enthusiasm for the both of them. She talked about it for a week straight—that, and trying to push him into going back to school, and to write more, play more.

Now here they were, going to her parents' house on Christmas day—the same folks that would just as soon tell him to kiss their aristocratic asses as say hello.

He was losing himself little by little, like a rock that keeps getting hit with water. And he didn't like it, even if the water was Nikita, even if it did make her happy.

Things were going to have to change.

Nikita peeked at Quinn from the corner of her eye. He'd worn the copper-colored Armani suit she'd bought for him, and he looked fantastic in it. He'd trimmed his locks and had them tied back. He'd started to grow a goatee that outlined his full mouth and strong chin. She liked it, and told him so.

She sighed silently. All of her hard work was paying off. Quinn was settling down…working…planning a future. He'd even begun to clean up his language, at least around her. His music was getting better, and Nick was definitely going to use one of Quinn's pieces on the album. She had him learning the magazine business, and he was really good.

So what if they argued a little more than they once had, and he seemed more quiet than usual? They still made love every night, she made sure of that, just like in the beginning. And she knew he loved her, even if he never said the words. He was giving up old habits for her, shedding old friends that were nothing but bad influences, anyway, and building a life together with her. So what if he never said the words? Didn't Amy say that some people showed love by the things they did for you?

And she loved him for it.

Quinn took the Christmas gifts from the trunk of the car, gifts that Nikita had purchased for her parents—"from the both of us," she'd said—while she trotted up the three freshly shoveled front steps and rang the bell.

He still couldn't figure out why she was so anxious to be up under people who gained pleasure from making her life—and especially his—pure hell.

As he stood next to her waiting for the door to be opened she turned and looked up at him, her eyes sparkling. That tiny dimple under her right eye was winking at him, and she said, "Thank you for this."

His heart softened, and there was that familiar rush he got in the pit of his stomach whenever she looked at him as if he could save the world.

She squeezed his hand and stole a quick kiss just before Amy opened the door.

Amy seemed delighted to see Nikita, hugging and inspecting her. She even seemed happy to see Quinn, giving him a good hug and wishes for a happy holiday.

"Come on in, you two. Everyone is in the front room. We have the fireplace going and everything, and there's plenty to munch on until dinner."

She took their coats and ushered them inside like honored guests.

Well, the pleasantries just about ended at the front door. He could taste Nikita's parents' distaste on his own tongue. Not that they weren't "cordial"—they were too uppity to act any other way. It was in the lift of their noses, as if they'd just stepped in something. And Nikita didn't help matters any by putting him on display as if he were going to be auctioned off and she had to show off all of his saleable qualities to the new masters.

"Did I tell you that the music Quinn produced is going to be on Nick's next album?"

"Isn't that wonderful?" Cynthia said in a tone that really meant, "So what?" "You must be very proud."

"Nikita seems to be. I'm just havin' a good time." He almost laughed out loud when Cynthia cringed and Lawrence grunted.

Quinn leaned back against the couch and crossed his legs at the ankle, just as Nikita dug in her bag and pulled out a copy of the magazine.

"Look at this." She flipped the magazine open to the dog-eared page. "Quinn wrote it." She pointed to the boxed-off poem.

Cynthia briefly looked at him over the top of her glasses, then down at the page.

"Very interesting style," she said, returning the magazine to Nikita. "Where did you study?"

Quinn frowned. "Study what?"

"Writing, of course."

He took a breath. "I didn't."

"I see. Where did you attend school, by the way? I don't think Nikita ever mentioned it to us."

Quinn looked at her the way he looked at the gamblers who owed money that he intended to collect. He leaned slightly forward, his gaze zeroing in on her. He saw her withdraw. "No place you'd know."

Things got a little better after that. Mom and Pop just ignored him altogether, which was fine with him. At least he didn't feel like a sitting duck.

The doorbell rang and Cynthia seemed to brighten. She actually smiled. It made him nervous.

She pressed her hands together and looked at Nikita with something close to glee.

"That must be my surprise," she said, standing when Amy came into view with a guest trailing behind her.

"Grant!" Cynthia gushed.

Quinn cut a look at Nikita and her face was frozen. He looked back at the brother in the doorway, and his eyes had targeted on Nikita. Oh, yeah. There was going to be some mess tonight. Ho, ho, ho.

"Grant, I'm so glad you could come," Cynthia greeted, walking over to kiss his cheek. She took his hand as if he were a little kid and led him into the room. "Look, Nikita, it's Grant. Surprise."

Nikita threw her mother a withering look, while Grant spoke to her father. Then he turned to Nikita.

"How are you, Grant? It's been a while."

"It has. Too long." He leaned down and pecked her cheek.

He had the kind of voice that sounded as if it belonged on the radio, Quinn thought. He gave him the quick once-over. One of those light-skinned brothers with the curly black hair and light eyes. They were about the same height, but Brotherman definitely looked like he worked out, from the fit of his suit and the width of his shoulders.

"Grant, this is Quinn Parker." She possessively took Quinn's hand. "Quinn, Grant Coleman."

Grant looked from one to the other and finally stuck out his hand, which Quinn reluctantly shook. "Nice to meet you."

Quinn just stared at him for a minute. "Yeah. You, too."

"Grant, you know where everything is," Cynthia chimed in as if this whole awkward experience were an everyday occurrence. "Help yourself to whatever you like, dear."

"Thanks. I think I could use a drink."

"So could I," Lawrence said, having uttered his first sentence since their arrival.

"Can I get you anything?" Nikita asked softly.

"Yeah, the hell outta here," he whispered under his breath. "And what's wit' you and Brotherman?"

"It's a long story, Quinn. I'd rather not talk about it right now." *She had Quinn now. That's what counted.*

But the truth was, she didn't want to talk about it at all. She thought she'd pushed her feelings for Grant way down deep beneath the surface. But suddenly seeing him again brought everything raging back with a vengeance. She was shaking all over. The sparks were still there, even if it wasn't a fire.

Dinner was the longest event of Quinn's life. Little by little he felt more and more like the outsider her parents wanted their daughter to see him as, and him to be. What hurt him most was that Nikita seemed unaware of the toll it was taking on him.

He listened to her and Grant compare notes about the places they'd been in Europe—she as a student, he while on his tour of duty in the air force—places he'd only heard about or seen pictures of.

Grant entertained the diners with heroic stories of Desert Storm, of being under enemy fire. Briefly, Quinn wondered if it was anything like being shot at by a rival gang. Did you get the same rush, have the same fear?

Nikita's mother just fell all over herself making sure that Grant had anything he needed, and had elected herself chief moderator to keep up a steady flow of "remember whens" any time conversation began to lag.

Finally, the ordeal was over. Quinn stood off to the side watching them all say their goodbyes.

"It was good to see you again, Nikita," he heard Grant say. "I'm glad to see that you're looking so well."

Nikita smiled. "Thank you. It was good to see you, too, Grant." And she really meant it. She hadn't realized just how deep her feelings had been for Grant Coleman until he'd walked into the room and she was in his presence again. She repeated her mantra, "That was behind her now." She had Quinn.

She turned, sensing him watching her, and her heart nearly broke. He looked so lost, almost as if he'd stumbled into the wrong party and wasn't quite sure what to do. It wasn't in his manner, or his unaffected stance. It registered in the hollowness of his eyes.

How different they were. But maybe they weren't. How comfortable would Grant be in the midst of Quinn's world?

"I really have to go, Grant. We have a long drive."

"I'll walk you to the door. I wanted to say goodbye to Quinn."

Grant stuck out his hand. "It was nice meeting you. Take care of this lady." He smiled, looking at Nikita. "She's something special."

"Yeah. She's somethin'. You ready?"

Nikita nodded.

"Later," he said to Grant.

"Take care, Grant." She walked behind Quinn to the door.

"You too, Niki."

"I hope you see what I mean, Grant," Cynthia said, sidling up next to him as he stared at the closed door. "She has no business with…that, that…thug."

Grant blinked away visions of Nikita and turned his attention toward her mother. He smiled sadly, putting his arm around Cynthia's narrow shoulders. "Let's leave it alone, Mrs. Harrell. Whether you want to accept it or not, Nikita is happy."

Cynthia puffed up her chest. "She'd be happier with you. *I* know she would. And you do, too, Grant."

"Niki will have to figure that out for herself." He leaned down and kissed her cheek. "Thank you for a lovely evening. And Happy New Year. I'll be leaving day after tomorrow for Virginia to finish up my tour."

"And then what? You'll be back, won't you?"

He shrugged. "I don't think so, Mrs. Harrell. Not this time."

Quinn couldn't get home fast enough to get out of the monkey suit. He felt like a model in a catalog ad.

Never again. The last place he would ever set foot in was her parents' home. He didn't give a damn how important it was to Nikita.

Nikita didn't know what to say. Should she apologize? Should she ask if he enjoyed himself? No. That was a stupid question.

She wanted to say something—anything to break the tension-filled silence. Quinn hadn't uttered a word since they got in the car.

They shouldn't have gone. She should have never subjected him to "them." And then Grant showed up. But all she'd wanted to do was show him off. Show her parents that she made the right choice, that Quinn was about something. All of her energy and input over the previous months proved what she'd known all along—Quinn Parker could be somebody.

"Can I turn on the radio?" she asked, her voice a thready whisper.

"Whatever."

She reached over and pushed the on button. Soft jazz wafted through the speakers. She sat back and tried to relax.

Quinn reached over and pressed the scan button until it locked onto his favorite rap station. Then he pumped up the volume until he could hear nothing but bass, not even the sound of his own restless breathing.

Nikita opened her mouth to say something, looked at his scowling features and changed her mind. She'd save whatever it was she'd decided to say until they got home.

By the time they pulled to a stop in front of their door she had a booming headache, intensified by the relentless blast of the music. She opened her door, grateful to get out. Quinn's voice stopped her.

"I'll see you later."

She turned. "What?"

"I said, I'll...see...you...later."

"You're going to leave? Just like that? I think we need to talk, Quinn." Her heart started pounding in concert with her headache.

"I don't think so."

She stared at him, her mind scrambling for something to say, something to make him stay.

Nothing.

"You're letting all the cold air in," he said without looking at her.

She pressed her lips together, grabbed her purse and got out.

Before she even set a good foot on the sidewalk he'd sped off down the street.

He knew if he'd stayed it would have been something. He would have said something that he might regret later. He needed a clear head when he talked to Nikita. If she had been any other woman, any other person, he would have truly lost it. But even though there was no respect given to him, he'd tried to maintain it, even if that meant leaving, now…and in the future.

* * *

Maxine stretched out her hand and looked at the perfect little diamond on her ring finger.

If you turned it just right it picked up all kinds of light, making it look as if there were truly a rainbow inside. She smiled.

Engaged. Hot damn. She was getting married. Maxine Martin. Hmm. It would take some getting used to, for sure. Maybe she'd hyphenate her last name or something.

She could just see herself now, walking down the aisle, in a white dress, of course, with everybody boo-hooing because she looked so beautiful.

She'd never planned a wedding before. Matter of fact, she'd never even been a bridesmaid. She was definitely going to need some help. They hadn't set a date yet, but hey, it was never too early to start preparing.

She plopped down on her bed. She needed somebody to talk to. Val was out of town. She'd called her mother already with the news, and Dre had to drive up to Philly to see his family and wouldn't be back until New Year's Eve. He'd begged her to go, but she wasn't quite ready to "meet the folks" yet.

Now, she wished she had gone. Damn. She didn't feel like being alone. Not on Christmas. Not on the biggest day of her life…so far.

She reached for the remote control on top of the headboard and aimed it at the television. The doorbell rang in time with the volume.

She couldn't imagine who it was. Everybody that she knew was away, or otherwise occupied.

She pushed up from the bed and walked, barefoot, down the hall. "Who?"

"It's me, Q."

She opened the door, but her heart was beating so fast she just stood there with her hand on the doorknob. *God, she'd missed him.*

"Hey, Max. Merry Christmas." He kinda smiled at her, the same smile she saw in her dreams.

"Hey, yourself." Her eyes ran up and down his long frame.

"You…busy?"

She blinked. "No. Come on in." She patted her hair and stepped aside.

Maxine followed him down the hall and into the living room.

He took off his full-length black shearling coat and folded it across the back of the couch, then sat down.

Maxine just stood there looking at him, trying to figure out why he'd come. *And where was Nikita?*

"Can I get you somethin'…hot? I know that wind and snow is kickin' out there."

"Naw. I'm cool."

She sat down on the love seat and tucked her feet under her. "Long time, Q," she said, with a tinge of regret in her voice. "How you been?"

"Hangin' in. I just wanted to stop by and see you…for the holidays. You know…with Lacy being gone and all…you're like family."

Family. She wanted to scream. "Yeah, I know what you mean." She took a breath and put a smile on her face. "So how was your first live-in Christmas?"

"Nothin' like what I expected."

"Is that good or bad?"

"Depends." He shrugged. "Anyway, I didn't come out in all this freezin' snow to talk about me." He grinned. "What's been happenin'? How's business?"

Maxine leaned back and began to chat on about everything, from the kooky customers at the bank to her booming business. She had Quinn rolling with her anecdotes and longshoreman lingo. He hadn't felt this good, this loose, in months…since…the last time he saw her. The realization hit him with a one-two, tempering his laughter. What was happening to his life? Where had it gone?

"Q? You okay?"

He blinked and focused in on her. "Yeah. Just thinkin'. Glad to hear everything's working out for you, Max. Real glad, ya know." He swallowed and took a breath. "So, how's André?"

For the first time since Quinn stepped through the doorway, she remembered André.

Maxine took a quick breath. She couldn't hide it from him, and really there was no reason to. He was just a friend. A friend with a woman in his life, just like she had a man.

She proudly stuck out her hand, the diamond twinkling in the light. "I'm getting married."

Time suddenly came to a screeching halt, then spun blindly backward. In his mind's eye he saw Maxine at each stage of his life. Always there. Always there. Until now.

The words felt as if they were sticking in his throat, but he forced them out, anyway.

"That's phat, Max. Congrats. Where's the lucky man?"

"He had to go to Philly to see his folks."

Quinn nodded, not really hearing, struggling to put the right words together. "So... When's the big day?"

"We haven't set a date yet."

He nodded, then stood up. "Hey, I better get rollin'."

She watched him put on his coat, straighten his shoulders, then look at her.

Her heart thumped wildly. What was it that she saw in his eyes? Everything seemed to be moving in some sort of slow motion. She saw him coming toward her and stand there looking down into her face. The very essence of him wrapped around her. Hypnotized, she watched his finger extend and run along the line of her jaw. The corner of his mouth quirked upward—sad almost, she thought.

His voice came to her, then, low, private, personal. "I knew some lucky man would snatch you up. Be happy, Max."

She swallowed and reality slipped back into place. "I will."

He leaned down and dropped a featherlight kiss on her lips. A shiver ran through her.

He pressed just a little harder, his lips slightly parting against hers. And then he moved away.

"Take care, baby."

"Yeah." She smiled. "You, too." She moved back and looked at the floor, clasping her hands behind her back.

Quinn started moving down the hallway, with that slow, easy walk.

She took her time following him. She didn't know what she

was going to do when she got to that door, but she knew he'd better cross it to the other side before something jumped off that they couldn't handle.

He pulled his coat collar closer to his neck, turned and smiled, those dimples going full blast.

"Later, Max. And have a good New Year." He looked at her a minute and shook his head. "Gettin' married... I'll be damned. See ya."

She waved because she couldn't say anything, then shut the door behind him.

What in the hell had just happened? She wasn't imagining things. Two minutes ago she would have bet her last dollar that Quinn wanted to be with her, really *be* with her. Then, next thing she knew, he was grinning as if everything were just lovely.

But everything is lovely, fool. You and your man are getting married. You were just readin' somethin' into that kiss that wasn't there. That's all...that's all.

Quinn drove through the snow-white streets of the city. Twinkling lights hanging from rooftops, in windows and on doors cast kaleidoscopic colors across the brilliant white night.

Looking outward, with the city wrapped in purity, the bleakness, grit and grime were temporarily camouflaged, turning what looked like a war zone most of the time into a Hallmark card.

The windshield wipers swished hypnotically back and forth, pulling him under their spell, tossing his thoughts back...and forth.

He was glad for her. Really. Maxine deserved all the happiness. André seemed like a nice enough brother.

Then why did it feel like he'd lost another something special in his life that mattered? First his mother, then his sister, now Maxine. All in different ways, but the end result was the same.

How long would it be before Nikita was gone, too?

Where was he with that? Part of him wanted to grab on to everything he could from his relationship with her, not take for granted that it would always be there. The way he had in the past.

Then there was that other part, the part that had taken the full force of his hurts. That part told him, "Keep it close to your chest. Don't let go, 'cause when you do, you lose."

Yeah, that was the unwritten rule of the street, the code of survival, what had kept him safe. And every time he strayed away from that clear, cool, irrefutable logic, he paid the price.

He went home that night and buried his confusion, his fears and his pain deep within Nikita, for those moments washing them all away.

And Nikita knew he loved her with every movement of his powerful body, every moan, every utterance of her name. Even if he never said the words.

They never spoke of that night again. Because everything was going to be all right.

Chapter 24

Just Like That

The club was quiet after rehearsal. Everyone was packing up to leave. Nick pulled up a chair, sat next to Quinn and plopped the cassette tape in his hand.

"You did some fantastic work, man. We'll be going into the studio in about two weeks. I want this as part of the album."

Quinn looked at the tape in his hand and then at Nick. "You sure?"

"Hey, listen, I told you in the beginning you had talent. All you've done is used what you knew and blown it up. So, yeah, I'm sure." He smiled.

Quinn looked at Nick, the moment of disbelief slowly dissolving into acceptance. His work was actually gonna be on an album. He grinned. "Thanks, Nick. For everything, man. Really."

"You did it." He clapped him on the shoulder. "We'll work out all the financial details to something that we're all comfortable with. I'll have my attorney draw up the agreement papers for you to take a look at."

Quinn nodded.

"In the meantime, I'll be working out the recording schedule.

I should know something definite by next week, so you'll have time to adjust what you have to do."

"No problem. Whenever. I'll be there."

Nick stood. "This could be the start of something big for you, brother. Just hang in."

"Yeah. I will."

"Later. I have to run. See you Wednesday night."

Quinn sat, immobile, digesting what had just happened. Sure, Nick had said he wanted to use his work, but a little twinge of doubt had had him thinking otherwise. Maybe the doubt didn't have anything to do with Nick coming through, but with doubt in himself.

Hey, this was real. His music—the music he'd only heard in his head—was going to be heard by millions of people. Him. Quinten Parker. He wanted to jump up and shout. He'd done it. He'd actually done it.

He picked up his jacket from the back of the chair and headed for the door.

Some celebrating was in order.

Nikita tried to keep her mouth from gaping open as she listened to Lillian.

"I'm planning to retire at the end of the year, Nikita."

"But why? What are you going to do about the magazine?"

Lillian sat down, took off her glasses and put them on top of a stack of papers on her desk. "I've been thinking about that, too. And I'd like to make you an offer."

Nikita's stomach started to jump. "Me? What offer?"

"I'd like you to buy the business from me."

Nikita blinked. "Buy the business—"

"I know you can handle it, Nikita. You've done a remarkable job during the past year and a half. Sales are up. Circulation has expanded. You've hired an excellent assistant. The issues look wonderful. The entire business is running more smoothly because of you. You have vision, Nikita, a strong will, and determination that is rarely seen in someone so young. I have no doubt that you'll continue to do a fantastic job. And most of all, I trust you. If you don't buy it, I'll just let it go."

She swallowed down the knot in her throat. "That means a great deal to me, Ms. Ingram. I wanted to do a good job." She sucked on her bottom lip, slowly shaking her head. "But I don't have the kind of money to buy your business from you." She looked at Lillian with sad eyes, the brief moment of elation vaporizing.

Lillian smiled. "I'll sell the business to you for a hundred thousand dollars." She stood up, crossed the semi-carpeted floor and took her wool coat from the brass coatrack by the door. She turned to Nikita. "You're a resourceful young woman, Nikita. You'll think of something."

Nikita tapped her ankle-booted foot against the wood floor, while her recently French-manicured nails tapped out a beat on her desktop.

Her thoughts raced around in her head, keeping a steady pace with her heart. One minute her spirits soared when she envisioned herself as a publisher. A real live publisher! She looked toward the wide plate-glass window. This was her dream. She was here. She'd made all the right moves, all the right choices, and she'd gotten what she'd desired.

But in the next breath, reality took a choke hold, squeezing and squeezing the dream until it burst. Where would she ever get the money? If she borrowed it from a bank, she'd be paying it back for the rest of her life.

But she had to have it. No matter what it took. An opportunity of a lifetime had been handed to her on a platter. She wouldn't blow it.

Yes. She would find a way. Whatever it took.

Dre had set up shop in his apartment to cut down on overhead. The small business loan that Maxine had helped him get through the bank had financed the purchase of three video cameras, a stockpile of tapes, an enviable computer system and his business license.

He'd drafted tons of introduction letters to all of the major insurance companies and corporations in the tri-state area of New York, New Jersey and Connecticut.

In less than four months after Systemwide Investigations had officially opened for business, he had more cases than he could handle. Two of his former coworkers helped him out part-time, but if business kept up at this pace he'd have to start looking for some more help.

He was feeling good. Back in charge of his life. Again. The only thing missing was his wife at his side.

He pushed out a breath and turned off the computer. Every time he talked to Maxine about setting a date, she always came up with "Not now," "We have time," "What's the rush?" answers.

He was beginning to think that, maybe, she really didn't want to get married at all.

Naw. Maxine had always been straight with him. If it wasn't what she wanted, she would have said so.

Wouldn't she?

Val pedaled on the stationary bike in the gym, building up a sheen of sweat. "So, when are you going to set a date, girl? I'm dying to go wedding shopping."

Maxine put down the five-pound weights and wiped her face with a light blue towel. She draped it around her neck.

"I don't know, Val." She looked away.

Val stopped pedaling. "What's up, Maxie?"

Maxine heaved a sigh. "I don't know, Val. I…just… I'm just not sure."

"Sure about what…when to set the date, how you feel about Dre, or if you should get married at all?"

"If that was a multiple-choice question, you forgot 'All of the above.'"

Val hopped down off the bike and took a seat next to Maxine on a wooden bench. "You want to talk about it?"

"I just don't know if I'm doing the right thing. If Dre is even the right one." She dropped her hands between her thighs. "I just got caught up in all the fantasy, ya know. The white dress, church full of people, organ music, the whole nine. But… I'm just not sure if it's what I want."

"Don't you mean *who* you want?" Val put her hand on top of Maxine's knee. "You gotta let go, Maxie. Maybe Dre isn't the one, but let that reason stand on its own. Not because you have some notion that Quinten Parker is gonna come ridin' in on his white horse and sweep you away. It only works like that in romance novels and on television. This is the real deal, girlfriend."

Maxine covered her face with her hands. "I don't know what to do, Val. I care about, Dre...a lot. I don't want to hurt him. I could probably make him very happy."

"But would you be happy? Let it go, Maxie...and you know what I mean. For your own sake. And one way or the other you have to be straight with Dre, before you *do* hurt him."

Quinn made a quick trip uptown. He felt like massaging himself with the essence of the neighborhood. Inhale the aromas, move to the pulse, drink in the camaraderie.

Driving along Malcolm X Boulevard, he caught a glimpse of all the familiar hangouts, all the regulars in their regular spots.

It had been a while since he'd been to the old haunts. His trips were limited to just working for Remy, and even that had been cut back. T.C. had his own area to run, and from what he'd heard he was doing a damned good job.

He parked in front of B.J.'s and got out. He could already hear the music coming from the beat-up jukebox every time somebody swung through the blacked-out door.

A knot of young brothers were standing near the entrance when he approached, whiffs of smoke hanging over their heads like stagnant cumulus clouds.

One of them, with a red-and-white bandanna tied around his head, pants hanging low on his young, narrow hips, seemed to be the leader, as the others hung on his every word and mimicked his "don't give a damn" stance.

New crop.

Quinn looked them over, instinctively adjusting his body, the rhythm of his stride, the angle of his head, realigning himself with the cool, controlled melody of the street, becoming one with the unheard sounds.

They all gave him a look as he approached the door, his eyes cutting across all five brown, yellow, black and in-between faces at once, and they seemed to almost imperceptibly step back.

"Whatsup?" he acknowledged in a low mumble, not waiting for but expecting the same in return.

"Whatsup," they each rejoined out of sync.

Respect. He hadn't lost it.

Quinn pushed through the doors and immediately felt at home, as if he'd been sent away and had finally returned to familiar surroundings.

Smoke, stale liquor, cheap perfume and burnt onion rings greeted him like old friends. The semi-darkness, still hiding the stains, scratches, nicks and peeling paint, welcomed him into its warmth.

Home.

"Hey, brotherman. Long time," Turk greeted, still wearing the same stained undershirt.

Quinn smiled and slid into a vacant seat at the bar. "How's it goin', man?"

"All good. The usual?"

"Yeah, and make it a double."

Turk's bushy brows rose. "What's the occasion? Never seen you take down more than one Jack at a time." He chuckled, pouring the drink with the deftness of experience.

"Feel like celebratin' tonight, Turk. Things are changin'. Know what I mean?"

"So long as they good changes, brotherman. Here ya go." He placed the glass in front of Quinn. "Hear anything else about what happened wit yo sista?"

"We got the lawyers workin' on it." Turk didn't need to know that the police department was trying to settle out of court to avoid a trial and yet another police cover-up scandal. So far they'd kept it out of the papers, but Nikita kept saying that the fastest way to get results was to go to the press. He was beginning to believe her. But the fact was, he didn't want Lacy's memory spread all over the place for people to be eyeballing, because then the questions would start again and the dam that he'd been working on sealing shut would burst open again.

"Remy in the back?"

"Last I saw, yeah."

Quinn placed a ten spot on the table. "Later, man."

"Take it easy. Don't be no stranger. You know yo money's good 'round here." He laughed.

"You gon be on an album? No shit."

Quinn chuckled. "Yeah, for real, man."

Remy shook his head and smiled. "Who woulda thought it?" He looked at Quinn through the smoke of his cigarette. "Didn't know you had it in ya." He tapped a long ash into a cutoff can that he used for an ashtray. "Knew you was gon be 'bout somethin', just didn't know what." He coughed a smoker's cough. "Don't forget yo friends now, when you get big and famous. Just mention old B.J.'s when you get yo Oscar or whatever they called."

Quinn laughed. "Yeah, I will. Listen—" he pushed up from the lopsided wooden stool "—I gotta roll."

"See you Friday night, right?"

"No doubt."

Riding down 135th Street, he glanced at Maxine's building. He wanted to stop, but didn't. Her fiancé might be there, and he didn't feel like trying to be nice to the brother.

He hadn't seen or spoken to Max since Christmas. He kind of missed her, and knew that she would have all the right things to say. She'd be thrilled for him, and make his special moment even more special.

He kept driving.

Nikita could make it special, too.

Nikita felt as if she was walking on hot coals as she paced the length of the hardwood floors of the living room. Somehow, she'd have to convince Quinn to help her, and maybe, if all else failed, her parents. She couldn't let this chance slip through her fingers.

She checked her watch. It was already eleven and no sign of Quinn. She hoped this wasn't going to be one of those nights where he stayed out until the sun came up.

She heard an engine cut off and ran to the window.

"Here he comes. Thank goodness." She knew she couldn't hold on to this until tomorrow.

Quinn trotted up the steps, making just enough noise to let Mrs. Finch know he was home.

Nikita practically leaped into his arms as soon as he opened the door.

He started laughing. "What's with you, Little Bit?"

"I have something exciting to tell you."

"Must be the day for good news. Let's hear yours." He took off his bold orange fleece Chicago Bulls warm-up jacket and tossed it across the couch. Before he got a chance to sit down, she launched into her story.

"So the deal is, the magazine business can be yours if you can come up with a hundred grand?"

"Exactly." She let out a breath, stopped her pacing and plopped down on the couch beside him.

"So… How you gonna get it?"

"That's just it," she hedged. "I don't know."

Quinn stretched out his long legs and crossed them at the ankles. He leaned his head back and closed his eyes. He had a few thousand stashed away. He'd been ready to use it to help Maxine. But she hadn't needed it. She'd figured it out on her own. Nick had said there'd be some loot involved with this music deal. He could probably throw in part of that.

"Quinn!" She nudged him in the rib with her elbow. "Don't you dare go to sleep on me."

He slowly opened his eyes. "I ain't sleepin', just thinkin'. How soon you need this money?"

Her heart started to beat faster. "The end of the year, if not sooner."

He stood up. "I could probably lend you some of it. The rest you gonna have to figure out yourself. I got some of it, and since Nick offered to buy my recording, I'll be gettin' some more."

Her eyes widened and she let out an earsplitting screech. She jumped up straight into his arms, wrapping her arms and legs around him.

"I knew it would happen! I knew it, knew it, knew it," she babbled, planting kisses all over his face.

Quinn was laughing so hard he almost dropped her. "Woman, you goin' crazy, or what?"

"Yes. Crazy about you, baby." Her eyes softened. "I knew you could do it, Quinn. All those months of hard work paid off. There's no telling where this could take you."

"Things ain't gonna change that much. I'm still the same person."

She gave him a big kiss on the lips. "Of course things are going to change, silly—for the better. You'll see. Success changes everyone."

Chapter 25

It's Just So Hard

"Max, we need to talk," Dre said, sitting on the edge of her bed.

Maxine stretched her long, nude body and curled on her side. "About what?" she mumbled, totally satiated from their hours-plus of much needed sex.

"About us, Max."

Uh-oh. She squeezed her eyes shut for a hot minute, took a breath and sat up, pulling the floral-pattern sheet up to cover her apple-sized breasts.

"I'm listening."

He turned, angling his body to face her. "You've been wearing that ring for six months, Max. And every time I mention setting a date, you go into your bag of excuses, why 'now is not a good time to discuss it.' Now. Tonight is the time, Max. I get the feeling that marrying me is not really what you want to do."

Her throat tightened when she looked into that Michael Jordan look-alike face. He loved her. Really loved her. And as much as she'd tried, she didn't feel the same way.

"Dre, I—"

He held up his hand. "Don't. Don't give me a long story and try to save my feelings. Just answer me in one simple word, Max. Do you want to marry me, yes or no?"

She drew her knees up to her chest and lowered her head. "No," she mumbled into the softness of the cotton sheets.

Dre filled his lungs with much needed air, nodded his head and stood. "That's all you had to say, baby."

She watched him through tear-filled eyes as he kept his back to her while getting dressed.

Finally he turned around and looked down at her. He reached out his right hand and caressed her damp cheek. "It was good, Maxine Sherman. You were good for me. I'll always remember that. But your heart was never really all there for me. I thought I could make you love me the way I love you. But that's a hard thing when your woman's heart is with someone else."

"Dre—"

He shook his head. "I always knew. I saw it in your eyes and it scared the hell outta me. But I figured once we were married you'd forget." He straightened. "That'll never happen, Max, until you deal with how you really feel."

He picked up his nylon windbreaker from the back of a kitchen chair that she'd pulled into the room. "Hope you find what you're looking for, Max."

He turned, never looked back and walked out.

Parris ran her hand along the rows of suits and dresses in her closet. "Why don't you ask your parents for the money, Niki?" she asked into the mouth of the closet that resembled a designer's warehouse.

Nikita rested her head on her palm. "Believe me, I've thought about it, and if I don't come up with some other miracle, I just may have to."

Parris turned around, holding up a silver sequined cocktail dress with spaghetti straps.

"There's my dress!" Nikita sputtered, pointing her finger at the shimmering creation.

"Really? I had it so long I thought it was mine, chile. You want it back?"

"At some point," she answered dryly.

She returned it to its spot in the closet. "So how much is Quinn giving you?"

"He said fifteen thousand. He's using his savings and some of the money from the record deal."

"That's a pretty generous loan, Niki. I mean besides the money from the deal, where did Quinn get all that money from?"

"He said he'd been saving it."

Parris arched a brow. "Hmm."

"What's that supposed to mean?"

"Not a thing. Anyway, why don't you just take out a bank loan? I mean, Nick and I would love to lend it to you, but we have everything tied up in the club and he's in the process of trying to open another one on the coast."

"I appreciate the thought." She blew out a breath. "I've thought about the bank thing, but I don't want to get myself into that kind of debt, Parris. If anything goes wrong, I'll be liable and could lose everything."

Parris sat down on the paisley chaise lounge. "People take out business loans every day. If you're going to be a businesswoman, then you're going to have to start thinking like one."

Nikita tossed around the advice for a moment. "Maybe," she said finally. "I'll think about it as a last resort."

"Even the money that you get from Quinn and your parents, if you decide to ask them, you're still going to have to pay it back sometime."

"That's different."

Parris simply looked at her friend, at a loss for something to say. Nikita was so accustomed to everything being handed to her that she didn't know any other way. She sighed. Nikita would just have to learn sometime. Even if it was the hard way.

"So you finally told him, huh?" Val asked from across the cafeteria table.

"Yeah." Maxine stuck her fork in her salad, which she'd

drenched in diet Russian dressing. "I think he took it pretty well. I'm the one who's all bent out of shape. I just feel so awful about how everything turned out."

"It had to come to a head at some point. Would you have preferred to have that conversation after you married the man?"

"Definitely not." She ate a mouthful of salad.

"You'll be all right, girl. It'll just take some time. And you have plenty to keep you busy."

Maxine smiled. "You got that right. I'm about beat. The girl who helps me out is cool, but there's still so much to do. I'm gonna hang on to this gig at the bank a little while longer, and then I'm callin' game."

"Still thinking about opening an office?"

Maxine took a breath. She'd been thinking about that, all right. Now that it was over between her and Dre and she was planning to leave the bank, anyway, now was the time to tell Val what she'd been thinking.

Maxine put her fork down, crossed her forearms on the table, and leaned forward. "Val, I've been thinkin' about…not just leavin' the bank…but leavin' New York."

"Max, you can't be serious."

Maxine slowly nodded. "I am. Val, this past year and a half has kicked my butt. After Lacy was killed nothin' seemed the same no more. Ya know. I figured gettin' married would plug up the hole in my life, but hey…you see what happened with that." She fiddled with her water glass, slowly spinning it around. "And I just need to put some distance between me and the memories. Go somewhere and start fresh."

Val looked at her childhood friend—all grown up, successful, smart, funny as all hell, pretty and so very unhappy.

"Girl, lemme tell you something. You could go from here to the ends of the earth and it'd never be far enough away to keep your heart from feelin' the way it does."

She reached out and covered Maxine's hand, ceasing the spinning.

"You're going to have to find a way to settle what's inside,

Maxine, or you'll be running for the rest of your life. But, sister friend, if this is what you think you need, I'm behind you one hundred percent. And you know it."

"Thanks. I can't ask for more than that."

Quinn and Nikita sat across the paper-piled desk listening to Sean and Khendra bring them up-to-date.

"The district attorney had set up a complete investigation of the incidents surrounding your sister's death. Their conclusion is that it was accidental," Khendra said.

Quinn reared up from his seat.

Sean held up his hand.

"But, in order to avoid a civil suit, they have agreed to pay you damages for wrongful death, if you're willing to settle out of court," she continued. "Internal Affairs has dismissed the two officers involved for attempting to cover up what they'd done. The two boys they arrested have been released and all charges have been dropped."

Quinn was silent. It was Nikita who spoke up.

"In other words, if we keep our mouths shut they'll give us the money without a hassle?"

"Exactly," Sean said. "We could still take this to trial, reject the offer. But as I said before, it could drag on and get very ugly. The P.D. will do whatever it has to, to save as much face as possible. Even if that means trying to discredit your sister in the process. They'll close ranks on us."

Nikita looked at Quinn, whose face was unreadable.

"I don't want that. Make the deal." He stood. "But you'd better squeeze them for every dime. Their blood money will never replace my sister, and draggin' her name through the mud ain't gonna bring her back, either. But if the digits ain't high enough, take 'em to court. I'll just have to handle it."

"Done." Sean closed his portfolio. "What are you willing to settle for?"

"Nothin' less than a mil."

"We'll start at three."

"How long you think this is gonna take?"

"It's hard to say. A couple of months just to work out the deal. Getting the actual money is when the real wait begins."

Chapter 26

Pressin' On

Quinn was finished with his classes at ASCAP. There was no studio time today, and he didn't feel like going to Nikita's office.

Matter of fact, he felt like going there less and less, the same way he felt about going home. And she was starting to complain about that again, too.

He drove down Malcolm X Boulevard, seeing who he could see. Felt like hanging with the fellas for a minute. Get himself grounded again.

He wasn't sure what was happening to him lately. He just felt that he was pretending to be somebody else all the time. Putting on a front.

He slowed as he approached Shug's and spotted T.C. and his crew.

"Yo. T.C.!" He honked the horn.

T.C. turned and, seeing Quinn roll to a stop, moved away from the group and strolled toward the car.

He was still long and lanky, looking like he could use a good meal, Quinn observed. But there was something else about him that he noticed as he approached. There was a new swagger, a defiance, a hardness that he'd never noticed before.

T.C. came around the front of the car and leaned down against the driver's-side window. "Whatsup, man?"

They exchanged the handshake of the day.

"It's all good."

"Ain't seen you around much no more," T.C. said.

Quinn could have sworn he heard a challenge in his voice. "Been busy, brother." He smiled.

T.C. didn't return it. "Yeah, so I hear. You all big-time now that you outta the hood."

"Naw, man. It's still me. Ain't nothin' changed."

"*You* changed." He cut him a look. "Yo, I gotta roll. Take it light." He turned and walked away to rejoin the group, who then moved down the block.

Quinn sat for several minutes in the car, replaying what had just transpired.

Was he different?

Finally he pulled away and headed downtown. Maybe he'd stop by and see Nikita, anyway.

Nikita sat at her desk reviewing a pamphlet about soliciting an international contingent of authors, editors and publishers for a symposium in Nigeria. The group was just forming and needed volunteers to help with the coordination.

She read the information again, her adrenaline flowing like the Nile. She crossed her stockinged legs and began tapping her foot.

It sounded fantastic, something that she definitely wanted to be a part of. She and Quinn could work on it together.

Maybe that was just the thing they needed to get them back on track. Lately he seemed so distant, detached. He was coming home at more normal hours, more or less…since she'd put her foot down. He was working at the studio, and had finished his classes. Things looked as if they were going to work out about his sister's case. Their sex life was great.

She sucked her teeth and sighed. She just couldn't figure him out. She'd done everything within her power to enhance his life, open up new avenues to him, but…

A knock on the door pulled her away from her thoughts.

She pushed away from her desk, crossed the room, the seashell on the end of her lock swinging with her hip-swaying stride. She pulled the door open.

"Maxine..." She sort of frowned in confusion.

"Hey, Nikita. Sorry to bother you. I thought Quinn might be here."

Nikita's gaze moved quickly over Maxine's long, toned form, the mint green linen skirt suit showing off those damned hips and dancer's legs.

"He's not here...at the moment. Come on in. Something I can help you with?"

"No. Not really."

Nikita caught the hitch in her voice. "Everything okay? You...look a little upset."

She smiled and Nikita noticed the little gap between her two front teeth. Men had a thing for that, she'd heard. That and bowlegs. She wasn't sure why, though.

"Everything's cool. Listen, just tell Quinn that I dropped in to say goodbye."

"Goodbye?"

"Yeah. I'm leavin' for San Francisco in the morning. Just wanted to see him before I left."

"Oh." *San Francisco.* "Big move."

"Somethin' like that. Anyway, just tell him for me."

"Sure."

Maxine turned to leave, then turned back. "How are things with Lacy's case?"

Nikita braced her hand against the doorframe. "We've agreed to settle out of court. We just have to see how long it's going to take them to pay, and how much."

"That's good. Glad to hear it. It's been a long time comin'." She smiled again. "Take care, Nikita."

"I will. And good luck," she called out to the retreating form. She shut the door. *Well, if that wasn't the strangest visit. Maxine gone. Hallelujah.* That was the one element in Quinn's life that she feared more than his love of the street— Maxine Sherman. He always said they were "just friends." Ha.

She felt the vibes. And she knew that given the chance something would get going between them. But she'd made sure that never happened. Not on her watch. She had no intention of losing Quinn. Not now. Not ever. She'd worked too hard to get him, and them, to where they were.

With Maxine out of the picture her life became that much simpler.

Maxine walked toward the train station. She shouldn't have gone there. She shouldn't have put herself in that position... facing his woman. But she took a chance. She hadn't heard from Quinn since Christmas, more than six months ago.

Be real, girl. You wanted to see Nikita. Wanted to see *her* face again, and maybe that would, once and for all, knock reality past first base, all the way home.

They were a couple. Nikita and Quinn. Still together. End of story.

Nikita couldn't dial Parris's number fast enough. Parris picked up in time with her answering machine message, and had to shout over Nick's recorded voice.

"Hey, girl. Sorry about that. Just got out of the shower. Hang on a sec." She hugged the phone between her shoulder and her ear, draped a towel around her wet hair, and tugged on the belt of her robe. "Whew. Now, I'm listening."

"Guess who just paid me a visit?"

"Those guys from Publisher's Clearinghouse?"

"Parris...please."

"Okay, okay. Who?"

"Maxine Sherman."

Parris jerked her long neck back, her green eyes squinting. "Say what?"

"You heard me."

She went on to tell Parris about the impromptu visit and Maxine's announcement. "So what do you think about that?"

Parris sat on the edge of the chaise lounge. "Do you really want to know what I think, Nikita? Or is that just a rhetorical question?"

"If you have something to say, tell me."

Parris took a breath. "First of all, I think you're too happy, for all the wrong reasons."

"Too happy! Shouldn't I be?"

"You want to hear me out, or what?"

"Go ahead."

"Maxine, from everything I've gathered, has been a good friend to Quinn for more years than you've even known him. If the man loves you, his friendship with Maxine wasn't going to change that.

"He's lost a lot over the past two years. But you've been so hell-bent on proving something that you haven't taken the time to see what it is that he needed in his life…just your own."

"That's not true."

"Isn't it?"

"Parris, I've only wanted the best for Quinn. To see him reach his potential. If that meant doing some of the things I did, then so be it. Look at where he is now, from when we met."

"Yes. But is he happy? Was all that work, effort and energy really for him, or for you?"

Quinn got halfway to Nikita's office and turned around. What he really needed was some peace and quiet. He knew that wouldn't be the case with Nikita. She'd find something for him to do, or talk him to death.

He headed home, and for the first time in months, he began to write again.

Chapter 27

Your Love Is All I Know

Nikita couldn't have been more surprised to find Quinn at home if the guys from Publisher's Clearinghouse really had paid her a visit.

He was sitting at the piano, intent on putting together what seemed to be a new song. He didn't even hear her come in.

She stood quietly in the doorway just watching him. Her heart seemed to swell in her chest. He was exquisite. From the moment she'd laid eyes on Quinten Parker, she'd thought she'd died and gone to heaven. He was like a black Messiah, with an energy that radiated from him as easy as the air he breathed.

He'd lit a fire in her soul that she couldn't deny. Nor did she want to. She loved this man to the depths of her being. Maybe she had done some things that might have been selfish, but it wasn't because she didn't care. It was because she did. Perhaps too much. And it scared her. Scared her to think that she could ever lose him. He'd been the one constant in her life that mattered. The only thing that made everything in her life seem worthwhile.

* * *

He sensed her presence and slowly turned around on the piano bench. When he saw her standing there in the doorway, looking all soft, tiny and vulnerable, his heart knocked in his chest, and he wondered why he'd been staying away. Maybe not physically, but in spirit. His body had been there, but his heart and soul had been adrift. He wasn't sure for how long.

She'd been good to him—good for him—and he'd been fighting it and her. Keeping that one part of himself out of her reach. Maybe if he just let go…

"Hi," she said in that soft, sexy voice.

"Hey, baby."

She walked toward him, sensing a change in him. Sensing his sudden need for her.

She stood in front of him looking down into his eyes, which seemed to glow with a growing intensity.

His gaze stayed fixed on her while his hands began stroking her waist, her hips, down her thighs, until they found the hem of her skirt, inching it upward.

Her eyes slid shut when his fingers found the waistband of her panty hose and panties beneath, pulling both down her thighs, her legs, until she was completely exposed to him.

She trembled, emitting a soft whimper, a sharp intake of breath when he pulled her close, the tip of his tongue tantalizing the tiny bud until she cried out his name.

And he took…

And took…

There on the hardwood floor, on the slick black leather of the couch, on the plush softness of their mating bed, until there was nothing left for either of them to give.

They slept, then. Wrapped in each other's arms.

And she pushed all thoughts of her fears to the back of her mind.

Along with her promise to Maxine.

Val sat next to Maxine in the waiting area of the airport, dreading the moment when her flight would be called. She'd promised herself that she wouldn't cry and make sad matters worse. But Maxie was the last of the old gang. Her one true friend. Now she'd truly be alone.

"Flight number eight seventeen direct to San Francisco is now boarding," the nasal-toned announcer said. "Those with small children, seniors and those needing assistance, please come to gate B."

Val and Maxine looked at each other, both fighting back tears, trying to smile.

Maxine sniffled. "I won't start if you won't." Her smile trembled at the edges.

"Then don't start," she uttered in a shaky voice.

"Passengers in seats eighty through sixty-five, please begin boarding."

Slowly Maxine stood. She picked up her carry-on bag and her pocketbook. She turned toward Val. "You promised," she choked, seeing the tears thread down Val's high-arched cheeks.

"I lied."

They embraced long and hard, as only true-to-the-heart friends can.

"Be happy, Max," she said, pressing a kiss to her cheek.

"And you come see me. Anytime. You hear?" She wiped away her tears.

"Count on it." Val ran a finger under her eyes.

Moving away, hands outstretched, their fingertips touching in those final moments...

Then Maxine hurried off and was soon swallowed up in the knot of boarding bodies.

As the jet soared out of JFK, Maxine looked down, as the only city she knew began to disappear beneath her.

Quinn had never called to say goodbye.

"Sounds good, Nikita, but it don't sound like somethin' I want to get involved in right now. I told you that before." He stepped into his jeans, and pulled his Polo jacket from the closet and tossed it on the chair.

He moved around the bedroom, picking up discarded clothes

and putting them in a pile. Got his latest pair of Air Jordans out of the closet and put them on.

"Quinn, this symposium is something that's never been tried before. It's history in the making, baby." She huffed and put her hands on her hips. "Just think about having black writers, editors and publishers from all over the world coming together in one place to exchange ideas and put mechanisms in place to further African-American literature.

"Besides, it's not something that's going to happen right away. It'll be at least a couple of years down the road just to get everything and everybody together."

He angled his head in her direction, seeing the set of her smooth jaw and the determination in her light brown eyes.

It would be easier to just say *Yeah* than to spend all his time and energy debating it. She'd never let it rest, otherwise. Once Niki got her mind set on something there was no turning her around. Damn. She'd been at him about that thing for the past couple of weeks.

"I'll think about it. But I ain't makin' no promises. Got my hands full as it is. Going back in the studio to finish up the album. That's gonna take a while. Plus I got other stuff to do, ya know." He gathered up the clothes from the floor.

She put on her best "Do this for me, Quinn" voice. "There's a planning committee meeting in three weeks."

He cut his eyes in her direction and just grinned. He knew perfectly well what she was trying to do. He put on his jacket. "Yeah, I hear ya, Nik. Later. Okay?"

"Try not to be too late," she called out after him.

She spun around and flopped across the bed, a big smile brightening her cinnamon-toned face. He'd do it. Of course he would. He hadn't denied her anything…yet. And since things seemed to be going her way, she'd decided to pay her parents a visit and somehow get them to give her the money for the magazine.

Man. If it wasn't one thing with that woman it was something else. Every time he turned around she was shoving something else in his face. Just when he figured things were cool. *Bam!* Here she comes with more stuff.

He turned up the volume on the car stereo until the sounds of R. Kelly boomed through the speakers.

He dropped his clothes off at the cleaners, then headed uptown, figuring he'd hang out at B.J.'s, see what was happening. Then he changed his mind, as if suddenly tugged in the opposite direction, or something had whispered in his ear, *"Hey, Q."* A sense of Maxine came to him, just as strong as if she'd been sitting right next to him.

He shook off the strange sensation and headed toward Chambers Street. Sometimes Maxine worked on Saturdays. Maybe he'd catch her at the office.

The closer he got to his destination, the better he started feeling. That tightness that had gotten a lock on his insides seemed to loosen.

It had been so long since he'd seen her, heard her voice. He knew he should have stopped by long before now, but the thought that she'd be holed up with her husband-to-be had always turned him around.

She'd stopped calling long ago and might not have much to say to him now, after the way he'd dissed her. It wasn't right. And he knew it.

He found a parking space across the street from the bank. He watched the door, seeing people come and go, and for a minute he had second thoughts.

Finally he shut off the music and got out. Darting in and out of traffic, he jogged across the street and pushed through the revolving door.

He walked past the teller to the new accounts department and spotted her desk. Someone else was sitting there.

He stopped for a moment to get his bearings. Maybe that wasn't her desk. Or maybe she'd moved to a new area. He walked toward the woman, who had her blond head down, reviewing some papers on her desk.

She looked up when Quinn's dark shadow fell over her.

"Yes. May I help you?" Sparkling blue eyes focused on him.

"Yeah. I'm lookin' for Maxine Sherman. She usually sits here."

"Oh." She pursed her red-painted lips. "Ms. Sherman is no longer with us."

"No longer with you?"

"No. She left about three weeks ago. Did you open an account or a loan with her? Perhaps one of the other officers can help you."

"Naw. Thanks." He turned and walked out, wondering why Maxine would just up and quit her job. Maybe that traveling thing was really taking off.

He trotted around an express bus that had stopped for a red light and got back in his ride.

Since he intended to go uptown anyway, he'd just stop by her crib. And it was just too damned bad if *André* was there. He'd just have to chill a minute.

He pulled up in front of the building and got out of the car, the locks clicking into place with the tiny telltale beep.

Still hadn't fixed the front door, he noticed. He went right up.

He stood in front of her door for a minute, getting himself together before he knocked. He knew she was going to read him for staying out of touch. But he could take the weight. Actually, he was looking forward to it.

He knocked.

And waited.

And rang the bell.

Then he heard footsteps coming down that long, narrow hallway that he knew so well.

"*Sí?* Who eez it?"

He frowned, looked at the apartment number on the door. *That wasn't Maxine's voice.*

"Uh, I'm lookin' for Maxine Sherman."

The door creaked open, the security chain in place. A tiny, white-haired Puerto Rican woman peeked out.

"No Maxine here. Gone. Move away." She shut the door before he could say anything else.

He stood there, stunned. A pulse began to pound in his temple. His thoughts started jumping around.

Where was she? She'd quit her job. Moved out of her crib. And hadn't said a goddamned thing.

He zipped in and out of the weekend traffic, challenging lights and pedestrians, until he pulled to a rubber-burning halt in front of B.J.'s and jumped out.

Dismissing the pleasantries, he breezed by the group outside the door, passed Turk and went straight to the back, after being checked by Smalls.

"Yo. Sylvie." He signaled from across the murky room. The usual group was assembled around the ratty green felt table with the dull single bulb hanging over their heads. Several men looked up, grunting in acknowledgment, but quickly returned to the game at hand.

Sylvie sashayed across the room, her skintight sky-blue dress one with her body.

"Hey, baby. You're early. What's up?" She moved out of the twisting shadows into the dull yellow light.

"You seen Maxine around lately?" His chest pumped in and out, seeking some fresh air amid the stale stench of the back room.

"Naw. Heard somethin' 'bout she moved a coupla weeks back. Ain't sure, though." She shrugged. "Ya'll was tight. I should be askin' you." She popped her gum.

"Thanks, Sylvie. Check ya later."

Maxine gone.

He couldn't get it together. He just drove around for the next few hours, aimlessly.

A heaviness settled over him, a sadness that he couldn't explain. It felt like something, another part of him, was gouged out.

It never occurred to him that Maxine would ever be *gone.* Really gone. Not *his* Maxine.

Maybe she'd just moved to a bigger crib. Maybe she moved in with André. Damn. Maybe she was married already.

He found himself back at B.J.'s, located a quiet corner booth, ordered a burger and fries and a round of drinks.

"What in the world makes you think you can run a magazine, Nikita?" her mother asked, demurely sipping tea from her favorite cup.

"I know it. Ms. Ingram knows I can do it. I've been running the business virtually by myself."

Her father returned his coffee cup to its saucer. He cleared his throat. "You've disappointed your mother and me terribly, Nikita. We had plans for you. Worked hard to build a solid future for you."

He puffed out his chest and Cynthia smiled a secret smile behind the rim of her teacup.

"But you were always determined, Nikita." He swallowed. "I've always admired that in you."

Cynthia's eyes widened.

Nikita's throat tightened. She tugged on her bottom lip with her teeth.

"Before I make a decision, I want to meet with Ms. Ingram. I'll want my accountant to go over her books and do some projections for the next five years."

Her heart was racing. He was going to give her the money! Oh, God, she was going to have her dream.

Cynthia couldn't stand it another minute. "Lawrence, are you sure you want to do this? I mean, after all, she's asking for an enormous amount of money. She has no experience—"

"Yes, Cynthia, I'm very sure. *We* are going to do this for our daughter."

Cynthia's back straightened. She put down her cup and got up from the table. "Do what you want. I don't want to hear about it when it all falls apart, or she changes her mind and wants to leap off to some other foolish lark." She stormed out of the dining room.

They both watched her walk away. Nikita saddened. Lawrence resigned.

"She'll come around." He stretched out his saffron-toned hand, covering her soft brown one. He patted it gently.

"I'm going to make this work, Daddy. I promise you."

"I know I may have seemed harsh, overbearing and distant over the years. But I've always loved you, Nikita. More than I've ever said. You have been my pride and joy. Maybe I pushed you, *we* pushed you, too hard. But we thought it was for the best."

He swallowed, searching for the words that had lived within

him for far too long. "When you came back, even though I was upset, I was glad to have you home again. Then when you moved in with Quinn I was devastated, but I couldn't help admiring your determination."

He stood and slowly shook his graying head. "Even though I still think you can do much better than Quinn, I realized after you both left here at Christmas that if you really love someone you have to love them enough to let them go, spread their wings and make their own way."

Tears flowed down her cheeks. In all of her twenty-seven years, her father had never told her how he truly felt.

"Daddy, I've waited so long to hear you say that. I grew up believing that you didn't care. That I was just someone you took care of because you had to."

He walked over to her and she stood up, moving into the warmth of her father's embrace. She pressed her head against his chest, inhaling the familiar scent of his Old Spice aftershave. And she felt like a little girl again, as if her daddy could make all the bad things go away, not just make her go away.

"I...love...you, Nikita," he said tightly.

"I love you, too, Daddy."

Nikita tried to stay awake, to share her news with Quinn. But she couldn't keep her eyes open. The last time her bleary eyes looked at the clock it was four-thirty.

He wasn't quite sure how he'd made it home in one piece. He was wasted. Remy had tried to convince him to stay, not to drive in his condition, but he'd refused. He had to get home. He'd promised.

He felt his way along the staircase up to the bedroom and stripped out of his clothes, tossing them in a heap on the floor. He crawled into bed, his stomach and his head spinning like a top. He'd never let himself get like this before, and wasn't quite sure why he had this time.

He snuggled against the warm body next to him, and began drifting, images of his day floating through his head.

* * *

He'd been drinking, Nikita realized through the haze of sleep, the odors of cigarette smoke and alcohol enveloping her. She tried to inch away without disturbing him, and then he mumbled something that set her heart and her conscience to racing. Her petite body stiffened.

"Can't…find…Maxie. Maxine's gone, Nik." He laid his head on the cushion of her breasts. "Just…gone."

Chapter 28

All That Glitters

"The district attorney and Internal Affairs have settled on two point five million, if you sign a waiver holding up your end of the agreement not to go to the press," Sean said, passing the lengthy document across the desk to Quinn.

He looked it over, making sure to read the fine print. Here it was, Lacy's whole life reduced to a piece of paper. All that she was. All that she could have been. Just some lines in black and white.

He started to feel sick. His stomach roiled and his head began to pound. He reached for a pen and signed, pushing the paper back across the desk.

Without another word he got up and left, never wanting to set foot in those offices again.

Nikita rushed around the office, getting everything in order for her assistant, who was going to cover for the rest of the afternoon. Monica was a treasure. From the moment she'd hired her, she'd jumped in with both feet. With Quinn staying away from the magazine more and more, Monica's help was invaluable.

He'd been spending a lot of time away from everything lately.

He was back to those early morning hours, and she'd heard from Parris he'd even missed a few rehearsals. He hardly spoke, and if he did it was brief and uninformative. It was as if he'd withdrawn to a place that she couldn't reach. She was beginning to worry. The only time they seemed to communicate anymore was when they were in bed.

But tonight he'd promised her that he would come to the meeting about the symposium and then have dinner with her and her parents in celebration. Her father was completely satisfied with his accountant's findings and he was going to finance the balance of the money she needed.

By this time tomorrow when she presented Lillian with her check, she would be the CEO and publisher of *Today's Woman* magazine!

She had big plans. If everything went according to them, she intended to start publishing books in another year. From the few meetings that she'd already attended, she'd seen just how many talented black authors there were out there with no outlets for their work. She intended to change that.

Val stood on the corner of Chambers Street, looking to hail a yellow cab. She had an appointment with Sean and Khendra in twenty minutes. He'd offered her a position with his firm as a paralegal until she finished her degree and passed the bar. Then she would work for him on a full-time basis as a real live attorney. A cold gust of wind whipped around her. She pulled her coat collar up around her neck. Winter was on its way, for sure. You could smell the crisp air, see it in the heavy gray clouds.

On her ride to Midtown, seeing the cars, buses and people whiz by, she thought that maybe it was time to make that promised trip to the coast to see Maxine. Get away from the hustle and bustle of New York City to the balmy air of San Francisco.

From everything that Maxine had said it was the most beautiful city, with its hilly streets, trolley cars and old-world charm. Her business was doing extremely well and she was feeling good again, about herself and her life.

Val spotted a man's hat sailing down the street.

She smiled. Yeah, maybe it was time to make that trip.

The cab pulled to a stop in front of the building that housed Sean's office.

"Eight-fifty," the cabbie grunted in some accent she couldn't place.

Val paid her fare and got out.

As she walked toward the building's entrance she could have sworn she saw Quinn getting into his car a little farther down the street. But she couldn't be sure without her glasses. She squinted, and he came into focus.

"Quinn!"

He looked for oncoming traffic and opened the door.

"Quinn!"

Her shout was blown away by the force of the wind.

He got in the car and drove off.

Quinn headed uptown, taking the FDR by rote. He didn't want to think about anything at the moment, or talk to anyone.

Had he done the right thing by just giving in? Maybe he should have put up more of a fight. But there just didn't seem to be any more fight left in him. For anything. And that wasn't like him. Between dealing with Nikita and her wants and needs, the demands of the music business, and still trying to keep a piece of himself for himself, there just wasn't anything there.

He didn't even know who he was anymore. There wasn't anybody he could really talk to, who would understand. Nikita would just tell him to try harder. And tell him how wonderful he was.

That wasn't what he needed, hadn't in a long time. He just needed someone to listen. Really listen to him, without asking anything in return. For just a minute.

He pulled up in front of Shug's Fish Shack, and as usual there was a line, even in the cold. He smiled. At least some things never changed.

He got out, suddenly having a taste for some fried whiting, and was happy and surprised to see T.C. on line, with his arm around a girl, no less. *Hmm.*

Walking up to him, he clapped him on the shoulder.

"Hey, man. How's it goin'?"

T.C. turned, and that familiar smile spread across his face. "Q. Whatsup, man? Long time." He really seemed glad to see him.

"How 'bout that." He put his hand on T.C.'s shoulder. "I'm really sorry about that, man. Know what I mean?"

T.C. looked at his one-time brother, father, mentor. He smiled, just a little bit. "Hey, it's cool. I'm in college now. Started in September." He beamed. "Followed your advice, ya know."

"Way to go, man. That's the move." Quinn nodded, feeling a lot better, as if he'd made a difference. "Been waitin' long?"

"No doubt." He grinned, using Quinn's phrase. "This is Tichia."

"Hey, Tichia."

She smiled a little-girl smile.

T.C. tightened his arm around her thin shoulders, grinning with pride. "Gettin' cold quick, man. Hope we ain't got to wait too much longer."

"I hear ya."

"Bet Maxie ain't worried 'bout no cold in sunny Frisco."

Quinn's whole body tensed. "Say what?"

T.C. kinda frowned. "Maxine. San Francisco. No cold weather." He looked at Quinn's startled expression. "Didn't you know she booked?"

"Yeah, yeah. Just caught me in the mix, that's all." He smiled. "Lost her number so I haven't been in touch in a while."

"Yeah. I ain't got it, either."

"Sure like to kick it with her for a minute. Ya know, for old time's sake."

"I hear ya."

The line inched up a bit and they moved forward.

"Hey, maybe her friend, what's that chick's name… Veronica—"

"Val." His heart started to pound.

"Yeah, yeah, that's the one. Maybe she has it."

Quinn's thoughts started running in circles. Why hadn't he thought of Val long before now? He had to find a way to get in touch with her. Knew she'd moved out of the neighborhood ages ago. Somewhere in Brooklyn. Then he remembered that she was the one who put them in touch with Sean. Maybe she had her digits.

"Listen, man. I'ma roll. Ain't got the patience for this tonight."

T.C. chuckled. "I hear ya."

They did the one-arm hug. "Check ya later."

"Yeah, stay in touch," T.C. called out, briefly remembering.

Quinn hopped in his car and pulled up his cell phone. Hunting through his wallet, he found Sean's business card and punched in the numbers. Maybe Sean hadn't left yet.

The receptionist picked up and informed him that Sean and Khendra were in a meeting.

"This is important. Could you please just tell him I'm on the line?"

"Hold please. I'll see if he'll pick up, Mr. Parker."

Sean's voice came on the line moments later. "Quinn. Anything wrong?"

"Naw. Sorry to bug you… But I just needed to know if you had a way of getting in touch with Val. You know, the one who recommended you to me and Maxine."

"As a matter of fact she's right here. Want to hold on a minute?"

"Yeah. Sure."

He held his breath. The blood was roaring through his head.

"Quinn? This is Val. Is something wrong?"

"Val." He breathed a sigh of relief. "Listen, uh, I was wonderin' if you'd spoken to Max. If you had a number or somethin' for her."

"Yes, I do. Hold on." She rummaged through her bag and pulled out her phone book. "Got a pen?"

"Yeah, go 'head."

She recited the phone number. "You want the address?"

"Yeah, gimme that, too." He wrote it down. "Listen, thanks, Val. Uh, how is she?"

"She's fine, Quinn. Movin' on, as they say. But I guess you can find that out for yourself. Talk to you, Quinn." She hung up.

Quinn replaced the cell phone on the cradle, stared at the information on the tiny slip of off-white paper, and saw that his hand was shaking.

* * *

Nikita had gone straight from the office to the meeting in the Chelsea area of downtown Manhattan with the intention of meeting Quinn, as he'd promised. The meeting lasted for two hours. Quinn never showed up.

Standing outside with the wind whipping around her, she contemplated beeping him, then decided against it. He was a grown man and had to take responsibility for his actions without being reminded of what he was supposed to do.

She pushed back the sleeve of her short mink jacket and checked her watch. Seven-thirty. He had half an hour to get to the restaurant for dinner with her parents.

She headed for her car, and a sinking sensation settled in her stomach.

Quinn pulled up to a parking space right in front of the house and got out. He would have tried to call from his cell phone, but he knew that the reception would be terrible, if he was able to reach her at all.

He trotted up the steps, unlocked the apartment door and went inside.

Silence.

Then he remembered his promise to Nikita.

He checked his watch. Seven forty-five. He'd said he'd meet her at eight. He'd already blown that damned meeting and knew he'd have to hear her mouth, anyway. What the hell.

He went straight upstairs to the bedroom and to the phone on the nightstand. Sitting down on the bed, he pulled the piece of paper from his jeans pocket.

For several moments he just stared at the numbers.

Maybe he should just leave well enough alone. She'd moved on, as Val had said, whatever that meant.

But there was still that need, a deep and unyielding need to hear her voice, her laughter, to listen to her tell him, "You go 'head on with your bad self." He smiled at the recollection.

She was the familiar. The roots.

He punched in the numbers and listened to the clicks while the fiber optics kicked into place. His heart pounded.

The phone began to ring. And the answering machine came on.

"Sherman Travel and Tour. No one is available to help you right now. Please leave your message after the beep."

B-e-e-p.

He started to hang up. Just forget it. It obviously wasn't meant to happen. At least not now. But hearing that familiar voice again…

"Hey, Max, this is Quinn. Just checkin' on ya. See how ya don' and all." He paused. "I'll try you again…another time."

Maxine was just walking in the door and heard the tail end of the message, the familiar voice. She dashed across the room and snatched up the phone.

Quinn slowly lowered the receiver, feeling worse than before.

"Quinn!"

He jerked the phone back to his ear.

"Max?"

"Hey, Q."

Her voice washed over him like a soothing balm. His muscles began to relax, and his heart slowed its pace.

"Hey, yourself. Tell me what's good." He leaned back against the pillows and put his sneakered feet right up on the bed. What the hell.

She laughed, that deep, rich chuckle that made him smile. "Some of everythin'," she began, and eased right back into their old routine as if the last time they'd seen each other was yesterday.

He told her about the music contract and she squealed with delight and swore that she was gonna make all her clients buy the album.

They laughed and talked for more than an hour, making time and space slip away.

"So what ever happened with you and André?"

She sighed. "Wasn't for me, ya know. Thought it was. But it just wasn't happenin'."

"Hmm. Know how that is."

"What about Nikita?"

"She's cool. Gettin' ready to buy that magazine that she works for."

"Get out. Ya'll gonna be livin' large." She laughed.

"Ain't nothin' change but the day."

"I hear ya. So when you gonna come out and see a sista?"

He laughed. "I'ma make it a point to do that. Got good hotels around there?"

"Forget hotels. You stay with me. I got plenty of space."

"You got it like that, huh?"

"No doubt."

They both laughed.

"So make plans to come out and let me know."

"I'll do that."

She took a breath, not wanting to let him go, but knew that she had to. "Hey, listen, Q, I gotta run. So call me. Okay?"

His stomach did a slow dance. "No…doubt."

"Good talkin' to you, babe," she whispered.

"You, too."

She hung up before she could say something really stupid, then sat there and stared at the phone. She hadn't asked him why he never said goodbye.

Quinn lay across the bed and stared up at the ceiling, running the conversation over and again in his head.

He threw his arm over his eyes and wondered what life was like in California.

Nikita took a bite of her cherry cheesecake. "He probably just got held up in the studio."

"Hmm," her mother mumbled.

Her father signaled for the check. "Tell him we asked about him."

"I will." She smiled, fuming inside.

They parted at the door, exchanging hugs and promises to call soon. Nikita got in her car and couldn't get home fast enough.

He heard her the moment her key connected with the lock. He thought he was prepared for what he knew was coming. He wasn't.

The shrill whistle of the teakettle pierced in unison with the diatribe that Nikita hurled in Quinn's direction. Her petite body perched on shapely legs, paced with uneven footsteps across the hardwood floor, like a professor lecturing to an errant student.

She spun toward him. "Why do you do this, Quinn?" Her shoulder-length locks swung around her face, following his cat-like gait.

Apparently without a care, which only fueled her fire, Quinn took a short stroll to the far side of the living room and stretched out unceremoniously on the mud-cloth-draped black leather couch. Dark eyes cut at her from beneath his thick lashes. "Why we gotta go through this every time I don't do what you want me to do, be where you want me to be?"

Her light brown eyes widened. She expelled a long, exasperated breath between her teeth. She was the one who stayed up nights wondering where he was, worrying what had happened to him, until exhaustion lured her to sleep.

"We are on the planning committee for one of the biggest publishing events in ages, and you didn't even bother to show up. Not to mention that you never showed up for dinner. I was the one who had to pretend that your no-show was no big deal!"

Which had given her mother the perfect entrée to recite her laundry list of reasons why Quinn was wrong for her. Judging from this latest fiasco, maybe she was right. God, she didn't want her mother to be right. Not this time. Not about Quinn.

She took a breath. "Does it ever occur to you that I may be worried? Does it ever occur to you to call?"

A slow smile lifted the corners of his rich mouth. He eased his six-foot-plus frame to a sitting position. His shoulder-length locks swept the sides of his face, shadowing his dark, chiseled features in an erotic silhouette of light and shadow.

He was feeling too good after talking to Max. He didn't want to lose that sensation by fighting with Nik about something that was over and done with.

"Aw, come on, baby. I'm here now."

His dark eyes sparkled with that old, barely contained passion. He held his hand out to her in an offer of peace and she felt her anger begin to melt like skillet-heated butter.

His touch always aroused a level of sexuality that left her weak. The acceptance of that reality put her in a state of vulnerability, easily susceptible to Quinn's unorthodox lifestyle, which continually wreaked havoc with their lives. The only thing that had changed about Quinn in their two years together was his age.

She refused the olive branch he offered. "I…can't keep living like this, Quinn. I want more than you're willing to give this relationship. I want a man I can count on. Someone who is going to be there for me. Someone who is willing to share his goals and dreams with mine, and together make them come true."

"So this is all about you." His dark eyes narrowed. His voice grew dangerously low. "You sayin' that I don't have goals, that I ain't about nothing? What about what I want? What I need? Huh? Maybe I didn't wanna sit up in your people's faces all night and listen to the bull. Have them treat me like I was somethin' on the bottom of their designer shoes. Ever think of that?"

Nikita flinched. But she realized at that moment that if she backed down again, if she allowed his powers of persuasion to overrule what she truly felt, things would never change.

"What is it that you want, Quinn—to hang in the street till the sun comes up, to make a quick buck doing God knows what?" Her nostrils flared as she sucked in air. "Those seem to be your goals in life, you and that crowd you associate with." She shook her head. Her tone softened. "You have so much potential, so much to offer, and you waste yourself and your talents. You're a gifted musician and a brilliant writer, if you'd just stick with it."

Quinn pushed himself up from his seat and stood towering above her. His voice projected an eerie calm. "You don't know what you're talkin' about. I ain't like you, Niki. I never lived in *white* America. I didn't get to go to private school, or to the *continent*," he singsonged, "when I was seventeen. I was strugglin' for my life! I didn't have a mother or a father who gave a sh— what I did with my life. This is me. All there is. You supposed to love me? Then love me for who I am—not who you figure I oughta be 'cause Moms and Pops say so."

She felt as if she'd been slapped, and a sudden sensation of doom spread through her. "I do love you." She stepped to him.

"I do care what happens to you." Her heart beat faster when he wouldn't meet her eyes. "You've got to know that. If I didn't, do you think it would matter to me what you did, or with whom?" Her eyes frantically scanned the planes of his face.

She so wanted him to just tell her what was in his heart. What he really thought and felt, what dark corner it was that he always turned into and shut her out of. If he would only let his guard down just this once, and let her in.

He smiled a bittersweet smile, caressing her face with his large hand. He gently brushed her trembling lips with the pad of his thumb.

His darkly haunting eyes, eyes that had seen too much, trailed up and down her face, seeing himself through hers. It was then that he realized with vivid clarity that they would always be in two different worlds. How could he ever hope to cross the bridge that separated them? Yet he needed her. His unspoken love for her helped him to face each day, and the decisions that lay ahead of him.

Slowly he lowered his head until his mouth was inches away from hers.

Niki trembled.

When his warm mouth touched hers and his tongue parted her lips, she knew that all she ever wanted was to be with this man— to have him within her—always. She loved him with a desperate yearning that frightened her. She knew he was right about her parents. He was everything she'd been taught to stay away from, a parent's worst nightmare for their daughter. He was their eleven o'clock news.

But she couldn't stay away. Somehow they'd find their way. They'd find a middle ground.

She clung tighter to him.

Without words, Quinn led her upstairs to their bedroom, slowly undressing her along the way. With a patience that belied his need, he took his time, finding a slow, soothing rhythm that stoked the embers of her fire, only to be quenched by his eruption of release.

Quinn gave himself to her, body and soul, as he'd always done before.

She never did see the silent tears that slid down his chiseled cheeks.

This union was different.

So very different.

When Nikita awoke the following morning, her heart and mind were filled with a sense of peace. Something wonderful had transpired between her and Quinn the night before. Their souls had somehow touched, and she wanted to finally understand the shadows that haunted him.

She was mildly surprised to find that he wasn't sound asleep next to her. Rising early was not his strong point. She smiled. He was probably downstairs. Maybe working on a new piece.

She was eager to talk to him, tell him that she was really willing to work out their relationship—together, not just on her terms.

Quickly she got out of bed and hurried into the adjoining bathroom for a short shower. She was sure she'd find Quinn in the living room sipping his morning glass of grapefruit juice, his feet propped up on the coffee table, waiting for her to tell him to take them down.

What she found instead was an envelope stuffed with money for the next six months' rent, and a note that changed her life and shredded her heart.

BOOK TWO

Chapter 29

Startin' Over and Over

Nikita sighed and turned away from the puffs of cottony clouds that floated around the speeding Boeing 747. Three years. Three long years. A time that was behind her, and best forgotten.

She leaned back against the headrest and closed her eyes, letting the motion of the slipstream currents lull her into a light, dreamless sleep. She didn't want to think about Quinn anymore, and, oddly, she hadn't for quite some time. The trip to Nigeria from which she was returning—the one that she and Quinn should have taken together—coupled with faxes and letters of correspondence from her executive editor, Monica Frazier, had caused the old wounds to seep open.

When she'd received the fax from Monica about a fabulous new book by a Q. J. Parker that her entire staff was abuzz about, it had thrown her completely off balance.

But, of course, the notion that Quinn had actually written a book was ludicrous. Once she'd been able to dispel the notion that it could be Quinn, she, too, got caught up in the possibility of a bestseller. She was eager to get back in the driver's seat and see what all the excitement was about. Yet, as much as she'd tried, nagging memories of Quinn pricked the back of her mind.

To this day, three years after his unannounced departure from her life, Nikita still did not understand why he'd left her. She could forgive him anything—but not that. All that she had left of their two-year tumultuous affair was one of his favorite T-shirts and the hastily scrawled note saying that he was sorry. *Sorry.*

Fuck you, Quinn!

It had taken months for the shock to wear off. Day by day she'd discarded whatever clothes he hadn't taken. And then she'd slipped into a state of numbness. Maybe it was a good thing, she reflected, allowing the memories to settle over her once again.

Quinn's betrayal of her love had unwittingly been the catalyst that had propelled her to where she was today—owner and publisher of a growing black book-publishing company. She'd taken the money from her parents and what he'd given her and bought out Ms. Ingram's magazine, expanding it.

Now, her company, Harrell Publishing, had been responsible for launching the successful careers of several black authors that other companies had refused to touch.

She knew in her bones that Harrell Publishing was on the brink of national attention. What would put them solidly in the company of Dutton, Penguin and the like was a major blockbuster novel. And from the sound of Monica's fax, the new manuscript they had in their possession could be the one.

Nikita sighed. At thirty, she was in an enviable position. She had her own business, a solid circle of friends, and one of the few small female-owned black presses that were making inroads into mainstream America. And she had Grant, she added almost as an afterthought. Yes, she had it all, along with an unyielding sorrow that followed her like a shadow.

The voice of the captain filtered through her brooding thoughts.

"This is your captain speaking. Please observe the fasten-your-seat-belt sign. We are making our approach to Kennedy Airport. We anticipate touchdown in approximately twelve minutes. 2:00 a.m. eastern standard time. The temperature is sixty degrees. Thank you for flying with Delta."

Slowly, Nikita opened her eyes and looked around, shaking off the remnants of the intrusive memories. Within moments she would be back in New York, soon back to work and back to Grant.

Grant. Her glossy lips flickered with a smile. They'd finally started seeing each other again. Had been a couple for the past three months. He was the first man she'd been with since Quinn. Somewhere in her mind, going back was easier than going forward, starting again.

Grant Coleman was everything Quinten Parker was not. Grant, she knew, would be waiting for her at the airport, even at the ungodly hour of 2:00 a.m.

She frowned, knowing that if it were Quinn, he would be explaining how he'd overslept, or was hanging out with his boys and missed her flight. They'd have their yelling match, or at least *she'd* be yelling, and he'd soothe. Then they'd be in each other's arms, making love.

A shudder skipped through her. Or was it just the plane landing with a subtle thud?

Nikita unfastened her seat belt and stretched her legs before standing. No one paid any attention to those seat belt signs once the plane finished its taxi, anyway.

As she threaded her way through the web of straggling travelers, she spotted Grant's tall, lean form standing out amidst the throng. He was attractive—there was no question about that—in a quiet sort of way. She was happy that she'd decided to get back together with Grant. He almost filled all of the emptiness. And her parents adored him.

Her smile bloomed as she drew near.

Grant was what she needed in her life.

She stepped into his solid embrace.

Secure, dependable Grant. Her rock.

Quinn, her grains of sand.

"Six weeks seemed like forever. It's good to have you back again, sweetheart," Grant breathed into her hair, holding her close.

Nikita stepped back and smiled up at him. "It feels good to

be back." She kissed him softly on the lips, vanquishing the remains of Quinn.

"You look good enough to eat." He slid his arm around her waist, ushering her toward the exit.

"The motherland was good to me," she said, doubling her step to keep up with his.

"Not as good as I'm going to be to you."

"Hmm." Nikita smiled and snuggled closer, hoping to achieve the intimacy she craved, and failed. "There's so much I have to tell you."

"I bet you do. And I want to hear every detail. Later. We have the rest of the weekend to talk."

They stepped outside to where the chauffeur was waiting and took her bags.

"I didn't plan anything special. I thought you'd wind up with a whopping case of jet lag," he said, helping her into the backseat, then positioning himself next to her. "So I thought we'd just relax at my place. So I can take care of you."

The truth was, he was still too uncomfortable at her apartment—the one she'd shared with Quinn. He couldn't understand why she'd never given the place up.

"Sounds heavenly." Her stomach clenched.

Grant kissed the top of her head. "It's only just begun. I want to show you just how much you've been missed."

San Francisco

Maxine moved quietly through the two-story town house, humming softly right on key to Whitney and CeCe's tune from the *Waiting to Exhale* soundtrack—man, she loved that song—opening windows, pushing back curtains, watering plants and simply enjoying a lazy Sunday morning. "Count on me through thick and thin, a friendship that will never end," she crooned in her sultry alto. Yeah, that was *her* song.

She trotted downstairs and opened the front door to retrieve the papers. She was anxious to see what kind of deals the airlines were running this week. She grinned and shook her head, strolling into the sunny kitchen on the ground floor. If it wasn't one airfare war, it was another. Made her job an exercise in ingenuity. And hot damn if she wasn't good at it!

Her favorite mug, one that she'd found in an old antique shop in the downtown bay area one Saturday afternoon, hung from a little rack in the corner by the microwave. It was a good old mug, she mused, taking it from its hook. Had a little chip in it right along the rim. Sometimes it reminded her of the chip in Dre's front tooth. She smiled.

He'd called her about a month ago. Said he was doing well and was in the process of opening another location. Was getting married, too, some chick he'd met "on the job." She was happy for him, after she'd gotten over that New York minute of jealousy.

She filled the mug with water, put it in the black box and nuked it for thirty seconds. Sitting down at the white Formica table, she spread out the paper and took a short sip of her scalding mint tea. The sun beamed in through the window, streaming across the kitchen like "the force, Luke." She chuckled inwardly. She'd always liked that line.

She crossed her long, bare legs at the knees, swinging her foot in time to *her* song. Immersed in the ads and taking mental notes, she didn't know he had eased up behind her until his lips pressed down on her neck.

"Mornin', babe."

His locks brushed against her cheeks, making her tingle. "Hey, yourself." She looked up and pushed out her lips for a real g-o-o-d morning kiss.

"Hmm. Now that's better," she breathed against his mouth. She pecked him one last time. "What's happenin' with you today?"

Quinn pulled up a chair, turned it around and straddled it, folding his arms across its wicker back. He pressed his chin down on his arms.

He stretched out a hand and covered hers. "I need to talk to you about somethin', Max."

"Sure, babe. What is it?" She closed the paper and turned her full attention on him.

"I'm going to need to go to New York for a while, Max."

She went completely still. Her throat tightened, and her heart was knocking so damned hard that it was kind of hard to breathe. "Yeah?" She bit down on the side of her mouth, trying to be cool, like this was a regular event.

"Just for a while. Need to straighten some things out." There was no easy way to say this, no easy way to do it. *Just do it.*

She pulled her hand away and got up, nearly kicking him when she uncrossed her legs, and wished she had. She dumped her tea in the sink and began scrubbing the cup as if it had the plague.

"Max. Just listen for a minute."

She spun around, her long fingers dripping with water and Ivory dish liquid, flinging water on her freshly washed ceramic tile floor. "What you got to tell me, Q? Huh?" She planted her hands on her round hips and cocked her head to the side, her oversize T-shirt inching farther up, revealing the elastic leg band of her peach panties.

He got up and moved toward her. He placed his hands on her shoulders. Looked down into her face, into eyes that challenged him to tell her the real deal. "It's about the book deal, Max. You know that."

"Yeah. And? People write books from all over the world and never meet the publisher, Q. So cut the bull and get to the point. You're goin' to see Nikita. Just say it."

"I have to, Maxine. The book did a lot for me. It helped me to get out all those things, the confusion, the hurt, everything that's been buggin' me for years."

"So then why go, Q? You still haven't told me why."

"There's still unfinished business, Max." He took in a lungful of air. "I walked out on a woman who loved me. Leavin' her nothin' more than some loot and a note. Nobody deserves that. And it's been eatin' me for the past three years."

She stiffened under his fingertips.

"I ain't never gonna be free, Maxine, really free, until I see her face-to-face. That book that I wrote tells a lot. And maybe she'll see it for what it's worth. Me, tryin' to tell it like it was, and is. Straight. I don't want to go through the rest of my life with that weight hangin' over my head." He placed his forefinger beneath her chin and tilted her head up. "And I don't think you want me to."

She swallowed, hard. "I guess, somewhere deep inside, I always knew this day was comin'." Her smile flickered around the edges. "Can't say I wanted it to." She chuckled softly. She looked into his eyes, seeing all the years, all the shared hurts and triumphs, and most of all, the sincerity. She knew this man as she'd known no other. If they had never been more than this, right this moment, she knew they'd always been for real with each other.

"You do what you gotta do, Q. I always told you that."

She took a breath and the tension eased and flowed away between them. She wrapped her arms around his waist, pressing her body against his.

She pressed her body a little closer. "But, just so you don't try to get slick, I'm bookin' that *round trip* flight, along with a hotel far enough away from Miss Thang, with a three-day return. So travel light, my brother."

He threw his head back and laughed, hugging her close. "Max, you're the one, baby. You are definitely the one."

She pressed her head against his chest, an unnamed fear gripping her like a bad case of the flu. *They'd just have to see. Wouldn't they?*

They chatted on the drive to the airport as if the trip were a regular business trip—not one that had the potential to turn their lives upside down.

Maxine had gone to the hairdresser the day before, had her nails professionally done—something she'd never done in her life—worn some new lingerie instead of one of his sports T-shirts to bed, and worked him out last night so he wouldn't forget that ride for a long time to come. And had bought a slammin' new outfit for the drive.

And she was scared. Bad. She'd never admit it to Quinn, or to anybody else for that matter. The truth was, Nikita Harrell had a hold over Quinn that she never understood, had the ability to make him change his whole world, his outlook, his friend-ships. Even halfway across the country, four-hundred pages of a book and three years later, she still had that hold. How could she ever hope to fight against that kind of power? How?

Her heart was racing a mile a minute as she held his hand while the line moved up for boarding.

He got to the entrance and she knew this was it. One way or the other.

Quinn turned to her, sensing her hesitation. His gaze held on to her. And he kissed her, a fleeting but gentle kiss.

"I'll be back, Maxie."

"I know."

She smiled that smile that he loved, that little toothpick gap winking at him.

And then he was gone.

She stood against the railing, not sure for how long, watching the planes come and go, knowing that one of them was his, just as she had three years earlier, when he'd called during those early morning hours and said he was on his way.

When he'd stepped off that plane and she saw him coming down the gangway, all the years, the emptiness, slipped away. They hugged each other and laughed, just like old times. She didn't ask him why he'd come, or how long he was staying. She didn't want to know.

He'd rejected her offer to stay with her and checked into a hotel until he found an apartment through the same realty agency that had located her town house. It was only then that she knew this wasn't just a short visit.

She didn't know what he did with his days, and didn't ask, knowing that he'd tell her whatever he wanted her to know. What she did know was that he was going through a healing process, a taking stock of himself and his life. And that took time.

They spent their free time together and some afternoons and evenings, too, sitting out in the back of her town house, soaking up the sun, talking, listening and just being Q and Max. They shopped together, looking for things for their respective residences, combing the streets of San Francisco for just that perfect somethin' somethin'.

Then the letter came. And everything changed.

She'd just gotten in from work and was totally worn out. All she wanted was a quiet night, a hot bath and bed.

She'd slowly climbed the stairs and went into her bedroom, tossing her purse and briefcase onto the cushiony chair by her bed. Stripping out of her clothes, she dropped them in a heap and headed for the bathroom. Just then the phone rang.

She had a good mind to let the answering machine pick up, but whoever it was she'd probably have to call back, anyway. *Might as well get it over with,* she'd thought.

"Hello?"

"Hey, Max. It's Q."

"Hey, yourself." She sat down, a soft smile on her face, feeling her body slowly uncoil. "Whatsup?" She wiggled her toes.

"You busy tonight?"

"Maybe," she teased. "Depends."

He heard the smirk in her voice and couldn't help but smile. "I wondered if it would be cool if I came over. There's somethin' I want to run by you…ya know…"

There was something in his voice that put her senses on alert. There was never any formality between them. He'd never asked to come over before, and neither had she.

"What's wrong, Q?"

She didn't hear anything but his breathing.

"Q?"

"Is it cool, Max?"

"Yeah…sure. Come on by."

"Thanks. See you in about an hour."

She'd taken a shower instead of her desired bath, changed clothes, and then found herself pacing, her thoughts driving her up the wall. Something had shaken him. Bad. She could tell by the vacant tone in his voice. And she was chewing her gum so hard and fast her jaws were beginning to ache.

When the doorbell suddenly rang, she nearly jumped out of her skin. She ran to the door and pulled it open.

The whites of his eyes were red. His smooth face looked drawn, as if he hadn't slept in days. His usual overpowering aura seemed to have dimmed, like a bulb that wasn't bright enough for a room.

Her stomach muscles tightened. "Quinn, you're scarin' me. What's the matter?"

He dipped his head and stepped inside, brushing past her and into the living room. He sat down on the couch, stretching his legs out in front of him.

She sat on the love seat, opposite him, her heart in her throat.

He dug in the pocket of his shirt and pulled out a thick white envelope and handed it to her.

She blinked, took a breath and opened the envelope, noticing the New York address and Sean's law firm's name.

Slowly she unfolded the pages.

Dear Mr. Parker,

On behalf of the New York City Police Department and the people of the State of New York, we extend our condolences for the loss of your sister, Miss Lacy Parker.

Pursuant to our agreement, enclosed herewith is a cashier's check in the amount of one million dollars, which represents a portion of the agreed to compensation for the loss of your sister. The balance of the proceeds will be forwarded through your attorney within sixty days.

A copy of the signed agreement is also enclosed.

Thank you for your patience in resolving this very difficult situation.

She couldn't read any more through the haze of her tears. Her hands shook as she refolded the letter.

"Just a bunch of numbers, Max. Written off and filed away. That's all Lacy was to them. Her…whole…life. Shit! I thought I could handle it…Max…I…"

Then she saw them trickle slowly down his cheeks. Her heart nearly stopped beating. And her insides rushed up to her throat. She'd never seen him cry. Not even at the funeral. Not even when they put Lacy in the ground. And her own tears fell as she went to him, wrapping him in her arms, shushing away the pain, holding on to his shudders, making them her own.

She kissed away his tears, tasting the saltiness on her lips, brushing his hair away from his face, whispering over and again, "It's okay, Q. Just let it go."

He looked at her then, really looked, beyond the little girl he used to tease, beyond the woman who had it going on, past the friend and confidante that she'd always been, to the woman his heart had been fighting for far too long, the one who had always brought peace to his mind, smiles to his face and an ease to his soul. The one he'd always turned to, no matter what. The one who gave and never asked for anything in return.

His eyes danced over her face and she looked back, knowing that his heart had finally seen inside hers.

She smiled a soft, gentle smile and nodded slowly, her hand stroking his damp cheek. "Yes, it is okay, Q."

He cupped her face in his hands, bringing her to meet his waiting lips, and drank of what she offered.

They explored each other, slow and easy as it had always been between them. Whispers, laughter, soft moans and sighs of arousal filled the spaces, floated through the air.

As she stood before him, nude and exquisite, and led him upstairs to her bedroom, he knew that whatever had been would only be better, richer, fuller.

When they were together on the downy softness of her bed, moving to a secret rhythm, listening to the beat of their hearts, he realized that he didn't just want to satisfy her, hear her shout his name, ask for more. He wanted to make her happy, as happy as she'd always made him.

It seemed that she'd been waiting all her life for this moment. To give herself, her being, to the only man she'd ever loved. When she felt him enter her body, fill her and move within the wet confines of her walls, suckle her breasts, slip his tongue in her mouth when she cried out, she lost a part of herself that she'd never been willing to give up before. She'd been holding on to it, saving it, for this moment. This time with him.

There were no bridges to cross, no gaps to fill, no finding of a middle ground.

It was just *all good.*

They moved into a higher level of their relationship, then, a keener awareness of each other and their needs.

Although he kept his apartment, he spent most of his time at her place, except when he closed himself off to work on the book. That was hard for her, realizing that he was pouring out his relationship with Nikita onto the pages, and she preferred not to read it—not really wanting to know, just understanding that it was something he needed to do. He'd decided to use part of the money to open a recording studio, and with the other part he started the Lacy Parker Foundation for minority kids who had an interest in music but couldn't afford lessons or instruments.

Both had taken off. The studio kept him busy and he'd even recorded his own album. The foundation had helped more than a hundred needy kids in just over a year.

And in between it all, he wrote.

And day by day, she loved him more. Even if she never said the words.

She blinked back the memories, pushed away from the window and moved toward the exit.

Walking through the airport parking lot, she recalled an old saying of her grandmother's. *"If you love someone, love them enough to let them go away. If your love is returned they'll come back to stay."*

"Hope you're right, Grandma," she whispered.

Chapter 30

Ain't No Mountain High

The spring weekend was far too short, Nikita mused, pulling her Benz into the parking garage where her new offices were housed. She handed her monthly coupon to the attendant.

Grant had definitely lived up to his pledge to take care of her. There wasn't a thing she'd asked for that he hadn't given or done.

The only thing that Grant was lacking was an ability to totally satisfy her. He wasn't an inconsiderate lover, just an unimaginative one. She had yet to feel the sparks of undeniable desire boil in her veins for Grant. Never had. But back then, that first time around, she hadn't known the difference. Until Quinn.

There was no denying that she and Quinn, physically, had fit like two pieces of a puzzle. She squirmed uncomfortably in her seat at the titillating thought. It was the other aspects of their lives that stayed in turmoil.

But, now she had Grant. Grant was good for her. And she was finally beginning to accept having someone take care of things for her for a change. And it felt good.

She supposed.

Moving toward her office, she felt that old familiar rush surge through her veins when she looked at the gold lettering on the door. *Harrell Publishing, Inc.* Hers. Her hard work and determination had paid off.

Her heels clicked with purpose across the marble floors, the sound of a polished businesswoman who had the right contacts, the right clothes, a devoted staff and the right man. That old Virginia Slims commercial ran in her head—"You've come a long way, baby."

Nikita opened the entrance door of the office and was thrown into openmouthed shock when a thundering round of "Welcome back!" nearly hurled her back out the way she'd come in.

For several breathless seconds, she just stood there, her hand pressed against her chest, willing her heart to be still, while her staff of ten enveloped her in hugs and kisses of welcome.

Her eyes stung and her throat felt tight. This was the last thing she'd expected.

"I...don't...know what to say." She sniffed back impending tears.

"Just tell everyone how much you missed them so we can dig into these bagels," a familiar voice rang out from the back of the group.

Nikita looked up and her eyes widened, then narrowed. She pointed an accusing finger in Grant's direction. "You...you knew all along. You sneak!"

"I confess." He made his way toward her. "But they swore me to secrecy," he said, kissing her on the cheek.

"I'll pay you back later, bud," she said, low enough for only him to hear.

She looked around and beamed. "You guys are really something. This is great."

Monica slipped her arm around Nikita's waist. "'Scuse us a minute, Grant." She squeezed between the couple, pulling Nikita aside. "Girl, it's good to have you back." She ushered her toward the spread of donuts, bagels, juice and coffee. "Just want to warn you. I set up a lunch meeting with that new author I told you about. He'll be in town tomorrow, then we can talk contracts."

"No problem, as far as I know. I'd have rather had some more time to go over the manuscript before meeting with him. But I'll try to get through as much of it as possible between now and then."

"You would have thought, with a novel like this, he'd have gone to one of the major houses for the big bucks," Monica said, "but hey, don't look a gift horse in the mouth. Right?"

She was getting that funny feeling in her stomach again, as if she were on a roller coaster. She smiled faintly. "Right."

Grant stepped up to the duo. "Listen, sweetheart, I have to get back to my office."

Just that quickly, she'd forgotten he was there. "Oh, Grant." She blinked. "How did you manage to get away? Those tightwad accountants are sticklers for time."

He grinned. "I told my boss I had an appointment with the IRS."

Monica gave him a blank look, obviously not getting the joke. Grant's sense of humor somehow always reflected numbers or accounts in some form or fashion. It took some getting used to, and his years in the air force had only made him stiffer.

Nikita tiptoed and brushed her lips against his. "Thanks for coming, sweetheart."

"Pick you up after work?"

"I drove in. I didn't feel like being at the mercy of a cab-driver today."

"Then I'll see you at six. Try to be ready."

"Very funny." That was the one bone of contention between her and Grant. He was a stickler for time, just like that group he worked with. Often it bordered on annoying. Her thoughts had already shifted to the manuscript, and she was actually eager for Grant to leave so she could get to work.

After the staff had devoured the morning feast and returned to their desks, Nikita and Monica retreated to Nikita's office.

"Wow, this feels good." Nikita sat, then leaned back against her high-back leather swivel chair, just like the one she'd seen in her little-girl dreams.

She let out a breath. "Okay, so let's have it. What's the story on the new author?"

Monica sat down, a Cheshire-cat grin on her butterscotch

face, and crossed her long legs, purposely dragging out and dramatizing the moment. "W-e-l-l, as I mentioned in the fax, about three weeks ago I got this package—no agent, just regular mail. I started to just put it aside, but when I had some time on my hands I took a peek. Let's put it this way—I started reading and couldn't stop. It's that good, Nikita. It's hot. It had me laughin', cryin' and swearin'. I've read few stories like that, written by a man, with so much passion and insight." She shook her head. "This author has talent to the bone."

"Can't wait to read it."

"I'll bring it right in." Monica popped up from her seat, went to the door and stopped. "Hey, Niki, didn't someone named Quinn work at the magazine from time to time just before I started?"

Her stomach rose and fell. She focused on her appointment book while she answered. "Yes. Why?"

"Q. J. Parker. His name is Quinten. Wouldn't it be something if it was the same guy?" She hurried out.

Her world started to spin.

Moments later, Monica reappeared with the box containing the manuscript. "Here it is. Enjoy. I have a stack of stuff on my desk to take care of. See you later."

Nikita's eyes trailed to the box as if magnetically drawn. "Sure," she mumbled. "Thanks."

For several interminable moments, she just sat there staring at the covered box, teetering on the threshold of indecision. A part of her, the publisher part, was eager to read the contents. But the woman, the one who was still trying to put her life back together, hesitated. Hesitated, because if Quinn had written a book that took the reader's breath away, she didn't know if she would be woman enough to publish it. No matter what the rewards.

She turned her attention to her calendar, checking production dates for upcoming titles and reacquainting herself with appointments that had been made months ago.

She spent the next three hours returning phone calls, reviewing bills and catching up on correspondence. But her gaze and her thoughts kept drifting back and forth to the box.

"This is ridiculous." She swallowed and tossed her pen down on her desk. She reached for the cover and snatched it open.

There, staring at her in big bold letters was *A Private Affair,* by Q. J. Parker. She inhaled a shaky breath and reached for the first page when the phone rang, a momentary reprieve.

"Imani. How are you?"

"Not so good, Ms. Harrell. My contract says that I have no input about the cover art. That's totally unfair. Suppose the artwork is horrid?"

Generally, Nikita didn't take these calls. She let Monica handle them. But Imani Angoza was a brilliant, budding novelist who needed to be handled with kid gloves. Although she loved Monica to pieces, Monica had a way of expressing her displeasure that wasn't always too subtle.

"You did sign the contract. And I know you had your attorney look it over, because she returned it to me personally before I went away."

"But, Ms. Harrell. I—"

"Tell you what, when the cover layouts are submitted I'll call you and we'll review them together. How does that sound?"

"Great. Thank you, Ms. Harrell," she said, finally losing the whine in her voice. "I don't mean to be a nag, but this is important to me."

"Of course it is. It's important to me, also. I'll keep you up-to-date on the progress."

"Thank you. I'll call you. Soon."

Nikita smiled. *I know you will.* "Do that."

She leaned back in her seat, resting her head against the cool leather. She closed her eyes. Her head was starting to pound, and when she opened her eyes and looked up at the antique grandfather clock that sat in the corner of her office, it was past one.

Well, she'd successfully gotten through her morning without reading one word of the manuscript. She sighed. She'd planned to cut her day short anyway, in preparation for the evening. If she left now, she'd have plenty of time to take care of her running around, read some of the contents of the box and be ready in time for Grant to pick her up at six.

She shut off her computer, packed her briefcase and tucked the box under her arm. The office had cleared out for lunch by the time she came out front. She left a note on Monica's desk.

Impatiently, she shifted from one foot to the other, waiting for the elevator. Grant was such a pain about time, and could make her entire evening an exercise in misery if she weren't ready. She didn't want anything to ruin her reunion with Parris.

They'd made plans to meet after her show for a late dinner. Just the two of them. To catch up.

While she waited impatiently at a red light, she checked her watch. Time seemed to be moving at an incredible speed today. Then, when she looked up at the street signs, she realized that she'd taken the wrong route home and had completely bypassed the cleaners. She had to pick up the dress she'd planned to wear tonight and stop at the market, which was in the opposite direction. She took a left at the intersection and sped off.

What's wrong with me? Can't seem to stay focused. Maybe it's just the aftereffects of the trip.

She stopped by the market and selected the few items that she needed to prepare a light meal for her and Grant.

Jumping back into the Benz, she pulled out into traffic and zipped around a slow-moving Caddy.

As much as she didn't want to admit it, she knew it was the resurgence of old thoughts and feelings about Quinn that were playing havoc with her emotions.

Annoyed with herself—her weakness and inability to seal her heart against memories of Quinn—she slapped away the lock with the little seashell, the one that now reached below her shoulders, and turned on two wheels onto her block.

She was almost grateful that Grant would be coming in a few hours. If anyone could put order back in her life, Grant could.

Nikita hung the dress in the closet, chuckling on her way to the kitchen. She knew Parris would leap at the chance to steal it from her if she wasn't careful.

"Not this time, sistah." That dress had been pure extravagance. She'd paid nearly a month's rent for the creation.

She began gathering the ingredients for an early meal with Grant. She whipped together a pasta salad on a bed of fresh spinach, lightly seasoned with oil, just the way Grant liked it.

Yet, no matter how hard she tried, memories, visions and desires for Quinn seemed to taunt her, come to life with every blink of her eye.

Her hands had the slightest tremor as she replaced the condiments. Her heart beat a little faster when she briefly shut her eyes and imagined his scent. The assault on her senses was almost more than she could stand. What was worse was accepting how desperately she still missed him.

"Go away!" She pounded her fist against the yellow countertop that they'd prepared so many meals on together, and lowered her head. "Go away," she whispered.

Totally frazzled, she returned to the living room, the box with the manuscript calling out to her from the coffee table where she'd left it. She moved slowly toward it, picking up its weight and settling herself down on the couch.

She pulled off the box top and the cover page beneath and began to read….

Steam rolled off the New York City streets in waves, pushing intrepid strollers to seek refuge in the cool confines of cafés, malls and local bars. The heat this summer afternoon was beyond intense. But that wasn't why the folks on Malcolm X Boulevard and 135th Street would remember that day. No, it wouldn't be remembered for the heat, but for the many lives that were irrevocably changed by an ugly twist of fate.

The small church was packed. Neighbors and friends stood shoulder to shoulder, whispering among themselves how tragic it all was. Marcus stood alone—from the world and with his grief. He couldn't count how many times he'd asked himself: Why his sister?

Parts of him felt as if they'd break into a million pieces. Other parts of him were infused with an anger that was barely contained. The pain was so deep, so pervasive, that it stooped his proud shoulders.

He tried to pay attention to what the minister was saying. It was all a haze. The trip to Tracy's final resting place was a dream scene. Words of condolence were met with his vacant stare and empty smiles. The sultry, steamy days that followed blended together into a nothingness.

Marcus forced himself to go out every day, to the street that was his home. He seemed driven by forces that he could not control. He pushed himself with a vengeance. Maybe if he had worked harder, faster, none of this would have happened. He and Tracy would have been out of the clutches of the drive-bys, the drugs, the gangs. It was his fault. And he felt so alone—until he met her.

He'd been sitting in the local jazz club, nursing a glass of Jack Daniels, when she'd walked into the club. He felt his heart pick up just a notch, and the hair on the back of his neck began to tingle with awareness. Even the music seemed to pulse with a little more intensity, like a scene in a movie building toward the climax.

He tossed down the last of his drink and watched her move— in what seemed like slow motion—across the crowded room. She wore a white spaghetti-strap T-shirt that molded to the curves of her breasts from the dampness that clung to her body like a satisfied lover.

She was a bit on the short side, Marcus noted, but she was packaged well. The pale-colored shorts cupped her round bottom in a most appealing way. Her curved legs were a glistening bare brown, the color of honey, her tiny feet encased in white deck shoes.

Marcus swallowed hard, and swore that the air-conditioning must have burst a circuit, because it was suddenly damned hot.

She signaled for the waiter and ordered a Pepsi with lemon.

He slid slowly around on the bar stool until he had a view diagonally across from where she sat, apparently very content with her surroundings. She wasn't meeting anyone.

He didn't know how he knew it. He just did.

She seemed to sense his approach. Slowly, she raised her eyes. They didn't register alarm, Marcus realized, but acceptance. He watched her swallow the last of her drink, and followed the path of the cool liquid down the line of her slender throat. She smiled when he stopped and stood above her.

"I've been watching you for a while," Marcus said. He'd memorized the perfect slope of her brown eyes, the arch of her chiseled cheekbones, the curve of her full lips, but up close they were even more intense. The sensation had him reeling.

He took a quick breath and slid into the seat next to her. "I'm glad you're alone." He looked casually around the darkened room. "You aren't waiting for anyone," he stated more than asked.

"What makes you think that?"

Her voice was low and throaty, inviting, just like he'd imagined it would be.

"Because we've been waiting to meet each other for a long time. The time is now." He gave her a slow, lazy smile. "My name is Marcus Collins, and yours..." He reached across the table and took her hand. He felt her tremble, and instantly knew that she wasn't as full of all the bravado she'd displayed. That tiny realization inched open the doorway to emotions that he'd nailed shut.

And he was suddenly afraid. Afraid of what feeling again would do to him.

Through a veil of tears, she wiped her eyes and continued to read, reliving their life together, page after page, the loving, the laughter, the fighting, and his secret pain.

He wasn't sure anymore where he began and she ended. The more he gave, the more she wanted, never seeing that all he wanted, all he needed in his life, was for her to love him, just to be loved for who he was: a simple man. Maybe not the perfect man, but one who was willing to try, who was doing all that he could, in his own way, to make her happy. Even, it seemed, to give up a part of himself in the process.

That Christmas, at her parents' house, was the beginning of the end. He didn't realize it then, but it was.

In vivid, anguished clarity the eloquent prose painted a portrait of a man emasculated, humiliated, in front of the woman who claimed to love him. Why, the writer asked, would she have put him in that position when she said she cared? So he'd put on his front, his don't-give-a-damn attitude, hidden behind his facade of indifference, and she hadn't seemed to notice.

But it wasn't her fault. He couldn't blame her. Never would. It was all she knew. She came from a world where everything went according to plan. There was no struggle, no hard-core reality check. She stayed so busy planning the future, she couldn't see the now. But still he tried, until he couldn't try anymore.

And how could he tell her what was going on inside? He'd never really learned to share emotions. That was for women, he believed. She saw him as a tower of strength. No weakness. This vision of invincibility. He couldn't show any other face to her. Not now. Not after all this time. The only way he knew how to show her that he cared was by giving her what she needed. And giving her his body. It was the only time he could let go, bridge the gap that separated them. There was no other plateau on which he could reach her expectations. It was only there that he filled her.

And finally, even for him, it was no longer enough.

She didn't want to read any more. Didn't want to feel those feelings again. She'd never known. Never understood how deep his feelings went. How empty he felt without his sister, how guilty he felt about his mother's abandonment, the loss of the women in his life, his fear that it would only happen again. She'd tried to fill it by making him do, do more, do better.

And then it hit her like a surprise left hook. She'd done to Quinn exactly what her parents had done to her. And just as it had pushed her away, it pushed him away, too. He had to find his own way.

And he had.

"Oh, God, Quinn, I'm so sorry. So sorry."

She covered her face with her hands and wept.

On the ride to the club she tried to keep up a cheerful front, to smile in all the right places, say the right thing. But it took all she had not to come apart.

Grant looked at her after another bout of silence. "You want to tell me what's wrong, Nikita?"

She forced another smile. "Nothing. Just tired, I guess, and anxious to see Parris again."

"You sure? You seem totally preoccupied—"

"I'm fine, Grant, really. Just…please…leave it alone."

"I would if I knew what it was I was leaving alone." He focused all of his attention on driving, hoping that she'd finally tell him about whatever was bothering her.

The club was packed by the time she and Grant arrived. Michelle, still the hostess, wiggled around the patrons and showed them to their tables. Jewel and her soul mate Taj were already seated.

Taj stood and kissed her cheek. "Hey, lady. Long time."

"Listen to you, Mr. World Traveler." She turned toward Grant and introduced him to Taj.

They ordered drinks. Nikita stuck to her usual, but within the next few minutes she wished she'd gotten something stronger.

"Good evening, everyone," Nick said, stepping up to the mike. "Tonight we have a special treat for you. Not only will my lovely wife, the incomparable Parris McKay, be singing for you, but we have a special guest—a former member of the band who will play some selections from his soon-to-be-released CD…Mr. Quinten Parker. Give it up!"

Her heart slammed in her chest, arresting her breathing. Her head pounded.

The audience roared its approval.

Quinn rose from a seat at a table on the far side of the room, moving toward the stage in the slow, easy gait that she'd memorized, taking his place behind the black and whites, in the single spotlight that captured him.

She froze. Seeing him again…here, now, in the place where it really all began, pushed away all the time that was lost, the hurt that was experienced. And time suddenly stood still as he took them on a musical odyssey, his fingers caressing the keys the way they'd once played along her spine.

Grant had his arm around her shoulder and felt her stiffen, then begin to tremble, ever so slightly.

He whispered in her ear, "We can leave if you want."

She looked at him, really looked at him, and realized that he understood. Probably always had, without her ever saying a word. And he'd been by her side…anyway. The way Maxine had always been for Quinn.

She smiled and squeezed his hand. "No. I need to stay."

He nodded, kissed her temple and turned his gaze back to the stage.

The club had emptied out. The strains of music from the jukebox filtered through the spaces. Everyone was gone and, to her surprise, it was Grant who'd insisted that she stay behind and "work it out." He'd given her a soft look of understanding and perhaps regret. "I'll be home if you need me," he'd said.

Nikita picked up her glass and then put it back down, looking across at Parris. "When did you know he was coming?"

"About an hour before I went on." She looked at her friend. "Are you okay?"

"I will be. Finally, I think I will be." She took in a long breath and let it go. "I know everything now, Parris. Everything that went wrong and what went right," she said in a faraway voice.

"What do you mean, hon?"

She looked into Parris's green eyes. "He wrote a novel. Yes. Quinten Parker wrote a novel." She turned away for a moment. "About us. Our life together." She slowly shook her head. "I saw myself through his eyes, Parris. I was never able to see that before. Maybe I didn't want to."

"And?"

"He did the best he could. Loved me in his own way. We didn't give each other a real chance." Her throat tightened. She looked up and saw him walking across the floor, toward their table.

Parris got up, touched his arm as she walked past him, and disappeared into the back room.

His smile was soft, hesitant, but those damned dimples were still there, and she smiled.

"Still drinking that lemon Pepsi."

That old familiar voice surrounded her, worked its way down to her bones.

He reached out his hand to take hers, as the jukebox pumped out Chaka Khan's "Your Love is All I Know."

She stepped into his embrace, as if she'd never left. And they moved easily to the music, finding their own special rhythm, the poignant words touching them in their own way.

"I had to come back. To see you, Niki. Tell you I was sorry," he said in a ragged voice, hugging the familiar body close to his.

"I know," she whispered. "I know." She took a breath, stepped back and looked up into his eyes. "I read the book, Quinn. Most of it—"

"I needed you to… I found a way, Niki…just like you always said I would. I…tried to use what I'd always had, to say what I've never said to you…. It wasn't your fault, baby. Never was. And I can't keep runnin' away anymore. Runnin' to the familiar, takin' the easy way out, where it's safe. You never gave me no easy way, Niki, and it scared me."

She struggled for air.

"I'm not scared anymore."

"Where do I go…after all that we've been through…" Chaka cried.

Nikita swallowed back the lump in her throat, her eyes sparkling with the tears she'd sworn she'd never shed again.

And then he said the words he'd never uttered to another soul. "I love you, Nikita, from the depths of my soul…I know that now…maybe I always did."

Her world seemed to spin and she barely breathed. How long had she waited to hear him say he loved her? Those precious words. She inhaled deeply, and stepped out of his embrace. She reached up and stroked his cheek, pushing aside a stray lock of his hair.

She stood on tiptoes, touched her mouth to his, to those all too familiar lips, lingering a moment, just…long enough.

"You know how to find me, when you're ready."

She turned, picked her purse up from the table and walked out, knowing that her tomorrow, her forever, was now finally hers.

Quinn watched her go, his soul finally at peace, crossed the room to the bar and ordered a glass of Jack Daniels.

Nikita never made things easy. She was his light, always had been. He'd just been too blind to see it.

He smiled.

Chapter 31

Here All the Time

She'd made up her mind that if he didn't come back she'd be all right. She'd press on. But dammit, the past thirty-six hours had been the longest "I don't care" hours of her natural born life.

Work was one salvation. And she'd just about burned herself out at the gym, hoping that she'd be so exhausted she'd just collapse into bed.

Nothing happening.

She didn't know folks could stay awake for damn near two days without going into a coma or something.

One more night. Just one, and she'd know for sure. One way or the other.

She locked up the office and walked the half block to where her five-year-old Honda Accord was parked. Got a good deal on it and it ran like a dream. She stuck the key in the lock, thinking about her long night ahead. "Don't play with me, Q. Just don't even try it."

Taking the long route home, she stopped at some of the antique shops, just to look, then decided to pick up some fresh vegetables and a bottle of wine.

Everything else failed at putting her to sleep. Since she wasn't a wine drinker, maybe it would do the trick.

By the time she reached her neat little home, it had grown dark. And she felt the loneliness settle over her just like the clouds hanging up over the rooftops. Nights were the hardest. Always had been.

She opened the door, picked up the mail and flipped on all the lights as she went—saying "hey" to all her plants—needing the light, but needing more than that somebody to come home to, especially tonight.

He stood watching her from the top of the stairs as she fussed over her plants, cussed at the bills in her hand, in all her earthy beauty. And it made him smile, inside and out.

"Hey, girl."

She shut her eyes and breathed in and out real slow, wanting to make sure it wasn't the lack of sleep playing tricks on her.

Okay, she had herself together.

She turned around, slowly, because if it *was* her imagination she wanted it to last just a minute longer.

She looked up. It wasn't a dream. It wasn't a trick.

She tipped her head to the side and put her hand on her hip. "You here to stay, Q?"

He started down the stairs. He watched those perfect little breasts of hers rise and fall beneath her yellow silk blouse. *Only Max could wear yellow silk.*

He stood in front of her, looking down into those eyes that challenged him to answer her…with his heart…with the truth.

"I think you know, Max. You always have," he whispered.

And her eyes filled and tears ran down her cheeks even though she'd promised herself she wouldn't cry, one way or another. *Didn't make sense to let a man know he had you like that. But… What the hell.*

He pulled her into his arms, tight, feeling her all around him, in his heart, deep in his soul. Right there all the time. His friend…all that she ever could be.

She tilted her head back, smiling through her tears, that little toothpick gap winking at him.

"I know," she breathed. "I know."

And she knew she'd be okay.

Epilogue

After the Fire

The nationally syndicated television show *Like It Is* was just coming back on after a commercial break. Gil Noble turned to the camera.

"For those of you who are just tuning in, I'm talking with Quinten Parker, author of *A Private Affair.* Mr. Parker, just today your book hit the *New York Times* Bestseller List. The book has had a phenomenal impact on the industry, especially since you decided to go with a small, relatively unknown publishing house. What prompted you to write a relationship story?"

The camera zoomed in on Quinn's face. "Just a story that needed to be told."

"And judging by the sales, one that a lot of people want to read. How has the sudden success changed you?"

Quinn smiled, and every television viewer got an up-close glance of those dimples.

"The success hasn't changed me," he said. "Finally telling the story did."

Nikita stood in the wings ready to burst with pride, watching him on the closed-circuit television. She smiled and nodded.

"No doubt, Q. No doubt," she whispered.

REQUEST YOUR FREE BOOKS!

2 FREE NOVELS
PLUS 2 FREE GIFTS!

KIMANI™ ROMANCE

Love's ultimate destination!

ARABESQUE®

HELP CELEBRATE
ARABESQUE'S
15TH ANNIVERSARY!

2009 marks Arabesque's 15th anniversary!

Help us celebrate by telling us about your most special memories and moments with Arabesque books. Entries will be judged by the Arabesque Anniversary Committee based on which are the most touching and well written. Fifteen lucky winners will receive as a prize a full-grain leather duffel bag with the Arabesque anniversary logo.

How to Enter: To enter, hand-print (or type) on an 8 ½" x 11" plain piece of paper your full name, mailing address, telephone number and a description of your most special memories and moments with Arabesque books (in two hundred [200] words or less) and send it to "Arabesque 15th Anniversary Contest 20901"—in the U.S.: Kimani Press, 233 Broadway, Suite 1001, New York, NY 10279, or in Canada: 225 Duncan Mill Road, Don Mills, ON M3B 3K9. No other method of entry will be accepted. The contest begins on July 1, 2009, and ends on December 31, 2009. Entries must be postmarked by December 31, 2009, and received by January 8, 2010. A copy of these Official Rules is available online at www.myspace.com/kimanipress, or to obtain a copy of these Official Rules (prior to November 30, 2009), send a self-addressed, stamped envelope (postage not required from residents of VT) to "Arabesque 15th Anniversary Contest 20901 Rules," 225 Duncan Mill Road, Don Mills, ON M3B 3K9. Limit one (1) entry per person. If more than one (1) entry is received from the same person, only the first eligible entry submitted will be considered. By entering the contest, entrants agree to be bound by these Official Rules and the decisions of Harlequin Enterprises Limited (the "Sponsor"), which are final and binding.

NO PURCHASE NECESSARY. Open to legal residents of U.S. and Canada (except Quebec) who have reached the age of majority at time of entry. Void where prohibited by law. Approximate retail value of each prize: $131.00 (USD).

VISIT **WWW.MYSPACE.COM/KIMANIPRESS**
FOR THE COMPLETE OFFICIAL RULES

KPI5ARACONTEST